The Model Patient

The Model Patient

Lucy Ashe

**SIMON &
SCHUSTER**

London · New York · Amsterdam/Antwerp · Sydney/Melbourne · Toronto · New Delhi

First published in Great Britain by Simon & Schuster UK Ltd, 2026

Copyright © Lucy Ashe, 2026

The right of Lucy Ashe to be identified as author of this work has been asserted in accordance with the Copyright, Designs and Patents Act, 1988.

1 3 5 7 9 10 8 6 4 2

Simon & Schuster UK Ltd, 1st Floor
222 Gray's Inn Road, London WC1X 8HB

For more than 100 years, Simon & Schuster has championed authors and the stories they create. By respecting the copyright of an author's intellectual property, you enable Simon & Schuster and the author to continue publishing exceptional books for years to come. We thank you for supporting the author's copyright by purchasing an authorised edition of this book.

No amount of this book may be reproduced or stored in any format, nor may it be uploaded to any website, database, language-learning model, or other repository, retrieval, or artificial intelligence system without express permission. All rights reserved. Inquiries may be directed to Simon & Schuster, 222 Gray's Inn Road, London WC1X 8HB or RightsMailbox@simonandschuster.co.uk

Simon & Schuster Australia, Sydney
Simon & Schuster India, New Delhi

www.simonandschuster.co.uk
www.simonandschuster.com.au
www.simonandschuster.co.in

The authorised representative in the EEA is Simon & Schuster Netherlands BV, Herculesplein 96, 3584 AA Utrecht, Netherlands. info@simonandschuster.nl

Simon & Schuster strongly believes in freedom of expression and stands against censorship in all its forms. For more information, visit BooksBelong.com.

A CIP catalogue record for this book is available from the British Library

Hardback ISBN: 978-1-3985-4862-6
Trade Paperback ISBN: 978-1-3985-4863-3
eBook ISBN: 978-1-3985-4864-0
Audio ISBN: 978-1-3985-4865-7

This book is a work of fiction. Names, characters, places and incidents are either a product of the author's imagination or are used fictitiously. Any resemblance to actual people living or dead, events or locales is entirely coincidental.

Every effort has been made to obtain the necessary permissions with reference to copyright material. We apologise for any omissions in this respect and will be pleased to make the appropriate acknowledgements in any future edition.

'Four lines from 'The Wasteland' (*Collected Poems 1909–1962*) by T.S. Eliot is reprinted by permission of Faber and Faber Ltd.

Typeset in Bembo by M Rules
Printed and Bound in the UK using 100% Renewable Electricity at CPI Group (UK) Ltd

For Erik

April is the cruellest month, breeding
Lilacs out of the dead land, mixing
Memory and desire, stirring
Dull roots with spring rain.

(T. S. ELIOT)

PROLOGUE

A woman screams in the dawn. But it is silence that rises from her bed, a strangled cry that vanishes like the fading fragments of a dream.

She longs to wake.

It starts quietly, a simple journey to the past. She is in the passenger seat, a familiar blue car, her mother's hands in leather gloves, a drive through country roads. A house appears in the distance, a tree-lined approach, grass that shines a flawless green.

A scene change: time jumps. The car has vanished, her mother gone. She is walking towards the house, the trees closing their branches into the darkening canopy of a forest.

Reality is shifting, the edges ripping. It is an oil painting transforming into the weeping paint of watercolour.

Maybe she can stop, root her feet into the road, turn around, go home. But she keeps walking. This is the only way she knows.

Lucy Ashe

It is coming for her. She can sense it stir, an uncoiling from somewhere deep inside the house.

A reptile, its body thick and sinuous. She can feel the pulse of its breath, how it matches the beat of her heart. Its face hardens into view.

It comes closer, so near she can see flashes of fire in its lidless eyes. The corner of each enamelled scale is sharp, shining like mother-of-pearl.

The serpent flares up from the ground and the woman's fear screams into life. Awake now, the creature moves fast, finding her feet, the ground beneath her, the weight of her limbs. It is growing from her legs, circling and writhing above and around her, connected completely.

Its jaws are open, a mouth stretching wide. The serpent is unravelled.

The attack is sudden: first her head, next her shoulders, her body, her waist. It consumes her whole.

They become one: a serpent and a woman bound beneath the green armour of scales.

Every night it comes to her; there is only one way to make it stop.

The doctor closed the door, returned to his desk and pressed the record button on his Dictaphone.

'4 March 1963 – Westbrook, 11am.

'Mrs Evelyn Westbrook arrived at today's appointment fifteen minutes before our scheduled start time. Miss Simmons answered the door as usual, and I continued reading through the notes from last week's recording. I found myself distracted by her early arrival. Sometimes these things mean nothing, a patient hurrying to get out of the rain. At other times, they mean everything. I couldn't help but think about what happened between us last week.

'Today, she positioned herself on the same corner of the sofa and, as always, she took a while to speak, glancing around her as though checking no one else was in here with us. I noticed her gaze linger on the clock above the door. She must have been surprised to see that it was still a few minutes before eleven o'clock. Sometimes I find small changes can be helpful in disrupting the cyclical thoughts and barriers that patients create.

Lucy Ashe

'After everything she had told me last week, how much more open she had been, it was disappointing to see her discomfort today, how anxious she looked, the words she was trying to say eluding her. So, I suggested a more directed approach – a word association task to help her identify the troubles she was having in speaking how she felt. She was willing to try, though I was wary of the tightness in her lips as we began. I worried she was going to attempt to control and moderate everything she said.

'Her responses, plus the time she took to speak, any hesitations, signs of distress, are recorded in my usual projective testing folder. However, there was one response that struck me as being worthy of particular attention.

'The word was "sex". Always a difficult one for patients, particularly women who are not used to speaking openly about such things, especially with a man. She looked up at me then and asked me to repeat the word. There is no judgement, I said to her. I told her that she was safe with me, that she should let herself say the first thing that came into her head, she did not need to fight it, not here with me.

'It was only a whisper, but there was no mistaking the word she said.'

CHAPTER 1

Evelyn Westbrook had looked forward to the party all week. She needed this tonight, a reminder of how life used to be, before she was married, before everything changed.

And perhaps it was working. As the taxi pulled up outside the shop, Henry leant over and kissed her on the side of her neck.

A hot cloud of cigarette smoke closed around them as they stepped inside from the bitter cold. The party was to celebrate the opening of a new clothing store on the King's Road, and the room was already packed with guests shouting to be heard through the music and the laughter and the loud cries of greetings. Evelyn was glad to be able to shrug off her coat, revealing her bare arms in a new silver shift dress. The weather this winter was atrocious, intense waves of cold, not even the city centre escaping the snows and frosts, windows frozen on the inside in the mornings and treacherous sheets of ice on every pavement. The worst weather in two hundred years, everyone said. It was all people seemed to talk about, ever since the first snowfall on Boxing Day. Evelyn was sick of wearing the same practical clothes: she wanted to throw away her sturdy boots and tear her thick woollen stockings into shreds.

Henry mixed her a too strong concoction of gin, vermouth and Campari from the bar, a makeshift wooden plank that balanced across two stools, and they moved together between the mannequins and rows of bright dresses and blazers that hung along metal racks, returning twice to refresh their glasses from the sticky bottles and melting ice cubes. There was an easy energy between them, the argument from the night before forgotten. It suddenly seemed so silly to Evelyn, a trivial nonsense, and she blamed herself for putting Henry through all that drama. The argument had been over something his mother had said to her; but it was unimportant now. It was Henry, not his mother, she had married.

But then somehow they had separated and she found herself among a group of women, a few she remembered from her modelling days, but most of them brand new and fizzing with the strain of trying to fit in and to stand out. A difficult performance to maintain, Evelyn knew, but she missed it all the same.

It was a relief when her friend Lionel led her out of the crowd to a corner where they could talk, but too soon he was gone, called away by a fellow jewellery designer, and she was alone again. Without Henry or Lionel by her side, she felt at the edge of it all, too many new faces, youngsters who seemed to half-recognize her but could not quite place where it was they had seen her before. Her fingers itched for a cigarette, a sure sign she was anxious. Smoking at parties was how she covered her nerves, the unhurried activity of pulling out the cigarette, asking someone to light it for her, the rhythmic movement of her hands.

Evelyn was only twenty-seven years old. But tonight she felt ancient and her hopes for the night were quickly evaporating. She stood silently as she listened to three girls in matching burgundy skirts talk about their latest magazine shoot, a frozen, miserable experience in a wood outside of London. They described how many layers of make-up they applied to stop their skin turning red from the cold, the photographer bellowing at them when they shivered during the shoot. Despite her own memories of similar situations, freezing toes and bitter winds in outfits unsuitable for frost-coated fields, Evelyn had felt a painful spasm of longing.

Her last booking had been two weeks before her wedding day and she had cried on the way home, the taxi driver glancing anxiously at her in the rear-view mirror. Henry spoke about the end of her modelling career as though it was a liberation, an opportunity to escape the long hours, the early starts, travelling with the constant burden of a suitcase packed full of make-up, brushes, combs, rollers, stockings, bras, the aggressive demands of the photographers, the cancelled jobs just hours before a shoot. But even with all these trials, she had loved her work. She missed the satisfaction of earning a living, her own money to spend as she wished. And there was nothing like the thrill when a camera captured the curves and shadows of her body, her aching muscles trembling to be still, the pleasure of seeing the end product, her skin adorned and glowing in the permanence of a two-dimensional image. She loved the fashion awards and shows too, the appraising eyes of the audience, the first steps onto the stage when all heads would turn to her, the parties afterwards where, as a model, she was never alone.

But now all that had disappeared. She was a married woman, no longer one of the bright young girls with their daring haircuts and eye-catching outfits. Evelyn was struggling to understand where she fit in this loud, dazzling group.

She found Henry by the bar. A cluttered mess of tumblers, mostly dirty now, whisky bottles, orange peel, ice melting in a silver bowl, Evelyn looked at it all and felt that longing again. A desire to turn back time.

Henry was laughing loudly with two men, both magazine editors Evelyn recognized from her working days. Cigarette smoke drifted in the air between them. Nestling against her husband, Evelyn wrapped her arm around his waist. When the two men turned back to the bar, she whispered to Henry.

'Are you ready to leave?'

He nodded. Hand in hand, they wound their way between the guests, collecting their coats from the rack next to the door.

Their home in Pimlico was supposed to be Evelyn's pride and joy. When they moved in after a two-week honeymoon in

The Model Patient

France, Evelyn's friends had processed through every room, exclaiming in astonishment at the size, the light, the two spare bedrooms, the wardrobe already stuffed with Evelyn's clothes, the kitchen with all the newest cooking appliances, wedding gifts still in their boxes on the countertop. She had been excited then, sharing her friends' joyful curiosity for the direction her new life was taking, a life of picking out paints and curtains and cushion covers, a life of central heating that worked and a husband to take her out for dinner and love her every day. One man. Not the unsatisfying parade of boys who she hadn't even wanted, not really.

But tonight, when Evelyn and Henry closed the door on the bitter winter weather, salt from the road sticking to their shoes, Evelyn could not conjure that same passion. Married now for nearly two years, Evelyn was frustrated by how quickly the novelty of her new life had lost its shine.

When she turned on the light in the kitchen, the yellow tiles looked dull and domestic, and the familiar sound of Henry filling a glass of water from the tap made her feel tired. She tried to shake the feeling away by wrapping her arms around her husband's waist, pressing herself into his back. His shirt was damp, but she didn't mind, her hands moving lower to his belt.

Turning, he kissed her forehead and took her hands in his.

'Upstairs?' he said. It was a question that seemed to offer a promise of more. And yet Evelyn felt the low tug of disappointment, the spontaneous passion she needed to lift her mood vanishing fast. But she nodded, leading the way up to their bedroom. Reaching the top of the stairs, she turned, extending her hand to draw him to her.

There was only empty space, devoid even of shadows, no husband following her up the stairs.

When Henry finally joined her, she had nearly given up on him. She watched from the edge of the bed as he pulled off his trousers, folding them neatly over the back of a chair. Placing his shoes at the bottom of the wardrobe, he lingered there, fastidiously rubbing a mark off the leather with his handkerchief. Evelyn stretched out one leg, studying the long pale gleam of her skin in the dim lamplight.

She longed to find a way to make him come to her. If only he would look at her, truly look at her. She wanted hunger and urgency. She wanted desire. For two years she had tried to make him touch her in new ways, guiding him towards those parts of herself he knew nothing about. There would be moments of connection, fleeting sensations that gave her hope. But then, too soon, they'd return to routine, the same predictable motions ending with the same predictable frustration.

He got into bed behind her and she turned, crawling up the mattress until she was next to him. Slipping beneath the covers, she touched his chest, finding calm from the regular beat of his heart. Henry had a beautiful body, a sturdy athleticism left over from his days of school sports and National Service. Evelyn loved looking at him, how safe it made her feel to be close to him. He caught her watching sometimes, when he was getting changed for work in the morning and she was lying in bed. When they were first married, he'd wink at her in the reflection of the mirror on their bedroom wall, and she'd blush, pretending to hide her face in embarrassment. That playfulness – she longed to get it back.

Henry took her hand and kissed it, his lips at her wrist.

'Have you thought about our conversation?' he said, and Evelyn felt her heart lurch.

'I thought we could wait a little longer,' she replied, trying to keep her voice calm. 'There's no rush, is there?'

Evelyn's thoughts had, in fact, been dominated by their conversation, an endless cycle of indecision. It frightened her how quickly she'd considered giving in to him, even though it was not what she wanted. This was not a new discussion, but there had been a different intensity to his words recently. She worried it would not be long before his reluctant patience darkened into anger.

She pressed her pelvis into the side of his thigh. A distraction, anything to remind him that it was she that he had married, Evelyn, not a phantom baby who did not even exist. He sighed, barely perceptible, but Evelyn could feel it in the depression of his chest, a balloon deflating.

Reaching across to the lamp, he pulled on the cord, plunging the room into darkness.

'Goodnight, baby girl,' he said, finding the corner of her lips for a quick, chaste kiss.

And then he was gone, turned away from her, his shoulders forming a block in the dark. Evelyn blinked, her eyes slowly becoming accustomed to the night, the shapes of the room reforming themselves into grey and fragile shadows.

Once Henry's breath had loosened into the even rise and fall of sleep, Evelyn slipped out of bed, wrapping her dressing gown around her.

To sleep was impossible. She knew the nightmare would come to her again and she could not face it, not tonight.

As silently as possible, she descended the stairs, turning on no lights, instead letting the street lights of Pimlico filter in between the curtains. Taking a tiny key from an ornamental silver bowl, she unlocked her writing desk, the one Henry had bought her as a wedding gift with its pretty compartments for letters and pens, and pulled out her sketchbook. She lowered herself onto the rug in the middle of the room, her legs crossed and her bare feet tucked beneath her thighs.

Opening a new page, she closed her eyes, settling into the sensation of the pencil pressing lightly onto the paper. It was too dark to draw anything neat, so she sketched without looking at the page. Breathing deeply and letting her hand guide her, she thought back to the party, to her conversation with Lionel, to the decision she had made.

Lionel Diallo was always able to tell when something was wrong, not an obvious problem like the temperature being too cold or the photographer getting carried away with the physical impracticality of a pose. No, it was more that he could dig deep beneath her smiles and her make-up, sensing when she was too afraid to speak out. It was Lionel who had saved her many times when she was young and trusting and too keen to impress on those early jobs they did together.

And it was Lionel, a gifted designer himself, who had encouraged Evelyn to try jewellery design. It was he who had taught Evelyn how to harness her love of art and fashion, how to develop the precise skills of a designer, guiding her on types of metals, jewels, the avant-garde new methods of jewellers who combined precious metals with commonplace materials, how to conjure the dynamism of the creations with paper and pencil. She had taken a course at Goldsmiths, learning the basics of silversmithing, which helped her work to cross the border from sketches into detailed, meticulously planned designs.

But for Evelyn, with her marriage and all the changes it brought, the fantasy of designing jewellery with Lionel had come to an end. It was not possible to continue, not when everything else in her life had moved in a new direction.

Lionel had taken her by the arm when he saw her at the party, ushering her to the back of the shop where two small changing rooms were hidden behind thick red velour curtains. Extracting the drink out of her hand and placing it next to him, he had sat opposite her on the wooden floor of the changing room, the light from the party spilling through in dim red streaks. She imagined that he was a fortune teller in a circus tent, the music from the record player dampening into the strange magic of the air around her. Lionel's eyes found hers through the dark.

It wasn't long before she was telling him about the nightmare, her terror every time she woke, the cold sweat that seeped into the sheets. It always started differently: sometimes she was travelling in a car, other times she was packing a suitcase, once it was an obstacle course like the ones she used to do in the dreaded physical education lessons at school. Last night, she was on the school stage, walking up to collect a prize.

She shivered, unsettled by the throbbing pain in her chest that had grown as she was speaking.

'That sounds terrifying. How many times have you had this nightmare?'

'Nearly every night. It began a few months ago, but I don't know what, if anything, starts it. I just know that it is making me afraid to sleep.'

'I have an idea,' Lionel said, handing Evelyn back her drink, the condensation dripping onto her leg. 'A friend of mine, Theo, has been seeing a psychologist. His closest friend died, and he has struggled with the grief, especially when many people didn't know their friendship was so important to him. His parents can't understand why he has sunk into such a bad place.'

'I'm sorry,' Evelyn said. 'That sounds difficult. But is the psychotherapy helping?'

'I believe so. And my friend did mention that this particular psychologist is doing a research paper on symbolism in dreams. Apparently he asked Theo if he could use one of his dreams as a case study.'

The Model Patient

Evelyn played with the fold of the changing room curtain, testing the softness of the fabric. She knew she needed help if she was to be able to escape from the nightmare. And there were the other problems too, the ones she hadn't told Lionel, anxieties far more real than a serpent writhing through her dreams. The ones about Henry, her fear of having a child, the painful visceral panic she felt when she imagined a baby growing within her, the birth control pills she took, obsessively, every morning, despite Henry's pleas for her to stop.

Perhaps this psychotherapist could help her with that too, give her the courage she needed to move on with her life, to give Henry the baby he wanted, to be calm at last.

Standing and moving to the window, Evelyn peered at the page of her sketchbook, adjusting her eyes to the pool of light that shone down from the nearby street light. Her pencil strokes were uneven, some thick and dark, others barely marking the page. She had drawn the long neck of a woman, just the tip of the chin and the sloping lines of the collarbones in the faintest of pencil. Wrapped around the neck were scores of little circles. She examined them again, trying to work out what it was she had drawn. The shapes were familiar, their meaning just out of touch. Squinting a little, she looked at the drawing afresh.

She knew exactly what these were: four thick rows of pearls pressed tightly into the skin.

Shutting the book abruptly, Evelyn sighed, frustrated. She knew that necklace. She hated it; and she resented the disappointed look Henry's mother had given her when she refused to wear it on her wedding day, how the one time she did wear it to the opera with Henry and his parents, she had felt as though the air was being sucked from her lungs. A pearl choker, the precious family heirloom, the chains of motherhood, obedience, the safety of following the path of least resistance. Yet she had welcomed the gift when Henry's parents first presented it to her at their engagement dinner. It was only after Ruth Westbrook asked Evelyn if she was looking forward to giving up all that mucking around in front of a camera that her excitement at taking her place in the Westbrook family had darkened into a breathless panic. But Evelyn, then, was too wrapped up in her feelings for Henry to think to challenge him when he persuaded her that his mother didn't mean it.

Evelyn ripped the page out of the sketchbook.

As she walked upstairs, she tore the drawing into shreds, white strands of paper falling around her ankles. Tomorrow, she thought, she'd tidy it all away.

CHAPTER 2

A receptionist let her in, guiding her around the corner to a sleek wooden bench that lined one wall of the waiting area. It was the stillness that Evelyn noticed most, the doors to consulting rooms closed and not a sound slipping beneath them. The building felt empty, asleep, and it seemed to Evelyn as though she had left behind the reality of the outside world, entering instead that strange vacancy before the beginning of a dream.

It was only when the neat clip of the receptionist's heels broke the silence that Evelyn found something real to grasp on to, and she was able to take in her surroundings. The receptionist's desk was next to the front door, around the corner from the waiting area, and it was disorientating to Evelyn not to be able to see her. She had barely looked at the woman when she'd arrived. Too nervous to do her usual thorough assessment, what she did notice was that the receptionist was young and pretty, and that she smiled brightly with a strong red lipstick that reminded Evelyn of the Max

Factor make-up she used to wear in the fifties when she was preparing for a day at a catalogue shoot.

Extricating a magazine from a wooden rack to the side of the bench, Evelyn tried to distract herself. It was a recent edition of *Vogue* and she felt a faint tug of disappointment that it was far too new for her to be featured in any of the advertisements.

Today, when she looked up, she did see an image of herself, but this time it was a reflection in the mirrored door of a wooden cabinet, her body carved up into the neat squares of the glass. Wearing her coat and a large woollen scarf, she had not warmed up from the bitterness of this January day, and there was a red mottling on her cheeks as though she was slowly and unevenly starting to thaw. She had walked the entire way, an excuse to get out of the house as early as possible. By the time she arrived at Upper Wimpole Street and was ringing the bell of the attractive Georgian town house where the psychologist held his clinic, she was frozen, the soles of her feet stiff and numb.

Lionel had called her the day after the party with the details of his friend's psychologist, and Evelyn had set up the appointment immediately, before she changed her mind. She was to be a private patient, paying in cash, she told the receptionist on the call. The thought of explaining to Henry what she was doing was a step too far, so cash payments, drawn from her career savings, were essential. But she was willing

The Model Patient

to try anything to sleep calmly. And maybe, too, for Henry to turn to her again.

And now, less than a week later, she was here in his waiting room. The telephone call with Dr Daley, once the receptionist had put her through, was brief and formal and she had been relieved that he did not try to ask her any of the details of her problems over the phone. She did not know if she would have found the words to speak them, not from her living room with all the smiling photographs from her wedding day surrounding her, the cushions she had chosen with Henry, the soft trappings of domesticity.

Unbuttoning her coat and removing her scarf, she tried to arrange herself more attractively. Her hair was tied loosely in her usual half-ponytail, backcombed a little on the crown to emulate her idol Brigitte Bardot, and the ends were curled under. She looked untidier than she would have liked, the blonde layers around her face falling in her eyes. A smudge of black eyeliner had broken its bounds, and she dabbed at it anxiously, leaning forward to see the mirror more clearly.

At eleven o'clock exactly, a door opened nearby and the sound of footsteps travelled down a corridor towards her. She glanced up at the man walking into the waiting area, uncertain whether this was her doctor or a patient leaving an appointment. Dr Daley had explained to her on the telephone that this clinic was used by a number of psychologists, and that she may encounter other doctors and patients in the waiting room. It was reassuring how careful he was to put her at ease, to explain what to expect from the appointment, how to get there, who would let her in, where she would wait. He told her he was a clinical psychologist with a doctorate from University College London, and while it was true that he was conducting research on symbolism in dreams, their appointments would be confidential. On the call she had thought it was unnecessary how many details he was giving her, but now she was grateful.

The man smiled as he reached her.

'Mrs Westbrook,' he said. So this was Dr Daley. She stood and smiled too, offering her hand in greeting.

To her surprise, he did not lift his hand in return. Instead he clasped his hands lightly in front of him, his eyes fixed on hers.

'Shall we?' His smile was kind and if he had noticed her awkward attempt at a handshake, he did not reveal it.

He led the way, and she walked behind him, terribly conscious of the squeak of her Oxford flats on the wooden floorboards. She tried to focus on him instead, a trick she had learnt to ease the nerves of a new job, concentrating on the tics and eccentricities of the photographer when her poses were becoming tense. Dr Daley's shoes were also squeaking, she noticed with a disproportionate sense of relief. They were black ankle boots, one of his trouser legs partially tucked in at the back. He was wearing cream trousers and a collarless jacket, chequered red and brown.

Evelyn found herself staring at his hair as they walked along the corridor, trying to work out its colour: a deep dark brown, nearly black, that tinted auburn when he passed underneath the ceiling lamp. With thick and tight curls that fell untidily towards his shoulders, as well as the dark shadow of a beard, there was something just a little animal about him, she thought. Long hair on a man had always interested her, how deliberate it was, a refusal to conform to the unspoken rules of society. It was rare for the male models she had worked with to have long hair, most of them sticking to the safe choices of side-partings, a quiff or pompadours, or even a bowl cut if they wanted to be a little more daring. And then there was Henry with his regular trips to the barber, the neat trim of his hairline a product of his boarding school days of cadet corps drill practice.

'You take the sofa,' he said as they entered the consulting room.

Evelyn's gaze flicked over the room: all neutral tones, wooden furniture, a leather sofa with a matching armchair opposite, cream curtains hanging either side of the window, a light net curtain covering the glass. Evelyn could just make out a small garden at the back, a patch of frozen grass that surely never saw any sun. A desk was tucked into the corner, a row of books across the back.

She wasn't sure what she'd expected. A girl she used to work with, Bethany Graham, had seen a psychologist, 'to be analysed', she'd called it, rolling her eyes in self-mockery. It was her father who'd made her go, though Evelyn had never found out the reason why. Bethany had described how four times a week she'd lie on a couch while a psychoanalyst sat on a chair just behind her head, so she couldn't see him. She could hear him making notes every time she stopped talking.

Dr Daley was standing in front of the armchair, waiting for her to be seated. She sat down gingerly, perched far forward on the cushion. Surely, she thought, he would tell her if she was supposed to lie down. After the embarrassment of her greeting, she did not want to get anything else wrong. She placed her handbag and coat next to her, still clutching her scarf. In the silence that followed, while Dr Daley waited for her to settle, she realized she was grasping it tightly, twisting the fabric into an untidy mess. She relaxed her grip and moved her scarf onto the pile with her coat and bag. The room smelt good, a mixture of mint and eucalyptus, and she let the scent soothe her. It made her think of her mother, those steaming bowls of water and mint essence when Evelyn had a cold.

'Shall we start with you telling me a little about why you are here today?'

He had a low voice with an accent she found hard to place. British, she thought, but with an American inflection that came through in the way he rounded his 'r's. His voice, she had thought on the telephone call, had reminded her a little of an English teacher from her schooldays. She had fond memories of Mr Martin, newly graduated and on exchange from Princeton University. Young and full of energy, Mr Martin seemed so different from their other teachers, all women who at the time Evelyn had thought of as ancient and old-fashioned. Mr Martin often read to them in lessons, poems and short stories that set her imagination alight.

Today, however, seeing Dr Daley in the flesh, it was to

another time, another voice, another man, that her mind seemed to travel. But she pushed the thought away. That was not why she was here.

Evelyn nodded. She had practised this, thought about how to frame her problems, how to make it clear why she needed help, without sounding deranged. It was a difficult balance to find: she didn't want him to think she was wasting his time speaking to a bored housewife with a bad dream, a privileged woman who simply needed to embrace her marital duties and put her hysterical nightmares to bed. Nor did she want him to think she was insane.

'I am here,' she said in the words she had rehearsed, 'because I would like to be able to settle into my marriage. I have some problems that are, I think, stopping me from sleeping.'

Already, the sentences were slipping away from her, and she nodded again, gathering herself together. 'When I married my husband nearly two years ago in March 1961, everything was perfect, a new and exciting life with the man I love. I was sad to give up my job, but Henry didn't want me to continue with it. I was a model, you see, and the lifestyle wasn't suitable for a married woman, according to Henry.'

She looked up at Dr Daley, searching his face to see how he was responding to her. It was difficult to know how much she should say. But there was nothing in his expression to help her.

'Very few of the other girls were married, at least not to

someone like Henry: too much travelling, and I know he didn't like some of the working conditions.'

'What didn't he like about them?' Dr Daley probed.

'The demands of the photographers, I guess, and the long hours, me traipsing around London with my A–Z. And how I wouldn't really know what I was going to be asked to do until I got there. It worried him.' Evelyn could see Dr Daley was about to ask another question, but she ploughed ahead. There was so much she could say about her old career, but that wasn't why she was here.

'I accepted his wishes because I was in love and excited about the changes ahead. We had a wonderful honeymoon, moved into our beautiful home, and continued to do all the things we enjoyed when we first met and were courting.'

'What sort of things?' Dr Daley said. Evelyn was noticing the way he guided her out of vague statements; he wanted to know exactly what she meant, but Evelyn resisted. She would much prefer for him to work things out for himself.

'Oh, you know, parties and dinners and seeing friends. Weekends drinking too much and lazy Sundays, just the two of us.' Evelyn blushed, looking down at her hands. It wasn't necessary to tell him about Henry's insistence that they wait until they married to have sex, how Evelyn hid so much of who she was, how she moulded herself into the woman Henry wanted her to be.

'And something changed?' he prompted.

'It was a gradual change. At first I barely noticed it, this nagging sensation that there was a gap in my life. I tried to counter it by going out more, visiting galleries, shopping, seeing my friends, regularly dropping into the flat where I used to live with my friend Diana, spending time with her like we always used to. But I'd always have to leave in time to get home for Henry returning from work. He wanted me to learn to cook, you see. I thought he was joking when he brought up the subject. I could cook just fine. But he wanted me to cook the way his mother cooked, carefully selecting ingredients, wasting nothing, conjuring these miraculous dishes that she had made even during the rationing of the war. I had no interest in spending longer than necessary in the kitchen.'

Evelyn smiled at him, shaking her head with a nervous laugh. He smiled back at her, the tiniest of nods, and she felt her shoulders relaxing.

'Before I married, I lived with my best friend, in a little flat near Sloane Square. Diana and I have been friends since childhood. Diana is always working: either she's teaching, or writing, or training teachers, or attending lectures on child development at the Tavistock clinic. Our cooking was completely chaotic, but that was our preference.'

Evelyn paused, sighing. She was getting distracted and she knew she sounded exactly like a bored housewife. Here she was, apparently seeing a psychologist because she didn't want to cook.

She glanced up and met Dr Daley's gaze. He was looking at her intently, no sign at all that he thought she was being ridiculous, wasting his time with her petty problems. That look in his eyes, it gave her the confidence to continue.

'But then Henry started talking about trying for a baby. He wanted me to stop taking the birth control pill but I couldn't bring myself to do it.'

Evelyn could feel that blush creeping up her neck again. She focused her gaze on the fireplace to the left of Dr Daley, the grate replaced with a large, smooth ornamental stone.

'Can you tell me how Henry reacted to your decision?'

Evelyn was thankful for his prompt, the guidance she needed to feel that it was acceptable to tell him more.

'He was a little upset, I think. But he wasn't too concerned. I guess he thought that I just needed another month or two, that I'd be ready soon. But when he asked again, I still didn't want to have a baby.'

Evelyn's hands drifted to her stomach. Without thinking, she pressed them into her dress, gathering the soft wool between her fingers. 'In fact,' she continued, 'the thought of it fills me with dread. And I don't know why. I've always loved babies. When I was younger I used to enjoy imagining myself with a family. Now that the possibility is right in front of me, it all feels completely different.'

'And is this creating difficulties for you and your husband?' he asked. Evelyn nodded. She knew she should explain that her goal in coming to psychotherapy was to learn how to tidy away these concerns. Dr Daley, she hoped, would tell her how to find happiness in her married life, exorcizing her nightmares at the same time. She wanted to know how to embrace motherhood with all the excitement expected of her. But she suddenly felt exhausted, as though even the act of saying this goal out loud was demanding too much. Slumping back against the sofa, she closed her eyes, trying to find the will to continue.

When she opened her eyes, Dr Daley was watching her. As she briefly caught his gaze, she realized that he wasn't making any notes. His hands were empty and there was no notebook on his lap. It was comforting, she found, to be able to talk to him without the barrier of a notebook between them. Somehow that would have changed it all, made her nervous about what he was choosing to write down on the page.

She tried again, pulling herself forward so she was leaning over her legs, her elbows resting on her thighs. It was a gathering together, this physical change that drew her back into the moment.

'I want to be able to give him a child, I do. But I resent how quickly I have become, I don't know, not enough for him. When we met, when we married even, we loved to be together, weekends spent with no one else but each other. We were all we needed. He didn't mind my carefulness with birth control methods then. I think, maybe, he was relieved that he didn't need to deal with it himself.'

'So he was happy to use contraception at the start of your marriage? And before?'

Evelyn blushed again.

'We didn't sleep together before we were married.'

Dr Daley waited, silent, no apology for the assumption of his question. In the seconds that followed, Evelyn was surprised to realize that she wasn't offended. Rather, it was helpful. Once again he seemed to be giving her permission to say what she needed, no restrictions, no boundaries.

'I must have been one of the first women in the country to be prescribed those pills. It was the end of 1961, just after a Christmas spent with Henry's family. We'd been married for nine months already, but I knew I wasn't ready to have a child. I think I worried Henry would start suggesting I should stop using the diaphragm. And so I wanted something else, a safety net I suppose. I was afraid that my doctor would refuse to prescribe to me, that I wouldn't have a good enough reason. But I was lucky. Not every doctor would have asked so few questions.'

'Did you tell your husband that you were taking these contraceptive pills?'

She looked up at him, trying to hide her astonishment. It was frightening how quickly he had asked exactly the question she found most difficult to answer.

'No. Not immediately. I continued using the diaphragm, but I was taking birth control pills, too.'

'How long did this go on for before you told Henry?'

'A few months, I think. I did tell him eventually, when I was ready.'

It wasn't a lie, not really. She had told Henry, but only because he'd found the pot of pills hidden in her underwear drawer.

'And how did he react?'

'He understood,' she said, too quickly. He had not understood, not at all. They had argued for days, and she was certain the discovery had accelerated his attempts to persuade her to try for a child. The only way he could trust her again, he seemed to imply, was if she gave him a child.

Dr Daley nodded, but a faint line had appeared between his eyebrows. Evelyn could not repress the shiver that ran down her spine. She knew he did not believe her.

'It is certainly something important for us to think about together, if you would like to, that is.' He glanced up to the clock above the door and Evelyn followed his gaze. She felt a little burst of panic. It was forty-five minutes into the appointment and she had not even mentioned her nightmare. She braced herself. She couldn't leave without talking about it.

'There is another reason I am here,' she said, determined. Dr Daley nodded encouragingly and she spoke fast. 'I have been having a recurring nightmare where I transform into a serpent and then consume myself.'

She paused, doubt overwhelming her. Even though Lionel had recommended Dr Daley for his interest in dreams, she worried he would laugh at her. Here she was, an anxious housewife wasting his time with her fantastical dreams.

'That sounds very frightening.'

There was something about the way he said those four words that loosened a knot within her. Without any warning, her eyes swelled with tears and her face crumpled. The tears were fast and hot.

She reached for her bag, overwhelmed by a desire to cover her face and dry the tears. It was a relief to find a handkerchief folded neatly inside. As she lifted it to her eyes, she shook her head firmly and tried to push away that unsettling rush of emotion.

Dr Daley waited, the silence building again. Evelyn could feel her mind straining, desperate to find a sound on which to anchor her thoughts. But there was nothing, just a silent space in the gap between doctor and patient.

He seemed to sense, without looking, that the clock had reached eleven-fifty. The appointment was over.

'We are going to have to stop now,' he said. 'But let's return to this next week, if you would like to continue meeting with me?'

Evelyn nodded. She had barely started. 'Yes, I would like that.'

He stood, opening the door for her while she gathered her belongings. As she left, saying a brief thank you, she couldn't help feeling like a child who had overstayed their welcome.

The receptionist met her at the front door, opening it and ushering her out onto the street. The young woman said something to Evelyn, complimenting her handbag maybe or perhaps just a comment on the weather, but she forgot what it was as soon as she stepped outside.

Crossing the street, a freezing wind biting her skin and obstacles of dirty snow lining the pavement, she turned and looked back at the building. The door was shut and the curtains of the front room were drawn. But part of her was still inside, trying to find order in all the things she had said.

CHAPTER 3

Evelyn took extra care with the dinner that night, picking out Henry's favourite wine and lighting a fresh set of candles. She had trawled through recipe books in the afternoon, searching for a dessert that might conjure the ideal combination of indulgence with home-cooked comfort. Sometimes Evelyn suspected that the way to her husband's heart really was through food. He was obsessed with meals, in the same way that all men who have spent their lives in boarding schools, university halls, National Service, and then Whitehall, are drawn to the reassuring regularity of an institutional canteen.

'Good carrot cake, Evelyn,' he said as he cut himself another slice. 'Mum used to make this during the war. It was always delicious, despite having less sugar.' He swirled the tip of his fork into the cream cheese frosting. 'And definitely none of this icing.'

Evelyn tried to suppress her sigh. Of course his mother's cake was perfect, even with the challenges of rationing.

Evelyn, too, had grown up with a no-waste attitude, but she had never managed to master the effortless ease with which Henry's mother ran her home.

In the months leading up to their wedding, Evelyn made half-hearted attempts at learning how to be a good wife. Diana had dutifully tried to help, but they both found it impossible to be serious. Back then, there was no sign that Henry would expect his wife to be a devoted homemaker. If only she'd paid more attention: his mother was evidence enough of what was to come.

It was not only the homemaking. There was sex, too, how different it would be from Evelyn's previous experiences. Diana and Evelyn managed to find an old copy of *Married Love* by Dr Marie Stopes, and read out extracts to each other in the evenings, until their laughter became too much and they had to stop. When Stopes wrote of the necessity of knowledge and training to be able to achieve mutually pleasurable sex, Evelyn had not worried. Henry would know what he was doing. And she was not exactly new to sex herself.

But when it came to their wedding night, and they'd arrived at their hotel in the foothills of the South Downs, the pleasure of anticipation came to a disappointing end. As Henry pulled himself out of her, a self-satisfied haze in his eyes, her mind had drifted back to that little book, those words of warning she had assumed were not meant for her.

And yet she did have hope. They had their whole lives to discover one another, to find the right touch to make their lovemaking what she believed it could be. She remembered those lines from the book, how it often took several years for couples to discover the delightful results of marriage. But it also said that 'a noble frankness would save much misery'. There was no such frankness with Henry. Rather it was a courtly but predictable dance with occasional and fleeting attempts to introduce a new, wilder rhythm.

While she had imagined that his tales of adventure in war-torn Cyprus during his National Service were indications of an inner vitality and worldly experience that would emerge when he finally allowed himself to hold her naked before him, she soon realized this was far from the reality. Henry was educated on order and routine, the rhythm of a school bell punctuating his day. As head of his house at a traditional British boarding school, he thrived on drill practice, cadet corps kit inspections, the satisfaction of a perfectly polished pair of boots. When his National Service demobilization came around in 1956, transferring into the Civil Service had suited him perfectly. Evelyn found his annotated copy of *The Handbook for the New Civil Servant* on his desk one day when they'd just married. This orange booklet of rules and regulations must have been a comforting replacement for the customs of his school days.

Although the start of their sex life had not been what she expected, Evelyn never gave up. She often thought about the first time they met, a chance encounter in the foyer of Sadler's Wells Theatre. They'd chatted in the box office queue as they collected their tickets, Evelyn adding a special edition pack of Olivier tipped cigarettes for 3 shillings and 10 pence, and then they found themselves seated side by side in the stalls. Henry's sisters were on the other side of him, too absorbed in one another's conversation to notice their brother's attention shifting to the woman on his right. His presence had dominated her thoughts, as though if everything collapsed around her, he would be there to hold her. Stravinsky's opera-oratorio *Oedipus Rex* was simply a dramatic pulse beneath her alertness to Henry at her side.

She'd introduced him to Diana two weeks later, a supposedly spontaneous but in truth highly orchestrated meeting in a Sloane Square café. Diana said afterwards that she'd known instantly he was right for Evelyn. It was the look of genuine concern on his face when Evelyn told a story of a recent audition at an obscure studio an hour's bus ride out of the city. She described how she'd wandered in a growing panic through deserted streets, her trusty A–Z street atlas failing her, and how, when she finally arrived, there were already thirty girls waiting to be seen. Her agent had been mistaken: this wasn't a modelling job at all, rather a cattle-call audition, with Evelyn rejected and sent home after one brief glimpse from the casting manager.

'He looked exactly as your father does when you tell him about your London adventures,' Diana said later that night, the two women applying cold cream to their cheeks in front of the bathroom mirror.

'What look is that?' Evelyn replied, smiling at the thought of seeing Henry again the next day. He had tickets to the ballet, so different from the men who took her to alcohol-soaked house parties and showed her off to their friends, the men who didn't even try to hide their perverse delight in her stories of demanding photographers and daring outfits.

'The way he looked at you,' Diana continued, 'it was a mixture of wanting to murder the man who rejected you, and wishing he could wrap you up in his arms.'

They had failed to foresee that this endearing protectiveness would morph into a depressingly traditional expectation of the roles of husband and wife.

And now, with Henry barely touching her, she had no opportunity to draw him close. She did not know what she could say to challenge him, not when he behaved with such gentlemanly politeness, always respectful, little gestures of love like the flowers he bought for her on his way home from the office, how he praised her attempts at making the house attractive, how he kissed her when he walked through the door.

It was this patience, this promise of a gentle, tender romance, that had first drawn Evelyn to Henry. Diana was right: he was more like her kind, predictable school teacher father than the young men she met at parties.

'You're beautiful,' he told her at the end of their first dinner date together, the two of them walking slowly towards Covent Garden Underground station. Many men had said those words to her over the years. When she was a child she was too young to understand, but she had learnt quickly, too quickly, what was expected in return. Turning to look up at him then, she waited for his words to harden into a kiss, a change of direction, maybe a night club, a dark, hidden corner of the street. But there was nothing, no expectation for more, no suggestion that now she should thank him with her body.

That was the allure, she guessed, to feel she was enough for Henry exactly as she was. Evelyn longed to recapture those early days, back when Henry adored how different she was from his mother and his sisters, a bolder sort of marriage than the model provided for him at home.

Sometimes she wished she was more like Diana, unconcerned by whether she was doing the right thing to make men like her. But then Diana's sexual education had been so entirely different from Evelyn's. Diana was more interested in the way things were changing for women, taking every opportunity to challenge the conventions passed down from their mothers. She had queued for hours to be admitted into the public gallery of the Old Bailey to hear the *Lady Chatterley's Lover* court case. Evelyn couldn't help laughing when Diana returned and told her of the prosecutor's horror that anyone would let their wife or servants read such an indecent book.

Wife or servant. It had interested Evelyn that the prosecutor would place them in the same category.

'Shall I clear up later?' said Evelyn as Henry picked the final crumbs from his plate. She reached across to him and wrapped her fingers through his.

'I'm nearly finished,' he said, untangling his hand from hers.

The Model Patient

Evelyn could not bear the frustration that seemed to tighten in her throat. Standing, she pressed one hand to the white linen table cloth. Henry smiled as she leant forward to kiss his jaw.

But then he pushed his chair backwards and she stumbled. Standing abruptly, his napkin fell at his feet.

'I need to work, I'm afraid. A big meeting tomorrow.'

He kissed her gently, his thumb lingering at her neck.

'Don't wait up for me.'

He was gone, disappearing into the living room, a glass of wine in his hand. Evelyn stared at the remains of the dinner, the cake crumbs littering the table, the scarlet residue at the bottom of her glass.

This was what she had wanted, a life of safety, of predictability. A man who loved her.

She blinked away her tears. Crying would not make this marriage work.

In the kitchen, she stood at the sink, hot water running over her hands. Looking up, she fixed her eyes on the ghost in the window and suddenly she was a child again. She shook her head, a desperate attempt to return to the present. Evelyn thought she had left that girl behind, a girl who was frightened, too weak to escape from a trap she had never understood.

It was time to learn how to be someone new.

CHAPTER 4

'I want him to love me for me, not as the mother of his child.'

Evelyn felt bolder today, the anxieties from her first appointment less acute. Dr Daley was wearing a cream polo neck sweater beneath a woollen jacket. With no tie, no stiffly ironed shirt, his fashion choice seemed to give Evelyn permission to relax. She could be having a conversation in one of her favourite King's Road cafés, rather than a psychologist's clinic just off Harley Street.

'Are you worried he'll love the child more than you?'

Evelyn blinked, turning her head from side to side, uncertain. She hadn't thought about it this way before, never considered what would happen when and if a child arrived in their lives. Did she think Henry would love the child more than her? She wasn't sure. Her own parents loved her, their only child, a proportional, sensible amount, she had always felt. They put no demands on her, no expectations, never made her feel guilty for not visiting them frequently, unlike Henry's mother who called on them constantly, thinly veiled criticisms whenever they tried to miss a Westbrook family Sunday lunch.

'My parents love each other so much,' Evelyn said. She spoke slowly, unsure of the direction of her thoughts. 'They are happy to be alone, just the two of them. Having me made no difference to the strength of their love.'

Dr Daley leaned forward. 'And how does that make you feel about your place, as the child, in your parents' relationship?'

Evelyn looked down at her hands. She was talking about her own marriage, her desire to emulate the strength of her parents' love. Dr Daley's question seemed to throw her into a different place, a different emotion.

'I don't know,' she said swiftly, pressing her fingers into the chequered fabric of her skirt. 'I guess I'm lucky to be able to get on with my life and not worry that I am leaving them out. They are happy without me.'

He nodded, but said nothing. A silence built between them. Evelyn tried to control the direction of her thoughts, get back on track, find some way to talk about her goals, about why she was here in this room, seeking help. But it was impossible, not when a memory was rapidly encroaching, unavoidable like the current beneath a wave.

She found herself speaking, without even realizing why this felt so essential, why the words could not be contained.

'My father was the headmaster of a boys' boarding school in Surrey, until recently when he retired. We lived on the school grounds, a large house that was far too big for the three of us. I had a baby brother, but he died a week after he was born when I was a toddler: a heart problem, my parents said, but they rarely spoke about it.'

Evelyn frowned, remembering that day she told Henry about her baby brother. They were on the train down to visit her parents for the first time. She had felt this need to warn him, to prepare him for the quiet of her home compared to Henry's with his four brothers and sisters and the growing roll-call of nephews and nieces.

'It's a complex question, and we don't need to go into it now unless you would like to, but do you think you would have liked to have spoken more about your brother's death with your parents?'

'Maybe. I don't know. That loss was hard for me to understand, and I think I felt this unspoken need to make up for it, to be the model child who was enough for them.'

Dr Daley tilted his head and Evelyn thought she could see a look of sympathy in his eyes. But then it faded, and there was nothing for her to cling on to. She continued, savouring that fleeting look, how it helped her to find the words she needed to say.

'The first weekend of each school holiday was a special time because my father could relax at last, and we would spend it together, just the three of us, cooking a meal or going to the local cinema. But one of these weekends when I was about seven years old and it was the start of the summer holidays, they told me that there was a work event, a dinner with the governors I think, and I was to sleep across the street with my friend Diana, whose father was also a teacher at the school, though he was away then. It was the war, and many of the male teachers had signed up. My father needed to keep the school running; and he was too old, with a persistent knee injury from fighting in the first war.

'I went over to Diana's house in the early afternoon, and we played together for a while before Diana's mother cooked dinner. We did everything together, even then. I suppose it was our names to begin with, Evelyn Anderson and Diana Ashley, the first two in the class register, always in a pair,' she added, a fleeting distraction before she forced herself back to the memory she was trying to explain. 'When we were getting ready for bed, I realized I had forgotten to bring my toy rabbit, Margaret.'

Evelyn blushed. It seemed silly to be naming her rabbit in front of this man.

'Diana tried to cheer me up by offering one of her own toys. She was always kind that way. But they wouldn't do. So, when her mother was distracted by a new radio, we slipped outside and ran across the street to my house. I knew my parents were going to be out, but the back door wouldn't be locked. It was as we were running around the side of the house into the garden that I saw them.

'My parents were in the kitchen, seated at the kitchen table. It was summer, so the blackout curtains weren't drawn yet, and I could see inside. There were candles lit, I remember. They'd served up a meal on their plates, and they were holding hands. I watched as my father leant over and kissed my mother. There was a photograph on the table between them, a baby in my mother's arms. I knew, instinctively, that it was my brother, that tiny baby whom they mourned silently. They were supposed to be out at this boring work event, not hiding from me at home, wishing for a different child. That was when I knew, I think, that they would never love me the way they loved each other.'

Evelyn realized she was sweating, the room suddenly too hot. She hadn't thought about this for years. Perhaps not since the night itself.

'And how do you feel about this now?' Dr Daley asked, his hands clasped loosely in his lap. 'Do you think it is affecting the way you imagine what it means to be a parent?'

'I don't know. I always thought I wanted to be like my parents, finding that love they have for one another for myself, in my own marriage. But perhaps it has made me anxious that I won't find it, that Henry will love the child more than me, just like my parents preferred each other. And, of course, their memory of a dead little boy, a perfect baby for ever. It will just be another version of taking second place.'

In the silence that followed, Evelyn could sense Dr Daley watching her. She wanted him to say something, to offer a solution, some reassurance that she was not second place. But how could he do that, she reasoned with herself as the silence continued to grow. Only Henry, and maybe her parents, could give her what she needed.

A noise from out in the corridor broke through the silence, the sound of a door closing, footsteps, the murmur of voices.

The Model Patient

It was strange to think of others coming here, waiting for Dr Daley on one of those hard wooden benches. Was it the same for them, she found herself thinking, their thoughts circling and catching like a scarf trapped on a thorn bush?

Dr Daley's voice brought her back to the room.

'This is worrying for you, isn't it? This idea of being second place. Do you think your career ever brought up similar feelings?'

'Maybe. It was more that I never knew if I was going to get a call on the day of a shoot telling me the advertising company had changed their mind, that they'd picked someone else. Or I'd travel to a studio across London to be looked at, only to be rejected when I got there. I felt that every job I took had to be this huge success to make sure I was chosen again.'

'Yes. I imagine that must have been stressful.'

'I am not sure that I found it stressful. It's that saying, I think – you're only as good as your last performance. I could never settle until I was booked for my next job, as though that was evidence my previous photoshoot was good enough.'

'And now, without your work, how do you know if you're good enough?'

'It's impossible.'

'Yes, I can see it might feel that way.'

Outside, behind those thin chiffon curtains, a snowstorm was building. The frame of the window rattled and Evelyn shivered, pulling the sleeves of her sweater down over her

Lucy Ashe

hands. She did not want to go outside, back out in this frigid winter weather.

But the time was up, and she had no choice but to face the cold.

CHAPTER 5

The thought of going home was intolerable, not when her mind was scattered in too many directions, refusing to settle. Evelyn wrapped the scarf high around her chin and turned south towards Oxford Street. She wished she could meet Diana now, but she'd have to wait until the end of the school day.

Diana Ashley was a schoolteacher at an all-girls' school in South Kensington, not too dissimilar from the one Evelyn and Diana had attended in Surrey, though without the green playing fields and close access to countryside walks. The Bourne House School for Girls was nestled on the corner of two streets behind Sloane Square, and Evelyn would often meet Diana there after she finished teaching for the day, waiting for her on the pavement opposite while girls in their pristine uniform rushed out of the double doors.

It had been their Friday routine before she was married, Evelyn coming from the haute couture shop where she worked two days a week in the showroom. The only job that gave Evelyn any kind of regularity to her week, she enjoyed stalking around the room in stunning designs that she'd never be able to afford, nor, in fact, have an occasion to wear. The customers could be demanding, their underhand criticisms hidden behind patronizing smiles. While they might not look the way Evelyn did in clouds of chiffon or a structured suit, they wanted her to understand she'd never match their position in society. It amused Evelyn that she didn't care. She didn't want their life. And besides, that type of fashion was disappearing. Soon they'd be looking dated and tired, while Evelyn embraced the new fashions of the Mods, bought at a far cheaper price from the independent shops opening up along the King's Road.

By the time Evelyn reached the school, she had almost succeeded in calming her mind. After an hour in a café, followed by a bracing walk around the Serpentine, fresh snow brushing her skin, she was starting to feeling a little better. Hyde Park had glistened with ice, large stretches of the lake frozen and sleek. Snow had built up around the edge of the water, and it was difficult to tell where the grass ended and the lake began. Icicles hung from a 'Bathing prohibited' sign and a new board had been erected announcing a five pound fine for anyone who ventured out onto the ice.

Watching three geese moving in a slow procession along the surface of the lake, Evelyn had felt a strange lurch of fear. Just last week she had seen a Canada goose rescued from the frozen waters of the Thames, its feet stuck hard into the ice. She had found herself crying as she watched the goose, how valiantly it seemed to pretend there was nothing wrong, its body calm and serene. It was only once the men released it, chipping away at the ice with their chisels, that the goose started to panic, its legs moving fast and frenziedly through the snow.

It was too cold to stay out for long, so she passed the rest of the time wandering through Harvey Nichols, trying the perfumes and cosmetics, before finding herself in the jewellery section. Pearls and diamonds dominated, cutting the light beneath the sparklingly clean glass cases.

Evelyn moved quickly past the pearls, afraid of that unsettling sensation that she knew would catch her if she remained for too long among the chokers, bracelets and earrings. Smooth and pale and pretty, pearls made her think of porcelain dolls and bone china teacups, cream-topped stockings and the perfect silk folds of her wedding dress.

While her mother-in-law's pearl choker was stifling and old-fashioned, there had been one particular necklace that Evelyn had enjoyed wearing. She remembered the day well. It was just before she met Henry, and she was photographed in a twisting, snake-like strand of pearls. How cold they had felt against her skin, falling between her breasts and down to her stomach. She hadn't minded removing her blouse for this shoot. The photographer was, unusually, a woman, and Evelyn knew that the photograph would be unlike the typical advertising shoots. This was to be for the wall of a small jewellery shop, the photograph more art than advertisement, just a suggestion of the erotic but subtle, a little hazy, the boundaries between her body and the light around her blurred and beautiful. The designer too was female, a young and brilliant new jewellery maker who took the staid old styles of the pre-war years and transformed them into surrealist, modern artworks. While the pearls fell along the curves of her body, they ended with a bold, oversized charm that hung against her navel. It was an apple, moulded out of stainless steel, indented with the deep bite of teeth.

Evelyn had loved that apple, and was sorry to leave it behind at the end of the day. When the designer sent her a signed print of the photograph a few months later, Evelyn framed it and put it up on her bedroom wall. Henry, on visiting her flat and finding his way into her bedroom, had admired it, mimicking the fall of the pearls with his fingers as she lay back against the pillows. They had nearly slept together that afternoon, but Henry had suddenly removed his hands from her waist, kissing her chastely on her forehead. Sometimes, looking back, she wondered why she had never disillusioned him: Evelyn was not a virgin. But perhaps there was safety in being able to start afresh, a new Evelyn with a different sort of man. With Henry, she could stay silent and pretend the men from her past had never existed.

Now, in their marital home, the photograph was hidden away inside the tiny dressing room that linked the bedroom and bathroom. Sometimes, when she was hanging up the laundry, she fantasized about coming home to find the photograph on her pillow. Henry would be waiting for her, his need matching her own. But the image remained tucked away, forgotten and unremarkable.

The Model Patient

Diana hugged her when she finally emerged through the school doors, shivering from the shock of the cold. Since that first dramatic snowfall in December, the excitement of the weather had rapidly switched into frustration when snow turned brown then black, ice threatening to derail every venture outside. It was still grim, a grey pall arriving with the growing dark, and even the glistening shopfronts struggled to cut through the depression of so many weeks of bitterness. Diana and Evelyn walked fast, arm in arm, as they headed back to Diana's flat. Number Six, they called it, as though it was the only flat with that number in the entirety of London.

Two bedrooms, a kitchen, bathroom and living room on the top floor of a house on Markham Street, Diana and Evelyn had lived there together ever since they moved to London eight years ago. To pack up her bedroom, labelling the boxes that the men Henry had hired carried away without hesitation, had, in a fleeting burst of panic, made her want to call off the wedding.

The two girls rented Number Six from a governor of the school where both their fathers worked. It was a good arrangement, and they were left in peace to make the place their own, with limited rent increases over the years. Central heating had been installed two years ago, a relief for Diana in this freezing winter weather when many homes were suffering with frozen pipes and ice on the inside of the windows.

Climbing the stairs behind Diana, Evelyn ran her fingers along the bannisters. She still had a key, but she didn't come here without Diana; it felt like a weakness to need this so much, and she was determined to set herself some rules, at least, to help her move on. The second bedroom had remained empty since she'd left nearly two years ago, rearranged into an office for Diana to plan her lessons, mark essays, and prepare the lectures she gave at a London teacher training college. Diana had also found the time, somehow, to write a novel, and she'd work on it in furious bursts during her school holidays. She'd published some short stories in journals, and there was interest in her novel from a small literary press. But Diana was secretive about it, and Evelyn knew nothing of the book's plot or premise.

Now that she was earning more money as head of her school's English department, Diana didn't need a new flatmate. It was also better, she told Evelyn with a mischievous smile, for bringing back her many dates. How was she to know if another flatmate wouldn't judge her?

Diana didn't even bother asking Evelyn what she wanted to drink. A bottle of Babycham was waiting for them behind the sink, next to the cold draught of the window. Evelyn laughed when she saw it. Diana knew how much she loved sparkling perry, especially Babycham, served in their collection of branded champagne coupes with the famous prancing deer decorating the glass. It reminded Evelyn of parties in the mid-fifties. All the girls longed to be picked for the advertising campaigns, and Diana had caught her once standing in front of the mirror with a glass in one hand saying, in the poshest accent she could muster, 'I'd love a Babycham.' She was never chosen but, looking back, she didn't mind.

The Model Patient

The advertisements were comic to her and Diana now, the full skirts and bright red lipsticks of the fifties housewife no longer appealing.

Diana poured them a glass each and threw some biscuits on a plate. Evelyn realized she was starving. She hadn't eaten all day, too anxious and worked up after the effort of her psychotherapy appointment.

'Do you remember my rabbit?' she said suddenly, the threads of the morning still persistent.

'I don't think you ever had a rabbit,' Diana replied, frowning.

'No, not a real rabbit. Margaret. That scrappy toy.'

'Oh, Margaret. Yes, I remember Margaret. You wanted to bring her with you to the first day of senior school. I was the one who stopped you, I think, saying something about how it might not set the best first impression. Why are you thinking about her now?'

'I don't know. Nothing, really.' Evelyn pushed the biscuit crumbs around on the kitchen table. It was easy to believe that Diana had stopped her from bringing Margaret to the first day at their new school, when they were eleven years old. Diana always knew what to do at school. She was the brightest girl in the year, top of the class for every test, ranked highest in all the end-of-term reports. The teachers saw themselves reflected in her diligence, this brilliant girl who would go on to university, would train to be a teacher, following in their own footsteps.

It had not been so simple for Evelyn. She struggled to settle into each lesson, forgot to write down the instructions for her homework, and regularly failed the maths and spelling tests. Diana tried to help her, sending her little notes across the class with the homework task copied out in her neat handwriting, little tips listed underneath designed to help her friend. But Evelyn did not succeed in climbing up the academic ranks of the school.

No one minded though, and she was never made to feel as though her failure was a problem. She was a good artist, could dance reasonably well, and was frequently given a leading role in the school play. It was accepted, and she quickly allowed herself to match this acceptance, that the academic world was not for her. And why need it be, when she had such striking blue eyes, long, slim arms and legs, waves of thick blonde hair that framed her heart-shaped face. Sometimes the paintings she brought home from school were a little odd, her parents forcing out bright smiles as they tried to decipher the shapes and shadows hidden beneath swirls of colour, but she'd grow out of this, they reasoned, and it was best that she had some creative outlets to balance her academic struggles.

'Did I really try to take Margaret to school with me?' Evelyn said, shuddering as the memory returned with a blistering clarity.

'You grew out of it quickly,' Diana replied. 'Too quickly, perhaps.'

'What do you mean?' Evelyn frowned. There was something in the way Diana was looking at her that made her think of the appointment this morning, Dr Daley taking her back to the past.

'It's a thought I had the other day, actually, when I was at a lecture at the Tavistock clinic. How perhaps starting work when you were so young – as a model, I mean – might have disrupted the natural progression of your childhood.'

'I think I was ready to leave childhood behind,' Evelyn replied, swallowing the last inch of her drink. 'It was much more interesting to be a teenager.'

'For you, yes, I can see it might have been.'

Evelyn turned away, her gaze settling on the lists and reminders that Diana had attached to a corkboard on the kitchen wall. It was true what she said, how, as teenagers, Diana and Evelyn had been driven by very different goals. Although during the school day it was Diana who led the way, when they started walking together into town or taking picnics to the village green next to the river, it was Evelyn's turn to shine. Evelyn would pretend to ignore the whistles of the local boys, indifferent to their attention. But in truth she was aware of every look they gave her. Diana could sense an energy lighting up within her friend, this push and pull of attraction, the way Evelyn stretched out her legs and flicked her hair.

Diana never challenged her. Instead, she frequently found herself feeling protective of Evelyn. She remembered a party hosted by one of Evelyn's glamorous model friends. The two girls were newly arrived in London, aged nineteen and determined to make their mark on the city. But when a man had stalked towards Evelyn, beer splashing down his wrist, Diana had felt compelled to whisk her friend away from him. They hid for nearly an hour, more comfortable in the quiet intimacy of the host's bedroom than battling through the social introductions and flirtations outside. Evelyn had been happy to stay in that room with Diana, the two of them playing dress-up with the coats and jackets piled on the bed until they made their escape to the bus stop.

'Tell me you did something exciting this weekend?' Evelyn said, holding out her glass to Diana for a refill. She had been living vicariously through Diana recently, a strange craving for the details of her dates, the spontaneous house parties across London, the weekend trips to country houses with her writing groups. Now that Evelyn was married, Diana seemed to be living for them both.

It was embarrassing to acknowledge that hearing Diana's stories was becoming painful. Evelyn used to be the beautiful one, fitting effortlessly into the London set of artists, fashion designers, musicians, writers. And yet it was Diana taking on that role now.

Evelyn watched as Diana tilted the last of the Babycham into her glass. With an unnerving lurch of envy, she found her thoughts travelling back to the morning of her wedding day, the two of them getting ready in Evelyn's childhood bedroom, Diana pouring the champagne. She knew it was silly, but she'd been so angry with Diana that day.

It was all because of Diana's new haircut. Two days before the wedding, she'd walked into the most fashionable hairdresser in London, and had asked for her long brown hair to be brutally hacked off into a sleek and stylish cut. It had transformed her, evoking the look of Audrey Hepburn. It was confident, bold, entirely modern. Evelyn had been ashamed to feel frustrated with her friend. She wished Diana had waited, rather than choosing her wedding day as the moment to upstage her. Everyone commented on Diana's stunning new haircut, and Evelyn could sense eyes flicking too quickly to her bridesmaid when they walked down the aisle.

Evelyn tried to push the thought away. Her wedding was supposed to be the best day of her life. She preferred to think of it that way, ignoring the moments that made her feel hot with shame.

'This weekend,' Diana replied with an impish smile, 'I met a man in a bookshop who used the excuse of the book I was taking off the shelf to lure me into conversation. We went for a drink and I ended up in his hotel room. I doubt I'll ever see him again. He was here on business and probably has a wife back in a suburb somewhere. But we had a good time. A perfect twelve hours of romance.'

Diana shrugged, passion turned quickly into pragmatism. 'He tried to get my telephone number and address, for next time he's in the city, but I told him no. A second time would be disappointing. Sometimes you have to know when to capture a night, allow it to be one perfect, frozen memory. I don't want to ruin it with an underwhelming repeat.'

*

When Evelyn left an hour later, taking a taxi to make sure she was back in time for Henry, light snow was falling, freezing into ice as soon as it hit the ground. There in the taxi, punctuated by the uneven rhythm of her journey through the London traffic, she felt a deep yearning within her. Envy of Diana's life, for the men who chased her, the excitement of a first date; a desire to have it for herself. She clenched her fists, determined. Henry would not refuse her tonight.

CHAPTER 6

'There is a pattern,' Evelyn said. She could not look at Dr Daley directly; what she was trying to say was too awkward. Although Evelyn considered herself a modern woman, unburdened by the conservative prudishness of her mother's generation, she did not like to talk about sex, especially not here with this man she knew nothing about. The directness of language, the unambiguous signification of words, made her uncomfortable. It was so far from her own language of sex, spoken with the body alone. With the men before Henry, she had known how to get what she wanted. A fleeting glance at her navel would send their hands to her hips, a tilt of her neck lowered their kisses to the hollow of her throat, the wrap of her legs around their waist made them move with harder passion.

But here, now, with this doctor seated in his armchair across the room, her body was useless and she was going to need to find the words. It made her feel lost, like she was out in a turbulent sea.

As she struggled, she sensed him move, just the tiniest lean forward. She could feel his encouragement, an unspoken guidance towards the words she knew she needed to say. She tried again.

'Sometimes I have the nightmare and sometimes I don't. When it doesn't come to me, well, that is when I am feeling most relaxed.' She paused, that uncertainty kicking against her ribcage. 'As in, things have gone well with Henry.'

'What sort of things?' he prompted. Surely, Evelyn thought as she clutched her necklace with a tight, damp grip, he must comprehend what she was trying to say. She did not want to speak the words out loud. It would be easier if he could read her mind.

Glancing up at him and seeing such an open, neutral expression on his face, perhaps he did not understand her. Or perhaps he understood her perfectly. He needed her to find the words herself.

She sighed.

'When Henry and I sleep together, the nightmare doesn't come. It only comes on nights when ...' She paused. The phrasing seemed important, terribly important. She did not want to appear demanding, undesired. It was difficult when she did not know what was the right thing to say to make this man, this doctor, understand.

Dr Daley refused to finish her sentences for her. It was a habit of his, letting the silence expand and grow.

'It doesn't come if we have slept together that evening.'

There, she had said it. She was afraid he would ask her to

The Model Patient

clarify, to change the ambiguity of her phrasing to the precision of the word sex. But Dr Daley simply nodded. There was no change to his expression, no widening of the eyes, no exhalation of shock. It was just her, she realized, who was finding this awkward.

'And do you have any thoughts on why that might be?'

'No.'

Another pause. How could she possibly explain when she did not understand it herself?

Dr Daley was waiting patiently. She sighed. The silence would not break until she spoke.

'It's hard to explain. Although the nightmare doesn't come if we've been together that night, I wake up in a panic anyway. I worry that he resents me.'

'Resents what about you, specifically?'

Evelyn nodded. She was going to have to be more direct.

'Resents having sex with me.'

'Why would that be?'

'I worry that he only wants me if it will be a chance to get pregnant. And so, although I do feel better when we have sex, I become consumed with anxiety about it a few hours later.'

'Does he refuse to have sex with you?'

The question shocked her in its directness, its determination not to let her hide behind a subtler dance of ambiguities. She turned her head away, her gaze fixed on the garden, frozen and white behind the ice of the window panes.

'Mrs Westbrook,' she heard Dr Daley say. His voice was

kind, and she returned to him. 'I know it's difficult to talk with me about sex, but if we can explore this together then we will understand more about what is troubling you.'

Evelyn nodded. It *was* difficult. She had never really talked with a man about sex; it had not been necessary.

'It is not that he refuses. It is more that he makes it clear it isn't going to happen. But that hurts just as much.'

'Yes.' Dr Daley rubbed the edge of his jaw. 'I imagine that was difficult for you to tell me.'

Evelyn nodded again, but she wanted him to say more, to explain why her difficulty here, with him, was significant to the therapy. It was Henry she was trying to talk about, not this man in front of her, a doctor she had only met twice before.

'I wonder,' Dr Daley said, interrupting the confusion of her mind, 'do you have any thoughts about the serpent in your nightmare?'

'What do you mean?' Evelyn asked, perplexed. She knew that the serpent terrified her, that she woke in cold sweats, that its open jaws driving towards her face in vicious, jewelled splendour made her scream out in her sleep.

'Does it evoke any feelings? Or any memories? You said that the dream starts in a different way each time, often scenes or locations from your childhood. Can you tell me about some of those memories?'

'I often forget that part of the dream. It is like I have it there in my mind when I wake up, so clear and vibrant. And then, a second later, the image has gone, like a photograph that has failed to develop.'

The Model Patient

'You should try writing it down. Get a notepad and place it by your bed and that way you can write down the dream the instant you wake. You may find that the habit of this allows you to access more and more details from your dreams.'

He paused, shifting forward and pressing the palms of his hands into his knees. Evelyn felt the intensity of his gaze and she averted her eyes. 'If you wish,' he said, 'you could bring the notepad, those dreams you write down from your bed, to our sessions each week. We can discuss them together.'

Evelyn nodded, biting her lip as she thought. It would be a little like her sketchbook, the designs she let emerge from her, unplanned and raw, when she was feeling unsettled. She opened her mouth to speak, but quickly stopped herself. She didn't know why, but she wasn't yet ready to share her sketches with Dr Daley. It would be too exposing, like revealing the depths of her mind to a stranger.

He looked at her, his head tilted. 'Were you about to say something?' She blinked in surprise. This man noticed everything; perhaps, she considered, he really was able to read her mind.

He continued speaking. 'A memory, perhaps, a fragment from one of the dreams, something you do remember?'

An exhalation of relief escaped her. Dr Daley was simply trying to get her back on track.

'Yes, okay. I can remember some of them. Two nights ago, for example, it began at the school where my father is headmaster.'

Evelyn shivered, the details of the dream returning to her. It had stayed with her for hours after waking, new images returning as she continued with her day. This dream, no matter how hard she tried, had been impossible to ignore.

'In the dream I am an adult, as I am now, but I was being treated like a child, perhaps seven or eight years old. We were in the chapel and there were hundreds of schoolmasters, men wearing long black robes, facing inwards either side of a long aisle. My parents were at one end in the headmaster's box, and I was standing on the other end, an impossibly long distance away. Everyone was looking at me and I knew that they were waiting for me to walk down the aisle to join my parents. As I started walking, an eruption of noise hit me. The teachers were shouting at me, these loud animal jeers. They wanted me dead, I knew that instinctively.'

Evelyn stopped, uncertain if she could continue. Dr Daley seemed to sense it too, and he nodded. 'Can you try telling me what happened next?'

'It's difficult to put into words, but I think they didn't only want to kill me. They also wanted me, to possess me. I made it halfway down the aisle before the serpent appeared. The dream resumed its usual pattern after that, with one difference. The serpent was wearing tight rows of pearls high up towards its jaws.'

Evelyn's hands rose to her neck, her skin flushed and hot. So many details, very few of them she remembered before they appeared in the air in front of her. The necklace. She could see it so clearly now: four rows of pearls wrapped tightly around the reptile's scales. There was no doubting it was her mother-in-law's gift, the family heirloom that choked her.

'What are you feeling now, Mrs Westbrook?' Dr Daley's voice pulled her back into the present. Mrs Westbrook. It was her name, but it was also her mother-in-law's: she wished Dr Daley would call her Evelyn.

She realized she was grabbing the collar of her dress, wrenching the wool away from her throat. Letting go, she tried to calm herself.

'I am surprised by how much I remembered. All those details seemed to just slip out of me, without consciously thinking about them in advance. And the necklace. It belongs to Henry's mother. I hate it, but she likes me to wear it. She wanted me to wear it on my wedding day, but I refused. I don't think she has ever forgiven me.'

Dr Daley pressed the tips of his fingers together. It was what he did, Evelyn had noticed, when he was linking the strands of her thoughts, offering an analysis. 'It is interesting, we might think, that the setting for the dream was a chapel. You were walking down an aisle to join your parents. Perhaps it was a wedding of sorts, joining them as a married woman. Did you get married in that chapel?'

'Yes. Henry and I were married in the school chapel. And the reception was in the school's grand hall. My bridesmaids and I had joked that surely it was the longest aisle I could have chosen to walk down. But I'd definitely enjoyed walking down the aisle, Henry waiting for me at the other end. I know it's a cliché, but it really was the best day of my life.'

Even as she said it, she knew it was a lie. How could it have been the best day of her life when she knew who was watching her from the congregation, all the terrible things she had done, the shame that tormented her?

She pushed the thought away: that was not why she was here.

'And in the dream, how did you feel when the schoolmasters were shouting at you?'

'It was frightening, as though they were on the edge of breaking out from behind the stalls and attacking me.'

'Can you tell me more about how that felt?'

Silence again, growing between them like something hard and real. The weight of it pressed against her, and she found herself thinking of those snake-like scales shimmering with their dreadful beauty.

Evelyn was breathing hard, her hands gripped beneath her thighs. Her words were quiet, a whispered answer that Dr Daley had to lean forward to catch. 'It was exhilarating.' She looked up, holding his gaze. 'It felt wonderful.'

The smallest nod from Dr Daley, and she fell back against the sofa, closing her eyes.

A door slammed somewhere close by, the sound bringing her back to the room. She sat up straight, suddenly afraid. Shaking her head, she tried to claw back the words.

'No, I don't think that's right,' she said, too fast now, panic building. 'It was a nightmare. I was frightened and it was horrible. I don't know why I said that. Of course it wasn't wonderful.'

Dr Daley looked up at the clock. 'We've run out of time for today. Shall we continue next week?'

Evelyn struggled to compose herself. She wanted to challenge him, ask him why he had chosen now, at this moment of devastating self-disgust, to end the appointment. She looked up at the clock too, noting the time. It was eleven-fifty. Her time was up. But even so, how could he send her away now, right after she had said those awful things?

As she left him, turned out into the hostile cold weather, the noises of London refused to filter between her thoughts, the bustle of real life failing to return her to herself. A taxi screeched as it rounded the corner too quickly onto Weymouth Street; two women shouted loudly at one another from either side of the road; the whip of wind banged against a shop sign: she heard none of this.

All she could do as she started walking towards Pimlico was question over and over again what it was that she had done wrong.

CHAPTER 7

Evelyn's attempt at cooking their Monday evening dinner was not successful, and she resorted to heating up the Sunday leftovers, discarding the burnt fish cakes and making a mental note not to try that recipe ever again. It was one disaster after another, the tension within her building with every mistake. She cut her finger when slicing the onions, oblivious to the blood until it started staining the wood of the chopping board. Fish juice dripped out of the packet and onto the kitchen floor, and egg shells shattered into the yolk.

Her frustration was only eased by the sound of ice splintering as she poured vodka and vermouth into a glass. She garnished her drink with a slice of lemon, wincing as the citrus seeped into the cut on her finger. It was a strange sensation, the pain bringing her back to herself. She let the acid bleed into her skin for a beat too long before bringing her finger to her mouth to suck it clean.

Henry would notice the burnt fish smell when he came home, but if she successfully kept him away from the kitchen, she could make a joke out of her defeat. She had tried so hard yesterday for his parents. Lunch with Dr and Mrs Westbrook had become a non-negotiable Sunday routine. Evelyn was desperate for them to believe she was good enough for their son. If they could recognize her efforts each Sunday, that would be a start; but she never seemed to get it right.

They came to Henry and Evelyn's home far more than they visited Henry's four other siblings. At first Evelyn had hoped it was a sign of their favour, that she was successfully becoming a valued member of the family. But it didn't take long before she realized the real reason. Henry's four brothers and sisters were married and they all had children of their own, the eldest boy, Mark, the proud father of three. It was only Henry and Evelyn left to be monitored and cajoled into continuing the Westbrook dynasty. Christmas this year was at Mark and his wife June's home in Henley-on-Thames, and Evelyn had struggled to stay cheerful through an afternoon on the sofa with children climbing all over her. Ruth and June could not resist shooting comments at Evelyn about how happy Henry would be if he could watch a child of his own joining the other little ones.

Slipping off her two rings, an engagement and a wedding ring, Evelyn washed her hands, the stickiness of the lemon and the fish vanishing into the water. She loved her engagement ring because she had designed it herself. Mark had been granted the family heirloom ring when he proposed to his wife, and Evelyn was relieved she didn't have to wear such a heavy and ugly thing, a huge ruby encased in an inelegant gold band. It was Lionel who had found Evelyn's design in her sketchbook, had suggested it to Henry as the perfect engagement ring, and had commissioned its creation. He understood exactly how to take the clean simple lines of the sketch and transform it into a beautiful diamond ring.

Evelyn opened the refrigerator, trying to let the cool air soothe her irritation at the failed meal. Three Tupperware containers of different sizes were piled neatly on the middle shelf, and the sight of them made her shudder. Henry's mother had invited her to a Tupperware party a few months ago and she thought it might have been the most depressing night of her life. All married women, each one wearing a pristine pastel dress that matched the colour of their Tupperware bowl, Evelyn occupied the time counting the number of pearls accumulated from their necklaces, earrings and embellished cardigans. The conversation did not veer much further than home cooking and the shape and size of Tupperware ideal for their husbands' favourite dishes.

Ruth helped Evelyn clear after yesterday's lunch, scooping the remaining vegetables into each container with such efficiency that Evelyn could do nothing but hover anxiously by the refrigerator. But it wasn't so much Ruth's competency that put her on edge. It was her own compliance, how easily she thanked her, nodding obediently when told it was wrong to store her butter in the refrigerator when the pantry was perfectly cold enough, wrong to throw out the goose fat, wrong to dry the glasses with such a rough tea-towel. She hated the way she smiled at everything Ruth said and laughed obediently at her father-in-law's jokes.

The Model Patient

Dr and Mrs Westbrook arrived at midday exactly. Ruth slid her way past the two men to join Evelyn in the kitchen, placing a homemade Battenberg cake onto the kitchen counter. Evelyn felt nauseous looking at it, the perfect pink and yellow squares contrasting with the chaos of the kitchen. She was cooking a roast, and while the chicken was already in the oven, there was a disordered medley of potatoes, carrots and parsnips scattered over the work surface. Too late to hide the shortcuts she was taking, Evelyn positioned herself in front of the package-bought stuffing, hoping her mother-in-law wouldn't notice.

'Goodness, Evelyn dearest,' Ruth had said as she scanned the kitchen. 'You'd think you were run off your feet and cooking for a family of seven.'

Evelyn laughed nervously, fiddling with the oven as she tried to suppress the heat rising in her cheeks. Ruth knew exactly what it was like to cook for a family of seven. And even then, Evelyn assumed she would have never let a hair fall out of place. Pristine was the word that always came to Evelyn whenever her mother-in-law arrived at their door, the most brutal winter weather incapable of creasing the crisp line of her clothes. She was a petite woman, barely five-feet-two, and had a tiny waist which she made even smaller by wearing wide, stiff belts. Sometimes Evelyn wondered how she was able to breathe. Her make-up was perfect too, neatly drawn-on eyebrows, plum red lipstick, and hair arranged above her head in a smooth blonde sweep.

Evelyn had run out of time to think about what to wear

that morning, and she knew Henry's mother would not consider a casual grey sweater tucked into a thigh-skimming skirt to be the appropriate attire for Sunday lunch. It was only in the seconds before she appeared in the kitchen that Evelyn had time to slip on her shoes, hiding the worn toes of her stockings. Even in flat pumps compared to the heels that Ruth always wore, Evelyn towered above her. But that did nothing to stop her from being continually intimidated by this formidable woman, a woman who had, Henry told her, raised five children through a war, balanced the rationing of food and fabrics with ease, produced delicious, wholesome meals for her family as well as the evacuees they took into their country home in Wiltshire.

Now that her children were adults, Ruth filled her time by leading countless charity fundraisers and committees both in Wiltshire and London. As well as dropping in unannounced to her children's homes, of course. Evelyn was sometimes alarmed to hear the way Henry talked about his mother. In his eyes, Ruth was perfect, adoring, fiercely loyal to her family. Henry, as the youngest child, had probably been spoilt, Evelyn thought. It was foolish, she realized now, to think that his love for her would trump the lifelong love affair with his mother. Evelyn should have known that choosing to marry her was a short-lived attempt at rebellion.

Ruth came from a wealthy family of property owners, and it was thanks to her inheritance and her generosity that Evelyn and Henry had been able to afford the house in Pimlico. Evelyn longed for the day when they could pay off the mortgage, and give the deposit money back to Ruth and Alec. They hadn't asked for help; Henry and Evelyn would have been happy buying a flat somewhere less central. But Ruth insisted.

'I did say to Henry that he should have repainted the kitchen windows when we bought the house,' Ruth said to Evelyn, leaning over the sink and rubbing her finger along the faded yellow of the frame.

'It's the cold weather,' Evelyn offered, trying the hide the frustration that threatened to break through her politeness.

'You must be careful not to let small things slip,' her mother-in-law continued, peering at the smears of washing-up liquid behind the sink. 'Henry was always such a tidy child,' she said, and Evelyn felt her stomach clench as she thought of how he folded his trousers before bed, every item of clothing packed away.

Alec Westbrook, Henry's father, was a doctor, semi-retired now though still a senior partner at a private practice on Harley Street. When Henry told Evelyn that his father was a gynaecologist, she had found it hard to believe. The man she had met for the first time in the family's Kensington home was not someone she could imagine offering sympathetic words of advice to women dealing with their most private biological concerns. Certainly he was attractive, in a charming, old-fashioned way, a fatherly figure who made Evelyn feel like a small child again. He was flirtatious with her, little comments about stealing his son's heart with her beauty making her blush. But he was clever, staying just enough on the side of polite paternalistic charm that he could never be accused of crossing a line. According to Henry, he was in high demand, his patients so distraught by his retirement that he agreed to stay on a little while longer. Perhaps they saw him as a charismatic and attractive version of their fathers, but with the difference that he knew what sanitary products looked like and understood the intricate map of female anatomy.

Evelyn laid out the leftover meal, slowly spooning the food into a dish for reheating. She stopped frequently, setting down each Tupperware to take a long quenching drink of her cocktail. The sight of the thin and flaccid carrots was sending her into a deep exhaustion, and she could not bear to touch the greasy jelly of the chicken that quivered over soft beige skin. It was too much: all of her energy was depleted. Fragments of yesterday's lunch conversation had returned to her all day, infiltrating themselves between the anguish of her appointment with Dr Daley this morning. They could not have been more different, the platitudes she offered to her parents-in-law coming from an entirely different person to the one who shared the torments of her nightmares with a doctor.

It had all started with Henry's father wanting to know about the Minister of Health's progress on closing the large mental asylums, with the aim of transitioning patients into community care. Henry worked closely with Enoch Powell, the Minister of Health, and Dr Westbrook often saw his son's career as a useful way of accessing privileged information about the direction health policies were moving in. It had, over recent years, been helpful to Alec in ensuring his own medical practice was proceeding at the necessary pace to keep attracting patients. With the right education and contacts behind him, Henry had quickly climbed to a senior position in the health policy sector of the Civil Service. When, in 1961, Powell had delivered his messianic water tower speech about closing the mental hospitals in favour of increased community care, it was Henry who was tasked with keeping abreast of the intense debates surrounding the policy change, regularly meeting Powell to offer him a progress report. It was the same with the introduction of the birth control pill on the NHS in 1961. Evelyn had found herself in the midst of several discussions between Henry and his parents about the policy of contraceptive pills being only accessible to married women. Ruth refused to acknowledge that the question of sex might, frequently, be more complicated than the binary rigidity of before and after marriage.

'Of course Alec would never fall for the tricks of any of those unmarried young women who slip wedding rings between them in the waiting room. It is shocking that they think they can get away with it,' she had said one Sunday lunch.

'But not everyone agrees,' Henry had offered, his voice maintaining a careful neutrality. 'Every week there is another petition to our office, arguing that unmarried women should have access to contraception.' It was the first year of their marriage and the question of the contraceptive pill danced around every dinner table, debates about costs, taxpayers contributing to this controversial new medicine, the levels of freedom that doctors were given in deciding whether to prescribe. Henry had seemed excessively anxious about how his mother would interpret his interest in this medication. Evelyn wasn't entirely sure of Henry's reasoning. Sometimes she thought it was to protect her privacy; other times she saw it as a way to ease his mother's jealousy. Henry was supposed to love Ruth more than any woman in the world: sex complicated that devotion.

'What a ridiculous idea,' Ruth had replied. 'The whole enterprise is a slippery slope to moral delinquency.'

Evelyn suspected that Alec was a little more sympathetic. A woman with the right sort of pretty, biddable smile, and the bank statement to pay for private treatment, was likely to persuade Dr Westbrook that she should be prescribed the contraception women were starting to realize would change their lives.

At this Sunday lunch it was mental illness, a change at least from the endless conversations about the Cuban Missile Crisis, how close the world had come to another war. Several months on and it dominated everyone's conversations: either the Cold War or, more recently, this relentless cold weather. But as soon as the conversation began, Evelyn wished she could find a way to change the subject.

For Alec and Ruth Westbrook, there were people either with serious mental conditions who needed expert treatment from doctors, drugs, and in-hospital care, or there

The Model Patient

were neurotics who needed to get over it. Henry, despite his involvement in Enoch Powell's policy changes, had very little interest in arguing with them. His curiosity about mental illness had a distance, an almost clinical indifference that disturbed Evelyn. It was as though he could listen to hundreds of debates but still not see enough relevance to his own life to make it worthwhile building a personal opinion. Dr Westbrook, on the other hand, had very strong views. It was alarming to Evelyn how a doctor could spend a career attending to women and their bodies, hearing them talk about pregnancies, the menopause, ageing, sex, and still dismiss the realities of anxiety, depression, fear.

'All this talking therapy that is being offered now, whole clinics opening up for out-patients who spend an hour a week twisting themselves into contortions about something that once happened to them in their childhood. It is a waste of time and money.' Dr Westbrook was shaking his head as he poured the wine, and Evelyn, seated to his right, watched, transfixed, as a dark red drop splashed onto his shirt. She had a sudden urge to take her glass and throw it at him, filling in the clean white of the cotton with a deep red stain. Of course she did nothing of the sort, instead lifting the gravy boat and letting the thick sauce slowly coat the gaps of porcelain on her plate. It was soothing, like the tide coming in and filling the ravines between rocks on the sand.

'A new young doctor at my practice keeps referring his patients for psychotherapy, as if he can't fix them himself. It's pathetic, encouraging these women to mull over their hysterical tendencies. What they really need is another child to keep them busy.' He sawed through the chicken breast as he was speaking, the skin sliding over the flesh and collapsing at the edge of his plate. Frowning, he discarded the skin onto his side plate. Evelyn tried to suppress her sigh. As usual, she had failed to roast a chicken correctly.

'Women of my generation never had time to indulge in all these ridiculous anxieties,' Ruth said as she tapped a teaspoon of mustard against her plate. 'We were far too busy bringing up our children during a war, managing rationing, taking in evacuees, doing our bit. All this soul searching can only bring trouble.'

'It just makes these people more confused,' Ruth's husband confirmed, his knife and fork held aloft. Evelyn glanced up at him, wondering what would happen if he turned the cutlery on himself. What would he start on first, she thought? The hard paunch beneath his shirt, or the thick weight of his forearms?

Ruth's voice ended her fantasy, bringing her back to the reality of the dining room. She should have turned on another light before they sat down, the grey London sky already threatening to darken too early. In the gloom of the room, the pale blues and greys she had chosen so proudly two years ago took on an ill pallor, as though all the life was being slowly sucked away.

'Your sisters and I were shopping in Whiteleys this week,' Ruth said, turning to Henry and smiling brightly. 'There was a gorgeous wicker crib with such pretty baby blue fabric.

The Model Patient

I was saying to Elizabeth how well it would look in your second bedroom.'

Evelyn fixed her gaze on the window, mesmerized by a pattern of silver frost that was imprinted against the glass.

Henry coughed. 'Mother, we don't need to get into that now. There is plenty of time to think about starting a family.' Evelyn felt a surge of gratitude towards her husband. She knew that, in truth, he shared his mother's opinion, and it would have been easy for him to have taken the other side.

'I was pregnant with your older brother immediately after our honeymoon.' Ruth was looking pointedly at Evelyn, a smile hovering about her lips. 'It really isn't that difficult, dear.'

'Now, now,' said Alec with a loud laugh. 'Let's not embarrass them. I am sure they know what they are doing.' He turned to Evelyn, patting the top of her hand. 'And you know you can always come to see me at my clinic if it would help.'

Henry spluttered, his face turning a deep red. 'That won't be necessary, Dad.'

Evelyn poured herself another drink, pressing the ice out into the palm of her hand. It was nearly seven o'clock and Henry would be home soon. Something was nagging at her, a feeling of being out of place, or a problem that needed fixing. She went upstairs to their bedroom and through into their bathroom. It was a beautiful bathroom, much larger than the one she had shared with Diana at

Number Six. A bath dominated the space, a wicker chair in the corner. A lamp sat above a pale wooden cabinet, white towels piled in a basket, a towel rail bolted into the edge of the wood. There were two mirrors, one at the sink and another that filled the length of the wall next to the door, from floor to the ceiling. The effect of so much glass was startling, as though Evelyn's reflection was refusing to settle and be still.

Turning on the light above the sink, she stood in front of the mirror, scrutinizing her face. She looked a little tired, perhaps, the blonde strands of her hair too flat against her cheek bones. Retying her ponytail, she loosened the hair at the crown, unthreading a few wisps and letting them fall around her eyes.

Applying another line of black kohl, she shivered, her eyes watering against the pencil. She could not expel yesterday's lunch from her thoughts. Once the pink and yellow Battenburg cake had been devoured by Alec and Henry, their praise making it very obvious to Evelyn that this was the highlight of the meal, Ruth had disappeared, saying she was using the ladies' room. But when Evelyn had carried the tray of coffee through to the living room, she noticed the door to the downstairs bathroom was ajar, the light off. Ruth was nowhere to be seen.

A pressure had descended on her, a certainty that something wasn't right. Evelyn excused herself, Henry and Alec barely noticing her leave as they continued their discussion. When she reached the top of the stairs, she stopped, listening for her mother-in-law. She could sense her close by, the light floral notes of her perfume floating across the landing.

And suddenly there she was, coming swiftly out of Evelyn's bedroom and closing the door silently behind her. She turned to see Evelyn watching her.

'Goodness, you gave me a fright, Evelyn dear,' she said, as she moved to the top of the stairs. 'What are you doing standing on the landing like that?'

Evelyn frowned. Surely she should be asking Ruth the same thing, what she was doing in her bedroom, why she was creeping around her house? But she found herself apologizing, muttering that she was just coming up for some lipstick.

'You need to get more pillows for your bed, dear,' Ruth said. 'Henry prefers down pillows to feather.'

'I didn't know there was a difference,' Evelyn muttered, just loud enough to be heard, as she escaped into her bedroom. There was the tiniest exclamation of shock from Ruth, but Evelyn closed the door on her and stood entirely still in the deepening darkness of the room. Even in the dusk, she could see that Ruth had been sitting on the bed, a slight compression of the blanket on Henry's side. She felt herself starting to shake, a rage building beneath her skin. She tried to breathe, to let it go, to find calm. But then she heard the light laughter of her mother-in-law downstairs. Evelyn gave in to her anger, throwing herself on to the bed and pressing her face hard into the pillow. Her scream disappeared into the cotton and feathers.

By the time she came back downstairs, it was too late to

ask Ruth what she had really been doing in her bedroom. Perhaps it was simply a mother's curiosity, clinging on to the memories of her son as a little boy when she had been the only woman he adored.

A cold wisp of air found Evelyn before Henry had time to close the front door and take off his coat. She stood quickly, her head spinning. His presence was a comfort, a real solid body to take her out of her thoughts. Running into the hall, she smiled at him, stopping abruptly as she reached him, her hands behind her back. It was what they used to do, before he began to drift away: her unconvincing pretence at coyness, his laughter as he read her need.

He laughed now, pulling her towards him. Evelyn felt energy surging through her as their bodies collided. It was a kindness, she thought in a flash of gratitude, how he knew what she wanted, an antidote to the tension of yesterday's lunch. Her hands rose to his hair, and she pressed her fingers into the cool thickness of it, the chill of the outdoors still lingering on him.

Henry lifted her up in one determined spring, and she wrapped her legs around him, her arms tight against his neck. He carried her to the staircase and lowered her onto the steps.

He kissed her, a real kiss, so different from all he had offered her these past months. She did not stop to think why, to ask herself what had changed, whether one of them had done something new to end the coldness between them. Instead, she let her body go, a shudder of desire travelling from her throat down through her legs. He was right there with her, resisting nothing. He was lifting her hips, peeling off her stockings, sighing as he touched her, feeling how much she wanted him. She felt alive for the first time in weeks.

As her head fell back against the step, she closed her eyes. He had never kissed that place before, high between her legs, and when his mouth found her, she flinched. But then she let the sensation drive her closer and closer, a pattern of tension and release.

A wave of energy flooded through her body and her eyes flew open. She sank her fingers into the carpet of the stairs. Evelyn's head felt light, her breathing shallow, and she tried to fix her gaze on Henry, the staircase, the pale blue paint that she had chosen for the walls. But she could sense her mind travelling away from her, distracted, wild, a dangerous slipping out of control. She closed her eyes again, an attempt to find the focus she desired.

And yet too quickly she was somewhere else entirely. A sofa, the frozen garden behind the thin chiffon curtains, a man opposite her, his hands clasped in his lap.

As she grasped the balustrade, Henry rising up to kiss her, she remembered how she had pressed her fingers into the leather of the sofa, the dampness of her skin as she struggled through the appointment. It was frustrating to be back there again now, just at the moment she most wanted to feel free.

This time, when she kissed her husband, she kept her eyes firmly open.

CHAPTER 8

'This is our fourth appointment together,' Dr Daley was saying, the clock ticking onwards towards eleven-fifty. Evelyn had been on edge since she arrived, too aware of herself and her thoughts. Even the familiar scent of mint and eucalyptus was doing nothing to soothe her today.

When he had appeared around the corner to collect her from the waiting room, she had felt a wave of anxiety. She suppressed it, standing quickly and mentally running through the carefully planned talking points she had noted to herself in advance of the appointment. It would help, she had decided during this past week, if she could have a plan. She needed to prepare herself, a guide to help her stay on track, to keep their discussion to useful analysis of her marriage, her nightmare, her fear of giving up those precious birth control pills. There was no need to let her mind wander to anything else.

She had dressed carefully this morning, trying on so many outfits once Henry had gone to work that she was nearly late.

The Model Patient

In the end, she'd had to take the bus to make sure she got to the appointment on time. Shivering as she found a seat on the top deck, she had watched the constant curtain of near freezing rain shrouding the windows, a persistent breeze whistling in and up the stairs. She hated it, this endless rain and mist and cold, the damp smell of London clinging to her coat.

Now, pressing herself into the corner of the couch, she smoothed down the black-and-white dress she had finally settled upon. Bold shapes darted across the fabric, stripes and swirls that reminded her of the optical illusion paintings she had seen last year at an art exhibition at Gallery One in Soho. She liked the way the dress turned her body into an illusion of its own: Henry, when she had first worn it, had made her turn in front of him, while he leant back against the cushions of the sofa, losing himself in the moving shapes.

Evelyn found herself talking about Diana in today's appointment. Not, she realized after a while, anything from her planned discussion points. But it seemed important, the way she measured her own life against that of her friend. Dr Daley said very little, asking the occasional question, guiding her to be more precise in her words. It was not enough to simply tell him that she missed her old life with Diana. She must delve deeper, explaining how she missed tripping over the chaotic piles of books Diana left scattered around the flat, how it didn't matter if they fell asleep together on the sofa, the record player scratching around and around, how Diana would decide they were going to have bread and her favourite Wensleydale cheese for Sunday night dinner, with a bottle of six shilling red wine she'd picked up from a store behind Sloane Square station. They didn't need plans; every evening could be based on their spontaneous desires.

With only fifteen minutes until the end of the appointment, Dr Daley started to speak. Now that these first four consultations were coming to an end, he was interested in seeing whether Evelyn wanted to continue seeing him.

'My suggestion, if you would like, is that we start psychodynamic psychotherapy together. If you think it would be useful for you.'

Evelyn looked up at him in confusion. She thought that was what they were doing already, the psychotherapy part anyway. He had explained so much to her on the telephone before the first appointment, where to come, how to get in to the building, what to expect from the waiting area. And yet he had told her nothing about the treatment itself. The therapy, it appeared, was shrouded in mystery. It was strange to her that she had accepted this so readily, asking no questions about the method of treatment she was embarking upon. Now it was too late. The last thing she wanted was to come across as ignorant, throwing herself into a treatment she knew nothing about.

'Yes, I would like that,' she heard herself say, but despite the certainty of the words, her voice was quiet, nervous. Dr Daley shifted in the armchair, leaning forwards.

'Would you like me to explain how it will be different from these first four appointments?'

Evelyn nodded, unable to look up at him this time. She felt

The Model Patient

like a child, as though a kind but patronizing adult was trying to instruct her on some basic concept. Strangely, it reminded her of a man she had once known, though different in every other way, much older, wealthier, powerful. She pressed the thought aside. She could not think about him, not now. That girl, the teenager who would do anything to be adored, she was not that person anymore.

'From now on, you should say exactly what you are thinking. You must try not to moderate your words, no matter what it is that comes into your mind. Even if it is uncomfortable, or it seems trivial, or it is awkward, you need to try your hardest to tell me.'

Evelyn looked up at him now, horrified, her lips pressed tight together. In that moment she was attempting with every fibre of her will not to let the colour rise into her cheeks. How could she possibly tell him everything she was thinking? What purpose would there be in sharing how quickly and bewilderingly her mind could slip, how it had slipped back to this room one week ago, Henry's mouth against her thighs?

He continued speaking, no sign at all that he was aware of her unease. 'Think of it as a free association of thoughts, allowing yourself to speak whatever comes to you. Sometimes we will try word or image associations to help you access these thoughts, if we feel it would be helpful to us.'

Evelyn thought of her sketchbook, the way her drawings appeared beneath her hand when she was afraid, a substitute for the dreams she refused to let emerge when she was too unsettled to sleep. This psychodynamic therapy, the thought of it terrified her, how she might lose control, how it might reveal parts of her she did not want anyone to see.

'This is a safe space for you to say whatever it is you are thinking,' he was saying, but Evelyn was only half-listening, the other half of her mind attempting to build walls, fortifications to protect her. 'I will never judge you. My role here is to work with you to understand your individual experience of the world. I am here to help you discover how you can free yourself from the troubles you are experiencing, to help you become unstuck, as it were. We can break down those walls together.'

Evelyn's hand flew to her throat. For a moment she thought she'd spoken aloud, that she'd revealed herself to him. But no, she was certain that she had not.

He was silent, watching her. It was impossible for her to speak; she did not trust herself. Leaning back in the armchair, he crossed his legs and folded his arms, settling comfortably into the quiet of the room. Evelyn tried to do the same, but the cushions of the couch were too far away. She felt as though she was drowning inside the leather, her body weak and unsupported. Closing her eyes, she attempted to ground herself. She knew she needed to say something to make herself feel more in control. Dr Daley was not going to break before her and if she didn't speak then the silence would grow and grow.

'How do I know', she ventured, 'if I am saying something useful?' Dr Daley frowned, turning his head away from her.

The Model Patient

It was the wrong thing to say, she could tell. She had disappointed him, asking such a mundane, ignorant question, and she longed to claw it back, to try again with something interesting, something intelligent, anything that would make him return to her.

'What I mean is,' she tried again, 'how do I know if we can gauge something useful from what I am saying, or whether it is a distraction?'

He nodded, looking at her once again. She heard herself sigh, the pressure that was building within her dissipating a little.

'Anything you say will be of use. We will work together to explore your thoughts. Even the smallest detail can, often, be of significance. And remember that you can bring your dreams to me too and we can work through them together.'

'Bring my dreams to you,' Evelyn whispered before she could stop herself. Dr Daley caught her gaze and the colour rose in her cheeks. She brought her hands to her neck, looking down, embarrassed. 'Yes, of course, you mean write them down and discuss them with you.'

'Yes, exactly. If you would like. Your sleeping and your waking dreams. Your fantasies,' he added, and Evelyn heard his voice soften. She could sense him looking at her, his eyes missing nothing.

'You will, I think, feel better if you tell me everything, even if it happens to be something about me.'

She could not speak. How could she possibly tell him any of her thoughts about him: how she worried whether she was saying the right thing to hold his interest; how she watched for his reactions; how afraid she was of being ridiculous to him. How, this morning, she had spent longer than usual on her make-up in anticipation of seeing him. She did not understand how it would be helpful to tell him these things, what possible purpose it would have in easing her troubles. There was something infuriating about this doctor, how he insisted on placing himself at the centre of her thoughts.

It was a relief when he told her that their time, for today, was up.

CHAPTER 9

Lionel was already at the bar when she met him a few evenings later. The temperature had plummeted again, the depressing rain of the last week hardening into ice and snow. It was the bleakest February Evelyn could remember, and she resented the awkwardness of extracting herself from her scarf, coat and gloves, the thick wool of a sweater sticking to her, every time she walked indoors. The bar Lionel had chosen was too hot, a narrow space in Soho with a row of stools packed tightly together. Two bartenders worked at a relentless pace to mix drinks, low pools of light illuminating their work stations of orange peel, lime, olives, bowls overspilling with wilting mint leaves.

The taxi over had been slow, traffic on every road and a barrage of beeping horns at each junction. Snow had frozen into ruts across the streets and cars were forced to move at a snail's pace to avoid sliding over patches of black ice. Evelyn could feel tension straining across her shoulders, her nerves wound high. Ever since her appointment on Monday, she could not get Dr Daley out of her thoughts. *You can bring your dreams to me.* That was what he had said, and she could not help but feel the intimacy of his instructions. His words had thrilled her as much as they had frightened her, as though he was peeling back her clothes to reveal a naked need that only he could help her understand. Even though she knew it was irrational, she could not stop herself from continually looking for him on the London streets.

She winced as a bus tottered too close, a giant advertisement for the Flying Scotsman looming towards her window. The night seemed to hold the distortion of a nightmare, each double-decker Routemaster wavering as it struggled through the traffic. Evelyn closed her eyes, blocking out the sight of passengers slipping in the grime and snow as they climbed onto the back of their bus.

The heat and noise of the bar did nothing to relax her. But there was a cocktail waiting, and Lionel inched it closer to her as she climbed onto the stool. Wrenching off the remaining layers of her winter clothes, she exhaled sharply, her frustration refusing to dissolve. She was wearing a thin camisole, dark blue with a straight neck that cut across to slim shoulder straps. Lionel raised an eyebrow.

'Only you could get away with wearing your nightdress out for drinks.'

She looked down at herself, shrugging. 'It's not my nightdress. And it's your fault for choosing the tiniest, sweatiest bar in Soho.'

'The only way to get you to undress,' he laughed, looking

her up and down with a comic sweep of his chin. 'And why aren't you wearing any of my jewellery?'

'I forgot, Lionel. You know what it's like in this weather. I've lost too many earrings in my scarf already.' Evelyn could feel her sour mood bubbling beneath the surface and she tried to slow down, to settle into the evening and let her temperature drop now that her arms were free from clothes. But Lionel was right, she did feel naked without jewellery. She grabbed anxiously at her earlobes, wishing she'd remembered to wear earrings, some metal adornment and armour behind which she could hide.

Lionel watched her, his lips turned up in amusement. He was not going to let her simmer in irritation.

Sighing, she reached for her drink. Lionel waited for her to take the first sip.

'So, tell me. Have you been analysed yet?'

Evelyn smiled. It was just like Lionel to cut straight to it; no need to waste time dancing around one another with anecdotes about their day. What would Evelyn say anyway: that she did a food shop, tried and failed to make bread rolls, and lay in the bath for an hour willing herself not to think about Monday's appointment with Dr Daley. And yet, despite her efforts, she could hear his words repeating themselves again and again in her mind: tell me everything, he said, even if it is about me.

Lionel had always been able to read her moods, recognizing when he needed to step in and force a change in the dynamic playing out before him. There was the time when a designer had told her to wear a black swimsuit to model a collection of tiny clutch bags, their edges shimmering with jewels, better, he had claimed, to emphasize the shine. Evelyn, barely nineteen and desperate to find her place in this glamorous world that seemed to have no rules, did not even consider questioning whether a swimsuit was the right outfit for evening-wear accessories, even though her skin turned to goosebumps as she posed on the steps of a London hotel. Lionel had been the one to intervene, speaking firmly to the photographer about the advertising agency's instructions: accessories for a wife, not a shop girl. Lionel was often sent along to the shoots, the head office trusting him to be able to nudge the photographers and designers back in line, his tactful comments returning them to the brief they'd been given.

They had been friends for years, ever since Evelyn was booked for a jewellery advertisement, when she was seventeen and Lionel Diallo was twenty, the youngest and best of the assistant designers assigned to support the photographer for the day. The shoot was at the large department store, Selfridges, modelling their range of in-house jewelled hair pieces, necklaces and earrings. She had noticed Lionel's impeccable style immediately, the neat trim of his hair around the ears, a pompadour fashioned on top, the beige jacket he wore that crossed the boundaries of work and fashion, nipped in at the waist and balanced by an oversized collar. She was too intimidated to speak to him, but he was quick to seek her out, recognizing, he said, a fellow artist among the crowds. It was because of the way she had done her hair, he added, how instinctively she had known to counterbalance the heavy complexity of the necklace with the simplicity of a bun.

'My analysis has only just begun, it seems,' Evelyn said, trying to keep her voice light. It was impossible to express how distressing she was finding the therapy. It made no sense to her, and so it was easier to hide those thoughts away, present it instead like a comic story to entertain her friend. 'Though I'm not sure I'm going to like it. He wants me to say whatever comes into my head. Can you imagine?'

Lionel shuddered. 'No one wants to know the things that pop into my head. I wouldn't know where to start. What if you're thinking that the therapist needs to go on a diet? Or you hate the tie he's wearing? Are you supposed to say anything at all?' He laughed, his head thrown back. 'My thoughts jump around wildly and surely the ones about wanting to take home the man across from me on the bus are not going to be relevant.'

Evelyn laughed too, feeling the last remnants of her stress melting away. She knew Lionel would appreciate how difficult it was to speak one's most intimate thoughts.

'I think that would be exactly the sort of thing you are supposed to say. Though if you were with my therapist then he'd make you go into detail about what the man looked like, why you were attracted to him, and how it made you feel.'

'God, how awful. It's like taking something that you thought was an irrelevant passing thought and turning it into a massive deal. I don't see how that is helpful.'

'I agree, but it seems to be having some effect on me, even if it doesn't feel like a particularly helpful effect right now.'

'What about that nightmare you were having? Has he come up with any suggestions?'

Evelyn thought for a moment, trying to remember what it was he had said. If he had offered her an interpretation, it seemed to have vanished from her mind.

'Something about my marriage, I think. One of the nightmares took place in the chapel where Henry and I got married.'

'Well, that's not exactly a revolutionary analysis.' Lionel softened his tone. He could see the look of confusion on Evelyn's face as she tried to remember what Dr Daley had said. 'Well, these things take time, you know. You shouldn't expect answers straight away.'

'I know. You are right. But I guess I was hoping to feel at least a little better. But so far every time I leave the appointment, I feel terrible, much worse than before. He makes me feel …' She hesitated. It was impossible to describe how he made her feel. Lionel was watching her, a look of genuine curiosity on his face. She shook her head, her hands outstretched. 'He makes me feel like I'm getting everything wrong,' she said.

'How can you get therapy wrong?'

'I don't know. But that's how it feels, like he's watching me stumble around in the dark.'

'That doesn't sound right. I am pretty sure psychotherapy ought to be, I don't know, therapeutic?'

'You would think so.'

Evelyn swallowed the last pebble of ice from her glass, the cold edges pressing against her throat. She caught the barman's eye and gestured for another drink.

'Your friend, Theo, who was seeing him for help with grief. Did he ever tell you how he found it, if it was helpful?'

'He has stopped going, I think. I saw him last week and he said he was beginning to find a way through the pain.'

'Why did he stop going to therapy?'

Lionel shrugged. 'We didn't really talk about it. Though, he did say that the psychologist's analysis of his dream was all about sex, or sexual impulses, I think. It probably scared Theo, worried him he was going to say too much, reveal his sexuality. While some psychologists might be sympathetic, it's a risk to be too open. When Theo tried to suggest that maybe grief and love and acceptance came into it too, the therapist kept coming back to his own reading of the dream. Imagine!' he laughed, a little bitterly Evelyn thought. 'A therapist sitting across from you telling you that your unconscious is obsessed with sex. I mean, there must be more to it than that. A man in his twenties who's just lost the one person with whom he could be entirely himself. It's not easy navigating through all that again.'

Lionel's ability to understand the deepest fears and anxieties of others had not come without its share of personal challenge. He had confided in Evelyn over the years, the two of them growing ever closer. Born in Paris to French-Senegalese parents, he had moved to London when he was seventeen on an art scholarship at St. Martin's School of Art. It had not been an easy transition, leaving his home, his parents, the friendships that had sustained him, instead re-establishing himself in a new city surrounded by art students, many of whom did not bother to make him feel welcome. His parents understood how hard it was for him. When they had moved to Paris in the early thirties, they knew no one. But Lionel had persevered and now, thirteen years after making the move across the Channel, it was London he firmly called home. His dream was to set up his own jewellery store, stocking pieces from designers around the world. Every time he saw Evelyn, he told her that he was one day closer to making it happen. She had absolute faith in him; Evelyn believed that with his talent, his energy, and his brilliant personality, his dreams were going to come true.

Evelyn leant towards him, alert and focused despite the relentless noise of the bar. It was interesting to listen to Lionel talk about his friend, and she could imagine it, Dr Daley and Theo discussing the sexual symbolism of a dream. But there was another feeling too, an ache in her chest that made her afraid. It was this, a dream, sex, her own confused desire, that she wanted to talk about with Dr Daley; and yet she did not know if she'd ever have the confidence to say the words out loud.

There was something else tugging at her thoughts. Hearing that Theo, a man she had never even met before, had stopped seeing Dr Daley: it made her feel unexpectedly relieved. The thought of sharing him was unpleasant. While

The Model Patient

Dr Daley was frustrating, silent, patronizing, penetrating, she could feel his influence within every part of her. More than that, she wanted to be his alone. Between her Monday appointments, she wanted him to be waiting for her, thinking about her, writing his notes on her only, never making her share with other patients in the space of his thoughts.

It was ridiculous, she thought to herself as she took a large sip from the cocktail the barman handed to her. The bitter Campari brought her back to herself. He was a doctor and there was absolutely no reason he would think about her the way she wanted him to. She'd just have to try harder to forget about it.

Turning to Lionel, she smiled. 'Enough about me and my terrible dreams. Tell me about your new jewellery designs.'

It was nearly ten o'clock by the time Evelyn arrived back home. Henry was out at a work dinner, and Evelyn was relieved to see the lights were still switched off as she let herself in. She knew exactly what she wanted to do. And she needed to be alone.

As the taxi had driven her through the London streets, she gave up trying to push Dr Daley out of her mind. It was exhausting to fight the humiliating fixation of thoughts.

Perhaps, she mused, if she let her fantasy run through her mind now, if she fully indulged her imagination, she would have no need to return to it at her next appointment. She could purge it from her thoughts, instead devoting herself to the real, sensible work of therapy.

Ignoring the traffic, the horns and shouts along the road, the cold wind that infiltrated its way into the car, she stared out the window, her eyes seeing nothing but her fantasy playing out before her.

Evelyn's vision was of going up to her bedroom and taking off her clothes as soon as she reached home. The dark blue camisole would fall from her, sinking into a silken pile at her feet. She'd take the pearl choker from her dressing table, lifting those rows of cold smooth spheres from their satin bed. She did not stop to think about why she'd chosen this necklace, the pearls she hated with such irrational rage. Standing in front of the long mirror in her bathroom, only one lamp switched on, her skin would be lit dimly from behind, turning her into a shadow, a silhouette, not quite real.

Dr Daley would appear in the mirror before her, watching her, silent and knowing. He'd nod to her and she would kneel, the pearls draped through her fingers. She'd touch herself, the pearls sliding over and within her, their cool surface heating and slipping as she brought herself to climax. And she would hear his voice saying nothing and everything all at once.

She paid the taxi driver as fast as she could, too aware of the flush of her cheeks, the feverish shake of her hands. Running inside, she switched on the downstairs hall light, threw off her coat and shoes, and pulled the door closed behind her. She needed to be quick. Henry would be home soon.

Reaching halfway up the stairs, she paused. Something felt off, a smell perhaps, a faint scent that sent a shiver down her spine. Slowing her steps, she climbed the remaining few stairs. It seemed as though London had suddenly frozen beneath the deep winter chill, silent and motionless, no noise from the street slipping inside her home. All she could hear was the sound of her own anxious inhalation and the light depression of the staircase beneath her stockinged feet.

Her hand gripped the bannisters, an attempt to root herself in reality, to reassert control over her heated imagination. As she reached the top of the stairs, Evelyn stopped, fear thudding through her. There was a light turned on in her bedroom and, in the gap between the door and the floorboards, she saw a shadow moving inside the room.

Evelyn waited, her heart beating hard. She tried to stay silent and listen for the sound of footsteps. It couldn't be Henry. His coat wasn't downstairs and surely he would have left the hall light on for her. An image flashed before her, Dr Daley appearing from her bedroom, and she felt her body contract in a humiliating desire.

The shadow moved under the door again. This time she could hear the light tap of shoes, the intruder moving away from the rug and onto the wooden floorboards.

Before she could decide what to do, the bedroom door swung open and Evelyn screamed. A figure was walking straight towards her and it showed no sign of stopping. A hand reached out, thin fingers grasping onto her wrist. Evelyn tried to pull away but the fingers pressed tighter into her skin.

'Evelyn! What are you doing screaming at me like that?'

Evelyn blinked in the dim darkness, finally pulling her arm away.

It was Mrs Westbrook. Henry's mother with her perfect hair swept up in a neat twist, her signature floral perfume, her pale lipstick. She was wearing her navy swing coat and her handbag was tucked under her arm. Evelyn stuttered in shock, unable to find the words she knew she needed to say. It was she who should be asking the questions. Why was her mother-in-law creeping around her house in the dark?

Instead she found herself apologizing, once again, a vague concern about the tidiness of her bedroom slipping intrusively inside her thoughts.

'I didn't know you were here. Henry didn't tell me you were coming.'

'Henry said you were out at a dinner. You're back early.' She said these words with such severity, it was as though Evelyn had somehow inconvenienced her, turning up at her own home before Ruth had time to get in and out unseen.

'Can I help you with anything?' Evelyn tried to slow the beating of her heart. It was too much, the excitement of her fantasy thrown into chaos. She could not understand what Ruth was doing here.

'I am borrowing these,' Ruth said, lifting a box out of her handbag. 'They are mine, you know, and as you never seem to wear them, I'm taking them back for a few days. Alec and I are going to the opera this weekend.'

Evelyn stared at her, blinking slowly. Her mother-in-law was taking the pearls from her, the pearls she hated, that she had never wanted. Until tonight. They had, in her fantasy, taken on a new and thrilling role.

'I was planning on wearing them this weekend, Ruth,' she lied, trying not to let her voice shake.

'You can manage without them for a week, Evelyn dear.'

Ruth brushed past her, the floral notes of her perfume haunting the landing as she hurried down the stairs. Evelyn had an urge to push her, to grab the pearls from her handbag, to throttle her with them before throwing her out onto the street.

'Well, goodnight then, Ruth,' she said from the top of the stairs. 'I hope you get home okay.'

The front door banged shut and Evelyn went into her bedroom, all her energy gone. Getting changed as quickly as she could, she avoided the mirror, turning away from the sight of her nakedness.

Ruth Westbrook had turned Evelyn's desire into a dark and shameful monster. She wanted nothing more than to fall asleep and forget it all.

CHAPTER 10

By the time Monday morning arrived, Evelyn was worn out. The nightmare had come to her again, early on Sunday morning, and she had woken up feeling somehow uncoiled and exhausted all at once. It was, she realized with an uncomfortable flush, just like the feeling she'd experienced that night a few weeks ago, when Henry had held her against the staircase, his mouth between her legs for the first time. She often found herself thinking about that moment, wondering what had led him to her that night, touching her in a new way. And the response he'd aroused in her. Maybe the nightmare was changing, no longer the terrifying ordeal it used to be. But there was a shame in that too. How could she possibly tell Dr Daley that the nightmare she had come to him to destroy was now stirring something within her?

She knew she should be trying harder to put the complication of her feelings about Dr Daley behind her, so that she could move on and achieve the goals she was aiming for. The problem was that she was forgetting the reasons she had started psychotherapy in the first place. As she dressed and did her make-up on Monday morning, she whispered to herself in the mirror, reminding herself why she had made that phone call to Dr Daley's clinic one month ago.

'I want to be happy. I want to be calm. I want to sleep. I want to give Henry what he wants.' She stopped, her make-up brush pressed against her cheek. It was this last point that concerned her. Giving him what he wanted meant having a child. How could she do that when the thought filled her with dread? Perhaps the goal instead was to find a way to convince Henry to wait, to be happy with her and her alone without needing to expand their family so soon.

Or perhaps the goal was for her to learn a way to trust his love, to understand that he did love her enough, that a baby would not replace her. That was difficult, though, when he avoided her at night, turning over and switching off the light to punish her for taking the birth control tablets. In the last week, they had only had sex once, a rushed and urgent release in their bathroom before Henry went to work. Evelyn had been running the bath, her towel slipping from her as she tested the water. When Henry pulled her body towards him, leaning her over the sink countertop and pressing her wrists into the marble surface, she had watched him in the mirror. There was something in his expression, an anger perhaps, a frustration, that made her sense he hated giving in to his need. If he could, he'd refuse to touch her until she agreed to his demands.

She shuddered, a rush of an old and buried memory

flooding forwards. A bathroom, a man, a dressing gown discarded in a pool of water, her face, very young, reflected in the mirror. She pushed the thought away and continued applying the thin powder of rouge across her cheekbones. Turning her head from side to side, she checked the lines of her profile.

What she was absolutely not in therapy to do was to explore the forbidden memories of her past. It was over and she wanted to bury it deeply, not unearth it all again now.

When Dr Daley appeared to collect her from the waiting area, she felt a tremor of fear. It was his appearance today, how there was something different about the colour of his hair, the line of his clothes. He looked sharper, the neutral beiges and browns of the jackets he had worn in previous appointments replaced with black, and his hair was pushed back. As soon as she settled onto the couch, her cursory glance around the room complete, she let her gaze drift back to Dr Daley. The fabric of his jacket was embellished with black paisley swirls. Evelyn found herself staring at it, distracted by the coiling dark thread of the shapes.

He waited, silent, for her to begin. She must have been looking at him with a kind of despair, because he nodded encouragingly, leaning forward with his hands resting on his thighs.

'I found my mother-in-law in my bedroom last week.'

It felt good, at last, to be able to say this out loud to someone other than her husband. When she told Henry, he had frowned and then shrugged. 'I suppose she expected one of us to be in,' he'd said, before kissing her and switching off the bedroom light. Evelyn began to protest: his mother did not expect either of them to be at home. But he was no longer listening. It was to Dr Daley, then, that she poured out her fears.

'She was creeping around, taking back some jewellery that she'd given me. I don't understand why she wouldn't tell me she was coming over. It made me worry that she does this regularly, letting herself into our home and checking up on us. I already feel inadequate compared to her, like she could make our home much nicer for Henry than I can. Which I suppose is true. Her cakes are perfect; she always looks immaculate; she never leaves the washing up for the next day.'

Dr Daley nodded and Evelyn held her breath, waiting for him to speak. She wanted him to validate her concerns, to tell her what a disturbing woman her mother-in-law must be, how well she was doing to cope with Ruth Westbrook interfering in her life.

'Perhaps finding her in your bedroom felt as though the one place you have with Henry where she cannot intrude was being invaded?'

'Yes, maybe. Even our bedroom isn't private anymore.'

'Why do you think it was finding her in your bedroom, specifically, that upset you? Finding her anywhere in your house at night would, I imagine, have been disturbing.'

'As you say, my bedroom is where I have Henry to myself, without her influence.'

'You mentioned in a previous appointment that Henry is not having sex with you as much at the moment.'

Looking away, Evelyn tried to calm the leap of her heart. 'Yes, I feel as though he is punishing me for not wanting to get pregnant. And for being so insistent on managing my own birth control methods.'

'This is important to you, to be in control.'

'Yes, of course,' said Evelyn. She frowned. Perhaps Dr Daley did not realize what this meant to her. 'This new form of contraception has only been available on the NHS for a little over a year,' she continued, trying to make him understand. 'December 1961. I must have been one of the first in line.'

Evelyn and Diana had been visiting the same general practice since their early twenties, booking back-to-back appointments whenever they were available. While Evelyn could have gone to the Family Planning Association once she was married, she did not want to if it meant going without Diana. Unmarried, not even engaged, Diana would need to forge a letter from a vicar or family doctor if she was to be approved for any form of contraception. The FPA had strict rules about those they deemed worthy of support, despite claiming to be helping women control their bodies.

'It's humiliating,' she said, 'infantilizing, in fact, that to use the Family Planning Association, I'd have needed Henry's permission to be given the birth control pill.' She shook her head. 'I couldn't face asking him to sign the form.'

Evelyn sat straighter, daring Dr Daley to challenge her.

The Model Patient

She was an adult woman, she wanted to say, and she did not need the approval of a man to make a decision about her own body. The thought of it took her back to the past, to dangerous memories she refused to let resurface.

But Dr Daley did not challenge her.

'Perhaps you feel that I disapprove,' he said. 'That I think you should listen to your husband, to the FPA?'

Evelyn looked down at her hands. 'No, that's not how I feel.'

'I think you're angry,' he said. 'And we can understand why.'

She did not know what to say. It would have been easier if he had challenged her, if she could have fought him, argued her case. Dr Daley was a man. How could he understand? Diana was the only person she had ever talked to about birth control. And for Diana, it was even more complicated. Unmarried women were not offered the birth control pill, and so she continued to use the diaphragm. She did not trust a man to take the necessary precautions.

While Evelyn and Diana had tried to laugh about it, the embarrassment and associated shame of being fitted for the diaphragm weighed heavily on them, as well as the fear of pregnancy that accompanied every sexual encounter. But a new doctor had joined the clinic a few years ago, a progressive young man who had determined ideas about shaking up the culture of judgement around women's birth control. He had been prescribing Evelyn these bottles of pills since the beginning of 1962. He gave her three months at a time, three precious little bottles with the drug's name of Conovid printed on the label. For several months, Evelyn had hidden them in her chest of drawers, secret treasure she did not dare risk sharing with Henry. Until one day he found them while he was searching for a lost pair of cuff-links, and the secret was over.

It had made her feel lighter in some ways. While there were many things that must stay in the past, to add layers of deception to her marriage was not what she wanted. A flush of shame rose quickly, staining the skin of her neck. For what was she doing here, she thought, but constructing another secret, these intimate conversations with a man her husband knew nothing about.

Now she kept the birth control pills lined up in her bathroom cabinet. She liked seeing the neat row of the pots every time she opened the mirrored door, her face vanishing and replaced with the reassuring sight of contraception, mixed with make-up and face creams.

'So perhaps seeing his mother in your bedroom makes you feel as though it is her influence over Henry that has made him so keen to have a child, to please her. Which has translated into him not having sex with you unless you agree to stop using contraception. The bedroom has returned to her, his mother, and is no longer your place of pleasure and power as Henry's wife.'

Evelyn shuddered, that tremor of desire moving through her once again. It felt transgressive to talk to him this way, especially when he was watching her so closely, his eyes seeing everything. She could not help thinking of Henry pushing her pelvis against the sink, the steam from the bath clouding the mirror. How, when she let her vision haze, Henry's reflection morphed into a different man, the man who was seated across from her right now.

A silence had fallen between them again, Evelyn too afraid to speak. Who knew what secrets might escape from her lips if she felt that pulse of energy jolting through her body once again?

Evelyn wondered if Dr Daley could sense that she was closing in on herself. He sat back in his armchair and unbuttoned his jacket. Watching as the black paisley pattern fell away from his chest, she felt as though he was laughing at her, his ease against her suffering. When his gaze found hers, she blushed and turned away. It was infuriating to feel so lost in front of him. This felt like a terrible game, the rules of which she did not know.

'It is strange to be talking about Henry's mother this way,' she said at last. 'I've only ever told Diana how I really feel. Henry doesn't want to hear it.'

'Can you tell me more about Diana?' he said.

Tension fell away from her jaw. She was grateful to him, how he let her stay on the topic of Diana, back to comfort, to the familiar. Pausing, she frowned, unsure how to begin. He seemed to sense her doubt and so he clarified, guiding her once again.

'It seems to me that your relationship with Diana is very important to you. She has, as you said previously, been part of your life for a long time, since before Henry. I think it would be helpful to you to try to articulate what your friendship has meant to you at different points in your life.'

Evelyn tried to think what to say. Diana was her best friend, the rock in her life who had always been there, even when everything else was falling apart. They had known each other since they were toddlers, they had been to school together, left home together, lived in their first adult home together. She faltered, suddenly afraid again. If Diana was asked this question about her, would she say the same thing? She thought so, but there were memories tugging at her, painful uncertainties that she wanted to bury.

'When I was seventeen, I stole the boy Diana wanted. I regret it so much.'

Evelyn didn't know why she was telling him this. It was not a memory she enjoyed thinking about, and she was grateful to Diana for never bringing it up. It did not present her well.

Dr Daley said nothing, an impenetrable gaze that made her feel exposed. She had started the story now. She would have to continue.

'We were at a party, the birthday of one of the boys at our fathers' school. There were occasional social events between the boys' school and our local girls' school, so we had developed some friendships. Edward Greenly was his name. The party was at a gigantic house in a nearby town, with a dance floor set up in the garden, lights strung up between the trees, a band, and what seemed at the time like hundreds of teenagers. Edward was very popular.

The Model Patient

'I knew Diana liked him. She had developed a crush on him about five months earlier after a Christmas social between our two schools, but he seemed oblivious to her feelings for him. They had, instead, become very good friends, which always surprised me because she was much more intelligent than him. He was one of those athletic boys whom everyone adored, and I couldn't imagine smart, sensible Diana with him.

'It was obvious to me that their friendship was never going to change into romance. But they spent a lot of time together and had an easy familiarity which I envied. My friendships with boys were never straightforward. Too many had been ruined by a sudden declaration, an attempt to hold my hand, a kiss coming out of nowhere, and then a barrage of resentment when I told them I wasn't interested in them that way. Diana did once suggest to me that perhaps I gave them the wrong idea, that I led them on. I didn't like that. She made it sound as though I was deliberately drawing them to me, like a seductive siren, only to turn them down when they got too close. But perhaps there was something in what she said. I did want them to like me.'

Her face was hot and she fixed her gaze on the ornamental stone that decorated the fireplace. Dr Daley was watching her and she was terrified of seeing judgement in his eyes. Forcing herself to continue, she shifted her weight forward on the sofa, rooting her feet against the floor.

'At this party, Edward wasn't very kind to Diana. I knew she'd been hoping this would be the night, that he'd dance with her, look into her eyes and tell her he was in love with her or something like it. We turned over the possibilities endlessly while we were getting ready, planning it all, redoing her hair, trying on too many dresses. I think we both knew it was never going to happen, but it was fun to imagine it together. I was swept up in her desire and I really did want it for her. But as soon as we got there, he was dismissive of her. With all his popular friends around him, the rest of the school rugby team hovering at his side, he wanted to show off. Diana was not the prize he hunted for on his seventeenth birthday.'

Dr Daley's expression was quiet, entirely passive. Evelyn wondered whether he was even listening. She stopped talking, frowning as she stared at him. He looked back at her, his gaze still. While nothing changed, no movement, no smile of encouragement, she could sense an energy between them.

He was listening and he was right there with her. She continued, her stomach clenching as she remembered what happened next.

'It was late into the party, and someone had definitely slipped alcohol into the punch. We were all a little drunk. I was dancing, I remember the band had shifted from ragtime into these slow Frankie Laine covers, and I felt very alive. There was a wildness to the night, and I embraced it entirely. But there was a danger to the feeling too, because all evening I had sensed Edward's eyes on me. At first I thought he was looking at Diana, but as the evening continued I realized that wasn't true. Suddenly he was right there next to me, pulling at my waist and turning me around into the middle of the dancing. We were among all these swaying, dancing teenagers, the band loud and slow.'

Evelyn rushed through the story, too aware of the shame burning in her cheeks.

'When he kissed me, I didn't try to stop him. It was only when I saw Diana watching us from a few feet away that I pulled myself back to reality.'

Dr Daley pressed his hands against his thighs, sitting up a little taller.

'How did you feel when you realized what you had done?'

'Why does it matter what I felt? It was a horrible thing to do and I wanted to turn back time.'

'Did Diana punish you for hurting her?'

'I wanted her to, I think. I remember extracting myself from the dance floor. Edward didn't mind. He'd had his birthday conquest, his friends had seen the kiss, that was enough for him. I tried to find Diana, but she'd left immediately after seeing me and Edward, getting a lift with some friends.

'I was so nervous about seeing her the next day, but in the end I was surprised by how she reacted. There had been no need for me to be anxious; it was as though it had never happened. When I went round to her house in the afternoon, she smiled at me and asked if I enjoyed the rest of the party. It took me ages to be able to bring the conversation around to what had happened. But she dismissed it. She told me not to be silly, that it didn't matter at all. Edward was only ever going to be a friend to her, she knew that. All that talk about having a crush on him was stupid, she said; she'd never really believed he'd look at her that way.'

'Was it a relief that she didn't seem to mind that you'd kissed him?'

'He kissed me,' Evelyn snapped. Dr Daley said nothing, his expression calm.

She sighed, too aware that she sounded like a quarrelsome teenager. 'No, you're right. I did return his kiss. I guess it was a relief at the beginning. I was relieved to have my friend back after a sleepless night of feeling sure she was going to want nothing to do with me. But the more I've thought about it since then, the more uncertain I've become. She had every right to be angry with me.'

'Do you have any thoughts about why she responded that way?'

'Yes. I suppose I do. I think she was embarrassed that she'd let herself develop a crush on a boy who had no reciprocating romantic interest in her. And I think she was hurt that he'd chosen me, her best friend, instead of her, so she simply couldn't bring herself to think about it. She pushed it all away and decided to pretend that she'd never really considered him as anything more than a friend anyway. And it was easier for me to go along with her version, so that's what I did. Her friendship with Edward started to die away after that. I think he was probably embarrassed about it as well. It was a terrible thing that we did to Diana.'

'Why do you think it was this moment in your friendship that came to you when I asked you to tell me about Diana?'

The Model Patient

'I don't know.' Evelyn sighed. She didn't want to talk about it anymore. It was Dr Daley's turn, surely, to help her. She wanted him to reframe it all anew, to tell her that it was over, it was in the past, it didn't matter. Diana was still her best friend; she had never blamed her. Now, with the story confessed, Dr Daley could be the one to absolve her.

'Do you think there is still part of you that wants her to punish you? Her silence about it, refusing to discuss it fully with you, it left you full of self-doubt and conflicted feelings about yourself and what you did. You internalized all the blame, when if she had spoken it out loud, you could have moved on?'

'Yes, maybe. Or maybe she really didn't mind and knew it wasn't my fault. I couldn't help it that Edward chose me that night.' Evelyn knew she sounded defensive, but she didn't know how else to react. He wasn't making her feel any better.

'But you returned his kiss when you knew it would hurt your friend.'

Evelyn felt her body tense. He was refusing to let her escape the pain of the memory. His words placed her right back there, stripping away the comfort she had allowed herself to feel from Diana's indifferent reaction.

'Why did you do that, do you think? Did you have feelings for him?'

'No, I never thought about him that way. It wouldn't have occurred to me, not when I knew Diana liked him so much.'

Evelyn clasped the gold pendant of her necklace, pressing the ridges of the little heart into her thumb. It was a gift from

Diana, bought for her when they first moved to London together. Diana had a matching one, from Evelyn. On the back of the heart were their initials, the D & E intertwined.

'So what was it then?'

Dr Daley was pushing her, his questions driving her painfully into the memory and into herself.

'I liked how it felt when he looked at me.'

'How did it feel?'

'It thrilled me. It made me feel exceptional.'

'And now you want to be punished. You want to be punished for allowing yourself to feel exceptional, when you think you don't deserve it. You've punished yourself for it already, thinking about it over and over again, and it hasn't helped. So now you bring it to me.'

'Yes. I know it was wrong, but I also liked that he desired me. I'm ashamed of wanting to be desired.' Evelyn's words had faded into a whisper, her heart beating fast.

'Yes,' he repeated. 'You want me to make it neatly fall into place, your best friend's forgiveness and Edward's adoration, both at the same time.' He paused, leaning forward and holding her with that unsettling gaze. 'You want me to make you feel exceptional and you want me to punish you.'

'Yes, that is what I want.'

Dr Daley nodded and looked up at the clock.

In that moment, his attention shifting to the clock, the door, her departure, Evelyn hated him. Once again he had brought her to the edge, driven her to reveal her weakness, her need. And then he discarded her, saying nothing to put her back together again. Worse than that, he had led her further into her desire, placing himself firmly inside her mind. He would not let her escape.

And soon she would be alone, cast out, struggling to find a way to be calm.

'You're going to say our time is up, aren't you?' Evelyn could hear her voice coming out as a pathetic whine. She hated it, hated how she couldn't say what she really felt: that she wanted to kill him, that she wanted to kiss him, that she wanted him to walk over to her and take her in his arms.

'We can talk more next time,' he said, standing.

'Yes, okay, thank you.' The smile she could feel rising to her cheeks was unbearable, an entirely different expression from how she really felt. And so she left, walking fast out of his consulting room, down the hall, and towards the entrance lobby. She moved so quickly that Miss Simmons had no time to get up and open the door for her before Evelyn had wrenched it open and hurried out into the street.

In bed that night, Henry asleep beside her, she could hear Dr Daley's voice, her own in reply. It was a single exchange, going around and around in a relentless loop. There was only one way to make it stop.

'You want to be punished.'

'Yes, I want to be punished.'

And so she made it happen, her fantasy forming and her body responding. She was back in his consulting room, the dynamics between them changing into something real and alive.

Turning on to her side, she pressed her legs together. She let herself go, the fantasy travelling like fire.

She imagined him telling her to take off her clothes, how she undressed in front of him, removing her sweater, her skirt, her stockings. How he rose from his chair and came towards her, his hands moving over her hips, her stomach, her shoulder blades. How he peeled off her underwear, his hands grazing her thighs. How, when she tried to touch him, he wouldn't let her. How she waited on the rug until he returned from his desk, a black silk neck tie in his hands, the same paisley pattern as the jacket he had worn that day. How he bound her wrists, pushed her against the ground, his body lowering onto hers. How only then did he kiss her and she felt the roughness of his beard against her skin.

Evelyn could feel the heat rising in her neck. It was the detail of her fantasy that surprised her, how important each stage was to the narrative she was creating. Closing her eyes, she continued, imagining him rising away from her, turning her over, pulling her body up and in towards him. She imagined hearing him unbuckling his belt, pulling the leather out from his trousers and sliding it through his hands, leaning her over the edge of the couch, her wrists bound.

Too quickly, in a terrifying loss of control, her mind travelled to the past. She was back there again, a teenager, in a dangerous place with a dangerous man she wanted to forget. Evelyn heard herself cry out, a strangled nightmare of a sound.

Henry turned over in the bed, his arm falling heavily over

The Model Patient

Evelyn's waist. This physical contact, right when she needed it most, was more than she could bear. Moving closer to him, she whispered into his ear.

'Henry, are you awake?'

'Hmm, I guess I am now. What's wrong?'

She climbed onto him, her legs either side of his hips, her hands pressed into his chest. 'Now?' he said, sleep slowly dissolving. Taking his hand, she moved it gently to between her legs.

'Yes, now.'

In the midnight darkness, feeling how much she wanted him, he denied her nothing.

When morning came and Henry left to go to work, Evelyn made a decision. The next time Dr Daley wore that black paisley jacket, she would tell him everything. She would not moderate her thoughts; she would not hide within her discomfort. He told her she must say exactly what was in her head, no matter how awkward it seemed.

And yet there was another sensation, some primitive instinct for survival, that knocked in her chest. It told her to run from this man who seemed fixed on unravelling her.

But he was a doctor. He was trying to help her.

Evelyn was determined to put aside her fear. She was going to do what he wanted.

CHAPTER 11

Evelyn called Diana on Saturday morning. She could not endure another day of waiting for life to happen. For that was how it felt, each day a trial of patience while the world continued without her. Henry went to work; Diana taught her lessons; Dr Daley met with his other patients, forgetting about her until Monday rolled around once again. It reminded her of those days waiting for confirmation of a job to come through, afraid to move too far from the telephone in case her agent called. But at least then she knew what she was waiting for. There was a precise and hopeful purpose to that painful craving for the telephone to ring. Diana had commented on this one day, when they were living together in the flat off the King's Road. The two of them were lingering inside, Evelyn waiting for news of a magazine booking, Diana expecting an update from a publisher about a short story she'd written.

'How is it that humans put up with so much waiting?' she'd said, bouncing her pen against the kitchen table. 'It's unbearable and yet we do, somehow, seem to bear it.'

The Model Patient

'Perhaps we've taught ourselves to enjoy it, enjoy the pain, I mean,' Evelyn had replied. 'We imagine the pleasure to come and so we put up with it, need it even. How would you feel if every story you ever wrote was accepted immediately, no waiting, no suffering?'

'I'd love it,' replied Diana, shaking her head in amusement.

'Perhaps for a little while. And then what?'

'It would be sad,' Diana said, 'if the reality of getting my novel published never lived up to my imaginary version.'

'Yes, and the fantasy of this job will fall apart as soon as I arrive at the studio and the producer decides he doesn't need me.'

'So, you're saying we should enjoy this terrible waiting for the phone to ring?' Diana laughed. 'You always did have a masochistic streak, Evie.'

From her home in Pimlico, Evelyn waited anxiously for Diana to pick up the phone. She was already imagining the day the two of them were going to have together. The relief, when her friend answered the call, was immense.

The weather was taunting them still, the occasional day of thawing ice, and the dangerous floods that followed, replaced by three relentless nights of heavy frosts. Henry was desperate to play golf, but the ground was too hard. This weekend was supposed to be a friendly opening tournament at his home golf club in Wiltshire, with his father and two brothers, but it was cancelled. Instead the four of them were meeting at Dr Westbrook's London club to play squash and smoke cigars – hopefully not at the same time, Evelyn had said to Henry as he dressed that morning, his gym bag packed with his racket and sneakers. He had looked young and energetic when he left, and she kissed him at the door, enjoying the feel of him, how real and solid he was in her arms.

Evelyn had the day to herself. She met Diana a few hours later in Soho and they wandered arm in arm towards Carnaby Street. The transformation of this street over the past few years was astounding, and the two women liked venturing away from the familiarity of the King's Road to the growing popularity of this previously unassuming backstreet of Soho. The grey and faded tobacco shops from the last decade had metamorphosed into a growing number of men's fashion stores, and even the ruins of the old Central Electricity Board building had not escaped renovation. While most of the shops sold men's fashion, it was still an exciting street for the two young women, a few bars and cafés interspersed among the clothes shops. Evelyn often caught sight of people she knew from her modelling days, and had once spotted her fashion idol, Brigitte Bardot, leaving a shop with a large gift bag over her arm. The boxer Billy Walker was known to come here, too, drawing a new crowd of athletic young men.

Diana looked beautiful, Evelyn thought as she watched the reflection of the two of them passing along the window of The Mod Male. She was wearing cropped trousers that hovered above her ankles, the fabric tight over the hips, and a brightly coloured scarf was tied around her neck. Her

The Model Patient

exposed skin was stained red from the cold, but it just made her look younger and more alive. Evelyn wished she'd worn something brighter, an outfit to match the ever-changing displays in the windows of the male clothing stores lining Carnaby Street. Evelyn had met the Glaswegian tailor John Stephen at a fashion show just before she was married, and had been impressed by his energy. The Mod Male, Domino Male, Male W.1. – his shops attracted young men who wanted to break away from the safe suits and ties of their fathers.

Music filtered out from Domino Male, a fast beat spilling into the street every time someone opened the door. Two young shop assistants took a break outside the entrance, dressed in burgundy and brown collarless shirts, clusters of large buttons arranged down the front. Cigarette smoke hung in the air and the metallic smell of petrol hovered between the rows of scooters and cars that lined the pavement.

A window display in Male W.1. caught Evelyn's eye and she stopped still, turning around to take a closer look. There was a shop assistant climbing out of the window's alcove, brushing some stray cotton thread off a jacket as he did so. Three headless mannequins leant against one another, their wooden stands ending in a medley of shoes, belts and luggage accessories stacked on the floor of the display. It was the middle jacket that made Evelyn stare even harder, a tremor of fear moving through her.

Black, a paisley pattern stitched into the fabric: this was Dr Daley's jacket. He had worn it on Monday, in her appointment and then, later, in her imagination. She looked around wildly, afraid that he might be there on the street behind her.

'What's the matter?' Diana said, looking at her with concern.

Evelyn pulled herself together. 'Nothing. It's just I'm sure that I've seen that jacket before.' She looked again, taking a step towards the window. The jacket had changed right before her eyes. It wasn't black at all, but a deep blue, the paisley swirls embroidered in a thick grey and yellow stitch. Even the collar was different, a thin lapel that tapered away into nothing, not at all the same as the one Dr Daley had worn. She shuddered. This mistake, it made her feel unhinged.

'Let's get some lunch,' Diana said, taking her by the arm again and leading her down the street. Unusually, there was no queue at Cranks, the new vegetarian restaurant that Evelyn could still not persuade Henry to visit. A meal was not a meal, according to her husband, without a cut of meat. The waitress led them to a table downstairs, a small booth with a solid oak wood table and brightly coloured cushion covers. A woven basket lampshade hung above them, dimming the light into an orange glow. They ordered salads with a thick slice of nut roast, fresh wholemeal rolls on the side. Evelyn loved these lunches with Diana: the intimacy of the booths, the odd assortment of hand-thrown pottery, the vivid colours of the salads with the delicious citrus tang of the dressings. It was entirely different from the Sunday lunches that she dreaded, with matching white china, overcooked meat, and vegetables drowning in gravy.

The Model Patient

'What's that you're reading?' Evelyn asked, pointing to the slim novel poking out from Diana's handbag.

Diana lifted it out and handed it to Evelyn. *The Bell Jar*, by Victoria Lucas.

'It's not her real name. Everyone knows the author is actually Sylvia Plath, the American poet. I heard a rumour that she died less than a fortnight ago, not long after the book was published.

'Isn't she married to Ted Hughes?'

'Yes, but they've been separated for a while. This is what I've heard, anyway, from a friend who works in publishing. You should read the book after me. I think you'd find it interesting.'

Evelyn flicked through the pages. She liked the front cover, neat boxes of white, black and mauve. Her eyes settled on a sentence: *And I knew that in spite of all the roses and kisses and restaurant dinners a man showered on a woman before he married her, what he secretly wanted when the wedding service ended was for her to flatten out underneath his feet like Mrs. Willard's kitchen mat.*

She read quickly before handing the book back to Diana. There was something unsettling about this book, the thought of a bell jar descending over her head, like the serpent that consumed her in her dreams.

'I might have met someone,' Diana said as she tucked into her pudding, an apple tart topped with a crisp sugar glaze. Evelyn raised an eyebrow. Diana was always meeting someone. In her experience, this did not mean it would last more than a few weeks before Diana got bored with them.

Diana shook her head, laughing. 'I know, I know. But this feels different. We've only been on a couple of dates. But we have so much in common, and there is this energy between us. I can feel it every time he looks at me.'

'That sounds romantic,' Evelyn commented, truthfully. She remembered that feeling with Henry, the jump in her chest when she knew he was looking at her. There was no sensation like it. 'Where did you meet?'

'Don't laugh, but it was at an academic conference at the Tavistock clinic. I was there doing some research on child development for a paper I'm giving at University College, for the new intake of students at the teacher training college that's linked to the university. Well, I obviously wasn't expecting to meet someone, but he came and sat down next to me just before it started and, for the entire lecture, I could kind of sense him. It was like there was a physical bond in the air between us. And I just knew he could feel it too. When the talk finished, we didn't need to say anything to know we'd leave together. Ten minutes later we were in a pub, both of us asking too many questions and not even bothering to pretend our legs weren't touching beneath the table.'

Diana smiled, shaking her head as though in disbelief. 'I barely remember a word from the conference.'

'What's he like?' Evelyn asked. She was desperately trying to root herself in the conversation, to find the focus that she could sense was lacking, ever since she had seen the jacket in the window of Male W.1. It wasn't that she didn't care about Diana's new interest; she cared deeply, too much perhaps, with an ugly envy that made her feel monstrous. It was more that her mind kept shifting to an obsession of her own, to the man who was refusing to fade from her imagination.

Diana paused, her fork loaded with apple slices. 'His name is Patrick. He's hard to describe. There is an intensity to him, as though everything he does or says has a purpose. I know he loves listening to jazz music. He was telling me about all the records he collects: Duke Ellington, Ronnie Scott, Johnny Dankworth. And he dresses well. Both times we've met, he looked like he had stepped straight out of one of these Carnaby Street shops. We are going to a jazz club for our next date, Ronnie Scott's in Soho. There is a saxophonist he says I'll like: Johnny Griffin, I think. Though apparently this weather is stopping musicians from travelling, so we'll see. There are only so many times the headline "No Biz like Snow Biz" is going to work on an audience longing for live music.'

'Sounds dreamy,' said Evelyn, Diana's words drifting hazily over her. It was what she wanted, a date in a jazz club, the music rising and falling around them, a man's hand resting at the base of her spine. But for her, that world of romance and excitement and new, thrilling passion was over. It hurt to think Diana still had access to what she most desired.

'You and Henry should come too,' Diana said. 'Perhaps not this time,' she added, 'it's still too early to be bringing friends, but soon.'

'I'd like that,' Evelyn replied. She and Henry had been too safe in their choice of restaurants and bars recently. It would be good for them to join Diana and her date, a new romance reigniting their own.

Later that evening, back at home and waiting for Henry to return from Surrey, Evelyn turned on the radio and poured herself a large glass of Cinzano vermouth. She ran through the channels, the familiar sounds of the BBC giving her no comfort tonight. Finally, the notes she was searching for cut through from Radio Luxembourg, a station far more reliable in offering new music that went beyond a repeat of the most popular singles of the month.

The music that filled her living room now was a jazz record from a newly popular American musician called Wayne Shorter. She closed her eyes, letting the low swinging notes of the saxophone, the light syncopation of the drum underneath, dance through her. She thought of dark Soho bars, ice dripping onto her skin, the heat of a man's leg pressing against hers, musicians in the dim red light of the stage. She imagined herself in a silk dress, the back cut low and a necklace hanging down her spine.

Standing quickly, she went to her desk and took out her sketchbook from the top drawer. She drew fast with smooth arching strokes of the pencil.

A long chain, three silver strands wound together like rope. At the throat a pendant, the shimmering scales of a snake's head, a blue sapphire stone clasped in its mouth. And rolling down the spine, another length of chain, sparkling lightly. Evelyn longed for the sketch to come to life.

The Model Patient

She sighed, slamming closed the sketchbook in frustration. What was the point of any of this, her designs, her desires, her imagination? Switching off the radio, she moved back into the kitchen, her glass now empty. Evelyn ran the water at the sink, rubbing the cloth inside the glass with a furious intensity. It was only when the glass cracked and the water ran red with her blood did she feel the tension inside her release and the tears start to fall.

CHAPTER 12

Evelyn had taken Dr Daley's advice and was starting to write down her dreams. Untidy scribbles in a small notebook that she kept in her lingerie drawer, she wrote them down immediately on waking, slipping out of bed and into her dressing room before Henry stirred. There was a comfort, she found this Monday morning, in having her notebook with her for the appointment with Dr Daley. Dreams were a step removed from the embarrassment of her thoughts, the distance of her unconscious night-time explorations giving her an easier way in to discuss some of the troubles she found most difficult to express. It was as though the dreams did not truly belong to her: she could study them like a student analysing a text, taking no personal responsibility for the symbols and images and meanings.

The notebook lay open on her lap. She had exhausted all she remembered about the dream, Dr Daley guiding her back into the detail, trying to help her identify the place, the man, the feelings the dream had evoked. A country house,

The Model Patient

a row of sliced apples on a table, a white cloth, the flash of a camera. One moment she was taking a bath; the next she was standing outside, watching as a huge snake coiled and twisted inside the tub. A man walked towards her and she tried to run, but her legs were rooted into the ground. She lifted her fingers to her face, feeling rough grains of salt coating her lips. There were too many images, none of them coalescing into a coherent narrative whole.

'You remember flashes of a camera. Do you think this could be a place where you were once photographed?'

'It feels familiar, yes. But it's hard to place.'

'And the man. What does he look like?'

Evelyn stared up at the ceiling, trying to remember.

'He's older than me, smartly dressed. He is confident, relaxed, like he owns the house, perhaps.'

'And were you attracted to him?'

'Why would you think I was attracted to him?' She did not understand. What was it in the details of her dream that would suggest the man was anything other than a frightening figure from whom she wanted to escape?

'He walks towards you. You try to run, but you don't run, or you can't. Instead, you realize that there is salt on your lips. How did the salt get there?'

'I think he put the salt on my lips. But I can't remember how.'

'That's a very intimate gesture. To place salt on your lips. Did you like it?'

Evelyn shook her head. There was a memory creeping

forwards, a shadow that she knew she was powerless to stop. For years she had tried, distracting herself with work, the success of her career, relationships, sex, marriage. But here in this room, Dr Daley watching her, she knew her time was up.

'This man. Who is he?'

He could read her mind, she thought, her hands tightening into fists. Evelyn had turned Dr Daley into a man with supernatural powers: the ability to see inside her soul. She tried to relax, finding comfort in the scent of eucalyptus and mint. But there was something else in the air today, a base note of cedar, leather, a touch of orange. It puzzled her, this smell, how it took her back to the past with a frightening flood of feeling.

'It was a modelling job, one of my first, and I was keen to impress. I think I felt that if I could do this job well, then many more would come. And I was right about that: it was through the success of this photoshoot that I was offered more and more contracts.'

She stopped, struggling to grasp on to the details of the story she was trying to tell. That scent again, leather and orange, it seemed to be distracting her and guiding her, both at the same time. She slipped her hands beneath her thighs and continued.

'The shoot was taking place at a large estate not far from where we lived: Winter Manor it was called. I'd got the job through friends of my parents. Roland and Nora Hardy. My parents were often going to events at their house because Mr Hardy liked to host fundraising dinners for schools in the area. He was a businessman who had made his money in school uniform manufacturing. It was a lucrative trade, I remember my father saying once after they'd returned from a party there. Private schools often wanted bespoke designs and Mr Hardy made sure he was front and centre of their mind to be the supplier of choice. He had worked hard over the years to ensure all the big retailers stocked his uniforms, places like Selfridges, John Lewis, Harrods. The fundraising dinners were supposedly charitable events to raise money for school scholarships, but they were obviously useful business opportunities for Mr Hardy as well.'

Evelyn shuddered. It was strange to be talking about Mr Hardy, and she could feel herself slipping inside herself, as though she was a child again, uncertain and afraid. She looked up at Dr Daley, watching closely for his reaction. It seemed so important that he was on her side. But he was giving her nothing, just that silent passive waiting, hovering between attention and distance. She felt a desperate, sudden urge to be held by him, for him to wrap her in his arms.

'The point is,' she said with a determination to continue, 'my parents trusted him. I had modelled school uniform for his catalogue once, when I still looked like a schoolgirl. It had all been arranged very professionally, with chaperones for the children, plenty of breaks, Mum watching from the edge of the room. This time, though, everything was different.'

'Were you no longer a schoolgirl this time?' Dr Daley asked. His voice had an edge to it, his question harshly spoken, like a demand. It shocked Evelyn back into the moment, and she looked up at him in surprise. She nearly missed it, but for a second he had let emotion show in his eyes. A look of pain, Evelyn thought, as she desperately tried to understand. But it passed quickly and his calm, neutral expression returned.

'No, I was definitely still a schoolgirl. But the problem was that I didn't look like one anymore. I developed early, I was tall, and from my early teens I looked like an adult. Especially when I was wearing make-up, red lipstick and too much mascara, my hair styled in a sophisticated fashion, more appropriate for a young woman than a child.'

Biting her lip, she looked down at her hands. She tried to stop the weight of exhaustion from sinking through her. To hear the hardness of his voice was devastating.

Evelyn forced herself to keep going. He needed to understand.

'The shoot was at Winter Manor, Mr Hardy's house. Mum dropped me off before going out for lunch with Nora Hardy. They were becoming good friends and I think they realized they had a lot in common: both housewives keeping home for busy and successful men. Mr and Mrs Hardy had three children, but they were barely there. One was at boarding school in a different county, and two of them were adults who had already left home. I think Mrs Hardy was pleased to have my mum as a friend: she must have been lonely in that huge house with her children gone.

'I was taken straight to a bedroom where a stylist helped me get ready. The job was for a new range of women's watches. Mr Hardy knew the designer and he was doing him a favour in letting him use Winter Manor. The stylist did my make-up and pinned my hair into a loose bun and I was given a simple black evening dress to wear, strapless and tight-fitting. I remember looking in the mirror and barely recognizing myself. Although I was only a child, that day I could have been mistaken for a woman.

'The photographs didn't take long but I felt strange throughout, as though I was on the precipice of some great test. Mr Hardy was watching, as was the designer. They were drinking whisky or brandy, I think, and were talking loudly the entire time. I tried to block them out, concentrate on the requests of the photographer, but it was difficult. The photoshoot took place in a beautiful salon and I was seated at a grand piano. For some photographs I had to pretend to play the piano, in others just sit with my wrists crossed, the silver watch contrasting with the black of my dress.'

Instinctively, she clasped her fingers around her wrist. Dr Daley's gaze moved to her hands and she let herself wonder what it would be like if he held her there, if that was what he, too, was imagining.

'Tell me what happened next,' he said. Those words he chose, an order she could not disobey, they took her back into the memory.

'It was Mr Hardy who suggested the pose for the final shot. He came over to me and lifted me up by my elbow, leading me over to the side of the grand piano. "Like this," he'd said, pushing me into the wood so that I was leaning over the hammers and pins of the piano, my arms outstretched and falling forward towards the keyboard. I suppose it looked elegant, but I knew there was something else about the pose, something different that made the energy change in the room. Mr Hardy walked around to behind the photographer and watched me while the camera clicked away, faster this time. I remember feeling out of breath, even though I was standing entirely still.

'Mum collected me soon after. She asked questions about the shoot, what it was like, how it all went, with a cheerfulness that left no room to explain how it had really felt.'

'How *did* it feel?' Dr Daley asked, that same probing question, but harder. Evelyn could sense him pulling away from her, frustrated with her and her story.

'It felt wrong. It felt as though I should not have been in that house, with those men watching me, their laughter as they drank whisky and I posed in a dress that made me look like a woman far older than my actual age.'

He nodded, a simple gesture but enough for her to know she needed to continue.

'He called our house a week later and said that the photographs were ready and he wanted to give me one, as a memento. It was my mum who he spoke to on the phone, and she said we'd go back the next day. When we arrived, Mrs Hardy was already waiting at the front door. She'd booked a new restaurant a short drive away for the two of them for lunch, and they disappeared in her shiny black Austin Sixteen. I had no opportunity to say to my mother that I'd rather she didn't leave me alone. It would have sounded strange, like I was a child making a fuss. So I was left there in the house. Mrs Hardy said I could use the swimming pool: it was a warm day in early July, and they had a huge garden, a swimming pool, a tennis court, a summer house. I didn't have my swimming costume with me, but Mrs Hardy said I could borrow hers, that Mr Hardy would show me.'

Evelyn paused, her stomach tensing as she remembered.

'I didn't like the idea of wearing her swimming costume,' she said, frowning as she tried to find justification for all the ways that she, at fourteen years old, had failed. 'But there was nothing I could say that wouldn't have come across as rude.

'I waited in the hallway for a minute or two and then Mr Hardy appeared from his study. He told me to come with him; he wanted to show me something. I assumed it was the photographs.

'He led me into his study. There I was, so many photographs of me laid out on the desk. I was beautiful, sleek, looking much older than I actually was. My arms were long and thin, with all the different watches I had worn shining against the grand piano. He let me choose one, and I could hear his breath at my neck as I leant over to get a closer look. I remember feeling conflicted: I wanted to stay there for hours, staring at myself, taking in every little detail. But I also wanted to get away, escape from the sound of his breathing and the weight of his body getting closer to me.'

'Did he touch you?' Dr Daley asked.

'Not that time. Just light presses of his hands against my

arm, my shoulder, his fingers touching mine as we looked at the photographs. He asked me to sign the back of one of the photographs for him. He said he wanted to remember me in this moment. It was the final photograph, the one of me leaning over the side of the piano, that he'd chosen. Handing me a pen, he told me to sit at his desk. I didn't know what to write. I was too young to know what to do.

'So I asked him. He told me to write, "To Mr Hardy, in anticipation of more to come, with love, Evelyn." I didn't understand what it meant. But I was soon to find out.'

'He dictated the words to you?' Dr Daley asked. Evelyn stiffened. His words sounded accusatory, as though he didn't quite believe she was telling him a true version of events. For it was this that frightened her, the confusion and shame of her memories of Mr Hardy, all those times she met with him in his large house, her mother out for lunch with his wife, just a short drive away.

Evelyn had never rejected him, never challenged him. She signed the photograph, added a childlike 'x' after her name, a slip of the pen that she had not meant to include. But she always added an 'x' to the notes she wrote to her friends and family, birthday cards, thank you notes, Christmas labels. How was she to know how he would interpret that little kiss of the pen? Or perhaps it made no difference at all. Her fate was already decided.

'Yes, he dictated everything to me after that,' she said, determined to be clear. It was not her fault what happened. 'He organized my next bookings, put me in contact with an

The Model Patient

agent in London, ensured I was the first to be considered by all the retailers where he held influence. I learnt to be grateful to him and he made certain that I knew it was thanks to him that I was a success.'

'What did it require from you in return?'

Evelyn sighed. It was exhausting and she wanted to stop. Her fingers itched for a cigarette, but she knew there were none in her bag. All those feelings she had been trying to forget were flooding back. She had given into him so easily. And for a time she had even let herself enjoy it: the teenage girl adored by a wealthy man, a man who made her feel special, beautiful, exceptional.

'It cost me the end of my childhood,' she replied. 'And it cost him his family. A month after that photoshoot, his wife returned earlier than expected. She found us at the swimming pool. I wasn't wearing one of her swimming costumes. I wasn't wearing anything at all. He was watching me from the side and I was turning over and over in the water, feeling his eyes on me. She left after that, taking their child with her.'

'And did you stop seeing him? Did your mother realize what was happening?'

'That's what I find so hard, I think. Nora Hardy left, but she couldn't face the humiliation of it, her husband with a fourteen-year-old girl. So she never said a word. I remember listening to my parents talk about it at dinner one night, poor Roland Hardy whose wife had left him. There were rumours she was seeing someone else. Only I knew the truth. There was no one I could tell. And so it continued.'

'You were fourteen?' For the first time in all their appointments together, Dr Daley let his emotion show, revealed in the horror in his eyes, the surprise slipping into his words. It disappeared fast.

'Yes. I was fourteen when it all began. But it continued for years. He kept me a child in some ways, as well as hurrying me too quickly into adulthood. He always made me call him Mr Hardy, never Roland. I tried calling him Roland once, when I was an adult, nineteen years old. But he said I mustn't do that.'

'Why do you think that was?'

Evelyn shrugged, anger rising in her throat. She wanted to stop, to erase the memory and rewrite the past.

'Perhaps it made him feel powerful,' she said at last, filling the silence that pulsed between them. 'I was Evelyn, but he was Mr Hardy, the figure of authority to whom I needed to submit. It was only once I had been in London for a year and had begun to grow up that I found a way to end it with him. I had finally confided in Diana just before we moved to London together, and she tried to help me get out from his control. Sometimes I'd pretend it was all over, just to make her judge me less, but it was always a lie. Then one day, when we'd been living in London for a year and I was getting regular jobs through my agency, I realized I didn't need him anymore. When I told him it was over, that I never wanted to see him again, he laughed and told me not to be so dramatic. He had never forced me to do anything I didn't want to do, he said.'

The Model Patient

'And was that true?'

'It was complicated. You have to remember the context. After that, he never touched me again. He left me alone for the most part, though it was a shock to see him at my wedding. My parents still have no idea of the damage he did.'

Dr Daley was looking at her strangely, his gaze giving her none of the comfort she needed. It made her feel deranged, as though she was the monstrous one, her childish desire for love tempting a man into wanting her.

'It wasn't my fault,' she said. It was agonizing, this need to defend herself. Suddenly it felt essential that Dr Daley say something to help her. She needed him to exonerate her, to tell her she had done nothing wrong.

'Do you think you took so long to end the relationship because you enjoyed how special he made you feel?'

'Yes. Of course. I found it impossible to do anything that might make him dislike me. He made me feel as though it was only through the reflection of his gaze that I could be beautiful.'

A painful itch was running beneath Evelyn's skin, as though there was an animal trying to escape from within her. Dr Daley was refusing to give her any relief. She grabbed her necklace, trying to find a way to centre herself.

'I hate it when someone doesn't like me. I always want to adapt how I behave to make them change their mind.' It was all she could think to say, this weakness that had been there since she was a child and she had let a grown man touch her again and again.

'How does it feel now, to tell me this and not know if you're saying the right things to make *me* like you?'

'I know nothing about you,' said Evelyn, furiously. Her anger was building. 'All I know is that you're a man.'

'And what does that mean to you, my being a man?'

She stared at him, too shocked to unravel the confusion of her thoughts. Evelyn did not understand how they had travelled from the trauma of her memories to this terrible, tormenting question. It made her want to throw herself at him, to claw at his face and throttle him. She hated him, but even more she hated herself. She hated how the image of placing her hands around his neck shifted so quickly into a painful desire to kiss him.

'I like the idea of men looking at photographs of me and thinking I am beautiful,' she said, the words forming against her will. Evelyn shuddered, an urgent desire to defend her weakness flooding through her. 'Back then, I was a child, but I was learning that the only power I had over others was from the way I looked. The photographs of me were superior, compared to the real-life girl. I felt that men would need to see a photograph of me from a professional shoot in order to find me attractive. They provided the glamorous, beautiful, adult version of me. Not the anxious child with all the flaws exposed.'

'It must be hard for you to wonder whether *I* have seen photographs of you. Perhaps you like to think I've seen you in a magazine somewhere, or I recognize you from an advertisement.'

The Model Patient

Evelyn felt herself slipping inside her imagination, an image of Dr Daley cutting a photograph of her out of a magazine, placing it into his notebook. Specific photographs came to her mind, the ones where she looked most beautiful, irresistible, even: dressed in black lace with large diamond earrings falling down her neck, or stepping out of a car in a ballgown, displaying high-heeled satin shoes.

'Yes,' she said, barely thinking. 'I would like that.'

'You'd like me to look at photographs of you, to admire you, to think you are beautiful.'

'Yes,' she repeated. 'Yes, that is what I want.'

He smiled at her, his fingertips pressed together. 'Because if I had looked at photographs of you, it would make you feel that you were special to me.'

Evelyn nodded, but she did not understand him. She wanted him to start again, to reframe the words, to tell her that she *was* special to him: not like this, taunting her with specialness but doing nothing to make it come true.

'Yes, I would like to be special to you.'

He leaned forward, his smile vanishing and replaced with something hard that startled her. 'You would like me to desire you.'

'Yes, I would like you to desire me.' She gripped the edge of the sofa, her eyes fixed on him. He had to say more, to turn his words into something real. To leave her like this felt so cruel.

'I want to know how you feel about me,' she heard herself say, a childlike desperation in her voice.

'You know how I feel.'

She stared at him, her mind moving fast. She did not know how he felt. And yet perhaps, she thought with a burst of hope, he was giving her a clue. While he would not say it directly, maybe there was a chance he did feel something for her. But it wasn't enough. She needed to be certain.

'No, I don't know.' She paused, glancing down at the ground. There was so much more that she wanted to say.

He nodded and looked up at the clock. 'I see we need to stop now.'

The time was up and she was unravelled. It felt as though she had stripped herself naked in front of him, and he had watched, saying nothing. Lifting herself off the sofa, she felt an excruciating pressure pulsing inside her chest.

As she left, she could already sense her mind turning the conversation over and over. But worst of all was the rage creeping beneath her skin, a demonic energy that Dr Daley had done nothing to help her expel.

CHAPTER 13

Evelyn called her parents the next day and told them she was coming home. Just for a night, she said, as a break from the city.

'Won't Henry miss you?' her mother asked.

'He'll be fine for one night. Besides, he's going out for dinner with colleagues.'

'Well, it will be lovely to see you, Evie. I'll make up a bed.'

In truth, she needed to get away, not from Henry but from Dr Daley. The thought of him in his clinic, just a short taxi ride away from her home, was unbearable. She wanted to go back there and confront him, force him to think about her outside the boundary of those fifty-minute appointments. There was so much she wanted to say to him, to ask him: was he deliberately cruel, manipulating her emotions, refusing to provide her with any comfort while at the same time driving her to delve into her most painful memories? She did not understand how this was supposed to be therapy.

She could stop, she told herself over and over again in a

desperate attempt to find reason. No one was forcing her to turn up to those appointments. But she knew that was impossible: her feelings had rooted themselves too deeply.

Every minute of the train journey from London Waterloo to her childhood home was familiar. She could predict the exact moments the train would pick up pace, the corners it would turn as it pulled towards the stations, the view shifting from rows of houses to snow-specked woodland to the occasional church tower, a blanket of snow sinking down the tiles. Despite it being nearly the end of February, the world was still set in a deep winter freeze, the ground whitening as she travelled further out of London and into the countryside. A low snow-covered grassland to her left signalled the arrival of her station, and she peered out of the window to catch sight of the frozen river. Countless hours of her life had been spent walking along that river, arm in arm with Diana, or her mother, or the boys she dated. There had been snow most years when she was growing up, but never like this.

The sight of the river, so familiar and yet frozen into a winding silver mirror, made her think of her past. It took her back to how Mr Hardy had encouraged her to have relationships with boys her own age, as long as she returned to him whenever he felt like summoning her. He would ask her probing questions about the stages of her romances, demanding to know if the boys had touched her, how it felt, whether she enjoyed it. She learnt that he liked it when she teased him, just a little, telling him stories of a boy reaching for her hand in the cinema, kissing her outside her parents' house, fumbling with her bra in the grassland along the river. It made him want her more. Always some gift would arrive after those conversations, sent to her parents of course, but she knew they were for her: a box of chocolates or a tin of her favourite biscuits. How kind of Roland Hardy to send such generous gifts, her parents would say, handing the chocolates around their kitchen table after dinner. They had no idea what she'd done, she'd think, too ashamed of herself to do anything other than swallow the chocolate, the sweetness cloying in her mouth. And there would be the work too, contract after contract arranged through him. He was her patron, a generous man with all the contacts in the world of retail and design to make her dreams come true. Poor Roland, her mother would say, living alone in that big house, his wife and children never visiting him. Nora Hardy was the villain, a wicked woman who neglected her husband for whatever temptations had attracted her away.

Evelyn's mother was waiting for her in the car, a dusky blue Morris Minor, parked in her usual spot directly opposite the station's exit. She kissed her on the cheek as she climbed in. To feel her mother's arm reaching around her shoulders, pulling her into a hug, made Evelyn want to cry.

'Dad is at home, putting the kettle on.' Lydia Anderson drove carefully out of the station, avoiding a large mound of blackening snow. Evelyn rested her head back against the seat, trying to feel like a teenager again: the girl with her busy schedule, envied by her friends, special Evelyn Anderson, driven from place to place by her mother. But now, after all she had said in yesterday's therapy appointment, she could not find it in herself to feel good, or successful, or beautiful. Instead she hated that child, was repulsed by how she had allowed herself to feel so special.

When the reality was that she was not special at all. All she had were long legs and a seductive smile. Her value was fragile, dependent entirely on the judgement of others. She should have realized that earlier, of course: all the signs had been there when she was a teenager, the way her mother helped her choose outfits for parties through a careful consideration of what would make her most irresistible to the teenage boys she was meeting. Irresistible but also unobtainable, the beautiful and innocent girl who could be admired but not touched. Evelyn had never learnt how to untangle the mixed messages her mother had taught her, and they had followed her through life, a confusing rule book that made no attempt to allow for the double standards of the way men and women could express their desires.

Howard and Lydia Anderson no longer lived at the school. They had retired recently, moving to a house in a quiet residential cluster of streets, all large homes with neat gardens, trees shading each driveway. Evelyn had been sad to see them move out of the house in which she'd grown up. Packing up her room had been an almost impossible task. In an attempt to clear away decades' worth of clutter, her parents said they would take just one cardboard box of her belongings with them to their new house. In some ways it had felt good to throw so much away. It was Evelyn's first real attempt to discard parts of herself that she wanted to forget and leave behind.

She hugged her father when she arrived, gratefully accepting the tea he offered her. A plate of biscuits was on the kitchen table and she tucked into them, her hunger finally revealing itself. She had barely eaten since yesterday, her stomach tied in too many knots to be able to feel anything but an overwhelming anxiety.

'How's Henry?' her father asked. 'The two of you should come together for a weekend soon.'

'We'd like that. As long as his mother doesn't put up a fuss about missing a Sunday lunch with us.'

'His parents can come too, if they want. We've haven't seen them since the wedding.'

Evelyn nodded. She didn't feel like explaining how her attempts to find an accepted place within the Westbrook family had started fraying at the edges, descending into something close to fear ever since she'd found Ruth in her bedroom late at night.

'I'm cooking your favourite for dinner,' Lydia said, already opening the refrigerator and piling ingredients onto the counter. Fish pie, of course, cod and salmon in a creamy white sauce, mashed potatoes layered on top, peas in butter on the side. Evelyn's mother was the perfect headmaster's wife, and even now, with Howard retired, she hosted lunch clubs and tea parties for the wives of current and retired schoolmasters. It was a different sort of competency from

Henry's mother's, however. Lydia didn't hide the hard work and the mess; her devotion was cheerfully on display, evidenced by her flour-stained aprons, the mounds of laundry, weedy but colourful flower beds. She felt no need to present only the pristine shine, like Ruth did. Evelyn supposed it came from the chaos of life married to a teacher, the unpredictable schedule of a boarding school, dinners discarded and reheated, mud dragged through the house after an afternoon supporting the school rugby team. It was comforting, she found now, the mess of the kitchen, the crumbs sticking to her socks, the smear of grease staining the glass of beer that her father was handing to her.

'You're enjoying those biscuits,' her father said as she bit into her fourth. 'A gift from Roland Hardy. He dropped them around yesterday, on his way back from London. A new brand in Harrods, he said.'

Evelyn could feel the chocolate coating of the biscuit sticking to the roof of her mouth. She wanted to be sick. Swallowing as fast as she could, she took a large gulp of beer.

'He was asking after you,' her mother said as she started chopping an onion. 'You should give him a call, see if he wants to go out for lunch when he's in London. He said he hasn't heard from you since your wedding.'

'I don't know why I'd want to go out for lunch with Mr Hardy,' Evelyn said. It was surprising to hear herself say these words. Her parents looked at her, both of them frowning.

'Why would you say that?' her mother asked. 'He was

always so kind to you. Who knows whether you'd have made such a success of your career without him.'

Evelyn stood, the chair scraping loudly against the floor. She leant forward, her hands pressing into the table. This was it, the moment she could tell them everything, reveal the truth about the man they had brought into her life.

She looked up. Her parents were standing close together, a picture of domestic bliss, her father opening a bottle of beer, her mother smiling as he handed it to her. She couldn't do it. How could she throw a grenade into their lives? To tell them what had really happened would destroy them. They would never forgive themselves for letting Mr Hardy abuse her for so long, their actions, their blindness to what was happening leading him to her again and again. How could she tell her mother that when she dropped off her daughter to wonderful Mr Hardy, who was letting her daughter use his swimming pool and introducing her to modelling agencies, what the true cost of all those favours really was.

'I'm going to use the bathroom,' she said, forcing herself to smile. Her parents turned back to the cooking. They barely noticed her leaving.

Upstairs, she went straight to the bedroom, the one where she always stayed when she visited. Though it wasn't really her bedroom. That no longer existed. This, instead, was a beautifully designed guest room, as tidy and uncluttered as a hotel. It was the only room in the house that had avoided the inevitable accumulation of her parents' possessions, the newspapers discarded halfway through reading, recipe books stained with food, endless pairs of reading glasses, sweaters thrown over the back of every chair. Evelyn knelt next to the bed and lifted the edge of the covers.

Coming home and witnessing her parents' obliviousness to the trauma of her childhood had filled her with a devastating sensation of doubt. Dr Daley's hard-edged questions, his refusal to help ease her pain, the chocolate biscuits she had, just now, consumed: it was too much, making her question herself and her memories. She needed to know that she wasn't insane, that her version of the past was the truth.

Peering down underneath the bed, she could see her cardboard box, the sum total of her childhood possessions that her parents were willing to store for her. As quietly as she could, she dragged the box towards her. A layer of dust coated the top and she wiped it lightly, leaving a trailing imprint of her fingertips. Inside were photographs, letters, certificates from her tap and ballet exams, school sketchbooks, the black covers splattered with paint. Carefully, she lifted out the top items, searching further. There was a friendship bracelet, one from a pair she had made for her and Diana. She ran her fingers along the tightly woven cotton yarn, feeling the glass beads she'd threaded through the colourful fabric, before placing it back inside the box. Her rabbit, Margaret, was squashed beneath a photo album, one eye missing, the wool of the fur matted and thin. She let her be. Those memories would not give her comfort today.

The Model Patient

Finally she found what she was looking for. Her teenage diary. It was strange to see it buried among all the artefacts of her childhood. To have stored it here where her parents could, if they had wanted, have dug it out and read the most intimate record of her teenage years seemed bizarre to her now. But she knew they would have never thought to read her words. They saw her in the same way as everyone else: a model with her beautiful contented life, as sparkling as all those smiling advertisements for which she was photographed during the Fifties. She'd learnt a lot from the advertising industry: happiness was seductive, and she knew that she needed to seduce if she was to be wanted.

She was not a regular diarist, but she did have bouts of writing when she was younger, mostly accounts of working in exciting places, boyfriends, days out with Diana. And Mr Hardy. What would have happened, Evelyn thought, if her mother had given into curiosity and had read her diary? Surely that was every girl's worst nightmare, their mother reading all those shameful secrets, seeing their daughter's embarrassing self-obsessions recorded in blue ink.

Maybe it wouldn't have been so bad. The pain could have been cut short.

The diary might have been mistaken for a school exercise book. She had written her name in pencil on the front cover: Evelyn Anderson. And just below her name, she had added an 'x'.

Evelyn flicked through the pages, uncertain what it was she was looking for. It didn't take her long. Her attention was drawn by his name, Mr Hardy, and the house where it all began: Winter Manor. She read quickly, struggling to make sense of the words. She did not remember writing any of this, a 14-year-old girl trying to find order in something she did not understand.

20 August, 1950. Mr Hardy invited us all over to Winter Manor for dinner, me, Mum and Dad. Mrs Hardy left a few weeks ago, so he's been lonely, Mum says. I don't want to go to this dinner. But at least it's all three of us this time. My parents will be there too, so nothing will happen.

The rest of the page was covered in rough drawings, and Evelyn ran her finger along the pencil lines. She did not remember drawing these, a jumble of shapes, some impossible to decipher. But then she understood. They were watch faces, the ticking hands of a clock travelling between a mixture of wristwatch designs. Some were blurred and chaotic, as though the hands were moving too fast; others were hard and thick lines pointing with definite clarity to a combination of numbers and roman numerals.

She turned the page.

20 August. We are back from Mr Hardy's house and I am in bed. I am returning tomorrow because a friend of Mr Hardy who runs an advertising agency is going to be there and he wants to suggest me for a new advertising campaign. I think it's for a knitwear brand, which sounds very dull,

The Model Patient

but it's all sweaters and cardigans and wool skirts which has reassured my parents that I won't need to take my clothes off. No swimwear Dad said to Mr Hardy, and everyone laughed. I didn't know why it was funny, but I laughed too.

I helped Mr Hardy bring the pudding in from the kitchen. His housekeeper left after the main course and so Mum asked me to help. She tried to help too, but Mr Hardy told her to stay put.

It was when we were in the kitchen that he told me about the knitwear booking. He asked me whether I wanted it and I said yes, I did. He asked me how much I wanted it and I said that I wanted it a lot. Then he put his hands on my waist. I stood very still. He untucked my blouse from my skirt and put his hand inside. He asked me again, whether I wanted to be a model. I nodded and he squeezed my breast.

When we went back into the dining room with the pudding, he told my parents about the new job opportunity. They were so happy, and kept thanking him. Mum told me in the car on the way home that I should have said thank you too. It was rude of me to stay so silent. It made it seem as though I wasn't grateful.

I am grateful. I want to be a model. I'm never going to get good grades like Diana, or go to university like everyone says she is going to do. My secret wish is to be an artist but I don't think my paintings are very good. Mostly people look confused when I show them my art. I think there might be something wrong with me.

Next time I'll say thank you.

Lucy Ashe

The fish pie was ready and Evelyn tried her best to act normally. She ate the dinner, drank the beer, helped her mother with the washing up. When, at last, she said goodnight and went up to bed, the thought of that diary entry and the mistakes of the past were too painful to endure. So instead she thought of Dr Daley. It was still painful, but the pain was different. With Dr Daley in her mind, everything transferred to fantasy, and to hope, and to the exquisite and the agonizing imaginary relationship between a doctor and his patient.

CHAPTER 14

Evelyn noticed the jacket immediately. When Dr Daley walked towards her, she tried to stay calm, to concentrate on standing, smiling, following behind him into his consultancy room. He stood in the doorway as she passed by him, too close to her, his figure real and alive. This, here, was not a fantasy.

The room smelt different. The usual mint and eucalyptus fragrance was eluding her. As she tried to settle onto the sofa, she breathed it in, frowning as she felt her agitation rise. Rosemary and orange mingled with honey, leather, musk, cedar. She shivered, drawing her sleeves down over her hands. It was cold in the room, and she noticed the window wasn't quite closed, a tiny gap letting the freezing breeze seep inside. Dr Daley walked to the window and pushed it shut. Evelyn shivered again, unsettled by the sound, like a door closing firmly on a private scene.

Evelyn did not trust herself to speak. Glancing around the room, she was startled to see that it was not quite eleven o'clock. Dr Daley had begun the appointment early.

The silence was excruciating today. She watched him, his face giving away nothing. It made her feel like a child trying to get her parents' attention, only to be faced with blankness, no indication that they could see her at all.

He was wearing the black paisley jacket, and she had promised herself that this was the sign she needed to be able to open up to him. But now she was here, it seemed an insurmountable task. It was impossible to put into words. Evelyn knew that it would be easier to show him, to walk over to him, to kneel by his chair, to take his hands, to make him understand.

'If you would like, we can try something a little different today,' Dr Daley said. There was a clipboard on the coffee table next to him, a piece of paper attached. Evelyn could just make out columns of words, with blank rows marked out down the page.

'Yes, okay.' She was willing to try whatever it was, anything to end this silence.

'It's a word association task. A kind of projective testing, where I'll say a word and then you should reply with the first thing that comes to your mind. It's important that you don't try to moderate your thoughts. I will record the word or words you say, as well as how long you take to reply, and any physical responses that indicate an emotional reaction.'

She nodded. This, she thought, she could manage. It would be like her English lessons when she was at school, Mr Martin asking them to write down the connotations of imagery in poems. A line came to her now, the words so familiar: 'breeding lilacs out of the dead land'. It was strange how the image returned to her now, lines she had never understood.

'We will then spend some time discussing your responses afterwards. It might be useful to us to delve further into why certain words or phrases came to you.'

Evelyn could sense a tension winding its way through her. She was afraid of what she might say, especially today. Turning her gaze to the window, she tried to decipher shapes behind the gauze of the curtains. But there was nothing, just a grey sky, a sad patch of grass, the impenetrable brickwork of the house opposite.

Dr Daley held the clipboard on his lap. He leant forward and pulled his arms out of his jacket, the black pattern wrinkling as he placed it over the back of his chair. He was wearing a black shirt with a grey woollen waistcoat over the top, and he rolled up his sleeve to reveal a wristwatch.

Evelyn had never noticed him wearing a watch before. The clock above the door had distracted her from observing it, or maybe it had always been hidden beneath his clothes. This second clockface, it disturbed her, as though its existence made time tick on too fast. She could not compete against both a clock and a watch. A thought flicked through her mind, that perhaps he was deliberately showing her this watch, wearing it for the first time even. It was a manipulation, forcing her back to Winter Manor, to all those beautiful silver watches, how much they cost her. She quickly tried to discard the thought: it was shameful to be so paranoid, turning the simple act of wearing a watch into a methodical manipulation.

He turned his wrist and unbuckled the leather strap, before placing the watch flat against the clipboard. Evelyn could feel the colour rising in her cheeks, her breath shallow, and she looked away again, desperately trying to focus on something else: not Dr Daley, or his black paisley jacket, or the leather of his wristwatch.

'Are you ready?' he said.

'Yes, okay,' she replied, sitting up straight and forcing herself to focus. 'Can I ask you, though,' she added, 'did you come up with the list of words for this session? Or are they a standard list?' It suddenly felt essential to Evelyn that she know the answer to this question. This task, seemingly so simple, she knew it was going to dig deep inside her. There was an intimacy to what he was asking her to do. If the words were a standard list, compiled by an old, probably dead psychologist, she did not know if she could find the energy to engage in the test.

Dr Daley did not answer right away. There was indecision in his gaze, his eyes scanning from side to side. Evelyn watched him closely.

'I will answer your question,' he said eventually. 'But before I do, I'd be interested to know why this is important to you?'

It was frustrating for Evelyn. She didn't understand why he couldn't answer such a simple question.

'I want to know if you have planned the words with me,

specifically, in mind. Or whether you use the same list with all your patients.'

He nodded. 'Perhaps, you feel that if I had prepared these words specially for you, I'd have kept you in mind between our sessions, that you were special to me.'

'Perhaps.' Evelyn could feel the anger building inside her. It was infuriating, how he kept dragging her back to this place.

'Well, I can tell you that the list of words is partially based on a standard list, but adapted a little. The words were originally used by Carl Jung in the early 1900s, but with the language difference, German to English I mean, and the fact we are living in different times, I have made changes.'

'Thank you,' Evelyn said. It was only later that she realized he hadn't answered her question at all.

'Remember, there is no right or wrong response. You might say something completely different and seemingly unconnected to the word. And that is fine. We will discuss your responses afterwards and see if there is anything helpful to be explored.'

Evelyn nodded again, trying to relax the tension around her jaw. The room was still so cold and she was shivering. It had been unwise to wear such a thin sweater, but she had been determined this morning to ignore the relentless weather. Dr Daley tilted his head, his forehead furrowing with a look of concern.

'Are you cold?' he asked.

'I'll be fine. This weather, you know,' she shrugged,

unsure what to say. She had felt an unreasonable thrill of excitement that he had noticed. While she knew it was ridiculous, she longed for it to be evidence that he cared for her.

'You can wear your coat if you wish,' he said, but she shook her head. A moment's hesitation, and then he reached behind him. Evelyn tensed, her heart beating fast. He was holding his black paisley jacket. 'Would you like a jacket?'

She stared at him, desperately trying not to let the colour rise in her cheeks. He half-stood, reaching across to her with the jacket. Taking it from him, she placed it around her shoulders. He was watching her and the effort not to shake was exhausting. Evelyn wanted to give into the sensation of the jacket against her arms, the closest she would get to an embrace.

'Are you ready to begin?' he asked. Evelyn nodded, afraid to speak, even to breathe. She could smell that scent again, so much stronger now, and it made her want to sink down inside the jacket and disappear.

She tried to shift her attention to the word association task, focusing her eyes on Dr Daley and his clipboard. This was the first time he had held a pen during her appointments and she realized that she liked this change, as though he was engaging with her more actively, no longer so silent, so aloof.

The first word was 'house' and Evelyn responded swiftly with 'bedroom'. It had come to her immediately, but with an unnerving sensation of the bed covers floating up to the ceiling, like the billowing silk of a parachute. The next was 'glass' and she said 'wine'. But as soon as she spoke, it was the red of her blood dripping into the sink that came to her mind, and she grabbed her palm, tracking with her thumb the line of the nearly healed cut.

For 'bride' she said 'beautiful'. For 'plum' she said 'lipstick'. When he said 'lead pencil', she paused, thinking of her sketchbook with the jewellery designs. 'Pearls,' she said, and he looked up at her. She could feel the intensity of his gaze and she blushed, remembering her fantasy, the pearls sliding against her, Dr Daley in the mirror.

He continued: 'friend' was 'Diana'; 'carrot' was 'stick'; 'fur' was 'touch'; 'flower' was 'rot'. Some of her answers surprised her, and she could feel anxiety growing inside.

The words kept coming. It was an attack, wearing her down until she could no longer control any part of her response. He said 'child' and she paused, her thoughts darting about wildly. It felt like a trick, as though he was making her admit something she didn't really want. She shook her head.

'I don't know.' He nodded and wrote something down on his page.

'Woman,' he said. This was even harder. Was she supposed to define what it meant to be a woman, to condense herself into one hasty word? That scent, the leather and orange of the cologne: it came to her again, a smell so masculine, so potent. To smell it right now, the notes of cedar and dry grass, it was so different from her sense of herself: a woman sitting opposite a man.

'English Leather,' she said, unable to direct the journey of her thoughts. The scent was taking on a new dimension, transporting her back to a moment from her past she could not quite define. English Leather was the name of a men's cologne, and she could picture the bottle with its large wooden lid, but she could not remember where she had seen it before.

Dr Daley's face did not change; he simply scribbled something on the paper without looking down.

'To kiss,' he said. There was a tightening within her. He was getting too close. Evelyn battled, but her thoughts would not find an anchor. She touched her lips, leaving a light stain of lipstick against the tips of her fingers.

'My lips,' she said, but she was unsure what she meant. It must have been obvious in her voice, for he tilted his head to one side, waiting. She shook her head and looked down at her hands.

His eyes scanned down the list. Evelyn hoped he was going to skip some words and bring them closer to the end. The experience was becoming too fraught, and she thought she might explode. Sitting still was impossible. Her legs crossed and uncrossed; her body shifted back and forth on the cushions. She grabbed at the neckline of her sweater and pulled tightly on the chain of her necklace. His jacket was heavy against the back of her neck.

'Sex.'

'Can you say that again?' Evelyn was afraid. Perhaps she had misheard him, her fantasies intruding on reality.

'Sex,' he repeated, his voice steady. Dr Daley lifted the watch off the clipboard, dangling it by one of the leather straps. Evelyn watched him as he placed it around his wrist, pulling the leather through the clasp. Too many images were moving before her, a confusion of danger and desire. She clutched her necklace even tighter, her other hand pressed deep into the leather sofa. There was a creeping sensation beneath her skin, like a demon determined to possess every part of her.

'There is no judgement,' he said. He spoke softly, a gentle push to get her where he wanted her. 'You are safe here with me.'

'I want ...' she began, shaking her head.

'You don't need to fight it, not here with me.'

'I can't say it.'

'You want to say it. You will feel better if you tell me.'

She closed her eyes. When she opened them again, she stared right at him, her body poised and still.

'It's you,' she said. 'You.'

Dr Daley did not write anything this time. He placed down his pen, moving the clipboard onto the coffee table. Watching her, silent, he waited for her to break. It was unbearable, the penetration of his gaze. Her face crumpled and tears started falling down her cheeks.

'It might, I think, be helpful if we pause there. Your answers have given us plenty to discuss. If you are happy to do so,' he added.

She could not speak. He had said she would feel better, that she was safe here with him. But that was not how it felt at all.

'Your answers to the last two prompts, "to kiss" and "sex",

suggest that you have feelings about me, that it would be helpful for us to explore.' He spoke slowly, but without any hint of embarrassment. Evelyn reached for her bag, her hands trembling as she pulled out her handkerchief and dabbed the cotton beneath her eyes. A black stain imprinted itself, the thick lines of her eyeliner starting to smudge. She hated it, this exposure, this vulnerability, and she tried to pull herself together.

'Can you tell me why you are upset?' he said, leaning forward. There was a look of pity on his face, and Evelyn shuddered.

'Why do you think I'm upset?' she snapped. 'I've revealed that I have these feelings for you, exposed this terrible, shameful part of myself, and you question why I'm crying.'

'Why are they terrible and shameful? There is nothing wrong with how you feel.'

'Of course there is something wrong with how I feel. I'm married. I love my husband. And yet, somehow, you've brought me to this place where I think about you all the time. I have ...' she paused, her hands moving wildly through the air as she tried to think how to frame her thoughts. 'I have these strong feelings for you, and I don't know what to do with them.'

Part of her was relieved, painful though it was. She had told herself that she would explain her feelings to him if he was wearing the jacket. And that was what she had done. With the jacket around her shoulders, it had been impossible not to give in.

The Model Patient

It was as though a blockage that had been building within her had opened and released. It was up to him now to help her move on. Some indistinct part of her mind knew that her feelings for him were not real: it was a strange transference of everything from her past, her relationship with her parents, Diana, her boyfriends, Henry, all those photographers, Mr Hardy. But she couldn't think about that right now: the stronger drive was her desire. That was real, and she felt it in every part of her body.

'There is nothing shameful in your feelings. I told you that you should say whatever you are thinking, no matter how difficult or awkward. We can explore these feelings together.'

'How can we do that?' she said. 'What possible purpose would it have for me to sit here and tell you my desires?'

'You have brought these feelings here to me and we should not neglect the help they may give us in discussing the troubles you are having in your life.'

'Dr Daley,' she said, a ferocity building. 'I think you knew I was feeling this way. I think you encouraged me to fall for you. You wanted my feelings to intensify.' Evelyn could hear the resentment in her voice and she knew she sounded insane.

'Why do you think that?'

'You kept asking me to consider my reaction to you. You told me that I wanted you to make me feel special. That I wanted you to look at photographs of me. You taunted me with your hypothetical attention, driving me to want you this way.'

'Mrs Westbrook, you seem to think that I am able to read

your mind. I only know what you bring to me in these fifty-minute appointments, what you decide to tell me.'

Evelyn shook her head. She did not believe that he had been oblivious to her feelings until now.

'Your method of leading me to think about you, and whether you like me, it's manipulative. You suggest that I want to know what you think, but then you never tell me. Your silence, it's cruel,' she said, leaning back against the sofa, exhausted. 'You could have warned me that this was going to happen.'

He said nothing. Evelyn knew the time was up without even looking at the clock.

'And now you're going to tell me to leave, giving me nothing to help put me back together again. You deconstruct everything I've built in my life that protects me from the past and makes me feel safe. And then you watch as I struggle.'

'Do you think I want you to struggle?' he said.

She pushed the jacket off her shoulders, throwing it to the other side of the sofa.

'I don't know what you want. Maybe you pity me, how deluded I am. But I don't want that. I don't want you to pity me.'

She paused, looking at him with wide eyes. 'I'd prefer your cruelty to your pity.'

He really did glance at the clock this time. Evelyn followed his gaze. It was nearly midday.

Evelyn felt that familiar tremor of desire. He had given her more time: not much, but it was something. She had beaten the clock, breaking the boundary of the fifty minutes.

The Model Patient

They stood together, the space between them narrowing.

And then he was at the door, holding it open for her. As she passed by him, her body close to his, she could smell that cologne again. She inhaled, letting the scents establish themselves.

Perhaps she was going mad, an aromatic hallucination that seemed so familiar, evoking a complex web of sensations. But no, she was certain that she knew that smell: leather, orange, honey. It was not until she was walking towards Oxford Street that the smell faded, replaced with the fumes and dirt of London.

CHAPTER 15

'Come for a drink with me and Patrick after this,' Diana said as they arrived. They had been invited to the opening of a new shop on the King's Road, not far from Diana's flat, and they walked there together after Diana finished work. The two of them had drunk too much coffee and redone their make-up in front of Diana's bedroom mirror, just like the old days, but Evelyn could not relax the way she used to. Even the radio, the sounds of the popular new single 'Please Please Me', was doing nothing to settle her.

It was a Friday evening and Diana, finishing a long week at school, was ready for a night out. Evelyn said she'd see how she felt. Henry would be home tonight, and she wanted to spend the evening with him. The thought of watching Diana with her new boyfriend, that great passion she had described at lunch last weekend: it was too much.

The party was at one of the new stores springing up through Chelsea, each of them following the success of Mary Quant's Bazaar, with her constantly changing designs,

The Model Patient

vibrant colours, slim-fitting styles, and a shopping experience so different from the traditional shops of their mothers' generation. Evelyn had been invited to the opening by the designer, and it had given her a feeling of great satisfaction to receive the invitation. The card had arrived through her letterbox last week, a modern design patterned with bold circles of colour, and it made Evelyn feel relevant again. She had been remembered. They wanted her there.

Evelyn had never worried about being able to afford the newest fashions. A few years ago, designers and shop owners were happy to give her discounts, as long as she made sure to be seen wearing their outfits. It was disappointing, now that she was no longer working, not to get the same treatment. A married woman going to married woman dinner parties did not have the same allure as a model smoking in a café before an evening out. Evelyn rarely smoked now, just the occasional cigarette at parties, her hands feeling empty and uncertain without the routine of lighting up and contributing to the thickening air. Ruth had commented on her smoking once, just after they were married, when Evelyn pulled a pack of cigarettes out of her handbag at the dinner table. They were at a restaurant in Mayfair and Evelyn already stood out, her choice of dress too modern and too short for a restaurant where the waiters refolded the napkins whenever one went to the bathroom. Henry had glared anxiously at her across the table when Dr Westbrook politely lit her cigarette for her. Ruth, on the other hand, was far more direct. 'Not in here, dear,' she said. 'Smoking at your age looks gauche.'

The room was small and crowded, loud music competing against the shouted conversations of the guests. It was the same music they'd listened to while getting ready: Frank Ifield, The Beatles, Helen Shapiro. Everyone wanted to see The Beatles live: any music journal or teenage fashion magazine Evelyn happened to open seemed to have a feature on this brand new foursome.

Evelyn and Diana slipped through the space, finding the bar with its rows of white wine and bottled beers, before settling into a corner where they could talk. Mannequins were positioned about the space, the shop's signature raincoat on display. Bold and glossy, the coats were styled with big collars and hoods, large shining buttons down the front. Slim-fitting boots in matching colours were placed next to each coat, splashes of bright colours, red, yellow, blue, as well as a row of black-and-white coats in a monochrome pattern. It reminded Evelyn of the op-art and colour-field paintings she was seeing more and more in the small London art galleries, these clean canvases with their simple and confident strokes of paint. She was envious of these artists and their ability to throw colour onto a white canvas, or their mathematical precision in crafting squares and shapes into optical illusions. There was a painting at Gallery One that she had returned to twice after the opening exhibition. It was called 'Movement in Squares', by Bridget Riley, and when Evelyn stood before the painting, it was as though the rules of art, science and vision were breaking down around her. Every anxiety she had ever felt seemed to be overspilling into an endless nightmare. And yet as she continued staring at the painting, she felt herself drawn in and trapped inside, finding pleasure in the illusion. She had asked Henry what he thought of the painting, and he said he liked it: the symmetrical black and white squares were comforting in their repetitively precise movement. It was strange to her how differently they could interpret those shapes.

Evelyn's paintings when she was a teenager had none of this regularity, and even now with her jewellery designs, she found it impossible to match the clean, bold styles of pop art, or the self-assured minimalism of so many new artists, or the conceptual, hard-edge and colour-filled American painters such as Kenneth Noland and Sam Gilliam. Her designs were impressionistic, surreal, the tiniest detail emerging, uncontrolled, and taking on a meaning of its own. A few nights ago she had sketched a design for a bracelet, a complex plaited chain with a clasp made in the shape of lilac petals. That line had come to her again, from the poem she had studied at school: *The Waste Land*. She remembered a few more words this time: *breeding lilacs out of the dead land, mixing memory and desire*. That was Dr Daley's method, perhaps, mixing memories with her current desires, turning the past and the present into a strange chaos of emotions. She did not know what was more painful: discussing the traumas of her past or exposing her secret desires to the subject of her obsession.

'Would you wear any of this?' Diana asked, bringing her back to the present. Evelyn tried to laugh. She could not imagine either herself or Diana in one of these garish raincoats, but there was a time in her past when she would have worn anything, no matter how bizarre, to attract the attention of a fashion designer.

'Probably not,' she replied, pulling a cigarette out of the packet she kept in her handbag. Diana raised an eyebrow but held out her hand for one all the same. She, too, was not a regular smoker, but she knew that Evelyn felt the pull of those cigarettes when she was feeling anxious. It was not a trait that they shared: Diana was rarely anxious. She smoked when she couldn't think of a good enough reason to say no.

'What's wrong?' Diana said after the two of them had managed the awkward exchange of their drinks, a lighter, two cigarettes.

'Nothing's wrong,' Evelyn said. But she knew it wasn't a convincing lie. They had known each other for too long to hide anything from one another. She could sense Diana looking at her, but so differently from the way Dr Daley looked at her with his inscrutable gaze. When she turned to her friend, she saw concern, love, and genuine curiosity. It made her feel safe, and for a moment she longed to tell her everything. But she hadn't even told Diana she was seeing a psychologist. She had thought about it many times, but there was something stopping her. There was a shame, she realized, in admitting to finding life hard, especially when she seemed to have it all: a husband, a beautiful home, her youth and beauty still intact. And now, this obsession with her doctor. It was impossible to explain in a way that would make her friend understand. She didn't even understand it herself.

The Model Patient

She knew she needed to say something. Taking a deep drag on her cigarette, she tried to compose herself, filtering out the secrets from the truths she was willing to admit.

'I suppose it's Henry. And his parents. I want it to be like it was when we were first married. But now I have to act like the model wife, making these Sunday lunches and smiling at his father's jokes. It is always such a relief when they leave and I can turn on the radio. Alan Freeman's *Pick of the Pops* is the only way to save the weekend.'

Diana nodded, allowing Evelyn this brief attempt to lighten the mood with her talk of music and the radio. She flicked ash from her cigarette onto the floor. A spark landed on one of the raincoats, and the two women stared at it, mesmerized, before it fizzled and went out.

'And now he wants to have a baby. In fact it seems everyone wants me to have a baby. Apart from me. I'm sure I'll want to one day, but not right now. I'd be a terrible mother right now.'

'Can you talk to Henry about your feelings? Wouldn't he understand that you'd prefer to wait?'

'I've tried. And he says that's fine, but then he acts like he's so disappointed, punishing me for it all the time.'

'He needs to stop listening to his mother. That's his problem. I'm sure that if it wasn't for her, then he'd be happy to wait.'

'Yes, maybe.'

'Do you remember when he left his mother's dinner party to bring us groceries?'

Evelyn smiled, remembering the night she was talking about. It was a few months into her relationship with Henry, and Diana was sick with the flu. Evelyn was supposed to be at dinner with Henry's parents, but she'd called to say she couldn't come. Diana was unwell and she didn't want to leave her. A few hours later, Henry appeared on their doorstep, a paper bag full of fruit and biscuits in his arms. While Evelyn thanked him, Diana watched from the kitchen window. This was the first time a man had showed such uncomplicated devotion to her friend. He kissed her and walked away. Henry made no attempt to make her change her mind and go with him to the dinner party.

Since then, Diana's faith in Henry had never wavered.

'Yes, I remember. But recently it feels as though I can't compete with Ruth. Not without a baby anyway.'

The noise was building in the shop, the two women gradually retreating into a tighter corner as the space filled.

'Come on, let's get out of here,' Diana said, and they held each other by the hand as they wound their way between the guests and the mannequins and the rails of clothes, until they made it outside. February was over, but the cold was determined to haunt them. There had been a brief respite, ice replaced with a near-freezing drizzle, but it was back again now and Evelyn was shivering in a coat too thin for the weather.

'You know, Evie, there is no way you'd be a terrible mother.' Diana wrapped her arm around Evelyn, pulling her in towards her. 'I don't know why you'd say that. Fair

The Model Patient

enough that you don't want to have children right away. But the reason mustn't be that you think you'd be a terrible mother. You are kind, generous; you have this huge capacity for love that is so rare to find. And you're the best friend to me I could possibly imagine. You listen to me. You come to visit me more than anyone else, taking my mind off my giant piles of school marking. I wouldn't have survived being a teenager without you.'

'I wasn't always kind to you.'

Diana looked up at her. 'We were teenagers. Neither of us were perfect. For every unkind comment either of us said to the other, think of how many more wonderful, funny and silly things we shared to make up for it. Don't beat yourself up about the few mistakes, when it's the good times that I remember most.'

Evelyn could feel the tears building. These words from Diana had come exactly when she needed them most, reminding her that she was loved. She pulled her friend into a hug, a tight, solid embrace that felt entirely real. This, here, was not an illusion, nor was it a fantasy.

When they separated, they took each other's hands and started walking along the King's Road. For a few minutes, Evelyn allowed herself to be happy.

'Want to join me and Patrick for a bit? We're going to meet for a drink at the pub on the corner of Chelsea Common before I try to cook something for him back at Number Six. Though I'm hoping he will be the one doing the cooking while I mix us drinks.'

'That's kind of you to invite me. And I do want to meet Patrick one day very soon. But I think I should go home. I haven't seen Henry much this week, and we're going to Henley tomorrow to visit Mark and June. And their babies.'

'Of course. Get home safe, okay.'

'I'll get a taxi. I'm underdressed for this weather.'

Diana kissed her before continuing along the street towards the tiny triangle that was Chelsea Common. Tightening her coat, Evelyn stood on the edge of the street, watching as the world moved before her. Cars, buses, scooters, pedestrians crossing the road, they all moved with purpose, stopping and starting in tandem as they reached the junctions. Each individual was reliant on the others, like a band playing together on a stage. It made her think of her appointments with Dr Daley, the two of them reacting to one another, though more like a discordant experiment than a seamless musical performance. The appointments, though, they weren't real life. She lifted out her hand, signalling for a taxi. Tonight, she wanted to get back into the real world, place illusion and fantasy to the edge of her consciousness.

Her resolve only lasted for an instant. As the taxi began to pull away, she stared out of the window, determined to think of Henry and the evening they were going to have together. But right there in front of her, beneath the bright light of a streetlamp, a man was walking along the pavement. The familiarity of him caught her in the throat.

Dr Daley.

It was a shock to see him outside of his clinic. All of a

sudden she felt like a child about to be discovered somewhere they were not supposed to be. With her heart beating fast, she blinked, trying to establish whether it was really him, not some figment of her feverish imagination.

He walked fast, his head down and his long hair falling forward around his eyes. Evelyn pressed herself back against the seat of the taxi, but then she turned, wrenching her body around and keeping her eyes on him for as long as she could, taking in everything: the earthy tones of his suede jacket, his brown turtleneck rising out of the top, his black ankle boots.

It was definitely him. She watched as he made a right turn along Markham Street. Dr Daley, about to walk past her old flat, the place of so many memories.

As the taxi continued its journey home, she could feel her mind moving too fast, painful images emerging. It was strange to see him out in the real world. She wanted to know everything: where he was going, who he was meeting, what drink he would order from the bar.

She closed her eyes, but quickly opened them again. The sight she had conjured was too difficult, a nightmare that made her chest hurt. A beautiful woman, a candle-lit restaurant, Dr Daley standing behind her as they entered, his hand at her waist. Evelyn hated her, this imaginary woman she had dressed in seductive black silk in her mind.

Evelyn shuddered and rolled down the taxi window. The thought, it made her want to be sick. She longed to get home, to feel Henry's arms around her, to kiss him: for all to go back to normal.

Lucy Ashe

When the taxi pulled up outside her house, it was a relief to see the lights on and Henry's silhouette moving in the kitchen. But it was her mother-in-law's voice that greeted her when she stepped inside the threshold. She stopped, her fingers still gripped around the doorknob.

'Evelyn, dear, don't let in the cold.'

Slowly, Evelyn walked inside and pulled off her coat. The evening she had hoped for would have to wait.

CHAPTER 16

'I am finding it hard to know what to say to you,' Evelyn said. 'I don't want to get this wrong.'

Her natural response when faced with any task was to try to make it a success. Always it had been like this, ever since she was a child and the way to draw her parents' interest was to be the perfect daughter, never causing trouble, instead giving them updates on her achievements, the art competitions she was entering, leading roles in the school plays, and then contracts at fashion brands that even a country schoolmaster would recognize. It wasn't easy, competing with an entire school of boys, every one of whom her father knew by name, and her mother performing the part of the perfect headmaster's wife, mother to all.

Now, with psychotherapy, she wanted to be the model patient. She wanted Dr Daley to look forward to her appointments, for him to be fascinated by everything she said, and for him to feel that the progress she might be making was thanks to him and his talent as a psychotherapist. When she let herself stop to think about it, she found it frustrating that she could so desperately want to make him feel that he was appreciated and admired. From his side, he seemed determined to provoke her into feeling awful about herself. The relationship, if it could even be called a relationship, was unnervingly one-sided. While she poured out her heart, exposing her deepest vulnerabilities, he watched her in silence, occasionally, sadistically, reminding her that what she wanted most was for him to like her.

'What don't you want to get wrong?' he asked.

'I don't know. All of it. I want to be good at this, at psychodynamic therapy.'

He smiled, and it made her feel like a child who had just said something adorable but stupid to a benevolent adult. He was dressed in three layers of knitwear today, a mustard polo neck sweater with a scarlet wool waistcoat and a dark green chunky knit cardigan over the top. It was another freezing day, but Dr Daley looked warm and comfortable. Evelyn wanted him to enclose her in his arms, to feel his strength beneath all those layers of wool.

'There is no right or wrong here. All I am asking you to do is say exactly what you are thinking, as those thoughts come into your head.'

'That's not as easy as you make it out to be, Dr Daley. My thoughts are not always possible to share.'

'In this room, with me, everything can be shared without risk of judgement. What are you worried will happen if you tell me what is on your mind?'

The Model Patient

'I am worried you'll feel that I am breaking the boundaries of the treatment.'

'There are no boundaries, Mrs Westbrook. I think the only boundaries here are the ones you create in your own mind.'

'No. That's not true. Well, yes, I do build boundaries around what I can and can't say. But there are also very real boundaries.'

'Such as?'

'There is the boundary of the fifty minutes. When the appointment ends, I have to leave and you move on to your next patient. And there is the boundary of the treatment, a talking cure. I can say anything, but I can't do anything. I can't, for example, walk over to you and ask you to kiss me.'

'You really can ask me anything. If that is what comes into your mind, that is what you should say.'

Evelyn sighed, shaking her head. 'So if I did ask you to kiss me, what would you say.'

Dr Daley was silent, but Evelyn waited. It looked, this time, as though he really was thinking, myriad possible answers moving through his mind.

'I don't think it is helpful to discuss hypothetical scenarios. None of us knows exactly how we would respond to something in the future.'

Evelyn wanted to reframe the question, to ask him right then and there to kiss her. She wanted to find the confidence to say exactly what she was thinking. But she couldn't do it. The possibility of rejection would be too terrible a humiliation. And the chance of him saying yes, taking her in his arms and kissing her, had a terror of its own.

'Perhaps it would be helpful for us to explore in more detail the feelings you are having about me, the feelings that have made you anxious about the boundaries surrounding our time together.'

'I can try,' she said, playing with the cuff of her sleeve. It was a new shirt, white and silk, and she wore it beneath a black pinafore dress. Putting on a new outfit had made her feel stronger when she dressed this morning, an armour of confidence. That had all evaporated now and she felt trapped. She forced herself to hold her hands still. 'I am afraid,' she said.

'What are you afraid of?'

'I'm afraid you'll reject me.'

'What would that mean, for me to reject you?'

'I suppose it would mean you telling me that it isn't appropriate for me to be having these thoughts about you. Or you'd say you could no longer be my doctor, that you'd need to refer me to someone else.'

'I am not going to say any of those things, no matter what it is that you tell me. If it is of any help to you, I can promise you that there is nothing you say that I will think of as inappropriate.'

'Okay,' Evelyn replied, nodding slowly. She was getting closer, the words she wanted to say travelling forward.

'I have a strong imaginary life.'

'Yes,' he said. 'Tell me more about that.'

The Model Patient

'In my imagination, I have been having these thoughts about you.'

'Can you describe them to me?'

'It's difficult.'

'Because you find it embarrassing, or because you think I'll be shocked by them?'

'Both, I think.'

'And this is because they are sexual thoughts?'

Evelyn blinked slowly, embarrassment flooding through her. Fixing her gaze on a mottled mark in the wooden floorboards, she continued.

'Yes, sexual fantasies, I suppose. It's silly, but after you wore a particular jacket, the black one with the paisley pattern, I said to myself that if you wore that jacket again, I would tell you how I felt. And I did manage to do that, at least partially, last session.'

'That must have felt quite strange to you, uncanny even, that I offered the jacket to you to keep you warm.'

'It was unsettling.' She wanted to tell him what it was like to feel the weight of the jacket against her, the thrill that had spread through her body, but it was too humiliating to say the words.

'And now you are unsure whether you should tell me about these sexual fantasies you have been having?'

'Yes, I don't see what the purpose would be. And it would be so difficult to say out loud.'

'Well, I can tell you that you are likely to feel much better if you tell me your fantasy.'

'I want to try.'

She did want to tell him. If this was the way to be a model patient, his best patient, then she knew she could do it. Even though she had no idea how this was supposed to make her feel better, she was willing to try.

Silence hung between them. Dr Daley waited and Evelyn tossed the images she wanted to say around her head, desperately trying to find a way to speak.

'Part of the pleasure of the fantasy is that you know exactly what to do. I don't need to say anything to you for it to happen.'

'That's interesting, isn't it. Perhaps you worry that if you have to say the words out loud, rather than me instinctively knowing what you are thinking, it will take away the attractiveness of your daydream.'

'You should know that I do actually want these fantasies to go away, to get them out of my head. What is the point of allowing myself to indulge in delusions that can never come true? And I am not sure I would describe it as an attractive daydream.' She pressed her hands into the sofa, tucked them beneath her legs, and started speaking again. 'My most reoccurring fantasy about you is violent. There is pain, followed by pleasure.'

'And how does that manifest itself?'

He was pushing her, as always, into the details of her thoughts.

'I imagine that you . . .' She stopped. It was impossible, and she had said enough already.

The Model Patient

Dr Daley leant back in his chair and folded his arms. It was a closing off, a coldness descending and a distance growing between them. She had disappointed him.

In a panic, Evelyn started speaking. She needed to be better than this; she needed to do what he asked, putting aside her narrow-minded sensibilities and instead embracing the freedom to think and speak that he was offering her.

'I imagine that you tell me to take off my clothes, that you bind my wrists together, that you hit me with a belt. You punish me.'

'Is it my belt?'

'Yes, it's your belt.'

He nodded, his face impassive. 'And then?'

'And then we have sex.'

'Can you tell me more about that?'

'No.' Evelyn said. She could not tell him any more. Already it was too much, and her heart was pounding. There was a pain in her chest and her head felt light. 'It is too difficult to tell you more.'

'What's the difficulty?'

'How can I sit here and tell you where I want you to kiss me, to touch me? It is too painful and too erotic. It makes me feel insane.'

'Are you worried that it will be too much for me, that I will find it difficult to hear?'

'No. It's too much for me.'

'How does it make you feel to tell me your sexual fantasies about me?'

'You said it would make me feel better. But it hasn't made me feel better at all. My heart is racing. I feel uncomfortable, as though there is something moving beneath my skin. I know that I will not find calm again until . . .'

She stopped, unable to expose herself further.

'Until what?' he prompted.

'Fine,' she said, worn down by the questions and the prompts and the pressure to be the good patient who reveals all. 'Until I have sex with Henry.'

He nodded. 'And that will make you feel better. Why do you think that is?'

She shook her head. It was enough.

When he started speaking, for once filling the gaps of their silences by offering his analysis, Evelyn felt herself straining to take in every word.

'I think you'll feel better because you will be acting out your fantasy, physically. You've told me what you want with me, and now the only way to feel better again is to make the fantasy come true.'

'But it won't be the same.'

'No. It won't be the same.'

'And I'll feel guilty.'

'Why will you feel guilty?'

'Because I will be thinking of this fantasy.'

'You mean you'll be thinking about me while you have sex with Henry?'

'Maybe. I don't know. I can't talk about that.'

'There is nothing to be ashamed of. You seem to think

that it is wrong to have sexual thoughts about anyone other than your husband.'

'Of course. I don't think it's useful to encourage transgressive thoughts.'

'I think we could say that the dreams and fantasies you have are of particular use to the two of us, together, in helping us explore your current troubles.'

'It would be easier for me if it wasn't so one-sided. It makes me feel crazy.'

'You want us to have an affair,' he said, a matter-of-fact clarity to his words. 'You would like it to be midnight in a bar somewhere, the two of us sharing how we feel about each other.'

'That would be preferable to this, yes.'

The silence that fell was a respite, giving her the space to pull together the fireworks of her thoughts. She knew the appointment was nearly over, but she wanted to stay. She wanted the room to shift into that midnight bar that Dr Daley had made her imagine. He was looking at her, his eyes too penetrating. She had to turn away.

'Well, I see that we need to stop in a few minutes, but I think it might be useful to discuss whether you would like to start coming in to see me more frequently, twice a week I suggest.'

Evelyn froze. Out of everything he could have possibly said, she did not imagine it would be this. Her mind moved fast, trying to work out what to say. If she said yes immediately, without any reflection, she'd come across as too eager, her desire for him overspilling into obsession. But he already knew how she felt. This, now, an invitation for more, that maybe he was not repulsed by all the things she had said, this was real: no delusion, no fantasy, no transference of the dramas of her real life into the framework of therapy. By asking her to see him twice a week, the relationship had taken on a new angle, real and solid.

'Yes, I'd like that.' It was all she could manage.

'Okay. Good. Angela, Miss Simmons I mean, will arrange it for us, if you speak to her on your way out today.'

Evelyn did not move. There was so much she wanted to ask him, why he had suggested this change, what it meant, why he had chosen now, right after she had revealed the details of her fantasy.

'It seems there is something you want to ask me,' he said.

'I am interested in how often you see your other patients.'

'It really is idiosyncratic. Each patient is different.'

Evelyn looked away, frustrated by his answer. It was a surprise to her when he continued speaking.

'However, I can tell you that currently I am seeing all my patients once a week.'

'So why are you suggesting twice a week for me?'

'I believe it would be helpful for us in exploring the challenges you are having.'

He stood. 'We can return to this question next appointment, if you would like.'

Evelyn rose from the sofa, her hands shaking as she collected her coat from next to her. As usual, she smiled as she passed by him, looking down at the floor as she muttered a brief thank you.

She set up the second weekly appointment with the receptionist on her way out. It was the first time she had really looked at Miss Simmons, certainly the first time she had spoken more than a few words to her in person. Angela, Dr Daley had called her. It had made her feel strange to hear him use his receptionist's first name. There was an informality to it that startled her.

'Dr Daley can see you on Mondays at eleven and Thursdays at three. Does that work for you, Mrs Westbrook?' The receptionist had perfectly polished nails, a bright red that matched her lipstick. Evelyn nodded, watching as Miss Simmons made a note in a large leather diary.

Miss Simmons was barely out of secretarial college, Evelyn thought, as she took in everything, her auburn hair that curled neatly around her shoulders, the smooth shine of her skin, the clean press of her blouse tucked into a tightly fitting skirt. She was a little plump, and it suited her, the lines of her body curved and soft. The perfect life model, Evelyn thought, remembering those art classes she took in Chelsea in her early twenties, a rotation of men and women with their vastly different bodies, so many shapes and sizes, all glorious in their own vivid way. Evelyn had posed for the class once. It had been thrilling to slip off the dressing gown and hold her naked body as still as a statue in front of twenty artists, their gaze rising and falling from the top of her head to the white paper of their sketchbooks.

Lucy Ashe

Evelyn did not feel the cold as she walked home. She felt alive, her body aching with a different, dangerous energy.

Perhaps she was special to him. Perhaps it didn't need to be this painful, unequal dance. Maybe, soon, it was all going to change.

CHAPTER 17

Evelyn walked over to Number Six as soon as she thought the school day would be over. She was desperate to confide in someone, to unpick the confusion of her thoughts. It was disappointing when Diana didn't answer the door, but then she remembered that Diana ran a teacher training course on Monday evenings at University College. She wouldn't be home until late.

It was starting to rain in hard, freezing sheets and Evelyn was exhausted. The thought of going straight home again was too much. She dug through her bag, relieved to see that her key to Number Six was still tucked into a pocket inside. Letting herself in, she walked up the stairs and went straight to the kitchen. There was an open bottle of that familiar six shilling red wine on the table, two dirty glasses stained with its residue. Diana and Patrick, most likely, the two of them failing to tidy up after a Sunday night together. The crumbs of a loaf of bread littered the table, a serrated knife resting on the wooden board. After pouring some of the leftover wine into a clean glass, Evelyn opened the pantry. Diana's favourite Wensleydale cheese, half-eaten and rewrapped in its paper, was on the middle shelf.

It was strange to see the wine, the bread, the cheese: these were her and Diana's tradition for a Sunday night, and it felt like a betrayal. She shuddered, surprised at the strength of her anger, how upsetting it was that her friend would share this with a man. The cheese was different though, still Wensleydale, but from an unfamiliar grocery store, not Diana's usual.

The wine glass in her hand, she walked through the flat, trying to find comfort in the familiar. Diana's bedroom was tidier than usual; the bed was unmade but the rest of the space looked neat and ordered. Perhaps she had cleaned for Patrick, Evelyn thought to herself, trying to suppress the resentment that was creeping into her mind. She should be happy for Diana. It was disturbing to acknowledge how unreasonable she was being. Whether it stemmed from wanting to keep Diana for herself, or her jealousy of her friend's new, exciting romance, she wasn't certain.

This, a tidy room, was a sign that things were serious. Diana had never bothered to tidy the flat for most of the men she used to bring back here. Evelyn pushed open the door to her old bedroom, now Diana's study, and walked inside. Switching on a tall floor lamp, she looked around her, trying to piece together her thoughts. It looked so different from when it had been hers: the bed was gone and replaced with two armchairs, a desk, bookshelves. The desk was against the window, cluttered with books, literary magazines, a typewriter hidden under a mound of unmarked essays.

On the floor next to the desk was a pile of pages, loose but neatly stacked. The top page had the words 'A Novel, untitled' typed across the middle. Evelyn felt herself tense. She was desperate to read Diana's work, especially this mysterious novel that Diana refused to discuss. Kneeling down next to the pile of paper, she touched the top sheet lightly, afraid of leaving a mark. It was difficult, her curiosity fighting against her more sensible acknowledgement that to read these pages now would be a betrayal. Diana would ask Evelyn to read her work when she was ready.

And yet the temptation was so great, those pages right there in front of her.

Evelyn stood and moved to one of the armchairs, her wine glass gripped hard in her hand. Just one or two pages, that was all. Diana would never know.

She would wait, finish her wine, think about it a little longer. The novel and its mysterious existence stimulated her imagination. There was a part of her that wondered whether the novel was about the two of them, Diana and Evelyn, the great friendship, two women taking on the world. But there was an awkward embarrassment to this thought too, how self-absorbed it was to assume the book might be about her.

Diana had never given her the slightest hint what the book was about. All she knew was that it was, apparently, too obscure and weird to be taken on by a major publisher, and that the writing allowed Diana to combine her favourite styles of realism, horror and poetry. Standing, she walked to the desk, lifting up some of the books and magazines that were surrounding the typewriter. These, she hoped, might give her a clue, a small suggestion of the themes and concerns of the novel.

There was a collection of poetry by Anne Sexton entitled *To Bedlam and Part Way Back*. Scraps of paper marked a few pages and Evelyn opened to the first one. It was a poem called 'Her Kind' and Evelyn read it quickly, her mind too restless to find meaning in the image, a possessed witch haunting the black night. Underneath was a collection of poetry by John Keats, the page opened to 'Ode to a Nightingale.' Evelyn remembered the poem well: they had studied it at school with Mr Martin, and Evelyn had been hypnotized by the language. She'd translated her reaction to the poem into an art lesson the next day, though it was only Mr Martin who seemed to understand the link between the poem's haunting words and the explosion of paint on Evelyn's page: a deep purple globe hovering above a black mess. When Evelyn thought back to that painting now, she realized it must have been inspired by the Abstract Expressionism of the artists she loved, Jackson Pollock and his drip-paintings, Arshile Gorky and the surreal colours and shapes she had seen photographed in a magazine when she was a teenager, a painting called 'One Year the Milkweed'. The article had fascinated her at the time, how it described their painting as an unconscious act, an 'écriture automatique' that revealed the self without premeditation.

The Model Patient

She traced her finger along the words of the poem now, noting where Diana had scratched her pencil in thick strokes beneath the lines. As she was placing the book back in place, she noticed a cut-out photograph of a painting by Henri Rousseau stuck between the pages further towards the back of the collection. Evelyn picked it out, holding it lightly. The paper was thin and delicate and she did not want it to crease. 'Le Rêve', it was called: a naked woman reclined on a couch, immersed in her dream world of a jungle, green and vibrant, wild animals surrounding her. She was reaching out to a lion, lotus flowers opened towards the sky, a bright moon, the orange sinews of a snake.

Evelyn placed the image back where she found it, gingerly lifting the items on the desk and taking care not to disturb the order of a stack of school essays.

A book caught her eye, newer than the others, the cover clean and smooth. There was a picture of a man on the cover and the pages smelt fresh. The book was by the psychoanalyst Carl Jung, entitled *Memories, Dreams, Reflections*, and at a quick glance at the inside pages, she could see it had been published recently. Diana always knew how to get books early, sweet-talking her favourite booksellers into passing her copies before the official publication date. But she was surprised that Diana was reading an autobiography of Carl Jung.

Evelyn felt a shiver run down her spine. It was strange, uncanny even, that Diana's writing and Evelyn's psychoanalytical therapy seemed to be colliding, the two of them wading through the same ideas from very different angles.

For Diana, it was academic and thoughtful: books, articles, paintings, psychoanalysis approached from a safe, unemotional distance. For Evelyn, it was a painful battle that dug beneath her skin, splitting her open and devouring her whole.

Evelyn knew a little about Carl Jung and his ideas, how he had started as a disciple of Sigmund Freud but broke away with new theories of his own about which Freud did not approve. Jackson Pollock was a Jungian, she knew, and it was through her love of his art that she had learnt about Jung's analysis of dreams, the collective unconscious, the metaphors and symbols of the human condition. It wasn't until 1958, when she visited an exhibition of Pollock's drip-paintings in Whitechapel Gallery, that she had seen his work in the flesh, as it were. For that was how it felt, a confrontation, a physical experience that cut to the body itself, beyond intellect or emotion. It was a shock, Evelyn remembered, the transformation from seeing photographs of Pollock's paintings in magazines and press cuttings, to standing before a vast canvas, letting her vision sink into paint that had been dripped, hurled and poured. The conflicting opposites of light and dark, reason and madness, the layers of above and beneath, were impossible to decipher, so she had stopped trying. It had been both painful and liberating, she recollected, giving into the confrontation of the art without trying to force a union of the disparate parts.

Despite her fascination, she had never tried to find out more, never attempted to intellectualize the theories behind Pollock's art, or to read Carl Jung's work. All she knew was that Pollock had been through his own psychotherapy with a Jungian doctor in the 1930s; she'd read about it in an article after his death in 1956.

To think of this now was exciting. It made her own painful psychotherapy seem legitimate and worthy, transcending the shame and self-disgust into which her sexual fantasies had buried her.

Flicking through the book, she returned to the inside cover. Diana, ever since she was a child, had written her name in pencil in the top corner of the first page. Evelyn had asked her why she always labelled her books. Diana Ashley: a declaration that this was hers to consume and claim. Diana had shrugged and said she liked the idea of collecting books. One day she wanted to have a library of her own.

Evelyn moved closer to the light. The name written in pencil at the top of the page was eluding her, the handwriting irregular and thin, not the same as Diana's usual curvaceous letters.

Her hands froze, the bottom edge of the book's cover digging between her fingers. Diana's name was not written in the corner. It was a different name, one that made her chest tighten in a painful spasm. Patrick Daley.

She closed the book, pressing it tight between her hands. If she opened the book very slowly and looked again, surely the name would have changed back to normality, to Diana Ashley.

Her heart beating fast, she opened the book. The words were still the same. Patrick Daley.

Not her Dr Daley, she told herself, trying to find calm. She felt as though she was drowning, a deep weight of water sinking her down. All that she had felt after today's appointment, it was bubbling into a frenzy that she could not control.

She tried to think. It wasn't the same man; how could it be? There must be many Patrick Daleys. And she didn't even know the first name of her doctor: it might not be Patrick. Of course she had searched on the door of the clinic to find his full name, something to make him more human, more real. But all it said was Dr Daley. Not even an initial.

But how many Patrick Daleys would own this specific book? Only someone with an interest in psychoanalysis would have this, especially so soon after publication. And yet Carl Jung was famous, she reasoned; there would be others keen to read his autobiography. It might not be him.

But if it was her Dr Daley, then what did that mean? Diana said she had met Patrick not long ago, but Evelyn didn't know if it was before or after her appointments with Dr Daley had begun. She regularly talked about Diana in her sessions: surely Dr Daley would know if her Diana was also his Diana. He wouldn't pursue a relationship if he realized. There were too many complications: either he'd have to terminate his treatment with Evelyn, or end his relationship with Diana. And hadn't he just increased the number of her appointments? There was no sign he was planning on breaking off the treatment.

If it was a coincidence, then the universe was conspiring against her. It was cruel, Dr Daley and Diana finding each

The Model Patient

other, a legitimate, real relationship. They were free to love and be loved, whereas she was trapped in an impossible tangle. Intellectually, when she slowed down and considered the situation, she knew her feelings for Dr Daley were a fantasy. She had transformed him into a man who did not exist, the projection of her desires and delusions. And yet the reality of how she felt was entirely different. Her feelings were true, painful, torturous. He was both real and not real, a man and a ghost, a physical being she wanted to embrace and an elusive figment of her feverish imagination.

There was another possibility. Evelyn let her thoughts rush forwards, a new fantasy forming in all its irrational pleasure. Maybe he had deliberately sought out Diana in order to get closer to her. He knew, just like she did, that a relationship was impossible. But hadn't he shown her that he might want her the way she wanted him? There was the increased number of appointments, two each week unlike the rest of his patients whom he only saw once. There was the way he led her towards her sexual fantasies, encouraging her again and again to tell him what she wanted. How he reminded her that she wanted him to make her feel special; how he persisted in keeping her in that place of yearning, refusing to help her get over him. Why else would he ask her to articulate her longing, the details of how she wanted him to touch her? Either he was cruel, or he felt as she did, but was unable to break the boundaries of the therapeutic frame.

But then what about Diana? If Dr Daley was using her, then it was essential Evelyn fixed this now. She needed to force him to reveal himself before Diana became too attached. For Diana hadn't known Dr Daley, if it even was the same man, for longer than a month or so. She'd move on, as she always did.

Evelyn washed her wine glass and replaced it in the cupboard. It would be easier if she didn't need to explain to Diana that she had been here. Leaving everything as she found it, she ran down the stairs. Signalling for a taxi, Evelyn shivered in the freezing rain as she reached her hand towards the slowly moving traffic.

It was up to Evelyn to sort out this mess. But she'd need to wait until her next appointment to start to untangle the threads. Evelyn and Dr Daley; Diana and Patrick. Only one relationship could survive.

CHAPTER 18

Thursday morning arrived quickly. Evelyn was grateful for this additional appointment, how it alleviated the painful waiting a whole seven days to see Dr Daley. She woke early, a dream still vivid in her mind, and went into her dressing room to record it before the memory vanished. It was freezing out of bed, and her handwriting was untidy as she tried to loosen the tension in her hand. After writing it down in her notebook, she read it back to herself. She couldn't make any sense of the narrative. No serpent this time; instead a confusion of images: a large house, a wardrobe, a demon, a woman. It would be something to speak to Dr Daley about this afternoon.

Switching off the lamp, Evelyn wrapped her arms around her knees, trying to find calm in the darkness of her little dressing room. But it was impossible, not when her skin was stinging with energy. She shivered and returned to bed, wrapping her arm around her sleeping husband. He made no movement, no suggestion at all that he had noticed her leave and then return. Waking him, she gently ran her hands across his chest. He blinked himself awake, a bemused expression in his eyes. Henry pulled her under him and she felt her body sink into the mattress. She closed her eyes and disappeared into her fantasy.

Evelyn spent a long time getting ready, washing her hair, styling it into a ponytail, applying make-up with the precision of her modelling days. She chose a pale lipstick, subtle and fresh. When she looked at herself in the mirror, she decided her outfit looked like the sort of clothes Diana wore, slim-fitting black cropped trousers and an oversized sweater. It was a good look, casual but elegant, an effortless beauty that had, of course, taken close to an hour to achieve.

She took a taxi up to Marylebone, giving herself plenty of time in case the traffic was bad. While there had been no more snowfall this week, there were still great mounds of it, hard and blackened at the edges of the roads, patches of ice buried and dangerous. Everyone was waiting for spring to arrive, for life to reveal itself from beneath the ice and snow and mud, a hidden world finally making its way to the surface.

In the taxi, she was nervous. It was difficult when there was so much she wanted to say to Dr Daley, and yet she had no idea if she'd conjure the confidence to find the words. Are you Patrick Daley, she practised saying, the man who has caught the heart of my beautiful best friend? Are you trying to hurt me? Is this your way of driving me insane? But the silence that she knew would follow, the blank expression she imagined in his eyes, or, even worse, a bemused astonishment that his patient had fallen to such depths of delusion – it would take more than a few whispered rehearsals for her to ask him the questions that might tear her psychotherapy apart.

Most of all, despite her doubts about Diana and her Patrick, she did not want to disappoint him. If she was silent and dull, refusing to tell him the details of her thoughts, he might tire of her. He might regret giving her this increased attention. Since he'd suggested doubling their appointments, her mind was moving at a manic pace. Part of her was angry with him, how he must realize that he had sent her into a frenzy of confusion. But another part of her tried to be reasonable, how perhaps he was oblivious to the way she interpreted him, that maybe he simply thought two appointments a week would help her make faster progress.

Opening and closing her bag, she eventually settled on taking out her powder compact, checking the black pencil around her eyes was cleanly set, that her lipstick wasn't too strong, her skin smooth and clear. The journey was slow, but she arrived in good time, a little too early. She didn't want to come across as needy and emotional. Though perhaps that was a lost cause. He already knew how she felt.

Miss Simmons let her in and for the first time, she was not alone in the waiting area. The building was busy, a murmur of voices coming from the consulting rooms, the sound of footsteps around her. She took a magazine from the rack, flicking through the pages without seeing them. It was more interesting to glance across at the other patients seated on the wooden benches, to try to decipher why they were here, what was wrong with them, whether they, too, felt the same wild beating of their heart.

There was a man and a woman, both older than her, perhaps in their thirties. The man wore a flat cap and a waistcoat, a large driving jacket draped over his knees. It was impossible to tell much about him: he could be a poet, a painter, a taxi-driver, an off-duty lawyer, a doctor. Only the older generation of men, such as her father-in-law, Dr Westbrook, maintained the same strict uniform of suit and tie no matter what day of the week. The woman looked tired, and there was a large stain on her dress: a new mother, perhaps, struggling to cope with the demands of a child. A man came around the corner and the woman stood, her face barely registering him. Evelyn's attention shifted to this doctor. He was a stocky man, a stomach bulging beneath his woollen waistcoat. His face was round and smooth, his skin a ruddy pink, as though he'd been left out in the sun for too long. It was interesting to consider how different her appointments would be if he was her psychotherapist. Was it possible, she wondered, for her to feel the same passion for this man as she did for Dr Daley?

When it was her turn, Dr Daley walking towards her, she studied him, trying to work out if there was a difference between the man she held in her imagination and the man in front of her now. But he was exactly the same, no change to his eyes, his lips, the way he pushed his hair back from his face. Even his hands were as she imagined them: fine and expressive, capable of making her come alive.

She did not know where to begin. While she could ask him, directly, whether his name was Patrick, whether he was seeing her best friend, whether the Carl Jung book was his, she could not bring herself to do it. She was afraid that the answers would be yes. And then what? It would drive them to a crisis that she was not yet ready to confront.

'It is good to come in again, so soon after Monday,' she said, determined to start positively, to find a thread of connection between them. The problem of Diana, she decided, could wait a few more days. It was safer to speak to her friend, to ask Diana the questions that might give her the certainty she needed, than risk Dr Daley's pity.

He said nothing, but she could feel his eyes watching her, waiting for more.

'I have some questions, some more questions, about why you suggested doubling the appointments, when you said you saw all your other patients once a week.'

He nodded, but remained silent.

'I guess I'm not certain about your motivations.'

'What do you think my motivations might be?' he said.

'Can't you tell me? What is the point of me guessing, and working myself up into this confusion, when you could just answer my question?'

'It would be helpful for us to consider the thoughts you have been having which have led to this confusion, as you describe it.'

She sighed in frustration. It was maddening, the way he refused to answer her questions. 'I have thought about it a lot over the last few days, too much perhaps. My mind kept turning over and over with different possibilities. In fact, I wrote down a list of options.'

'Options?' he prompted.

'Yes. Reasons why you might have suggested this, from the most likely to the least likely. Or perhaps from the most boring to the most thrilling.' Evelyn smiled, remembering how she had sat at her writing desk yesterday afternoon, her dream journal in front of her, a fresh page open. It seemed fitting that she'd write the list among her dreams, for what was this other than a waking fantasy, a delusion or an illusion, she wasn't sure.

'Would you like to read your list out to me?'

It was a terrible thought, to expose the depths of her mind to him this way. But perhaps she could do it. The words were already written; all she had to do was open the page and read. With her hands damp from nerves, she pulled the journal out of her bag and opened to the page. Her chest was tight and she felt nauseated, but she spoke firmly to herself. She had no choice; this was the only way to draw him to her.

'Okay. I think I can do it. But I want to say before I start that the second half of the list is obviously delusional and I don't really think these things. They are just thoughts that passed through my head, that I recorded in order to help me process them.'

The Model Patient

He smiled. 'Remember, Mrs Westbrook, you really can say anything here with me. I am not going to judge you.'

She took a breath and began to read. 'Number one: he thinks meeting twice a week will help me to trust myself and him, to be able to open up more and talk freely, therefore making progress. He thinks I have become stuck in the therapy process and that changing up the routine might help. He is deliberately cruel and is manipulating my feelings because he enjoys having people fall for him. He likes listening to me talk about my feelings for him, because perhaps not many of his patients tell him such intimate things.'

She paused. It was already too much. The next and final three points on her list were excessive. They made her sound a combination of insane, narcissistic and desperate. She looked up at him but his expression told her nothing.

Gripping the pages of her journal, she felt as though her body was slipping off balance, the edges of the room warped and strange. Taking a sharp intake of breath, she forced herself to continue. She had to finish the list if she was to engage him.

'He is attracted to me. He wants to have sex with me, turning my fantasy into a reality. He is going to have sex with me and then murder me to stop me from regretting it and risking his reputation.'

Evelyn closed the journal and leant back into the sofa. She was exhausted from the effort. Either she was being ridiculous, making assumptions about him that couldn't possibly be true of a professional psychotherapist, or she was being naïve and not acknowledging the signals he was giving her. Either way, she felt as though she was going insane.

She had no idea where the idea of his murdering her came from, other than the fever of a delusion. It had emerged out of her unconscious like a monster from a nightmare.

Every moment of his silence was unbearable. She knew that he was probably processing what she had just said, trying to work out what he could possibly draw from such a deranged list, but she wished he would hurry up and put her out of her misery.

'It is interesting that you felt you should explain the list in advance, to reassure me that you didn't really think those final few points. But perhaps it is in those final possibilities, as you describe them, that we can find the most to discuss. You think I am attracted to you.'

'Is that so bizarre an idea?' she said. 'Am I impossible to find attractive?'

'You feel that the only way I can show my interest in you is through sex.'

'I don't know. Maybe. Sex and murder.' She heard herself laugh nervously. She did not want him to murder her. 'I suppose I want something other than indifference. Do you not see how painful it is? I sit here and tell you these intimate things about myself, my past, my feelings for you. You encourage me to go further and further as though I am stripping myself naked. And then I am naked and offering my body to you, and what I get in return is silence or these terrible questions that dig even deeper beneath my skin without you giving away any of yourself.'

'Why murder, do you think?'

'Maybe because cruelty would be another way you could show your interest in me. I would prefer you to be cruel to me than to forget about me.'

'Yes. I can see that. Murder is, in some ways, the opposite of indifference.' With his brow furrowed, he drew his hands together in his lap before continuing. 'One of your possibilities was that we have sex, turning your fantasy into a reality. Can you tell me more about your fantasy?'

'What do you want me to tell you? What is the point? Do you not see that it would be agonizing? I am sitting here telling you everything I feel about you, while you're opposite me, calm and in control, being sadistically professional.'

'Are you afraid that I am enjoying this at your expense?'

'Is that so unreasonable a thought?' she replied.

'I think you're afraid of what would happen if you did tell me your fantasy. Part of you wants to tell me, and for me to make it come true; but another part of you is terrified of that idea.'

'No. I'm terrified of the rejection. I'm afraid of the silence once I've told you; I'm afraid nothing will happen, the fifty minutes will be up, and you'll tell me to leave.'

'As I've said before, nothing you say will make me reject you. On the contrary, haven't I just doubled the amount that I see you?'

Evelyn shook her head, her lips pressed tight in frustration.

They were talking at cross-purposes. While she wanted this to mean that he wouldn't reject her attempts to seduce him, what it really meant was that he wouldn't reject her as a patient. They were two very different things.

'I had a dream I wanted to talk to you about,' she said. It was simpler to change the topic than continue with this torturous discussion. 'Can I read it out to you?' she said.

'Of course.'

She opened her journal again, finding the most recent entry. To read out a dream was far easier, the unconscious images a step removed from herself.

'I'm in a large house and suddenly everyone starts to run and hide because terrible, strange things are happening outside. I hide in a cupboard, a wardrobe with coats and dresses hanging over me. Another woman comes in. I haven't met her before, but she seems familiar. She looks like me, only older. She tells me that there is a demon on the loose. It attacks people in their sleep, playing on their insecurities to make them do horrifying, crazy things.

'I can sense the demon getting closer and I know for certain that it is going to find me. I brace myself and I feel it slide through my body. It's trying to destroy me and possess me. I feel strange, weak and vulnerable, but then it's gone and I'm fine. It did not harm me. I ask the woman why it didn't hurt me, and she said it was because I understood the demon and did not try to reject it.'

Closing the notebook, Evelyn shrugged. 'I don't know what it means.'

The Model Patient

'How did it feel?'

'Which part?'

'All of it. What was the sensation of the dream?'

'It was frightening to start, especially when I was hiding and I could feel the demon getting closer. But when the demon moved through me, I was not afraid. Instead it was like a challenge, as though if I could endure it for long enough, everything would be fine.'

'What did the demon look like?'

'It didn't have a body. It was like a spirit or a demonic energy. It moved through me, and I felt it like a weight inside me and pressing down on me, and then it was gone. I didn't fight it. I just lay there and then it ended.'

'And do you recognize the house, and the cupboard?'

'No. It was familiar, but I can't place it.'

'Was it a sexual experience?'

'What do you mean?'

'The demon possessing you, moving through your body. That sounds to me like it was sexual.'

'It didn't feel sexual.'

'How did you feel when you woke up?'

'I felt unsettled. That was all.'

'And what did you do when you woke up?'

'I got out of bed and I went to my dressing room where I keep this notebook. I wrote down the dream. I was cold so I got back into bed and . . .'

'And?'

Evelyn closed her eyes. She could not tell him how Henry

had kissed her, how strangely he'd looked at her when his hand moved between her legs, how he pressed her closer when he felt her desire.

'Nothing. That was it. I don't think it was a sexual dream. Isn't there another interpretation? Perhaps it was about this, my treatment with you, about how I should be trying to embrace the way you make me delve into unwelcome thoughts, how I should be working harder to endure the pain of it all, rather than reimagining it into a sexual fantasy.'

'So you think you should be rejecting your sexual thoughts about me, instead focusing on the difficulties from your past, as well as the challenges you are having in your marriage?'

'Yes, of course. Although Henry and I are having more sex at the moment, I feel guilty about it because I know the real reason is because of you. How can I make changes in my marriage if every time Henry touches me, my mind returns to this room?'

'Could we look at it another way, that in fact it is through embracing your sexual fantasies and exploring them in more depth, with me here in this room, that you might find yourself understanding and accepting some of those more challenging aspects of your past.'

'I don't understand how that would work. How I see it is that I tell you how I feel and you tell me nothing in return. It's unequal. The power you have is frightening.'

'What power do I have?'

'You have the power to give me everything and nothing both at the same time. You have the power to make me feel insane. But you also have the power, if you wanted to use it, to make me feel loved.'

'How I see it is the only way you think I could make you feel loved is by having sex with you.'

'No. That's not true.'

'How could I make you feel loved?'

'Maybe, rather than saying the time is up, opening the door, and sending me out feeling as though the world is falling apart around me, you could say or do something in the final few minutes to help put me back together again. Is there nothing you can say to me to make it all stop hurting?'

'What is it that you want me to say? Or do?'

It was infuriating, the way he turned everything back to her. It was already nearly four o'clock and Evelyn knew there was only so long he would let the appointment overrun. She knew that what she was about to say would sound pathetic. Even before she spoke, she could hear the neediness, the vulnerable and weak side of her that she hated anyone to see. But she did not have any choice.

'All I want is for you to hold me.'

'I know you do.'

'And will you?'

He said nothing, his gaze turned away to the window. At last he turned back to her, his face brighter.

'I think, considering the situation, we can shake hands.'

This was unbearable. She had asked for him to embrace her, to hold her, and he was offering her a formality, a brief touch that would do nothing to make her feel better. She stood, her body shaking as she looked at him. He reached his hand out to her and she took it. His grip was light, his fingers barely making contact with hers. At that instant, it felt like the most humiliating moment of her life.

She wanted to kill him, to pull him towards her, to wrap her hands around his throat. She wanted to make him notice her. If he wouldn't love her, then maybe he could hate her.

Letting go of his hand, she took a small step towards him. She opened her arms. Evelyn could feel the tension stretching along her shoulders.

Gently, he took her wrists in his hands. He was not going to let her embrace him, or kill him, or whatever it was she had been about to attempt. She did not know what was driving her more, the desire to hold him or strike him.

'Mrs Westbrook,' he said, lowering her arms to her sides. 'Evelyn.'

She blinked, trying to hold back her tears. His grip tightened around her wrists, his thumbs pressing hard against her pulse.

'Evelyn,' he said again. It was the first time he had called her by her first name. It made her want to cry even more. 'I will see you on Monday.'

She nodded, taking a step away from him. He let go of her wrists and moved to open the door. As she walked along the corridor and out into the street, she dug her nails into the palm of her hands, trying to shift the pain away from her heart.

CHAPTER 19

'Come round for dinner tomorrow,' Evelyn said to Diana. She was in her bedroom, winding the cord of the telephone round and round her fingers. Her skin was warm and soft, her dressing gown loosely wrapped. As soon as she'd arrived home from her appointment, she'd run a bath, the steam filling the room and clouding the mirror. Frozen after the long walk home, she was exhausted and numb. When her reflection vanished in the steam of the mirror, she sank down into the water, her skin instantly turning pink from the heat.

All she could think about as she pressed herself down beneath the surface of the bath water was the way he had held her, how he had tried not to hurt her, the gentleness of his touch that hardened against the pulse in her wrist. But it wasn't enough for her. She wanted him to seize her, to cause her pain, real, physical pain, not this internal conflict that made her chest ache.

When she finally emerged from the bathroom, she phoned Diana and set up dinner the next day. Henry was going to his father's club and so she would have Diana all to herself. This was her chance to learn all she could about the man who had found his way into both women's hearts.

Henry and his father were heading out when Diana arrived.

'Hello, Henry, Mr Westbrook,' she said, kissing them both on the cheek.

'You're looking lovely, Diana,' said Mr Westbrook, patting her on the shoulder. 'Breaking hearts again?' At their wedding, Henry's father had enjoyed teasing Diana about the young men who stared hopefully at her across the reception hall.

Diana laughed. 'When did I ever break any hearts?'

'Come on, Dad. Let's leave the girls to their evening.' Henry winked at them before ushering his father outside.

'I can't believe that man is a gynaecologist,' whispered Diana. 'Imagine him telling you to lie back on his examination table.'

'I'd rather not, thank you,' Evelyn replied. But she couldn't help but smile; Diana's laughter was infectious.

Kicking off her shoes, two-toned Oxford pumps that were stained from the salt and grit of the icy roads, Diana handed Evelyn four bottles of Double Diamond beer.

'I don't know if they'll go with what you're cooking, but you can save them if you don't want beer tonight.'

'Thank you, honey,' Evelyn said, pulling her friend into a hug. She held her tightly, wrapping her arms all the way around her, and she felt Diana return the pressure, a real embrace, their bodies close and warm. Evelyn felt that tension in her chest again, imagining a different embrace, the one she had wanted from Dr Daley. It hurt to think that he might hug Diana this way, drawing her firmly into his arms.

Diana watched while Evelyn boiled the potatoes and cut the vegetables, saying nothing when she drew a pre-bought quiche Lorraine out of the refrigerator.

'It's from the Harrods food hall. Much better than I could possibly make, so be grateful,' Evelyn said with a smile, as she opened two of the beers and poured them into glasses.

'I didn't say a thing.'

'And I bought us some French desserts. Look in the refrigerator if you want.'

'I can wait.' She walked over to where Evelyn was cooking and wrapped her arms around her. 'You're the perfect hostess.'

Evelyn grimaced. 'Don't joke. Henry's mother would boil me alive if she knew I was serving ready-made food to a guest, even if it is my childhood best friend who I know lives on bread and cheese.'

'You shouldn't care what she thinks.'

'You're lucky, not having to worry about fulfilling the expectations of a husband and his mother.'

'Henry isn't his mother, Evie. And he doesn't want you to be a copy of her either.'

Evelyn shook her head. She knew she should be honest with Diana, but it was difficult when it was her friend who had encouraged Evelyn to trust Henry back when they first met. It was easier to change the conversation.

'Tell me, how is it going with Patrick?'

'It's good, very good. He stayed over at Number Six on Sunday night, actually. For the first time.'

'And? What was it like?'

Diana laughed, pinching Evelyn's waist. 'You want to know all the details?'

'Of course,' Evelyn said, forcing herself to laugh in return. 'You know you can't keep anything from me.'

'Well, we drank wine, he managed to bring my favourite cheese without even knowing what it was, and we listened to a jazz record. I showed him around the flat and he asked how my writing was going. He's been very helpful actually, lending me some books.'

'You talk about your novel with him?' Evelyn tried not to sound hurt, but this was difficult to hear. Diana had told her nothing about her book, whereas it seemed Patrick Daley was given access to it all.

'Yes, he's a doctor, a psychologist, and one of my characters has personality issues about which he has been giving me some insight.'

'What sort of personality issues?'

Evelyn tried to stay calm, but she could feel a terrifying fear build inside her. This, surely, was confirmation that her Diana and her Dr Daley were together.

'There is a woman in my novel, the main character, who is a combination of neurotic and narcissistic, which makes her quite volatile. She falls in love easily, but is constantly doubting herself and what others think of her.'

'In what way is she narcissistic?'

'Well, it's a kind of vulnerable narcissism. She wants everyone to love her. When she worries that they don't, she becomes hyper anxious.'

'What does Patrick say about this type of person?'

Evelyn's heart was beating fast, struggling with the effort of revealing nothing. She had been very close to calling him Dr Daley. There seemed no point in resisting the truth anymore. Diana's Patrick and Evelyn's Dr Daley were obviously the same person. Tightening her grip on the knife, she continued chopping the carrots into smaller and smaller pieces.

'He was very helpful, actually, telling me how this might play out in psychoanalytical therapy. I might change the plot a little now, perhaps include a doctor like himself, to heighten the psychological drama of the novel.'

'You've never spoken about your novel with me before,' Evelyn said, refilling Diana's glass with beer.

'You're right. I'm sorry that I haven't shared this with you before. I think I haven't felt confident enough about the story and the research behind it. But now, after working on it with Patrick, I feel better about it. It's amazing how much confidence he has given me. The way he speaks to me, it's empowering.'

'How so?'

'I suppose he makes me feel intelligent. He tells me how special I am, how clever and interesting. And beautiful,' she added with a smile. 'It's very validating.' Diana blushed, and Evelyn had to turn away. It was rare for Diana to speak so fondly of anyone.

'Does he tell you about his patients, if any of them are similar to your character?'

'Not really. I don't think he would do that. But he does tell me about some of the theories that underpin the type of psychoanalytical therapy that he practises. His is a form of analysis he calls psychodynamic therapy. Apparently it's like psychoanalysis but only requires one or two appointments each week, rather than the three or four necessary for more traditional analysis. It's fascinating and hard to imagine, but apparently it's very effective.'

Evelyn felt ill. It was torture, listening to Diana speak this way, but she couldn't stop. It was as though she was drinking a poisonous wine, intoxicating now but would leave her sick and exhausted.

'Like what? Isn't psychoanalysis just examining your dreams and delving into your unconscious?'

'Yes, but to do that, you have to draw out those feelings, make them visible. Sometimes projective testing like word or image associations can work well. Or the therapist themself can become like a blank slate for the patient onto which they transfer their desires and fantasies and vulnerabilities.'

'How does that work?'

'Well, how Patrick explained it to me was that by the doctor being a neutral figure who is able to abstain from gratifying a patient's desires, such as for affirmation or love, the patient may start to see them as someone from their past, such as a parent or a lover or a sibling, someone with whom they had a complex relationship when they were a child. Therefore the doctor reflects the patient's unconscious desires, bringing them out into the open through the transference.'

'But then what do they do with all this. It sounds very messy and emotional?'

'They talk about it, analyse it together, work it through. The important thing, apparently, is for the doctor to maintain the strict boundaries of the psychoanalytical frame – never giving the patient extra time, never changing the routine of the appointments, or the frequency of appointments, never accepting or giving gifts, or doing anything that offers tangible evidence that they are more than an impartial, bland figure on which the patient themselves is transferring all their emotions.'

'So seeking out ways to learn more about the patient outside of the appointments by, I don't know, befriending people in their lives, would not be seen as appropriate?'

Diana laughed. 'That would definitely be inappropriate. Though Freud analysed his own daughter, apparently, so rules do get broken. It must be hard, I think, to maintain this distance when someone is sat across from you telling you all these intimate difficult things. I couldn't do it. I struggle not to cry when one of my students gets upset after failing a test.'

'Don't you think there is something quite troubling about this method, though? It seems to give so much power to the doctor, whereas the patient is left feeling bewildered and tormented with their unrequited desires and fantasies.'

'Yes, I did think that. I asked Patrick about it, whether he ever thinks it has gone too far, or is harmful to a patient. Imagine if his patient fell in love with him. It would, I expect, be confusing for the patient because they'd be encouraged to talk about their feelings, with no chance of any relief or return of how they felt. He said that this is common, actually. But he's learnt to tolerate this and, with time and commitment, the patient will learn about themselves, their patterns of behaviour, and even their unconscious.'

'*He's* learnt to tolerate this?' Evelyn said scornfully. She tried to calm herself, swallowing the last inch of her beer. 'What about the patient? How do *they* learn to tolerate this?'

'I have no idea,' Diana replied with a shake of her head. She smiled, pushing her hair out of her eyes. 'Well, good thing neither of us are in psychotherapy then.'

All of a sudden, in a cold blast of realization, Evelyn was sure that she knew. They were laughing at her, Diana and Dr Daley together. Diana was punishing Evelyn for all the mistakes she'd made over the years, kissing Edward that night, how pathetic she was, unable to extract herself from the relationship with Mr Hardy just because he gave her work and made her feel special, how irritating it must have been for Diana to listen to Evelyn's cycles of self-destruction. For years Diana must have resented her, waiting for her moment to tear her down, balance the scales, show her what she really deserved. Now, with Dr Daley, she had found her revenge.

The Model Patient

Evelyn poured the boiling water out of the saucepan, potatoes tumbling into the colander. She was too quick, her anger spilling out, and the water splashed onto her hand. The pain was bright and she exclaimed, raising the edge of her hand to her mouth. Diana was at her side instantly, taking her hand and running cold water over the burn.

'You'll be okay, Evie,' she said. 'It's not going to leave a mark.'

Diana wrapped one arm around Evelyn, the other held out in the sink, supporting her hand.

It was frightening how quickly Evelyn had let the paranoia descend. Of course Diana didn't know that Dr Daley was her psychologist. The idea was ridiculous. Diana was her best friend and despite the difficulties of the past, nothing could tear them apart.

'You're crying,' Diana said, looking at her friend. 'What's up?'

Evelyn shook her head. It was pointless to say that it was the burn. Diana was right: there was no mark and the pain had nearly vanished.

'It's just, you know, all this.' She gestured around her: an enviable kitchen, the refrigerator stocked with leftovers in their pastel Tupperware, the wedding gifts filling the cupboards. 'I don't know how to make this life work for me. I don't know how to be happy.'

Diana nodded, gently wiping the water from Evelyn's hand with a kitchen towel.

'Do you think maybe you're putting too much pressure

on yourself to feel good all the time? You look around you and think how much you've got, how idyllic your life looks, and then when you feel the sadness creeping in, it makes you feel guilty.'

Evelyn did not try to stop her tears, the tension in her neck falling away. Rather than judging her, it seemed Diana already understood.

'Yes. I feel that I don't deserve to make a fuss; but I also don't know how to be happy. I am not sure I even deserve to be happy.'

'That's not true, Evie. You deserve to feel happy. And it's also okay to let yourself feel low. Do you know what might help?'

Evelyn shook her head.

'I think, and please don't be angry, this is just a suggestion and you can tell me to leave it alone if you want, but I think you should tell your parents about Mr Hardy.'

Evelyn shook her head. 'You know I can't do that. And besides, it's over. What good would it do to drag all that to the surface? I don't think I could bear the shame of it.'

'He'll never be gone from your life until your parents reject him too. He was at your wedding, for god's sake. I wanted to murder him when I saw him in the chapel.'

Evelyn laughed. It was good to hear Diana's anger on her behalf. 'Yes, I did too. But a white wedding dress would have shown up the blood far too clearly.'

'We can murder him together, wearing black this time.'

They laughed as they dished up the dinner and poured

The Model Patient

more of the Double Diamond beer. But beneath the laughter, Evelyn could feel a tension loosening within her. It moved inside her, something dangerous and thrilling, full of an awesome rage, and it took her to new depths that she did not know she possessed. The good girl, the dutiful daughter, lover, wife: they were slipping away. Instead there was something darker, a monster, or a demon, rising to the surface.

CHAPTER 20

They meet near the edge of Regent's Park, inside the entrance closest to Baker Street. It is only a short walk from his clinic and he arrives first. He is waiting for her on the bridge above the boating lake, the water clear and calm. The winter ice has vanished at last.

Evelyn has discarded her coat for the first time in months, and she wears a charcoal dress, a thin jacket over her shoulders. She should be cold, but not today. Dr Daley is wearing the same cream trousers he wore the first time she met him, a burgundy sweater, a beige jacket. She smiles when she reaches him and he nods in greeting. They start walking, silent at first but then they begin to talk, the conversation moving easily between them. She tells him about her latest jewellery design, how it started as a tiny diamond burrowed into thin silver wire, like an egg inside a bird's nest, how it grew across the page of her sketchbook into a tangle of branches, a necklace that spread, decadently along the collarbones. He tells her about his research, his interest in dream analysis, how he searches for

The Model Patient

what is hidden in the symbols and images of fantasies, teasing out the latent content that lies buried, waiting to be discovered.

The park is quiet, even quieter when they drift off the main path and into the shade of the trees behind the rose garden. A breeze is moving through the grass and the spring flowers are emerging tentatively: the winter is not long gone and the flowers are fragile.

He removes his jacket and lays it on the ground. 'Please take it,' he says, gesturing for her to sit. She crosses her legs, spreading her fingers through the grass either side of her. Dr Daley sits opposite. This is how it should always be, she thinks, the two of them outside together, no furniture and walls to frame the boundaries of their connection, no clock, no time ticking onwards.

She reaches her hand out to him. He takes it, pressing her wrist to his lips. Leaning forwards and coming up onto her knees, she kisses him. He returns her kiss, his hands moving up to her hair, pulling it back from her face.

Gently, he pushes her down so that she is lying in the grass. He continues to kiss her, taking her hands and pressing them into the wild flowers above her head.

There is no violence; she doesn't ask him to hurt her, not now. Together, they are slow and tender and she feels her body sinking into the ground.

Once they leave each other, saying goodbye next to the bridge, Evelyn looks at her watch. They have been together for hours, far longer than the allotted fifty minutes.

*

She could not wait until Monday to share her dream with Dr Daley. A compulsion had led her, lifting her from her bed, leaving Henry asleep, dressing in the first thing she found in her wardrobe. Henry rolled onto his back as she walked past him, reaching out his arm across the empty side of the bed. Pausing by his pillow, she kissed him lightly, trying to suppress the stirrings of guilt in her stomach.

'I can't sleep,' she whispered. 'I'm going for a walk.'

Turning onto his side again, he took her hand. 'We're going to Henley later,' he murmured.

'I know,' she replied, wriggling free. 'I won't be long.'

Downstairs at her writing desk, she recorded the dream as swiftly as she could. She wrote it all down, every little detail, forging each moment afresh. It felt real, so much more than a dream.

Rising swiftly, the letter tucked inside her coat, she left the house. While the sun rose over London, Evelyn made her journey, walking with purpose along the familiar streets. A two-hour round trip, all the way to Marylebone and back, through Westminster, Green Park, Mayfair, the city woke around her. For the first time in months, there was no frost.

When she posted the note through the door of the clinic on Upper Wimpole Street, addressed to Dr Daley, she imagined what would happen when he found it. He'd arrive at his clinic on Monday morning and he'd read it. It was the only way to make sure she told him everything when she saw him at eleven o'clock for her appointment.

The Model Patient

This time she wouldn't need to say the words: he'd already know.

It was still early by the time Evelyn arrived home. She crept upstairs, determined not to wake Henry again. To explain why she'd been gone for so long at this early hour on a Sunday morning was impossible. There was a time, before they were married, when he'd have wanted to come with her, though it was more likely to be a night-time walk with Henry, the two of them kissing on a bench along the Thames, bottles of beer in paper bags at their side. It was many months since they had done anything that broke the routine of their lives together.

She undressed quickly, shivering as she wrapped her dressing gown around her. Switching the light on in the bathroom, she leant against the sink, staring at her face in the mirror. The morning light was coming in through the window, bright and determined. Winter really was on its way out; that, at least, was not a dream.

Her cheeks were pink, a pattern of freckles emerging faintly around her nose. She stared harder, her body straining as she leant towards the mirror. She could not believe that one morning's walk through London on a cool March day had made those freckles appear. And yet all else she had was a dream, Regent's Park, the rose garden, wild flowers between her fingers.

There was a dress hanging on the back of the door. Her gaze settled on its reflection in the mirror as she shifted her focus away from her face.

Turning abruptly, she blinked hard: she couldn't believe what she was seeing, the reflection in the mirror now solid and real. She tried to steady herself, her hands finding the edge of the sink behind her. The charcoal dress from her dream was hanging on the back of the door, the fabric crumpled and stained. She moved slowly, afraid it would disappear. Finally she was holding it in her hands, plucking at the cotton, trying to remember when she had last worn this dress. Not since the autumn, surely. It was too thin for the winter they had endured.

Henry appeared in the doorway, marks from the bedsheets lined into his skin.

'That was an early walk,' he said, pulling a towel off the rail and wrapping it around his waist.

'It's a beautiful Sunday,' she replied. 'I wanted to make the most of it before we have to drive to Henley.'

'I thought you liked visiting Mark and June,' he said as he reached around her for his toothbrush. 'We haven't seen the children since New Year.'

Evelyn attempted to hide her grimace as she turned back to the mirror. She remembered the New Year's Day gathering all too well, the freezing car journey to get there, a crawl along icy roads, her nephews and nieces playing in the snow outside the house, their screams swiftly morphing into tears. Ruth was immaculate as always, stoking the flames of her two daughters' anxiety as they watched, hungrily, for their mother's approval. Evelyn had been oddly enthralled by the way the three sons, Mark, Peter, even her own Henry, had instinctively mirrored their father, jostling to be the one to open the wine, carve the beef, lead the charge of toddlers desperate to help carry in logs from the shed. Evelyn had tried to relax into this choreographed chaos, convincing herself that it was the contrast to her own family dynamic, her as an only child, that made her feel on edge.

And now, today, they had to do it all again. At least this time there would be no Ruth or Alec. They were away for the weekend to celebrate their wedding anniversary. It was, however, Ruth who had organized this Sunday's get-together in Henley, despite not being there herself. Evelyn was suspicious: it was as though her mother-in-law could not allow Evelyn and Henry one weekend to themselves.

'When did I last wear this dress?' she said to Henry. Holding it up along the line of her body, her mind drifted to the dream, a welcome fantasy that took her away from the challenges of a Westbrook family Sunday.

'No idea. Why?'

'It was hanging on the back of the door, and it's dirty. Did I get it out last night?'

Evelyn had been sorting through her wardrobe before they went to bed, an attempt to pack away the winter coats once and for all. Moving the thick coats into the spare room wardrobe, she'd swapped them over with dresses and skirts. Her woollen scarves were folded up on the top shelf, replaced with her favourite suede jackets, a grey and a beige that she could not risk spoiling in poor weather.

Perhaps it was this that had created the spark for her dream, she realized with a tug of disappointment. It was pathetic really, a mundane household chore transformed into fantasy. She shuddered, trying to dispel the thought: was that all she was, a housewife searching for a thrill?

'You must have done,' said Henry. 'Did you think it would hurry up the spring?'

He stood behind her, the two of them reflected in the mirror. As he touched her hips, Evelyn relaxed, pressing the back of her head against his chest.

'And it worked, didn't it,' he said. 'The cold is vanishing at last.'

This dress, the one from her dream, must have been dirty from the autumn. But she wished she could remember hanging it on the back of the door, ready to put in the laundry.

'What I do know is that I like that dress,' Henry said. Evelyn laughed as he squeezed her waist. He kissed her and she shivered, remembering her dream.

When she thought about this moment later, she could not recall which of them had taken that kiss, deepening it into something more. On the bathroom floor, the soft wool of the rug below her, they had moved together. She closed her eyes, and she was back there in the rose garden of Regent's Park, feeling it all. It was only afterwards that she wondered what had changed Henry's mind. The question of a child seemed to have vanished, and his reluctance to have sex with her was fading into the past. The sex, too, was different. What she didn't know was whether it was Henry who was changing,

The Model Patient

or whether it was her, the fantasy of her desires transporting his touch into something new and thrilling.

Her husband watched as she gathered a towel between her legs. She glanced up, his face caught in the reflection of the mirror, and in that instant it was a relief to see that he was smiling.

And yet as she ran the bath and steam began to spread across the mirror, she found herself thinking that there had been something unsettling about his expression, a look of satisfied pleasure that made Evelyn want to take him by the shoulders and shake him. She wished she knew how to ask him whether he could see her at all. Was he oblivious to how she had changed? Did he notice nothing of the fever of her thoughts?

Standing before him now, the sound of the running water like a curtain between them, she did not know how to find the words.

CHAPTER 21

'Don't tell Mark about the car,' Henry said as they finally left London behind them, the MGA spluttering into life.

'Why does it matter?' Evelyn replied. But she did understand. Henry envied his eldest brother, desiring everything that Mark possessed: the big house in Henley, three children, a garage for his car, his name on the office door. Mark was much further along the journey to transforming into their father, the successful family man, Dr Alec Westbrook. When the car hadn't started this morning, the battery dead after too many weeks of standing motionless in the freezing cold, Henry had not been able to contain his frustration. It didn't help that it took many attempts with the crank handle before the engine sprang to life, the choke pulled out and Henry swearing as he crouched down in the road. Evelyn had teased Henry when he swapped their sensible Morris Minor for an MG sports car, but she didn't push him too far. There was a limit to his sense of humour when it came to competing with his brothers.

The Model Patient

'You know what he'll be like,' Henry said, his hands gripping the wheel too tight. 'He'll make some annoying comment about how I should keep it in a garage. How exactly am I supposed to do that when I live in the centre of London?'

'You mustn't let him get under your skin. And I thought you liked visiting Mark and June,' Evelyn couldn't help adding with a smile.

Henry turned to her, an eyebrow raised. 'Yes, okay, very funny. But you know what I mean.'

'At least your parents won't be there. Your siblings are more relaxed when they aren't trying to impress Ruth and Alec.'

'It's not always like that, Evie.'

'I'm sorry. I know.'

'Elizabeth and Carol are very close to Mum.'

Evelyn fixed her eyes on the car in front of them. 'You're all close to Ruth. It's not only your sisters.' She tried not to sound resentful, but she knew she wasn't doing a very good job. Evelyn wanted so much to be accepted by his family, but she never seemed to get it right. Perhaps the only way was to carry a new Westbrook into the world, a painful and bloody rite of passage.

Henry didn't reply, instead playing with the car's radio controls. When no sound emerged, the audio system dead despite the car's violent reawakening, he pressed his foot on the accelerator. Closing her eyes, Evelyn sank back into the car seat and slipped further into the memory of her dream.

*

Henry drove too quickly through the country roads, his entrance along his brother's winding tree-lined drive waking Evelyn as the car lurched over the potholes. Elizabeth and Carol were talking in front of the house, a child in each of their arms. Carol and Kenneth had a 6-month-old, while Elizabeth and Frank had two little girls whom they liked to dress in matching velvet dresses, bows in their hair. Evelyn could see Lily standing by the front door, failing to stop her manic 3-year-old son, Graham, from hitting her on the leg with a toy policeman's baton. Mark and June would be inside, she imagined, managing the chaos of feeding their twin toddlers, two wild little boys who, at Christmas, had succeeded in ripping Evelyn's sweater as they climbed over her on the sofa. Their 10-year-old daughter Miriam had a habit of disappearing for hours, escaping the noise of the twins. Evelyn liked Miriam, this quiet awkward child who preferred to wander through the garden, taking photographs of leaves and flowers, than endure an afternoon in the playroom with her younger siblings and cousins. Henry and Evelyn had given her the camera for her ninth birthday, a Kodak Retinette, after she showed an interest in Evelyn's work. It wasn't the fashion that attracted her, rather the changing styles of photographs, the light and shade, the decisions each photographer had made to craft the composition.

'What is she supposed to do with that?' Ruth had said as Miriam ran her fingers across the buttons. It took all Evelyn's self-control to stay quiet.

June appeared from the house, her arms open like a mother

welcoming home her brood. Dressed in a large smock dress, an apron tied around her waist, she had changed dramatically since the last family gathering. Evelyn felt her shoulders tense as she glanced up at Henry. June was pregnant again.

Ushering them inside, the front door closing behind them, June was giddy with excitement. She hurried them into the living room, leaving no opportunity to remove coats or shoes. Here was a woman determined to have her moment.

Stepping into the centre of the room, a beam of sunlight finding her through the latticed window, she untied her apron. She turned three times, like a child showing off a new dress, and pulled Mark towards her. Evelyn noticed the gold band of the family ruby ring pressing into her flesh.

'We're pregnant,' she exclaimed, her face beaming. 'Before you all panic,' she said, holding up her hand for quiet, 'Ruth and Alec know already. It was Ruth who suggested we reveal it today for you all. We did want to tell you earlier, but there wasn't a good time, not with the weather this winter.'

Evelyn glanced around the room, noticing the wide smiles of the adults, the way Mark watched his wife with unreserved pride. The twins were sprawled on the floor, colourful wooden blocks tumbling around them, and Miriam had pressed herself into the corner of one of the sofas, a book partially hidden in the folds of her skirt.

Among the inevitable rush of congratulations, Elizabeth, Carol and Lily placing their hands over June's stomach, Evelyn felt Henry pressing her lightly against her back. She stepped forward to join the women.

'It will be you next,' said June, tilting her head for a kiss. 'Ruth and Alec said we could be sure of it.'

'Did they?' Evelyn said, a laugh escaping her. 'I don't know where they got that idea.'

'You don't need to be coy with me,' June replied, wrapping her arm around Evelyn's waist. 'Come and help me in the kitchen.'

'I'll be there soon,' Evelyn said, extracting herself and gesturing to the hallway. 'I better wash my hands. We had a minor car incident on the way here,' she said, instantly regretting it. Henry had asked her not to mention the car, and there she was, blurting it out within minutes of entering the house.

It was only later that evening, when they were driving home and the lights of London were building around them once again, that she let herself process the fragment of conversation she had overheard from the kitchen door.

'Your mother was quite clear about it,' June was saying to Elizabeth and Carol, their heads close together as they peeled the lids off the Tupperware. 'It won't be long. Henry is desperate to have a child.'

'But Evelyn doesn't want to? Or can't they get pregnant? Is Alec helping them?' said Lily, her curiosity getting the better of her as she listened in, all the while stirring the soup on the stove.

Evelyn had hoped Lily would be an ally when they first met, another Westbrook newcomer who might share some of her frustrations with the power Ruth and Alec seemed to wield over their children. It was quickly clear that she had misread her. Lily was as obsessed with making Ruth like her as all the others. Evelyn had been invited to Peter and Lily's wedding, just six months before hers and Henry's, and had been horrified to see how Lily had deferred to Ruth for every decision. Maybe, Evelyn had thought, she was looking for a mother and did not care if she had to sacrifice herself to find one. Lily's mother had died when she was a child.

June lowered her voice. 'All I know is that Ruth said Henry wouldn't have to wait much longer.'

And then the conversation was over, the twins rushing in and knocking Evelyn into the room.

Evelyn glanced at Henry as he drove, trying to untangle her fears. The line of his jaw was fixed and frozen, his eyes forward on the road. So many times during the journey she came close to asking him what his sisters were talking about. But she stopped herself, too afraid of the paranoia she knew would creep into her voice, how it would expose her. Henry seemed entirely unaware of everything that was happening to her, the nightmares, her obsession with a doctor he did not even know she was seeing, the wildness of her thoughts, the shame of her fantasies. She preferred to keep it that way. To tell him what was happening would only cause him pain.

And yet she was desperate to be close to him. She wanted him to stop the car, to turn to her, to hold her, to make her feel safe again. But he gave her nothing, just a silhouette in the dark of the car, the sound of the road heavy beneath them.

CHAPTER 22

'Did you receive my note?' It was up to her to begin, but she was afraid. He was impenetrable, his expression giving her nothing. And yet, when she allowed herself to see reality, she knew that he was encouraging her, driving her to dive further into her fantasies with him. Evelyn did not understand it: did he want to keep her in this place of torment and desire, or was he trying to help her access the trials of her past, a terrible re-traumatization that she did not want? Either way, it made no sense.

He was wearing the black paisley jacket. This time there could be no mistaking its significance, not when he knew what it meant for her. She had told him not long ago about how her fantasy had emerged, the jacket at its centre, how, when he wore it, she would tell him her desires.

'Yes. I read your note this morning.'

'I'm sorry if I overstepped in writing it down. But I couldn't wait until today.'

'You don't need to apologize.'

The Model Patient

'It felt so real.'

'Yes.'

'I was thinking earlier today, on the way over, how it felt for you, when you read it?'

'You want to know if it felt real for me?'

'Well, perhaps not real, but whether you felt anything.'

'You want to ask me if I feel the same way about you as you feel for me?'

'Well, yes. I do want to know what you feel. I don't think there's anything unusual about that.'

'Evelyn,' he said, and she held her breath. 'I think you are worried that I don't feel anything, that I'm this cold, rigid doctor who does not understand the pain that you are experiencing.'

He paused, looking across at the window before turning back to her.

'But that isn't true,' he said. 'I can feel what you are feeling.'

Evelyn bit her lip, her hand flying to her chest. She wanted to understand him, but his words were not enough for her to be sure.

'You feel it too?' she whispered. 'This connection between us.'

'Evelyn.' His voice was gentle. 'You know I do.'

She was afraid to speak. In her dreams, this would be the moment he embraced her, the distance between them vanishing at last. But Dr Daley did not move from his chair.

'And, if it is of any help,' he continued, 'I can tell you that

I'm glad you brought your note to me. I'm glad that you wrote it down.'

'Why? Why are you glad?'

'It seems to me that we shouldn't miss the connection you felt, and that you describe me as feeling. That connection between us does, as you say, feel very real. I am interested in why you think it wouldn't be real?'

The way he was looking at her, that intensity in his gaze: it stirred her, and she struggled to sit still. She had practised everything she wanted to say today, but now that she was here, words were failing her. With her hands digging into the leather of the sofa, she tried to remember what it was that she had rehearsed.

'Because,' she said, trying to suppress the heat rising in her neck, 'while it feels real to me, I worry that you see me as another of your patients who is acting out the transference that has made them feel this way about you. You can tolerate it, push it to the side and treat it with clinical distance, while I feel it all. And now you've got me here, you do nothing to help me escape.'

'It is interesting that you say this after I have told you that I can feel what you are feeling,' he replied. 'And yet you seem to think that the appointment ends and I move on. Are you not able to consider the possibility that I might keep you in mind between appointments?'

'I don't know. You have never told me that you do.'

This was her chance, she knew, to confront him about Diana. Do you think of me, she might say, every time you

The Model Patient

kiss my best friend? But she couldn't do it. To hold this secret within her, it gave Evelyn a rare power that she did not want to lose. She would wait until the moment was right.

Dr Daley stood and for a heart-stopping moment Evelyn thought he was going to come to her, to make it real at last. But instead he went to his desk and picked up a folder. He handed it to her and returned to his chair.

'Open this please,' he said, and she did, her hands unsteady.

The folder was made of grey card, the words 'Dream-Images' written across the front in pencil. Inside were ten stiff pieces of paper, each a little smaller than the standard A4 size. Evelyn looked through them, unsure what she was supposed to be seeing. Each was a strange explosion of colour, shapes, shadows, the strokes of a brush, splatters of paint. They looked to her like crude and unfinished versions of the Abstract Expressionism paintings that she loved: Rothko, Pollock, Frankenthaler, Gorky, Krasner. In fact they reminded her most of her own artwork from when she was a teenager, those fierce layers of paint, hidden figures and stories beneath the colours.

'If you could think back to the word association task we did together a few weeks ago. In that, I asked you to say the first thoughts that came to your mind when hearing the word. We found that to be an illuminating moment for us both.'

Evelyn nodded, her eyes fixed on the cards. She did not want to think about the word association task, how she had revealed to him her most intimate thoughts. It was humiliating to be reminded.

'For this, I want you to focus on the note you delivered to me, our encounter in Regent's Park. We will explore it together more deeply, through the emotions these images spark. Some might evoke nothing for you, and that is fine. You can move through them until you find an image that takes you back to our time in Regent's Park.'

It was strange to Evelyn that he did not describe it as a dream. His choice of words – our encounter, a connection between us – it took her to a dangerous place.

'Think about those moments you described, the two of us together, and look at each image one by one. As you look at the image, tell me what you see. Describe whatever it is that comes to you when you look at the card – maybe a literal description, or how it makes you feel, an emotion, or a sensation.'

The first was tightly packed circles of black, grey and yellow, their edges seeping into one another. It was impossible to find the pattern, but it gave an impression of order, as though if one looked for long enough, there might be a unifying structure within the chaos.

'I wonder whether you painted this yourself,' she said. 'It reminds me of a painting by Lee Krasner.'

'No. I'm not a painter. But I can tell you, if it is helpful, that I worked on designing these with an artist, a colleague who shares my interest in dream analysis. The idea is, as you have observed, to emulate some of the Abstract Expressionist artists who were most engaged with psychoanalysis, the theories of Carl Jung in particular. There is much to be found in the work of those painters, the way they allow their unconscious to drive the creation of the work but also the deliberateness of how they play with ideas of submerging and emerging images, as well as the intuitive and the emotional.'

It was exciting to hear him speak this way. She liked how he was letting her into his world, sharing the mysterious secrets of his psychotherapy methods. Just like he did with Diana. For the first time, she felt, he was treating her like an adult, an equal. And there was the uncanniness of their shared artistic interests. It brought them closer, another thread between them.

She looked at the first painting again, letting her vision sink into the circles.

'Try to think of Regent's Park, the memories of that time with me.'

'The bridge. How I felt when I walked up to you. It was confusing, because I didn't know what you would do. This painting makes me feel trapped in my own mind. It's like I both know and don't know what is happening.'

'Can you tell me more about that?'

'I know that you desire me, but I also don't know it. You never let me know it for certain, but you lead me there again and again.'

He nodded. 'What about the next picture?'

She drew out the card beneath. It had the look of one of the Rorschach inkblots, but without the symmetry. Grey, cream, splashes of yellow, a red shape that looked, at first glance, like a wild animal melting into the page. The animal was facing out, almost at the edge of the card.

'An animal trying to escape,' she said. 'It's a landscape, a strange dream world, and the animal knows it needs to wake up and get out of there.'

'Is that how you feel, with me?' he said. 'You are trapped in a dream world you want to escape?'

'Maybe. No. I don't believe I'm putting any effort into trying to escape from how I feel about you. I wrote it all down. I brought it right back to you.'

'Who or what is the animal, do you think?'

Evelyn looked again and her stomach clenched painfully. Something came to her this time, the memories clawing their way out like an animal awaking from beneath thawing ground.

She saw herself, a teenager, beautiful and vulnerable and desperate for love. It was the day after her sixteenth birthday and Mr Hardy had driven to her house to deliver a gift. Her parents were out that afternoon: it was the parents' meetings at her school. Evelyn was anxious as she waited for them to come home, wondering what her teachers were saying about her. She knew she was struggling with her academic subjects, but then again, no one seemed to expect any more from her. Now, she felt herself wondering what it would have been like for her brother, if he had lived, whether her parents would have held him to a higher account.

'Mr Hardy gave me a bracelet on my sixteenth birthday. It was silver with a rabbit charm. There were two tiny diamonds for eyes. We were in the kitchen; my parents were not there. He watched me as I opened the box and then he clasped it around my wrist.'

The memory came back to her, an uncontrollable flood.

'He pulled me on to his knee. You're sixteen now, he said. Do you know what means, he'd asked me. I think I'd shaken my head. I did know, though. I knew exactly what it meant. We all laughed about it at school. Sweet sixteen. Not that any of my friends would have considered the age of consent to mean anything other than a hypothetical joke, something to make us feel grown up at last. I was the only one sitting on a man's lap, letting him put his hand inside my dress.

'He said to me that we could finally do what he knew I'd wanted for so long, ever since I first met him. It puzzled me, then, how he framed it that way. This was what I wanted, he said. He spoke nothing of his own desire. It was a week later, when my mum dropped me off to use his pool, that we first had sex. He'd told her that he was going to be away all week, that I could make use of the pool as much as I wished. But he was there, hiding away in his study. As soon as my mum drove away, he took me up to his bedroom.'

Evelyn stopped herself, her hands pressed together in her lap. She did not need to say this. It was enough. The memories, how his gentleness became hard and urgent: it could not be put into words.

'Looking back now, I know that it was rape. But he told me I had agreed. He told me that it was what I wanted. I remember the exact words he said to me. He said that I wanted to be adored. And he was right. But not like that.'

'And had you agreed?'

'No. Of course not.'

'Did you say no?'

'I was vulnerable. I didn't know how to say no.'

'Because your modelling jobs would have been taken away from you?'

'It was beyond that by then. He had rooted himself deep into my self-worth.'

'Did you enjoy it?'

Evelyn looked up from the picture, searching his face for anything that would help her understand what was happening. She could feel her panic rising. These questions, taking her further and further into the pain, it was humiliating. But his expression gave her nothing. There was no judgement, no criticism. But more frighteningly, there was no compassion either.

'I think I learnt to enjoy it,' she whispered. 'It was the only way to survive.'

'Shall we try another image?'

Evelyn looked down at the cards in her hand. The colours were losing their meaning.

'Please, just one more. I don't know how much more of this I can take.'

He was silent. She placed the top card at the bottom of the pile and looked at the next one. Evelyn gasped.

She knew this painting. It was identical, the same

brush-strokes, the same colours, the deep purple globe hovering above a confusion of black, as though someone had tried to hide an image beneath thick black paint. This was her painting.

She had been fourteen years old, in art class and responding to the poem Mr Martin had read to them the day before. She'd lost the painting not long after. It was impossible that it had appeared again now, more than ten years later, in Dr Daley's office.

'Where did you get this?'

'My colleague painted it, as I said.'

'That's not true.'

'It's inspired by a painting by Adolph Gottlieb, one of the *Blast* paintings. Perhaps that is what you are thinking about?'

'No, that's not it. I painted this.'

Dr Daley smiled. 'It's interesting that you've had this reaction, don't you think? We shouldn't miss the suggestion that you have found something in this painting that connects with you deeply.'

'Dr Daley, I am telling you that I painted this. When I was fourteen years old. I lost it soon after.'

'Tell me, what do you see in it that reminds you of when you were fourteen?'

Evelyn clenched her fists, a rage building within her. He didn't believe her, and it made her feel unhinged. She remembered it so clearly, the way the painting had emerged from her, the purple globe, the black paint that hid an image beneath.

'There is something under the black paint,' she said.

He leant forward. 'Yes, tell me what you see.'

'I don't see anything. I just know there is something under there.'

'What is under there?'

She closed her eyes, returning to that day in the art studio. It was not long after Mr Hardy had first touched her. Everything in her life was changing, possibilities opening, contracts appearing, and yet part of her had wanted to disappear. Evelyn, at fourteen years old, had not been able to reconcile the confusion of wanting love and death all at the same time.

'It's a clock, a watch-face.'

'Why do you think you see a clock?'

'I told you. I don't see a clock. I just know it is there.'

'Okay. Let's imagine you did paint this. Why is there a clock beneath the black paint?'

Time terrified her. The clock above the door; the watch around Dr Daley's wrist; the boundaries of time, fifty minutes that would soon be over; Henry's urgency, reminding her of the limitations of her own body, how she could not wait for ever to give him a child.

'The watches I modelled for Mr Hardy's friend. I suppose it was that.'

'In your note to me, you wrote about how we were together in Regent's Park for hours, far longer than fifty minutes. The length of time was significant to you.'

'Yes, that felt very good, I remember.'

'Tell me how you feel now, to think about that.'

'It feels dangerous.'

'What do you mean by that?'

'The way I feel is dangerous. If you make me think about it, I am afraid I won't be able to control the sensations in my body.'

'Can you tell me about those sensations?'

'I don't know if I can. It is too much. It makes me feel ashamed, the sensations I feel, how my body responds. It's confusing: it's sex with a ghost, with nothing. It makes me feel insane.'

'It's arousing?'

Evelyn nodded, unable to speak.

'Why are you ashamed to feel arousal when you are with me? This is a place where it's safe for you to feel whatever comes to you.'

'Don't you see that for me to be sitting across from you, feeling it all so physically, while you are so calm, so powerful . . . it's humiliating.'

'The physical feeling you are experiencing, is it like an orgasm?'

He watched her. She was shaking and she did not know what to say.

'Evelyn, there is no need to be afraid of this.'

She looked up at him. 'Yes. It's like that, close to that. Every time.'

'Like in Regent's Park, when I kissed you. When we had sex.'

'Yes, like in Regent's Park.'

It was quiet in the room, not a sound filtering in from outside. Evelyn was still holding on to the folder with the paintings. She looked down, seeing the purple and black painting once again. It seemed different now, a little neater than the one she remembered painting, smaller, the purple globe a unified colour. She blinked, uncertain. She hated this, to feel so fragile, her grasp on reality slipping.

'This is a hard place to stop, I know, but we have run out of time for today.'

'It's too difficult. I don't know how to endure it.'

He stood, and his expression was full of pity. She wanted him to understand the pain he caused. It seemed impossible that he could encourage her to feel it so physically, and then leave her with nothing.

But it was not pity that she wanted.

'I'll see you on Thursday.'

'Yes. Okay.'

Out on Upper Wimpole Street, she walked a few steps before she found herself stopping, her hands moving to her stomach. A pain surged through her, and she doubled over, gasping. It was as though the knots of tension she had held inside were escaping, a slow agony of release.

'Evelyn.'

A voice, a man's voice, was close to her, the sound of his footsteps getting nearer. For a moment she let herself imagine it was Dr Daley. He had followed her. He wanted to check that she was going to be all right.

The Model Patient

But it wasn't him. The man moving towards her was a different doctor, not at all the person she wanted right now.

Her father-in-law. As he reached her, she righted herself, smoothing down her coat. She tried to plaster a smile onto her face and blink away the tears.

'Evelyn, what's happened? You look dreadful.'

She let him put his arm around her. There was comfort in feeling supported. 'I'm fine, really. It was just a spot of dizziness. I don't know what came over me. I must have forgotten to have breakfast.'

'You need to be careful. You can't go passing out on the London streets.'

'I wasn't going to pass out.'

'Come to my clinic with me. I can ask my secretary to make you a cup of tea.'

She shook her head, but he wasn't going to let her refuse. 'I insist. It's just around the corner on Harley Street. And then I'll put you in a taxi.'

As they walked, he chatted cheerfully to her, telling her about his weekend away with Ruth. It was their wedding anniversary, and he'd taken his wife to a hotel in the foothills of the South Downs. The same one, she suspected, from her own wedding night two years ago.

'And I gather you were all partying without us in Henley.'

'June and Mark hosted a lovely lunch,' Evelyn said, tempering her words.

'What are you doing in this part of town, anyway?' he asked her as they arrived at his clinic. It was the first time she had been there and the reception area reminded her too much of Dr Daley's clinic. The receptionist was young and pretty, like Angela Simmons, but with a sharper, fashionable look. Evelyn could feel the woman's eyes following her, appraising and critical, as Dr Westbrook led her through to his consulting room. 'A cup of tea for my daughter-in-law,' he said as they walked past the receptionist. 'And some biscuits.'

'I was seeing my dentist,' she lied. 'Just a check-up.'

'Is your doctor's clinic around here?' he asked as he took her coat and led her to a chair next to his desk. 'Your gynaecologist, I mean,' he added, seeing the confusion spreading across her face. She had thought, for a second, that he was referring to Dr Daley, her psychologist.

'No, I always go to the same general practice doctor, near Sloane Square.'

'Well, you know you're always welcome here.'

'Thank you. I appreciate that. But it's easier to keep things as they are.'

There was no way she was going to let Dr Westbrook poke around her body. She glanced over at the examination table, the foot stirrups held aloft, and shuddered. It was unsettling, to go from Dr Daley's couch to this room, her father-in-law handing her orange peel and chocolate biscuits as though she were a child.

'Evelyn, if you and Henry want any advice, you can always come to me. I have helped many couples in your situation.'

She looked up at him in surprise. It was intrusive, this

assumption they wanted his help. He was treating her like one of his patients.

'I'd prefer not to discuss this, if that's okay, Dr Westbrook.'

'Evie, dear, you know you can call me Alec.'

'Alec. Sorry.'

'Well, perhaps it's not my place, but if you want my help, now or another time, you let me know.'

'Really, Alec, it's fine.'

Evelyn knew that what she said next was a mistake, even before the words left her mouth. But it felt essential, anything to claw back some control.

'We aren't trying for a baby yet. I don't know where you got that idea. I'm taking the birth control pill, and I have no plans to stop just yet.'

Dr Westbrook's expression did not change, no shock, no disapproval. He knew, she realized. He already knew she was taking the contraception. Henry must have told him.

He patted her arm and she felt her body tense. 'Well, be careful, Evelyn. Those pills only work if taken in a very specific way.'

'Yes, I know.'

It was patronizing, this assumption that she was incapable of managing the medication most important to her. The routine of taking the tablets, it was a sacred ritual that gave her a power of her own.

As her father-in-law's hand rested on her arm, she suppressed a shudder, remembering Mr Hardy, how he had reassured her he was taking precautions, the fleeting glimpse of a French letter every time he lay her across his bed. But as she grew up, her body becoming accustomed to the patterns of the way he touched her, she realized she had never actually seen him wearing a condom. It was a relief when her period came each month. She had decided, when it was finally over with Mr Hardy, that never again would she let a man control the fate of her body.

Evelyn shifted her arm out from under Dr Westbrook's hand. She was desperate to get out of there.

'It's kind of you to look after me, but I'm much more myself now. I'd better go home.'

'I'll get you a taxi,' he said, standing and moving to the coat rack. She followed him, letting him guide her into her coat.

Three women were seated in the waiting area, magazines on their laps, their hair perfectly curled and their lipstick neat. She wondered whether Dr Westbrook would hand his patients their coat in the same way that he did for her, holding it open for them as they slipped in their arms, re-dressing themselves after he had explored between their legs. Evelyn shuddered again; there was something terrifying about being a patient. Or maybe it was simply being a woman alone with a man – a man with the power to judge her health and her sanity.

Once they were outside, Evelyn was thankful that a taxi pulled up quickly. Dr Westbrook opened the door for her and she got in as fast as she could. He leant in towards her, filling the space of the door. His suit was perfectly pressed and she smelt the orange of the biscuits on his breath.

The Model Patient

When he kissed her, a light press against her cheek, she felt a bead of sweat running down her back. Her body was worn out and she longed to get home. At last, the taxi pulled away and she leant back against the seat.

She'd give herself one night to think and then she'd make her plan. This humiliation, it had to end.

CHAPTER 23

Thursday's appointment took on the same pattern as Monday's, a battle of intimacy and rejection. This time, however, she endured it all. For she would see him the next evening, Friday night, at dinner with Diana.

It was Evelyn's suggestion. She called up Diana on Tuesday and apologized for not staying to meet Patrick for that drink a couple of weeks ago.

'You know I'm dying to meet him. Let's have dinner together, the three of us,' Evelyn suggested. The effort to keep her voice steady was immense. It was only the distance of the telephone line that gave her the confidence to ask the question, her burning cheeks and shaking hands hidden from her friend.

'A lovely idea. I'll host at Number Six. Friday should work as he's coming over anyway that evening, after he finishes work. Why don't you come early and we can attempt to cook something.'

'I'll bring dessert.'

'From a fancy bakery, I assume.' There was no judgement in Diana's voice, just a fond amusement.

'I'll plate it onto my own dish and no one will ever know.'

They laughed, but Evelyn was gripped with emotion.

'It will be fun,' Diana said. 'Patrick will be delighted to meet you at last.'

'Does he know about me?'

'Of course. How could I not talk about my best friend?'

Evelyn thought of Diana's novel, the book by Carl Jung, the help she suspected Dr Daley was giving Diana in creating her character. She had to fight hard to suppress the creeping paranoia which a part of her knew was irrational. But the torture of her imagination was too strong, and she couldn't expel this terrible image of the two of them laughing at her as they analysed her anxieties, her neuroses, her pathetic need.

'Let's make it a surprise,' Evelyn said, suddenly worried that Dr Daley would not turn up if he knew she would be there. She had analysed it from every angle but still she could not understand what he was doing, whether he knew that her Diana and his Diana were the same. He must know, especially if Diana had spoken about her. There would be too many coincidences for him to ignore. Evelyn turned his motivations over and over in her mind: there were endless possibilities, none of them settling, none of them making sense. And yet there was one explanation that made her heart beat wildly, whenever Evelyn let herself imagine it. He was with Diana because of her. He felt the same way. He was in love with her. Her obsession was also his obsession and he had found a way to infiltrate her life. Somehow all of the ethical lines he was crossing didn't seem to matter, not if it brought them together.

'Tell him it'll just be the two of you and that you're making him beans on toast. And then we'll work together to put on a surprise feast.'

'That will be fun,' Diana agreed. 'Come over at four and we'll attempt to make this feast a success.'

For the rest of the day, Evelyn was lost in her thoughts, imagining how the dinner might play out. Dr Daley would reveal no hint of their connection until they were alone, a shared moment in the hallway perhaps. When they met on Monday for their next appointment, they would not be able to continue with the same cycle of desire, silence and confusion. All that power he wielded over her: finally she would have a way to balance the scales.

But when Diana rang her up that evening and Henry reached the telephone before Evelyn had the chance to peel off her marigolds, she could barely conceal her panic as the two of them talked, a friendly back-and-forth that gave Evelyn no opportunity to interrupt.

'I'd love to join you,' said Henry, turning to Evelyn and smiling widely as he held the telephone against his ear. 'Evelyn didn't tell me you had a new man.'

'Was that okay?' asked Diana a few moments later, when Henry had finally handed the receiver to Evelyn. 'I should have checked with you first.'

'Yes, of course,' she replied, too aware of Henry standing a few feet away. 'Was that why you called?'

'No, sorry,' said Diana. 'I only thought of it when Henry picked up the phone.'

When the call ended, Evelyn having muddled through Diana's question about a recipe for Friday, she turned away from Henry, rummaging unnecessarily among the cool shelves of the refrigerator. This changed everything, the dinner taking on a new and dangerous dimension she did not know if she was ready to face.

Perhaps, she tried to convince herself as she continued with the washing-up, there was no reason to be concerned. Henry would suspect nothing. And Dr Daley was unlikely to reveal the truth in front of him. It would be their secret, the tension building, silently, between them. It might even be easier, Henry at her side, a man to take the edge off her need.

The kitchen had exploded with ingredients, every work surface hidden beneath a mess of vegetable peelings and half-mixed sauces. Evelyn arrived just after four o'clock to find Diana unloading bags of groceries. They laughed when they saw each other. By chance, they were wearing nearly identical outfits: pullover pinafore jersey dresses that came to just above the knee. Both were dark blue, the skirt flaring out into pleats. Diana wore a white shirt underneath; Evelyn's arms were bare.

'Do you want me to change?' Diana said as she pulled

Evelyn into a hug. 'We look like sisters. Though you got the long legs gene.'

'Don't be silly,' she replied. 'Henry already thinks we're secretly sisters. And Patrick will have to get used to it.'

There was, in truth, something a little thrilling about dressing the same as Diana today. If it would serve to unsettle Dr Daley, then so much the better. She longed to find a way to break through that infuriating exterior, a man affected by nothing. How calm he was in the face of her discomfort: it made her feel like an experiment, a creature on which he tested his theories.

They had planned the meal together over the phone: cheddar and walnut on sticks, served with brown ale or Babycham; prawn cocktails to start; duck à l'orange with roast potatoes and carrots; the Black Forest gateau from a bakery in Mayfair, re-plated onto Evelyn's white and blue cake platter, a wedding gift from one of Henry's aunts.

Turning on the radio and kicking off their shoes, they started to prepare the meal. Cliff Richard and the Shadows dominated the radio, with both of the new singles 'The Next Time' and 'Bachelor Boy' playing, interspersed with Helen Shapiro's 'Walkin' Back to Happiness' and 'Love Me Do' by The Beatles.

'Where did you get all these ingredients from?' Evelyn said, rummaging through the medley of little packets on the counter. There were thyme sprigs, marjoram, parsley, coriander, cumin, black pepper.

'I thought I'd make an effort for once. It isn't every day

that I get to host a dinner party for my best friend and my boyfriend.'

Evelyn was in charge of peeling the vegetables while Diana prepared the duck. It was good to have something to do, a distraction from what was to come.

When the sounds of Cliff Richard singing 'Move It' came on, Diana threw down the orange rind she had been grating. She rocked her hips and lifted her arms above her head. 'Come on pretty baby,' she sang, pulling Evelyn into the middle of the kitchen. They loved rock-and-roll, and this song was one of the first of the genre to come out of Britain. Finally, in 1960, the American music they listened to in their teens had been embraced by British musicians. Holding hands, they swung each other around the room and Evelyn was seventeen again, bare feet, no make-up, dancing with her best friend in one of their bedrooms. She tried to keep her mind there, hiding from the reality of the evening. For a few minutes, it was just the two of them, no parties, no competition, no boys and their possessive gaze.

But it was difficult. That memory, the one that made her seethe with shame and self-disgust, was creeping forward. Kissing Edward Greenly at his birthday party. It was an insidious reminder that once again, tonight, Evelyn had let a man come between her and her best friend. Now that this was really happening, she was afraid. She did not know what drama was going to unfold when he walked through that door.

At six o'clock, they laid the kitchen table with Diana's

mismatched collection of crockery and cutlery. Evelyn folded cotton napkins under each plate and stuck white candles into old wine bottles.

'Let's light them now,' Diana said. 'They look too perfect like this.'

'You want romance for Patrick,' Evelyn said, thinking what it would be like for the four of them to be seated around the kitchen table, the candles flickering. 'I'll light them. You get us a drink. We both deserve it after all that cooking.' The kitchen was still a mess, but at least the food was in the oven and the starters prepared. Diana opened a bottle of Babycham.

'I'm oddly nervous,' she said as she handed a glass to Evelyn.

'Why? We're all going to get along just fine.'

'You're right.' Diana tried to wipe potato peelings into the rubbish bin, but scattered most of them at her feet instead. Evelyn helped her pick the pieces off the kitchen floor. As she knelt next to her, she could feel her own hands shaking.

It wasn't too late to stop. She could go home now, pretend to be unwell. She could cancel her appointments with Dr Daley and never see him again. It would be the hardest thing she'd ever done, but if she really tried, she knew she could do it.

'I guess I do know why I'm nervous,' Diana said as they settled onto two kitchen chairs, their glasses on the table in front of them. 'There is something I want to announce during the dinner. I need to check with Patrick when he gets here, to make sure he's okay with me telling you and Henry.'

'That sounds exciting. And intriguing. Can you tell me now?' Evelyn's chest was tightening painfully in the effort to be cheerful.

'I was going to wait until dinner, but it's true that I'll feel much more relaxed if I tell you. But you need to promise to pretend that it's the first time you've ever heard this, when I announce it at dinner.'

'Of course. What is it?'

'Well, I know it seems really sudden. We've only been dating for a couple of months. But Patrick asked me to marry him.'

'He did what?'

Diana did not seem to notice the aggression in Evelyn's words.

'It was on Monday evening. Not the most romantic day of the week for a proposal, but it felt right.'

Monday evening, not so many hours after he had asked Evelyn if she felt aroused in front of him. How was it possible to humiliate her, to strip away all her defences, and then to move on so quickly? How could he go from encouraging one woman to feel the intensity of all her desires, to proposing marriage to another?

'How did he do it?' Evelyn asked, her eyes fixed on the table setting in front of her. She wanted to take the knife and plunge it into her thigh.

'I met him at Baker Street station after school. It was a beautiful day on Monday, not cold at all. We went for a walk in Regent's Park.'

Slipping the knife off the table, Evelyn held it tightly in her lap. Diana didn't notice; she was too busy relighting one of the candles that was failing to build a flame. Evelyn pressed the edge into her palm, but it was too blunt to give her anything other than a dull, unsatisfying pain.

'And then?' she asked. It was torture, but she had to know.

'We walked to the rose garden. It was lovely there, an early rose starting to bloom and wild flowers in the grass. He couldn't have chosen a more perfect setting. He led me off the main path and into the tree line. And then he proposed. He said that meeting me had changed his life and that he loved me.'

'Was this before or after you had sex?'

'What do you mean?' Diana looked at her strangely; there was no denying the hostility in Evelyn's voice this time.

'Did you have sex in Regent's Park?'

'God, no. Of course not. Can you imagine? We're not animals. No, we went back to his flat on Blandford Street in Marylebone. He made me a gin martini. And then, yes, we had sex.'

'He doesn't love you.'

'Excuse me?'

Evelyn could feel her heart beating fast, a pounding ache in her chest that made her feel that she might explode. But she continued. It was too late to stop.

'I'm really sorry, Diana. This is going to be a shock, and I really didn't want to have to tell you this way. But Patrick isn't who you think he is.'

'You're not making any sense. What do you know of Patrick?'

'I know him as Dr Daley. He's my psychotherapist.'

'No, he isn't. Don't be ridiculous. Surely I'd know if he was. And you never told me you were seeing a psychotherapist.'

'I didn't tell you because I didn't want you to know that I needed professional help. And then the appointments became very intense and strange. And he knows about you. He started seeing you after I told him about you.'

'What is that supposed to mean?'

'It means that the only reason he is with you is because of me. I don't understand it myself; I don't know why he is doing this. But I have these feelings for him, very strong feelings, which he encourages and asks me to tell him such intimate details.'

'You're in love with him?'

'I don't know. Maybe. I desire him, and I think he desires me too.'

'You think he desires you? Has he told you that he does?'

'It's not that simple. He's my doctor. He isn't allowed to tell me what he thinks about me. But he makes it clear, from the questions he asks me and the signals he gives, that he is interested in me.'

'As a patient, obviously. You're paying him to be interested in you. Evie, you know not everyone is going to fall in love with you? Do you think it's impossible for a man not to find you attractive?'

'That's a cruel thing to say, Diana. Of course I don't think everyone finds me attractive.'

'So why do you think Patrick can't resist you?'

'It's not that. It's deliberate; he's done this to me.'

'How?'

'He brings everything back to him and how I feel about him. After I finally managed to tell him my feelings about him, he suggested we increase the number of appointments. And now, he is using his relationship with you to drive me further and further into this obsession. He found you because I told him about you. His proposal is a replica of a fantasy I explained to him where the two of us go for a walk in Regent's Park.'

'Why would he do that?'

'I don't know. I think about it endlessly, and I don't understand it. Sometimes I think maybe I am insane, that I'm making this all up. But I know I'm not crazy. Maybe he simply enjoys the power he has over me; or maybe he is attracted to me.'

Diana pushed her chair away and stood. Her fingers were pressed white into the table and she leant forward towards Evelyn.

'I should have predicted you'd do this, Evie. It's always the same, isn't it? You have to be the most loved, the most beautiful, the most desirable. You did this to me when we were teenagers, with Edward Greenly. I pushed it out of my mind then; our friendship was more important than a boy.

There have been other times, too, when a man I'm interested in suddenly shifts his attention to you, unable to resist your flirtation. It's like you have to have everyone for yourself. But this time I won't let you hurt me. Can you not allow me to be the one who is desired for once? What was it? You couldn't cope with the way I spoke about Patrick, how exciting it was, how much I liked him? You had to sabotage it, make him want you instead.'

She was shaking her head, and Evelyn could barely look at her. It was mortifying to see the lines of disappointment imprinted between Diana's eyes. Evelyn pressed the edge of the knife harder into her hand beneath the table.

'I don't know what to believe anymore. Did you seek him out as your psychotherapist after I had told you about him?'

'No. That's ridiculous. You started seeing him after I did.'

'Don't tell me what's ridiculous.'

Diana pulled herself up, her hands flying to her neck as she walked away from the table. Evelyn had never seen her so upset. 'You need to go. We obviously can't have this dinner party.'

'Diana, please. I am telling you this for your own good. I don't want you to get hurt.'

'No, you're the one who is hurting me. Just get out. Now.'

Evelyn stood, the knife still gripped in her hand. When Diana saw it, she took a step back, pressing herself into the kitchen counter.

'Please don't do this, Diana. I can't lose you.'

'Put the knife down, Evie.'

She looked down at her hands. The knife was blunt, but she'd pressed it into her palm, hard enough to leave a deep purple indentation. Placing the knife back onto the table, she folded her arms.

'Did you think I was going to hurt you?'

'I don't know what to think anymore. Just go, please.'

'I'm going. But ask Dr Daley why he chose to propose in the rose garden in Regent's Park.'

'It's not an unusual place to propose, Evelyn. You don't get to claim every romantic spot in London for yourself.'

'You don't understand. He did this deliberately.'

Diana said nothing. There was such fury in her eyes and for a moment Evelyn wished she could take it all back. But more than that, she felt a fury of her own. Diana did not believe her. Her best friend, the girl who had shared her life and knew every detail of her past, had decided to put a man before her. Worse than that, Diana had told her a brutal truth. She had revealed exactly how she felt about their friendship. Evelyn had been deluded to think that Diana had ever forgiven her for the past.

Out on the street, night had fallen fast. She knelt, pulling the heels of her shoes on properly. Henry would be here soon, as would Patrick. She put her coat and bag on the ground next to her and tried to find calm; despite the cold, she was sweating.

Waiting for Henry here was best; she did not want Diana to come up with an unconvincing excuse. Evelyn should be the one to see him first.

The Model Patient

As she stood, she saw a man walking towards her, his face and figure in shadow. Henry or Dr Daley; she couldn't decide which man she hoped would emerge out of the dark.

Dr Daley. Instinctively, she pressed herself back against the wall, but it was useless. There was no avoiding him.

She needed to know why he was doing this, why he insisted on keeping her in this place of terrible uncertainty. It was cruel, to taunt her with his affection, withdrawing it when she asked him directly how he felt. And now the Regent's Park proposal. There was no denying the similarity to her fantasy. He had made it come alive with Diana, knowing that she'd find out. He was trying to drive her mad.

'Dr Daley.' They were outside the door to Diana's building. The light from a streetlamp reached them in a faint glow, and Evelyn could see the look of surprise on his face. Diana had not told him she would be there after all.

'Evelyn, what are you doing here?'

'You'll have to ask Diana.'

He took a step towards her, his hand finding her arm.

'What's going on, Evelyn? Are you all right?'

'Don't you think it's too late to be asking me that question, Patrick? Or do I still need to call you Dr Daley, the great doctor who humiliates me again and again? Why are you doing this to me?'

'I'm not doing anything to you, Evelyn. You bring your feelings about me to the appointments. I help you understand them.'

'Do you believe that? Do you really take no responsibility for how you've made me feel?'

'Tell me how I've made you feel.'

'I've told you a hundred times. All we do is talk, you pushing me further and further, refusing to let me get over you.'

Still he held her arm and she could feel the pressure of his hand tightening. Her arms were bare, her coat on the ground next to her. Taking a step towards him, she lifted her face, closing the gap between them. He looked into her eyes and she could feel the intensity of his gaze.

She kissed him. For the briefest moment, she felt his lips soften. His hand rose up the length of her arm and around to between her shoulder blades. Evelyn wanted the moment to last for ever.

But then it was over and he was pulling away.

Evelyn couldn't stop shaking. It was too much, the way he was looking at her, that pity she could not endure. She picked up her bag and coat and started to run.

At the corner of the King's Road and Markham Street, she saw Henry coming towards her. She ran to him, flinging her arms around his neck. As he returned her embrace, she could feel the beat of his chest against her ear.

'What's going on?' His voice was gentle, and she could sense her tears threatening to spill. It was impossible to explain to him how she was feeling. There was no choice but to pull herself together, to hide away the pain.

'Diana and I had an argument. It was stupid, but it's thrown me a little.'

The Model Patient

'What was it about?'

'It was nothing really, just something about the past.'

'Do you want to talk about it?' he said, taking her arm as they started to walk.

'I don't think so, if that's okay with you. I'll call her tomorrow and I'm sure we'll forget all about it. Sorry to ruin the evening.'

'You haven't ruined anything, Evie. And I'm sorry about the argument. It's not like you and Diana to argue. Home or a restaurant?'

'Home, I think. Let's walk back.'

Evelyn went straight to bed when they got home. As Henry kissed her goodnight, it took an immense effort to stop herself from changing that kiss into a different sort of embrace. But she did not dare. There was too much shame in knowing where her mind would fly.

She woke early, the silver light spilling through the curtains. Her dreams had been feverish and wild, and she was exhausted. Sitting up, she felt an ache in her back, as though she'd spent the night in twisted contortions. Slowly, she swung her feet around and placed them against the ground. It was a shock to feel a cold movement of paper beneath her feet. She looked down, confused at what was there on the floor of her bedroom.

Her sketchbook. It was open to a double page, packed with drawings. Barely any white was visible. She knelt, her fingers running along the lines of the sketches. A pencil rested across the middle of the page and her sharpening knife was poking out from underneath. Pencil shavings were scattered across the rug.

Evelyn did not remember any of this. She did not remember waking, fetching her sketchbook from downstairs, returning to her bedroom, sharpening the pencil, covering the page with these terrifying sketches. A drawing of a necklace wound around the page: it was a serpent, its huge jaw open. It seemed to seethe and hiss from the crease at the centre of the page. A grotesque mermaid, her hair falling in long plaits, sat astride its scales, and a bracelet in the shape of a lizard circled its coils. A tree grew out of the base of the page, its branches piercing through the paper. She must have pressed so hard, the strokes of the pencil ripping the page.

If the drawings had been more precise, these would be interesting designs, she thought as she peered at them more closely. She could imagine recreating the tree into an upper arm cuff, the branches winding around the bicep in delicate silver strands. But this was a mess, as though she had drawn with her eyes closed, letting the compulsions of her hand move the pencil.

What scared her the most were the three smears of blood that stained the page. They looked like uneven brush-strokes, as though she had tried to hide the sketches below a blood-red paint.

There was a dull pain in her hand, and she turned over her palm to look. The purple mark from where she had pressed

The Model Patient

the blunt knife into her hand last night had deepened into a bruise.

But there was more. Sliced through the middle of the bruise was a cut, the edges of the wound closed but bloodied. As she stared at it, the pain deepened.

She climbed back into bed. Henry stirred and she wrapped her arms around him. This time, when he kissed her, she did not hold back.

CHAPTER 24

Evelyn was back in Dr Daley's consulting room and from the way he was looking at her, it was as though nothing had changed. He gave no indication at all that just three nights previously she had kissed him outside Number Six, that she knew about him and Diana, that their relationship as patient and psychotherapist was irretrievably broken. Part of her knew that there was a madness in returning here again. But how could she stay away when there was so much unresolved between them?

He refused to help her. Instead, he fixed his gaze more firmly and pressed his hands together in his lap. His jacket was a deep salmon pink, a floral shirt beneath. It was not unlike the colourful outfits she had seen in the windows of Carnaby Street, formality destabilized in colour.

'I was worried you might not be here today,' she said at last.

'What do you mean by that? Where would I be?'

'I imagined that Miss Simmons would have a message for

me, instructing me to reschedule my appointments with a different psychotherapist.'

'Why would I do that?'

She sighed in exasperation. It was obvious why he might do that, and she should not have to say the words. He refused to make this easy for her.

'Because of Friday night, of course.'

'Tell me what happened on Friday night which suggests to you that I might want to end our appointments together.'

'I kissed you. And Diana knows you are my therapist. How is it possible for us to continue as we were before?'

'Tell me about this kiss?'

She looked up at him, a sharp pain stabbing through her chest. The way he asked that question, it was as though he was humouring her, a deluded patient making up a fantasy, like Regent's Park, like the black paisley jacket.

'You know about the kiss. I don't need to go through it all again.'

'It would be helpful, I think, for us to explore together what you think happened, so we can discuss why you are feeling anxious about the possibility of me stopping the treatment.'

'Fine. If that is what you want. But please, don't make me feel as though I'm crazy. I can't bear it.'

'It is not my intention to make you feel as though you're crazy.'

'So if I do feel crazy, that's my fault too? You've contributed nothing to the way I feel?'

'That is not what I said.'

'No, that's not what you said. But in framing it this way, that how I feel is purely a result of my own delusions, you are absenting yourself from any responsibility. It is all my problem.'

He said nothing, and his silence made her feel unhinged.

'I will explain why I'm feeling this way,' she said at last. 'I want you to understand.'

She tried to collect herself, remembering all the things she wanted to say, how she'd rehearsed repeatedly all weekend, her thoughts trying to find order in words. Her grip on reality, she told herself, was not broken.

'I want to connect with you. I want to find a true and meaningful connection, where you can support me and help to contain me while I discover why I am having all these problems in my marriage and my new life. I'm obviously struggling to understand who I am without my work, but even that career came out of my relationship with Mr Hardy. So it's painful to bring up all these difficulties, especially when my feelings about you add a whole other layer of challenge that I resent but also find addictive and compelling. Occasionally, I feel that we've found that connection, the kiss for example, how it felt when you didn't pull away, not immediately anyway, how your hand moved around to between my shoulders.'

She paused, breathing deeply. Her body was all tension, a pressure deep within her skin. She was afraid of what would happen if she let go.

The Model Patient

'But then there is Diana. She's my best friend and I don't understand why you are with her. If I let myself think that it's because you want to be closer to me, even in this awful way where you seek out my friend and start a relationship with her, then I sound entirely self-absorbed.' She shook her head, remembering back to the kitchen, how Diana's words had been a dagger to her heart. 'Diana found a way to hurt me when she said that I must think I'm irresistible to all men. I don't think that; I don't think that at all.'

'What do you think?'

'I think some men do find me attractive, yes. But the reason I place so much focus on being attractive is because it's the only way I know how to be powerful and successful and have value. It's been ingrained in me ever since I was a child. And therefore, with you, to not know for sure what you think of me, it's frightening. You've taken away my power, and given it all to yourself. You encourage me to feel physical desire, the fantasies, the questions you ask me about whether I am aroused in front of you: it humiliates me. Your power is in your silence after making me say so much, how you withhold yourself. No wonder I want to think that your relationship with Diana is because of me. It is the only way to stop myself from going mad.'

'You must think, therefore, that I have pursued your best friend in order to play some cruel game. You think I'm sadistic, deliberately trying to evoke these painful feelings in you.'

'I suppose I do, yes.'

'And you haven't considered that there could be something else going on here?'

'Of course I have. Every possibility has circled around my head, over and over. Can you please just tell me what is going on.'

'Well, what I think is that you are so terrified of uncovering the painful memories of your past that you fixate instead on the present. On me and on Diana. This is, of course, still painful for you, but it's a different sort of pain from the fear you have of looking too closely at what cannot be changed.'

'So you think I'm making this up?'

'I didn't say that. I do, however, think we mustn't miss this opportunity to discuss why you have interpreted a relationship between myself and Diana to be a way to manipulate you.'

Evelyn could feel the rage building inside her. She wanted to kill him. He refused to answer her questions, instead turning everything back to her and her problems. She closed her eyes, her hands gripping the edge of the cushions. The leather creaked beneath her and suddenly she was back there again, at Winter Manor. Mr Hardy was lowering himself down next to her, the sofa sinking and her body falling against his shoulder.

Opening her eyes, she could see Dr Daley watching her intently. He knew what was happening, how he had taken her back to the past. Clenching her fists, she tried to resist. If she went back there, she was giving into him. She was letting Dr Daley win; she was admitting that it was her past, her problems, that were causing the fracture between them. But she had no choice. The memory was too strong.

'It was the week before I moved to London with Diana. I wanted to end it with Mr Hardy, so that I could move to the city and start afresh. I was nineteen and old enough, at last, to know for certain that his influence was dangerous. Or at least I thought I did before I sat down on the sofa with him that Sunday afternoon, just the two of us in his beautiful empty home. There was a photograph of me on the wall, an advertisement hidden among five other photographs of different women from campaigns he had organized. His children rarely visited him, but I suppose, when they did, that photograph would have simply looked like part of a collection of anonymous models, not the girl who had led to the end of their parents' marriage. But for me, it was so much more than that. Mr Hardy placed me on his wall, while at the same time making it clear that I understood my own fragility. The career I loved could be taken away from me at any moment.

'Diana and I had spoken about it, planning together everything I was going say. I had finally told her the truth, though I think she had already suspected a lot of what had been happening.'

'Why didn't she say anything to your parents or her own parents if she suspected what was happening?'

'I don't know. Perhaps she didn't want to believe it was true. And she must have been able to tell I didn't want to talk about it. I was too ashamed.'

'Perhaps you didn't want Mr Hardy's attention to disappear.'

Evelyn's tone hardened. 'I think we've established now that I was drawn to the way he made me feel successful and special. But he did that to make himself feel powerful. You must see that.'

'Is that what you think I am doing? I'm encouraging you to explore your feelings for me to make myself feel powerful?'

'Yes. I think you are probably doing that. Your manipulation of me is narcissistic.'

He did not even flinch. It was terrifying how easily he could tolerate her anger. She continued, desperate to make him understand. 'I resent the way you think my reaction to you is because of what happened with Mr Hardy. It allows you to take no responsibility, as though you are simply a blank slate onto which I paint my issues. But there has to be more to it than that.'

He said nothing, the silent power he had to make her feel so uncertain growing once again. She needed to explain, to finish her story, so that he would understand.

'I told Mr Hardy that I wanted to end our relationship. I was moving to London and I needed to carve out my own career without his influence.'

'And did he accept that?'

'He twisted it. He told me that I'd never relied on him or needed him for my career. I was deluded if I thought that it was only thanks to him that I'd been successful. He'd taken my hand in his, kissed it like he was some benevolent grandfather figure, and told me that I was too beautiful to need him. It hurt him to think that our relationship was so transactional. Wasn't I enjoying my time with him, he asked me. Had I only accepted his love and his gifts because I wanted something from him?

'In those questions, he had found a way to hurt me but also confuse me. This was suddenly all my fault, that I was this repulsive and manipulative woman who had pursued him for her own gain. But that wasn't true. It is frustrating now to see how easily I fell for his tricks. Back then I was still too young and insecure to trust myself. So, when he kissed me, I let him do whatever he wanted.'

'What did you let him do?'

'I let him punish me. He said I had hurt him and that I needed to show him I was sorry. That I loved him.'

'How did he punish you?'

Evelyn shook her head. 'It's not necessary for me to tell you all the details of this. It will only upset me more.'

'Was it like your fantasy? The one in which I'm wearing the black jacket. Where I hit you with my belt.'

Evelyn looked away, a pain surging down her body. In the silence that followed all she could do was slowly return his gaze and nod, once. He held her there until, at last, he started to speak.

'It's interesting that you remembered a photograph on the wall, you with five other models. You said that his children wouldn't realize that you, in the photograph, were the girl who ended their parents' marriage. Do you blame yourself for ending their marriage?'

'No. I don't blame myself. It wasn't my fault. But I sometimes think about his wife and their youngest child, how sad it must have been for them to leave their home. I got the impression from photographs around the house that Mr Hardy and his son were once close, at least in a superficial way. All the photographs seemed to be from years earlier, when his son was a young boy. They played sport together, went fishing, trekked in the mountains. In the photographs, the two of them were always doing something impressive, catching a gigantic fish or reaching the peak of a mountain. I think his son idolized him. It must have been hard when he learnt the truth about his father.'

'Did you ever meet him?'

'Who?'

'Mr Hardy's son.'

'No, I don't think so. I saw him a few times when I was fourteen, coming and going in the driveway. But we never spoke.'

Evelyn did not want to think about Mr Hardy's wife and children. Their loss was a painful reminder of all those years she had given to Mr Hardy, her own loss bound inextricably to theirs.

A muffled sound of voices from the hallway broke into the room and Dr Daley looked up at the clock.

'We need to finish now. I'll see you on Thursday?'

The same routine, the same cycle. What was the point, she thought, of sharing these most intimate and painful memories if he refused to hold her together once she was undone?

The Model Patient

As she left his consulting room, Evelyn realized that he had avoided every one of her questions. She could not go home, not with this much rage inside her, not to her empty house, the clean shine of her kitchen, the laundry she needed to sort and pack away, her hollow evening of waiting for Henry to return from work.

Turning north, she walked quickly to Regent's Park. It was a cool March day, the frost and ice finally melted away, and she needed to be outside. She walked fast, but even that was not enough. Evelyn knew she needed more, a physical edge to take away the pain in her heart. Picking up her pace, she started to run.

By the time she reached the rose garden, she was out of breath, her hair falling around her face, sweat beading across her brow. It was quiet in the garden, just a mother and her two young children eating a packed lunch on one of the benches. She slowed her pace and took in the scene around her.

The cold winter had proven too brutal for most of the rose bushes. It was a shock to see each plant, these scrawling and barren branches that stood in shivering surrender. Evelyn could not imagine that they might eventually sprout leaves, buds, the bloom of flowers. Some sorrowful wild flowers grew in sparse groups at the edges of the garden, but not at all in the beautiful abundance she had imagined. She turned around, trying to see the early rose Diana had mentioned when she'd described the proposal. But there was nothing.

Sinking down to the ground, Evelyn pressed her hands

into the soil of the flower bed. She slowed her breathing, rooted herself into the dirt, and closed her eyes. She longed to feel calm, to expel the demonic creep beneath her skin. It crawled, trapped inside her, a monster that refused to settle.

When she stood, a thorny rose branch seemed to reach for her, tangling itself in her hair. As she pulled away, extracting herself from its grip, a thorn dug hard into her wrist. She let it run up her arm, leaving a long scratch. A bead of blood sprang out of her skin, the most beautiful jewel she had ever seen.

CHAPTER 25

Evelyn understood that Diana did not want to see her. But if they didn't talk soon, Evelyn knew that the edges of her reality would slip further and further into chaos. Of all the possible scenarios she imagined, the one she did not predict was that Diana would be waiting for her outside her house when she finally arrived home on Monday afternoon.

'We need to talk,' Diana said when Evelyn reached her.

'I agree. I'm happy to see you here.' Evelyn wanted to cry. She wanted to embrace her friend, and for this mess to go away, for the two of them to start again and return to the past, before it had all gone terribly wrong. But the coldness of Diana's voice warned her not to try to touch her.

'Let's go inside. You need to explain to me what's going on.'

Evelyn opened the door and followed Diana inside. There was a determination to her friend that scared her, as though Diana was bracing herself for a fight.

As soon as they were in the kitchen, Diana started talking. Her voice was hard.

'I stayed at Patrick's flat last night.'

Evelyn shook her head. She did not want to hear this, not now. It was cruel for Diana to speak this way.

'You need to hear this. And you need to explain.'

'Explain what? You're the one who should be explaining it all to me.'

Diana ignored her, instead snapping open her handbag and pulling out an envelope.

'I found this in Patrick's desk.'

Evelyn took a step forward, holding out her hand. She had no idea what was inside the envelope and there was no time to think, to imagine, to prepare. Unfolding the flap of the envelope, she reached inside and pulled out a single photograph. It was face down, the image hidden from her, but she knew exactly what this was.

Her childish handwriting was scrawled across the back. 'From Evelyn.' And signed with a kiss.

She turned over the photograph. There she was, sixteen years old, though in the photograph she could have been much older. Winter Manor was in the background, the setting for an automobile advertisement. She was perched on the bonnet of an open-top car, her head thrown back and her blonde hair catching the sunlight. There was a man in the driving seat, his arm resting on the steering wheel: she did not remember his name, and had never seen him again after that photoshoot.

It was summer in the photograph, and the sun was hitting her at a low angle, all golden and warm. She felt it all again.

The Model Patient

Beneath her, the metal of the car was hot. She had tried to sit on as much of her dress as possible, protecting her legs from the heat of the steel. The dress she had been given was full and billowing, blue and white cotton with an A-line skirt and a straight neck that ran across to sleeveless arms. Mr Hardy was there, watching from the deckchairs laid out on the grass, along with some men from the advertising agency hired to create the advert.

She remembered how, part-way through the shoot, Mr Hardy had stood and walked over to the photographer. He said something to him, all the time looking directly at her. He wasn't smiling, and it made her afraid that she was getting it all wrong.

The photographer nodded and then came up to her. Without any warning, he pulled the back of her skirt out from under her legs, the cotton fabric bunching up towards her waist. He pushed it up higher, his hands on her thigh as he rearranged the dress. She tried not to react, not to flinch as he prepared her for the shoot, not to reveal how hot the car's surface burnt against the back of her thigh. But she could see Mr Hardy watching, a smile on his face.

'How did you get this?' she asked Diana, her hands shaking as she held the photograph. 'It looks like an original.'

They hadn't ended up using this one for the advertisement. She didn't see the finished photograph until it was already published, several months later; Mr Hardy had shown it to her in a men's magazine when he came to visit her parents one afternoon. It was painful to remember how her mother had delighted in the advertisement, complimenting Evelyn on her smile, Mr Hardy on the beautiful roses flowering in the background, his estate shown off at its best. In the photograph they had chosen, she was seated inside the car, smiling at her partner, his arm draped around her shoulders.

She did not understand how Diana could have found this photograph. The only people who might possibly own a signed photograph such as this were herself, her parents, Mr Hardy, or someone from the advertising agency. Though the more she thought about it, there were other possibilities. Mr Hardy could have given it to anyone, his friends and colleagues, advertising agencies, retailers looking to find a model. And Diana. She, too, might have a copy. Evelyn had often left photographs of herself around the flat, mock-ups for advertisements or extra copies she used in her portfolio.

'I told you. It was in Patrick's desk. When he was in the bathroom this morning, I decided I needed to know for sure whether he was your psychologist. I asked him about it, but he said he couldn't discuss his patients. If it was a problem for me, he said, then I'd need to talk to you.'

'It's irritating, isn't it,' Evelyn said, a small smile hovering at her lips, 'his refusal to answer questions directly.' But beneath her smile, she was falling apart. Dr Daley had a photograph of her, the beautiful version of who she was, the attractive, polished professional. She could remember every moment of that conversation with him many weeks ago, how he'd taunted her with his hypothetical attention, asking her if she'd like him to look at photographs of her, drawing out her desire and then giving her nothing. And all that time, he possessed this photograph, hidden in his desk, an erotic secret.

Diana shrugged. 'I haven't felt that. It makes sense that he can't talk about his patients. He didn't even confirm that you were his patient.'

'I am his patient.'

'Okay, I do believe you about that.' Diana folded her arms, the hardness to her voice returning. 'While he was in the bathroom, I looked in his desk. I had no idea what I was looking for. Maybe his notes or an appointment diary, but he must keep all that at his clinic. I found this inside an envelope. There was nothing else; just this.' She took a step towards Evelyn. 'You gave this to him, didn't you?'

'No. Of course I didn't. I have never given him anything.' But as Evelyn said the words, she wondered why she hadn't. Rather, it was strangely reassuring, how she had kept some semblance of control, never desperately thrusting photographs towards him. The thought of it made her shudder with embarrassment.

'How can I believe that?' Diana said. 'You must have given him this. And he accepted it. What's going on between you?'

'I didn't give this to him. I don't know how he has it. Maybe he found it himself. It can't be impossible to find photographs of models.'

'You're saying he went on some secret hunt for a photograph of you? Why would he do that?'

'I don't know. I don't know anything.'

'Evelyn, please tell me the truth. You gave him this photograph.'

'I don't know what to tell you, Diana. Can't you see this isn't right? He only started seeing you once I told him about you. I know it sounds crazy, but that's the truth. It must be.'

'How can I believe that? He's a doctor, a psychologist. And you. Well you're the one who needs help. You're unwell. You're his patient. Your sense of reality is completely warped.'

'That's cruel, Diana. Are you saying I'm insane?'

'I'm saying that you're literally seeing this man because you're mentally unwell. How am I supposed to believe you over him?'

'Because I'm your best friend. Because we've known each other our whole lives. How can you do this to me?'

'I'm not doing anything to you, Evie. That's your problem. You think everyone is trying to manipulate you, to hurt you. But you are the one who needs to take responsibility here, rather than shifting the blame onto others. Just for once, can't you accept that maybe you are the problem.'

Evelyn stared at her. The kitchen walls seemed to pulse dangerously, the fabric of reality breaking. She blinked slowly, desperate to find control, but her vision was unsteady, the space around her changing. Everything was wrong, the window too large, the tiles on the wall shrinking, the table legs swelling into grotesque trunks. She knew what was happening. Doubt, that treacherous creep of uncertainty: it was destroying her.

Perhaps Diana was right; maybe she was the problem. It was terrible how quickly her mind could shift, all certainty she had been feeling disappearing fast.

'You need to leave Patrick alone,' Diana was saying, but Evelyn could barely hear her. 'I don't want to fight with you, Evie. I really don't. But until you've stopped seeing Patrick, then we can't be friends.'

Diana walked to the kitchen door before turning back to Evelyn. 'Let me know once you've found a new psychotherapist. And then we can talk.'

It was only once the front door had slammed shut and Evelyn had walked, numb, to the hallway, that she realized she was still holding the photograph. She looked down at her 16-year-old face, her smile, her golden hair, the warm sunlight shining on the bonnet of the car. There was no hint of the anxious teenager hiding beneath the gloss and the glamour.

She pressed the photograph to her chest. How dangerous it had been to conceal her vulnerabilities from everyone she loved, hiding her fears beneath a beautiful mask. The mask she thought was protecting her had been her undoing all along.

She could not accept Diana's ultimatum. Dr Daley needed to take responsibility for the way he had made her feel and Evelyn would do whatever it took to break him.

CHAPTER 26

'Where did you get this?'

Evelyn asked him the question the moment they walked into his consulting room. She refused to wait until she had taken her usual seat, the silence had descended, her anxiety had risen. Today was going to be different.

She watched him carefully, trying to ignore the swelling sickness in the base of her stomach. Handing him the photograph was a declaration of war, her first move on a complicated chess board that he seemed determined to avoid. Maybe he wouldn't make a move; but at least he might step onto the board. This was her opportunity to break down his defences, to reveal the human beneath his cold, calm exterior.

She'd rehearsed endlessly over the past few days to make sure she was prepared. For he was an expert, of course, and she knew he'd be deploying every fortification he possessed to resist her.

'Take a seat,' he said, smiling benevolently. She seethed as she obeyed him, never letting her eyes leave his face.

'Why don't you tell me what this is and where you found it?'

'No, Dr Daley. We're not doing it like that. I refuse to fall for this again.'

'Do you think I'm trying to trick you?' he said, the same calm tone, no sense at all that he was angry with her. 'As I've said before, I have no intention to manipulate you or deceive you. I would like us to discuss the significance of this photograph for you.'

'Diana found it. In your desk.'

Evelyn could feel the heat rising in her skin, an uncomfortable burn beneath her shirt. Even though she had no choice, to bring Diana into this felt like a betrayal. But he must already know, she decided, hardening her resolve. Diana must have asked him about the photograph by now.

'Is that what she told you?' he said, his head tilted.

'Yes. She told me this photograph was in your desk. She accused me of giving it to you and wouldn't believe me when I denied it.'

'Why do you think she didn't believe you?'

'Because she thinks I'm unstable. You're the doctor and I'm the patient.' Evelyn's voice was climbing and she hated the sound. Already, he was taking her in a direction that she knew would only lead to her frustration and his protection. He would reveal nothing of himself.

'Perhaps the reason this photograph, and all the circumstances surrounding it, has had such a profound effect on you is because of our conversation a few weeks ago. We talked about how appealing it was for you to imagine me looking at photographs of you from magazines and advertisements.'

'Yes. Of course that has significance here. But that's not relevant to our discussion right now. I am not interested in why, on a psychological level, this has affected me. I am interested in why you have this photograph. Why was it in your desk? And why are you with Diana?'

He smiled again and nodded. 'It comes back to this question of my relationship with Diana, your assumption that I am trying to hurt you.'

'Please can we focus on what I am asking you. You know it drives me crazy when you refuse to answer my questions. Whether your intention is to hurt me or not, you must see why this is so strange to me. I don't think it is irrational of me to ask these questions.'

'I can see that this has upset you. And I am sorry for that. But the photograph you have just handed to me now . . . this is the first time I have ever seen it.'

'That can't be true.'

He looked down at the photograph again and there was an attentive focus in his gaze, as though he was thinking deeply. Eventually he spoke, shifting his focus to the real Evelyn seated in front of him, not the 16-year-old girl smiling as she perched on the bonnet of a car.

'Is it possible, Evelyn, that Diana did not find this photograph in my desk?'

'Are you suggesting that she is making this up?'

'No, I'm considering that we should discuss how this

might fit into a pattern. You have spoken about your desire for me to look at photographs of you; there is our Regent's Park afternoon; you want me to say things to you that will make you feel loved. This, the photograph, is another method by which you have created a tangible connection between us. It is interesting that you cannot allow yourself to know that I care for you. You need more, these narratives, specific stories and fantasies, words that I might say to you, to feel that you are loved.'

His words were distracting her, weakening her. She tried to resist, but it was too hard to block the pathways of her mind. She thought of her parents, how she spent her childhood searching for evidence of their love, the pain she felt when she realized how superfluous she was to their relationship; how they closed their eyes to Mr Hardy's abuse, happily transferring the responsibility for loving their child onto another man; how she ran, open arms, towards the affections of others, trapping herself in the longing to be loved, desired, recognized. Dr Daley had refused again and again to give her the evidence she needed. Instead he kept her in a place of doubt and suggestion, sending her into turmoil every time he drew her close and then pushed her away.

He was still holding the photograph. That, at least, was not a delusion. To see the way his fingers touched the edges of the photographic card, a real image, a real object, it brought her back to the present.

'I won't let you do this to me,' she said. 'I am not making

this up. Diana found the photograph in your desk, and you need to explain why it was there.'

It was the tiniest of exhalations, but Evelyn had seen it: a sigh, an acceptance that this time he was going to need to change his method.

'I think Diana was mistaken,' he said. 'The photograph must belong to her. Maybe it was inside one of the books that she lent me, and it fell out. I must have packed it away without realizing what it was.'

Evelyn did not believe him. But it did not matter, because this felt like a victory. For the first time, he had revealed a fact about his life, giving away a detail that made him, even in the smallest way, as human as she was. He had admitted to a relationship with Diana; he had acknowledged that the photograph could have been in his flat; he had allowed her to know that she was not the problem. It was infuriating that he did this by blaming Diana, but at least, for once, it was not because of Evelyn and her delusions.

She was about to speak, to fight him further, but she stopped herself. A coldness had driven its way into the space between them. He was not looking at her, the photograph discarded on the coffee table to his side, and she could sense a hardness in his jaw. It was regret, she decided, how he resented his self-disclosure, how he wanted to turn back time and redirect the conversation: he wanted to regain his power.

It was an opportunity she could not waste. While every part of her longed to stay, to find a way to make him love her, to break him, to make him care, this was her chance to take control.

There were twenty minutes left of the appointment. Standing, she gathered her coat and bag into her arms.

'I'm leaving,' she said.

He looked up at her, the faintest shadow of surprise written across his brow. 'We still have time,' he said. 'We can talk about this more.'

'I don't think so. You're obviously not going to find the courage to tell me the truth.'

He stood and walked to the door. It was maddening how he refused to fight with her.

'Will I see you next week?' he said.

She wanted so much to be able to deny him, to say no, to forget about him, to move on with her life, with Diana, with Henry. There would be a satisfaction in walking away. But she knew she could not do it. As she looked at him, she imagined what it would be like to say goodbye, to never see him again.

'Yes, I'll see you next week.'

Once she was outside, she wanted nothing more than to turn around and run back to him. Those twenty minutes were hers. She had given them up. With an immense effort, she started walking away from the clinic.

Reaching the end of Upper Wimpole Street, she was forced to pause. Every step was becoming an ordeal, as though her body was refusing to obey her will. She had felt strange all day, but this was different, a deep pain surging at the base of her stomach. It was a cool day, but she was sweating inside her coat, and she felt a loosening within her. Stopping at the corner of the road, she leant against the black railings that enclosed the houses, waiting for the pain to subside. Trying to control her breathing and calm the tension swelling inside her stomach, she pressed her hands around the railings.

It felt as though her body was falling apart, disconnecting itself from within. She shifted her weight, trying to work out the source of the pain. Her head was light and there was a strange wetness between her legs, a frightening warmth inside her underwear. The street was quiet, no one to see as she reached down, inside her coat, beneath her skirt.

When she pulled out her hand, her body crumpled. Her fingers were covered in blood. She grabbed onto the railings once again, fear shocking through her. She needed to get home and yet there was no taxi in sight. Evelyn tried to stay calm, but she knew this wasn't her menstruation. This was something else entirely.

She couldn't bear it, the shame of her body treating her this way, punishing her, humiliating her. All she wanted was to sink into the earth and hide.

Another wave of pain lurched through her and she cried out. If she could just make it home, she would be all right. Reaching out her hand into the road, she prayed for a taxi to appear around the corner. But there was nothing, just a man on a bicycle who swerved away from her, calling out angrily as he pedalled away.

The Model Patient

Evelyn felt a shock cut through her, like a knife penetrating from behind. Sinking down onto the pavement, she tried to slow her breathing. If she closed her eyes for a moment, she'd find the strength to walk, she thought. There would be taxis on another road.

As her body fell forward, her palms slamming hard into the pavement, her eyes flicked open to see the blur of red patent leather shoes moving fast towards her. Evelyn tried to lift her gaze, to focus on the woman's face, but her vision was blurred, a white haze closing around her. All she could think as she fell into unconsciousness was that maybe Dr Daley had sent Miss Simmons to find her.

CHAPTER 27

When she woke, Evelyn did not understand where she was. The bed beneath her was hard, and there was a bright light shining into her eyes. Her feet were raised and when she tried to move, she felt metal pressing into her ankles. There was a white cloth over her waist, and she realized in a terrified confusion that she was naked from the waist down.

'I'm going to be sick,' she cried, her vision tightening into a nauseous white mass.

A woman held back her hair as Evelyn vomited into a bowl, the bile sticking to her chin.

'It's okay, Evelyn.' The voice that came from the end of the bed was familiar. 'My receptionist found you. You're safe now.'

It was Dr Westbrook.

Here she was, her legs strapped into his examination table. This was a nightmare too paralysing ever to have penetrated her consciousness.

A weight pressed at the pit of her stomach as though a

hand was gripping her from within. She shuddered: to be so scrutinized and prodded, she felt imprisoned like an injured creature in a trap. Evelyn longed to throw off the cloth, to pull her feet from the metal stirrups, to run out onto the street, away from this man whose hands moved between her legs.

She felt like a child again, any power she ever had stripped away. And yet she knew she had no choice but to stay: her body had failed her.

As she leant back against the table, Evelyn felt the nurse placing extra pillows behind her head. Dr Westbrook was at the end of the examination table, a white coat covering his suit. Evelyn could sense him touching her, his hands protected inside his gloves, all the while giving instructions to the nurse. She tried to pull herself up, to see what was happening, but the nurse took her hand, lowering her back against the pillows.

Somehow, the nurse reminded her of her grandmother, a woman about which she had only one recollection. The memory had taken on a fairy-tale hue over the years, each character cast in the bright neat colours of a children's book: Evelyn running around a tree stump in the school grounds, a fall onto a hidden shard of glass, the blood gushing out fast and hot. It had been her grandmother who had wrapped Evelyn's knee in bandages. It's normal to cry, she'd said. This nurse, now, with her soft grey hair, wrinkles forming around her eyes, her presence was a comfort. It gave her permission to be helped and held.

'There,' Dr Westbrook said, standing upright and coming around to the side of the table. He handed a pile of wet cloths to the nurse, blood staining each one. 'We've cleaned you up, but I'm not sure your stockings and skirt are going to survive these stains. You've lost some blood, and there'll be more to come over the next few days.'

'What's wrong with me?'

'It was very early stages, but I am sorry, my dear. It pains me too, of course, as the grandfather. But you've had a miscarriage.'

Evelyn shook her head. 'That's not possible. Are you sure it wasn't my monthly?'

'No, Evelyn. This was definitely a miscarriage. You were probably only around five or six weeks pregnant. But that doesn't make it any easier, I know.'

He took her hand and gave it a gentle press. She turned from him, staring instead at the painting on the wall: a storm rolling in at sea, a cottage tucked away at the edge of a cliff. If it was intended to calm his patients, it was having the opposite effect on her right now.

'You'll need to use extra sanitary towels over the next few days, changing them regularly. I can give you a supply of Dr White's, so that you don't need to go to the store. And take it easy. This is a hard thing for a woman to endure. I know how much you and Henry wanted to have a child.'

'No, you're mistaken. We weren't trying for a child. I was using contraception – I told you that.'

'Yes, dear. What I meant was that while of course you

were waiting for the time to be right, this is a hard blow for a married couple. To be pregnant and then to lose the baby ... it will be a shock for Henry, too, I expect.'

'As neither of us knew I was with child, the shock is more in how I could get pregnant in the first place.'

'Those birth control pills aren't perfect, my dear. You have to be strict with how and when you take them.'

'I am strict. I have never missed one.'

'Even so. I wouldn't worry too much, Evelyn dear. Miscarriages are common, far more than people realize, not that it makes it any easier for those afflicted. But you can take solace in the fact that your body knows how to get pregnant. Next time, I'm sure it will take.'

Evelyn's lips tightened into a silent line of protest. He wasn't listening to her, and it made her feel insane.

The nurse handed a bag of sanitary products to Evelyn. She peered inside, a shudder running through her. Like many women, she hated wearing these unyielding wads of material every month, how it felt like a regression to childhood, her body refusing to find the decorum and control she expected. Sanitary products made her think of nappies, but also of medical dressings to contain a wound. To wear these for the next few days would be a humiliating reminder of all that was wrong with her. It was another exposure, an unveiling, everything that she had thought was sacred and hidden within her, brought out in a disgusting external display. It was what Dr Daley did to her, penetrating her most intimate thoughts and turning them into the immutable tangibility of words.

Dr Westbrook cancelled his final appointment of the day and drove Evelyn back to Pimlico. She did not have the energy to resist when he tucked a blanket around her legs, patting her knee for a beat too long. Darkness was descending as they left Harley Street, the early evening light filtering with the street lights and shop windows.

'You sleep if you like,' he said, when it became obvious she was not going to join in with his chatter. She turned her head away from him and stared out of the window. It was a Thursday evening and the streets were busy. Usually she'd long to be out with the crowds, or to be getting dressed before a night out, selecting the lipstick that would complement her dress. But tonight she wanted to run a bath, turn off the light, stop the ceaseless chaos of her thoughts. Even a bath, she realized, would not be possible, not when she was still bleeding.

Her father-in-law waited until she was settled on the sofa before he left her. He had tried to insist on staying, at least until Henry returned home, but she convinced him she needed to be alone. From the quiet of the sitting room, she could hear him on the kitchen telephone before he left. She'd asked him to call Henry, to explain. It was easier that way.

As soon as she heard the front door close, she threw the blanket off her legs. She had been treated like an invalid for long enough.

Upstairs, she went straight to the bathroom cabinet. Her birth control pills were there as normal, the bottle tucked next to her morning face cream. She kept a small calendar beneath the bottle of pills, a simple folded-up piece of paper with each month blocked out in squares. It was her morning routine, to take a pill and mark out the day of the month with a pencil. Unfolding the calendar, she checked carefully. She had not missed a day.

She read the instructions again, self-doubt harassing her. The pill was to be taken for twenty days in a row, starting from five days after the start of a menstrual period. The next period would then start between one and four days after the last tablet in the bottle had been taken. Checking through the calendar, she saw that her period was overdue: this was not unusual. She often had irregular periods, so she kept an even rhythm of twenty days on the pill and five days off. This was the recommendation in the instruction leaflet, to allow a clear five days if the menstrual period did not occur. It was nothing to worry about, the leaflet said: 'This does not mean that you are pregnant or that the tablets are not doing what you expect them to do,' she read again now. She knew her periods were unpredictable when she was anxious, when she forgot to eat properly, when life refused to conform to her expectations. And so she had not thought too much about it.

She had started a new bottle of pills two weeks ago. Taking the bottle out of the cabinet, she carefully tipped the pills out onto the bathroom counter. She leant down, peering closely at them. She did not know what she was looking for, other than some indication why her usual reliable drug had failed her.

They looked the same as normal, though it was hard to

tell when the pills were so small. She usually took them in the morning light, the same routine every day. A sudden thought, a desire for thoroughness, made her straighten herself and go into her bedroom. She rummaged through her bedside table and found the package she had picked up from the pharmacy a few days ago. Her doctor had prescribed her the next three months, a rushed appointment in which he'd asked her the same questions as always, before scribbling an illegible few words onto a prescription pad.

She rattled the bottle as she walked back to the bathroom. Opening the new bottle, she tipped a few pills out onto the sink counter. Taking one from each pile, she placed them side by side.

There was no mistaking it. The pills were different. The pills from her open bottle were slightly larger, barely noticeable but detectable when placed next to the others. What was more conspicuous, however, was the missing trademark: no engraved letter 'c', just smooth and white and unmarked.

Evelyn started as the sound of Henry arriving home reached her. Downstairs the door banged, and he called out to her. She was silent. Henry would find her eventually, and she needed to think.

Henry had swapped her pills for fake ones. Her previous bottles too, she assumed. It was the only thing that made sense. For the past two and a half months, maybe even longer, she was not protected by contraception.

'Honey, there you are.'

Henry was in the doorway. She looked up from the sink

The Model Patient

counter, watching him in the mirror. There was concern written across his face. 'Dad told me what happened. I'm so sorry, baby. Are you okay?'

She turned around and stared at him.

'I'm fine. It will pass in a few days, apparently.'

He walked towards her. Evelyn saw an image of his naked body thrusting into her, his face determined, her eyes searching for his in the reflection of the mirror, and she shuddered. When he embraced her, she did not press her body against his. She was cold and stiff, her jaw tight. Shifting, she extracted herself and pushed him backwards.

'How could you do this to me, Henry?'

'What do you mean?'

'I know you wanted to have a baby, but I wasn't ready. Couldn't you have spoken to me about it, rather than do this?' She gestured behind her, the pills scattered in untidy piles. It looked, she realized, like the beginnings of a disaster, pills thrown in manic disorder in the harsh light of a bathroom.

'What have you done?' he said, taking her wrist and holding her tightly. She snapped away from him, her skin burning from the friction of his grip.

'I haven't done anything. How long have you been doing this to me? What was it? You couldn't bear to be disobeyed? So you punished me with this?'

'Evelyn, I don't know what you're talking about. What is this?'

It was pathetic, this performance of his, how persistently

he pretended ignorance. Remorse wasn't necessary, she realized. It would be enough for him to shout at her, to own what he had done, to acknowledge his cruelty.

'You swapped my pills. It's obvious that the pills I've been taking are different from the real ones. How long has this been going on for? What have you been giving me? Dummy pills? Aspirin? Or something else?'

A fear jolted through her. Perhaps he had swapped her pill for another drug, something to control her and weaken her. Her emotions recently, how unhinged she was, her grip on reality loosening. She shook her head, forcing the thoughts away. It was too terrifying to see herself as a victim, her husband and her psychologist manipulating her.

'You need to get out,' she said. 'I don't want to see you right now.'

'Evie, please. This is insane. I didn't do this. Why don't you come downstairs and I can make us some dinner. You must be exhausted.'

'No, Henry. I am not exhausted or insane or making this up. Don't do that to me.'

'I'm not doing anything to you, Evelyn.'

To hear him use those words, it was too much. They were eerily familiar. Dr Daley, Diana, and now Henry. They had all said the exact same sentence, turning it back to her. She was the problem.

Not this time.

'Get out, Henry. Go to a hotel. Stay with your parents, I don't care. You can explain to them what you did.'

The Model Patient

He took a step towards her, but she dodged him. 'Now, Henry. I'll go downstairs and you can pack a bag. But then I need you to go.'

He sighed, shaking his head. 'I hate to leave you like this, Evie. You're not well.'

'I am perfectly well.'

'I can see you're upset. I'll go, for tonight. But I am going to call you first thing in the morning. I'll come back after work.'

'I wouldn't do that.'

'We can talk when you've calmed down.'

It took every inch of strength she possessed, but she said nothing. If she had learnt anything over these terrible months, it was the power of silence. He wanted her to scream, to cry, to be the hysterical woman he had cast her as, sick and demented. But she refused to take on that role.

She waited in the dark of the sitting room until Henry had gone. Then, for the first time in months, she slept without dreaming.

CHAPTER 28

Miss Simmons answered the phone on Monday morning when Evelyn called to cancel her appointment. The bleeding had nearly stopped, but she did not have the energy to get in a taxi and navigate the labyrinth of give-and-take to which Dr Daley would subject her. She did not think she could endure the humiliation today, how he took her close and then denied her everything.

Henry called several times over the weekend, as well as turning up on Saturday morning with an oversized bouquet of flowers. Watching him from her bedroom window, Evelyn waited until he had stopped ringing the doorbell before she slipped on her dressing gown and went downstairs. When she opened the front door, he was still there, staring up at the first floor. He took a step towards her, but she shook her head, staying firmly on her side of the threshold.

'Let me in, Evie, please.'

'No, Henry. I don't know how to forgive you for this. Flowers are not going to help.'

'You're making a mistake. I didn't touch your pills.'

'Don't make me feel as though I'm the one to blame here. That I forgot to take the pills, or I'm making this up. I can't bear that.'

'There must be another explanation. Dad says this can happen.'

'The pills were swapped. You were the one person who stood to gain by doing that to me. You and your parents who were so desperate for me to fit into their idea of the perfect family. Did they help you? Is that what happened? Did they come to your rescue, plotting with you about how to make me conform, the good wife bound to you and your home with your child inside me?'

'Is that what you think? That I want to have a child so that I can control you?'

'That's what it feels like to me. I told you I wasn't ready but you couldn't cope with the disappointment. Couldn't you see that it wasn't the right time? You made me give up the job I loved. My life had changed already, too much and too quickly.'

'I thought it would be good for you, Evie. A baby would take you outside of your own head, give you something else to focus on rather than all those drawings, your crazy idea of designing jewellery. Lionel was humouring you when he signed you up for that silversmith course, you must see that. You were a brilliant model, so beautiful; you should be proud of the career you achieved. But that time is over. You need to let go of those old dreams and start focusing on the next stage of our life together.'

'Don't be cruel, Henry. I am allowed to have dreams of my own. I won't let you steal them from me.'

Evelyn and Henry stared at one another. A thought passed through her, how much easier it would be to invite him inside, to give into him, to acknowledge the sense in what he was saying, to apologize for letting her grip on reality weaken. Maybe she should be trying harder to embrace her new life. But she would not do it, not again.

'I'll come back in a few days. Maybe you'll be feeling better by then, once the miscarriage is over and you're less emotional.'

She stepped back inside the door and pushed it hard. Henry thrust the flowers towards her, and a rose disintegrated at her feet as she slammed the door shut.

Over the next few days, her mind would not find peace. One moment she'd be filled with longing, a desperate weakness that made her want to seek out someone who would hold her: sometimes Dr Daley, sometimes Henry, or Diana, or her parents. The next she would be bent over her sketchbook, jewellery designs emerging in sporadic bursts of creation.

She drew a red rose brooch, a snake curled up at the centre. In light pencil strokes, she sketched a necklace of interwoven threads made from silver wire, delicate as gossamer, with a tiny silver spider lodged at the neckline. She designed earrings that cuffed the ears, the head of a fox at the base. It was her consortium of creatures, crafted to adorn and protect the body. She had long been drawn to the complexities of jewellery, ever since she was photographed in the watches for Mr Hardy's friend, her arms draped over the piano. Wearing jewellery felt to Evelyn as though she was in conversation with her body, how she wore it in a quest to feel beautiful and adorned. She enjoyed transforming her body into an alluring work of art, and without it she was not complete. But it was also her armour. A necklace hiding her heart, earrings lining her neck, bracelets protecting her wrists from the grasp of others. She seduced and she hid – that had always been her power. But now, with Dr Daley, with her husband too, they had exposed her, stripping away the adornments that made her feel safe.

While she bled, the hidden secrets of her body seeping and soiling the pristine white sanitary products, she felt a deep yearning to cover herself in jewels, in silver, in the hard metal gildings of her designs.

By Tuesday morning, the bleeding had finally stopped. She dressed carefully, a dark burgundy dress over a silk shirt, brown suede boots that rose to just beneath her knees. Her gold necklace with the 'D&E' pendant was nestled under her shirt, and she wore earrings in the shape of golden leaves. With every bathroom light switched on brightly, she leant into the edge of the sink as she drew black pencil around her eyes, smudging the edges and blending the black kohl into her eye shadow.

She walked to Chelsea. It felt good to be outside at last, after a weekend of hiding indoors with her breaking body. It was the start of April and schools were out for the Easter holidays. The streets were full of energy, children hurried along by their parents, teenagers gathering in small crowds on every corner. It had rained in the night, washing the London dirt into puddles at the edge of the pavements, but now the sun was bright and clean and exposing. Beneath the familiar trees of Sloane Square, dandelions had spread, hundreds of them in all the stages of their growth, the bright yellow bloom, the white seed clock that would soon disperse in the April wind. Evelyn remembered how she had picked them with her father when she was a child, the two of them walking through the school grounds, delighting in blowing apart the dandelion head. She did not remember when they had stopped, how it had been decided that she was too old for such childish pleasures.

Diana knew she was coming over. Evelyn had broken her resolve just once over the past few days, picking up the telephone and calling her friend. She told her about the miscarriage, and for a moment she heard Diana's tone soften. It hadn't been easy, though, and she'd found herself faltering on the phone. What if Diana did not believe her that the pills had been swapped? And so she kept that part of the story to herself. There was too much vulnerability in hoping her friend would take her side.

She let her body relax when Diana hugged her, but she could sense a distance between them. It was not their usual embrace. They sat at the kitchen table with the cups of coffee Diana had made when Evelyn arrived, a silent and painful few minutes of waiting for the coffee to brew. Neither of them knew how to begin.

Evelyn remembered the last words Diana had spoken to her: let me know once you've found a new psychotherapist, she'd said. And then we can talk.

Evelyn had no intention of finding a new psychotherapist. It was Diana who needed to give him up.

'I spoke with Dr Daley about the photograph,' Evelyn said. 'He said it must have been inside a book you lent him, and it fell out. Is that what he said to you, too?'

'I don't want to talk to you about Patrick.' Diana's leg was trembling beneath the table, a nervous energy that Evelyn knew too well. She sighed, and suddenly Evelyn felt like a child who had disappointed a favourite teacher. Maybe this was how Diana's students felt when she reprimanded them. 'It's ridiculous that you call him Dr Daley. Why do you do that?'

'He has never asked me to call him Patrick. He never even told me his first name.'

'Are you going to stop seeing him?'

'It's complicated, Diana. I can't just stop.'

'Why not? He's your doctor, not your boyfriend.'

Evelyn looked down at her coffee. The conversation was already moving in a dangerous direction.

'I know that. But my feelings for him are too strong. Sometimes I imagine our last appointment together, and I can feel the panic building inside me.'

'Are you in love with him?

'Do you really want to know that? What is the purpose

of me telling you what I feel for him, when it will just hurt us both.'

'I want to know if you are in love with him.'

'Are *you* in love with him, Diana?'

'Answer the question, Evelyn. I'm allowed to be in love with him – he's my fiancé.'

An agonizing shudder travelled through Evelyn's body, spreading out from her heart. The thought of him married to Diana, the calm, intellectual conversations they would have, how they loved one another in a fond, balanced way, not like Evelyn's horrible obsession, it was too much to endure. It would be better if he was dead.

'Sometimes I hate him. I want to kill him. I suppose it is easier to hate him.'

'Easier than what?'

'Easier than letting myself believe that I might love him.'

'It's not real, Evie. You must know that. It's the way this psychoanalytical therapy works. You've fallen in love with a fantasy.'

'I can't accept that. It feels too real. He's real.'

'But he also isn't real. He's what you've made him.'

'So why does he haunt me all the time? Why can't I let go if it's nothing?'

'You need to try harder. It's gone too far now. You need to leave him. For me, please. He's real for me.'

'No, he isn't real for you, Diana. He's with you because of me.'

Diana slammed her coffee down on the table, liquid

spilling over the rim. 'You need to stop that, Evelyn. It's a delusion.'

'If it's a delusion then why doesn't he try to break me out of it? Why does he do nothing to help me see the difference between fantasy and reality? He encourages me again and again to delve deeper into my desire.'

'Just stop, Evelyn.'

'It's no longer up to me to make this stop. He needs to take responsibility. If he wanted me to get over him, then he would help me to do so. He knows I am trapped and he won't let me be free.'

'It is up to you to find the strength, Evie. He's never going to love you the way you want him to.'

'I'm sorry, Diana. But I can't accept that.'

'I'm going to talk to Patrick about this. I think he can't understand how far this has gone. It's dangerous. Have you told him how you feel?'

'Yes, I've told him. He makes me tell him everything.'

'I'll speak to him.'

'No, Diana. Please don't do that. I don't want you to do that.'

'This is about me, too. He's my fiancé.'

'Have you ever thought about the way you met, how he seemed to know exactly what to say to you, brought you your favourite cheese and wine, our tradition? It's because I told him about you, about us. I even told him that you go to lectures at the Tavistock clinic for your teacher training course. He planned everything to make you fall in love with him, just like he manipulated me in therapy to become obsessed with whether he was attracted to me.'

'That's crazy, Evelyn. He's a psychologist. It's totally normal that he would attend a lecture at the Tavistock clinic: not everything is about you. Look, Evie, it's obvious you need help, but Patrick is not the right person for you anymore.'

She stood, reaching across the table to remove Evelyn's mug, and walked to the sink. While the tap water ran and Diana turned away from her, Evelyn realized that the conversation was over. But she remained where she was, unmoving and silent.

'I'm going to leave,' Diana said, turning around from the sink. 'I need some fresh air. Stay until you've calmed down, and then please go home. I meant what I said before. We can talk again once you've found a new psychotherapist.'

Evelyn was frozen, her hands clasped in her lap. It took until she heard the door close and the sound of Diana's footsteps travelling down the stairs for Evelyn to understand what she wanted to do.

In her old bedroom, now Diana's office, she went straight to the desk. A manuscript was piled neatly next to the typewriter. It was strange how her bed, the site of passion, of love, those early days with Henry, that slow journey to their wedding night, had been replaced with this: a desk, a typewriter, a secret book written by her best friend.

She picked up the manuscript and took it to one of the armchairs. The title page was the same as she'd seen it: 'A Novel, untitled' printed across the middle. And yet in pencil

The Model Patient

underneath the typed letters were scribbled phrases, all of them crossed out. These were Diana's working titles, a list of possible options. It was terrible to think that she might have discussed them with Dr Daley, the two of them drinking wine, their heads close together as they came up with ideas. Evelyn read through them, deciphering the writing beneath the crossing out: 'The Single Flame', 'Obsession', 'The Burning Woman', 'Dangerous Dreams', 'The Shadow Self'. None of them, it seemed, had quite worked for Diana.

Placing the title page face down on the floor next to her feet, she started to read.

On the nights when the audience applaud most loudly, Miranda Hades does not seek out a lover. She goes home, strips naked and lies across the fur rug on her bedroom floor. She lets the sensation of the fur against her skin move her, and she remembers it all: how the men call out from the auditorium; how the sound of the cheers and the clapping vibrates inside her body.

But on the nights when she does not perform, or when the audience is distracted, quiet and indifferent, she ventures out into the night with one goal. One need.

Tonight is a special occasion. The man is her thirteenth lover. Thirteen is her lucky number: it was the age of her first kiss, the number she was given to wear for her first acting audition, the number of the bus that killed the first man she had wanted dead. Thirteen is fate; it is the number that understands her desires.

She kisses him. It is a cold night, but they are protected by the trees at the edge of the park. He is still warm, and she lifts his arms, placing them around her neck. When they fall back to the ground, stiff and heavy with death, she sighs. She does not have long before morning.

Evelyn did not understand what she was reading. An actress who roamed the streets, killing her lovers to assuage her emptiness after a poorly received performance? This must be the character Diana mentioned to her, the neurotic and narcissistic woman who falls in love easily, volatile, always doubting what others think of her. It was terrifying how when Evelyn read the description of this murderess, all she could see was herself.

Flipping forward to the middle of the book, she attempted to read a little more. But it was too much. The actress devours the heart of her victim, the blood trailing down her arms in deep red rivulets. Or she searches for a lover, indulging in his embrace, only to cut this throat when he tries to get up and leave.

This was not who she was. Evelyn was not a huntress, a wolf seeking the blood of men. She did not want to destroy those who would not give her the love for which she yearned. And yet hadn't she said to Diana that she wanted to kill Dr Daley? To kill him or to love him? Surely her thoughts of killing him were a defence, a way to stop herself from falling in love too hard?

She did want to kill him. It was what she repeated to

The Model Patient

herself over and over when she left his clinic, every time. But she knew she was fooling herself. More than wanting to kill him, she wanted to love him. If he let her, she would give him her heart.

This, Diana's grotesque surrealist story, was a betrayal. It was obviously based on her, an actress not too dissimilar from a model, how she yearned for the affections of others, destroying friendships, destroying herself, in the process. She quivered with fury.

Gathering up the novel, she returned to the kitchen. Opening the cutlery drawer, she searched for a pair of scissors. When she couldn't see any, she pulled out instead the largest, sharpest chopping knife she could find.

She held down each page as she sliced through them, one at a time. Starting slowly, she cut long, careful tears. Each rip was a balm to her anger. As scraps of paper fell around her, the wooden kitchen floor covered in the black ink of the story, she began to speed up. Soon she was working in a frenzy, the cuts no longer straight, the sheets splitting into ragged pieces as the knife slipped and the tears spread in all directions. Her neat attempt at obliterating the story tumbled into a determined rage.

When she cut her hand, she did not stop. Her skin was hot and slick with sweat, and the knife was slipping. Discarding it, she heard it clatter onto the floor, quickly hidden by the pages that continued to fall. Shredding with her fingers now, the blood from her wound stained the white paper in dark red strokes.

Lucy Ashe

Finally, the book was destroyed. Wiping her bleeding hand on a kitchen towel, Evelyn looked down at the chaos of the kitchen floor.

She left it all, Diana's work in pieces, and she made her way out onto the street. Evelyn knew exactly what she needed to do next. There was only one way to destroy the pattern; only one way to make the repetitions of her life come to an end.

CHAPTER 29

'He's not here yet, I'm afraid,' Miss Simmons said to her when she arrived at the clinic on Upper Wimpole Street. 'He only sees patients in the afternoon on Tuesdays.'

'Can I wait for him?'

Miss Simmons looked nervous. Evelyn understood how she was feeling, torn between disappointing the woman in front of her and making a mistake with her employer. She obviously did not know what to do, whether Dr Daley would be annoyed to see an unscheduled patient waiting for him outside his consulting room.

'He's not due for another few hours. Shall I tell him you were here, and then I'll call you to see if he can fit you in for an appointment at the end of the day? His last appointment ends at half past seven today, and it is possible he could stay later. I'll have to check with him,' she added, scanning the page of a large diary on her desk.

'No, don't worry. There's no need. Can I sit for a few

minutes in the waiting room? I'm recovering from illness, and I'm feeling rather tired.'

'Of course,' Miss Simmons said. She appeared relieved to be able to do something to help. Angela Simmons, more than anything, longed to be useful. 'Can I get you a glass of water?'

'No, thank you. You're very kind, but I'll feel better once I've sat for a few minutes.'

'Stay as long as you need. I've put some new magazines out.'

Evelyn smiled. She hid her feelings well, giving the receptionist no indication that here before her was a woman on the edge of destruction.

Settling onto one of the wooden benches that lined the waiting area, Evelyn tried to think. The building was quiet, no voices drifting out beneath the consulting room doors. All she could hear was the light tap of Miss Simmons's typewriter from around the corner.

The telephone rang, a shrill, sharp sound that made Evelyn jump. This, now, was her chance. She took her opportunity, walking as quietly as she could towards Dr Daley's room. The wooden floorboards creaked once, but Miss Simmons was already talking on the phone. The door opened easily, making no noise at all.

With the light switched off and no Dr Daley to usher her inside, the room seemed cold and melancholy. She wanted to touch everything, to kneel on the rug and press her fingers into the fabric, to run her hands along the back of his chair, to open every book on his desk. But there was no time. Miss Simmons would soon notice that she had left the waiting room.

Starting at the bottom, she pulled open the desk drawer, wincing at the sound of the wood sticking. She knelt, her hands moving over the objects inside. There were pencils, a few scraps of paper, some pens and ink cartridges. But it was the Dictaphone that made her heart beat wildly. She imagined him taking it out between appointments, recording his notes onto vinyl disc. Rummaging through the drawer, she longed to find those discs, but there was nothing – no evidence of a single recording.

Moving on, she opened his top desk drawer. Inside was a neat stack of notebooks. She took out the top one and flicked through it. The book was entirely empty, not one sentence hidden inside. In a panic, she pulled out every notebook, leafing through them quickly. They were all the same: empty pages that seemed to mock her with their cold indifference. She tried to stay calm, but she could feel a devastating depression sinking through her limbs, her chest aching.

When she opened the drawer below, the pain shifted, the tension within her releasing. There were a series of folders, pages spilling from the edges of each one. The top folder was familiar: grey card with the words 'Dream-Images' written in the corner. She lifted it out and looked through the folders underneath. In alphabetical order, these were his notes on each of his patients. Flicking through them, she found her folder right at the bottom: Evelyn Westbrook. It was strange to see her name written out in his hand.

Here, in this folder, might be the secrets she longed to understand. What he thought of her; why he was with Diana; whether he understood the pain his methods caused? There was no time to look at them now, and Evelyn knew that reading these notes would require the privacy of her bedroom. Her bag was too small to fit the folder, so she lifted her dress, stuffing the pages beneath her shirt and securing them against her skin.

She was going to read the notes. And then she would decide what to do. It was a delay, taking her off course from the decision she had made just one hour ago at Diana's flat. But this was important, vital. This was her chance to find out exactly what he thought of her. She wanted to know everything, no matter how much it hurt.

Miss Simmons was still on the phone, so Evelyn smiled and waved at her as she left the clinic. The receptionist waved back and returned to her call.

Digging her necklace out from beneath the collar of her dress, Evelyn played with the pendant as she hurried down towards the main road. She felt wild and alive, the edges of the folder digging into her skin.

Beneath her clothes were the words that would tell her what to do.

CHAPTER 30

Evelyn Westbrook: (D.O.B 20 June 1936)

21 January 1963 – presenting problem is a struggle adjusting to married life. Gave up her career as a model when she married, and is clashing with her husband over his desire to start a family, as well as other aspects of domestic life. She takes the birth control pill and does not want to give it up. She is suffering from a recurring nightmare, discussion of which led to an emotional response. Generally good presentation, keen to please, orientated.

28 January – anxiety about how life will change if she has a child. She shows signs of being dependent on the affections of others to feel content. More relaxed today, but still guarded and censoring herself in order to present herself attractively.

4 February – a developed discussion of her nightmare, linked to her relationship with her husband and her fear of getting pregnant and having a child. Serpent imagery clearly phallic, unresolved envy leading to resistance to becoming a mother. Strong anxiety about the changes in her life and her identity.

11 February – she has decided she would like to start psychodynamic psychotherapy with me, and is committed to the treatment. Signs of anxiety about the task of free association.

18 February – tensions with her mother-in-law and fear of being replaced in her husband's affections by his mother or by a child. Self-punishing with feelings of overwhelming guilt over failures to control her narcissistic desire for admiration as a teenager.

25 February – dream exploration, with resistance. Trauma from an early relationship, with unresolved split between conscious and unconscious elements of the experience. Painful memories explored which she attempted to contain by shifting the focus to the present. Signs of transference, a fantasy of specialness.

The Model Patient

4 March – projective testing, word association (results in clinic file). She showed anxiety about the test, but did manage to relax and was committed. Led to discussion of the transference she is experiencing, her anger and resistance.

11 March – the appointment was dominated by the transference and her obsession with the possibility of countertransference. She shared her fantasy, after initial resistance. Requires careful and intensive treatment, increased to twice a week.

14 March – continued obsession about countertransference and frustration with her own emotions. Unsettled psyche, constantly shifting between positive and negative transference. She attempted to act out her cathexis at the end of the appointment, which required sensitive management.

18 March – delusional fantasy, discussed together, with idealizing transference shifting quickly into a narcissistic injury and anger. Intervention with my original Dream-Images projective testing. This led to painful exploration of unconscious impulses, with a further delusion that she had painted one of the images herself. Unconscious yearning to make herself special to me acted out.

Lucy Ashe

21 March – a calmer affect, sitting more comfortably within her fantasy. Less combative and willing to engage in discussion of painful memories and dreams, with a return to the pattern of obsessional transference when the pain of the past became unendurable.

25 March – showing irrational fears of abandonment, projected onto a delusion about a relationship with her best friend. Paranoia personality type revealing itself: believes that she is being manipulated by people in her life. Likely to be a way of avoiding responsibility for her own thoughts and actions.

28 March – obsession with a photograph of herself that she believes I sought out – evidence of her fantasy needing a tangible outlet, the unconscious brought to the surface. Signs of struggle to understand the difference between reality and fantasy, no sign yet of individuation, or being able to bring her fractured sense of self into a harmonious whole.

Evelyn turned the pages back and forth, desperate to find something else. But this was it. A dull grey folder, a few sheets of paper, some of them still blank, a form at the front containing only her name and date of birth. Dr Daley's handwriting sprawled across the pages, a promise of recognition and understanding. And yet all that was contained in those sentences were cold words, indifferent and clinical. The woman described on these pages was alien to her, a patient reduced to psychological jargon, problems, symptoms.

This was a betrayal. It hurt so much, how distanced this was, giving nothing of the intimacy of the appointments, nothing of the part he played in the way their relationship had developed. There was no acknowledgement of how deliberately he drew out her desires, asking for the details of her so-called delusions, bringing her to the edge of sanity with the way he prodded and poked, never helping her to straighten out the difference between fantasy and reality. He had removed himself entirely.

It was nearly half past six in the evening. One hour until Dr Daley finished with his final patient of the day. It was naïve of Miss Simmons to give her that information. Little did she know how Evelyn would decide to make use of it.

Redoing her make-up and pulling her hair into a ponytail, Evelyn stared intently at her reflection in the bathroom mirror. She chose a pale lipstick, a soft peach that contrasted with the black of her eyeliner.

'I'm not mad,' she whispered to herself over and over again. She would not let him do this to her. Diana, she had dealt with, destroying the manuscript that had made her feel so enraged. It was Dr Daley's turn now.

She was caught within her conflicting desires, to love and to hate, to hold him and to destroy him. It was exhausting how quickly she could jump from one impulse to the next. These notes, how emotionless they were, they pushed her closer and closer to an overwhelming anger. It was frightening to feel so out of control.

She imagined him at his desk, writing his notes between appointments, deciding what he would commit to the page and what he would leave out. It made her furious, how easily he could dismiss her: a deluded patient, obsessional, lost in her fantasies.

Changing out of her dress, she pulled on a pair of cropped black trousers with a sleeveless black jumper. Slipping on her grey suede jacket and wrapping a large scarf around her neck, she nodded to herself in the mirror. She was ready. Taking the pages from the file, she folded them neatly and placed them in her pocket.

It was only once she had left the house, evening beginning to fall around her, that she realized what else was tucked inside her jacket pocket.

She had no recollection of going into the drawer of her writing desk. She did not remember taking the knife that she used to sharpen her pencils and placing it inside her pocket. But there was no denying that the knife was there, nestled beneath grey suede and resting against her hip.

Plunging her hand inside the pocket, she walked fast towards the main roads on the edge of Pimlico and Westminster where she knew she'd be able to find a taxi. Running her finger along the blunt side of the knife, she let the dull sensation of pain build into a deeper yearning.

The Model Patient

There was no more holding back. This time, when she saw him, she'd make sure she had no regrets. She'd give him her heart or she'd end it all.

CHAPTER 31

Evelyn ducked her head beneath the window line of the taxi. It was a shock to see Henry walking along the pavement, the sight of him hardening her mood into a deeper anger. No doubt he was heading home to Pimlico, another misguided attempt to end their conflict. As the taxi drove onwards, she straightened herself, catching the eye of the driver in the mirror. He was smiling at her and his expression was that of a bemused adult laughing at a child. She scowled at him and he returned his gaze to the road.

The taxi dropped her off a few streets away from the clinic and she walked the rest of the journey. It was nearly half past seven in the evening, and the sun had vanished beneath the unruly London skyline. A cool grey gloom had settled across the streets, and she tucked herself against the railings on the corner of Upper Wimple Street and Weymouth Street. It was quiet, as usual, just the occasional car arriving and disappearing between the crossroads. Evelyn pulled her scarf high around her face, and waited.

The Model Patient

Her hands were restless and she wished she'd thought to bring her cigarettes.

At last she heard footsteps coming towards her from the direction of the clinic. Dr Daley walked quickly, and Evelyn flattened herself against the railings on Weymouth Street until he had crossed the road and begun to head west. He was wearing the same outfit as the first time she had met him: cream trousers and a collarless jacket, chequered red and brown. Only his hair had changed, even longer now and nearly touching his shoulders. It was strange to think how ignorant she was back then, no understanding whatsoever of the journey on which she was about to embark. That first time she saw him, she had felt no attraction, no desire. Yes, she was anxious and she wanted him to like her — but that was it. The intensity of her longing came later, little by little, until she could stand it no more.

If she could turn back time, would she do it? Would she erase these months from her memory and return to life before meeting him? As she ran across the road, making certain to stay in the shadows, she realized that the answer was no. He had taken her to the edge of her desires, woken her to pain but also to love: he had shown her the depths of her soul. And now it was time for her to take control.

She followed him down Marylebone High Street, before turning right onto Blandford Street. The area was still in recovery from the war, new residential buildings emerging while the shops remained shabby and tired. As Evelyn tracked Dr Daley's route, she wished the street was busier.

The few shops and pharmacies in operation were closed and there was only a slow trickle of people moving up and down the high street.

Evelyn felt exposed, the road too quiet to cover her. If Dr Daley turned around, she would be easy to spot. How would he react, she thought, to see his patient following him down the road in the early evening? Would he run from her or would he draw her towards him? If it was anything like their appointments together, he would bring her so close that he'd get right beneath her skin. And then he'd discard her, and she'd be left alone to mend the wounds he had opened.

Staying as close to the edges of buildings as she could, Evelyn followed. Part-way down Blandford Street, she noticed him slowing, his hand reaching inside his jacket pocket. He was pulling out his keys.

Evelyn picked up her pace. He stepped up to a black front door, his hand moving towards the lock. There were three low steps up to the house, railings either side of him, four storeys rising above. She needed to get to him now, before he disappeared into one of the flats inside.

'Dr Daley.' She was right behind him, one hand gripping the black railing to steady herself.

He turned quickly, shock flashing across his face. And then it was gone and he composed himself.

'Evelyn, what are you doing here? How did you find my address?'

'Diana didn't tell me, if that's what you're thinking. I followed you, from Upper Wimpole Street.'

The Model Patient

'Angela said you dropped by earlier. Why didn't you come into the clinic? I could have seen you there.'

'No, I don't want to repeat the same pattern over and over again. It would achieve nothing.' She took a pace towards him, rising on to the lowest step. Dr Daley held his ground.

'You make me feel insane, that there is no reason for me to be upset that you are getting married to Diana, that I am delusional, that you have done nothing to hurt me.'

She took another step forward, just one level away from him now. 'How could you propose to her, in the Regent's Park rose garden of all places, on the same day that I told you my dream?'

He returned the keys to his pocket, the door remaining firmly shut behind him. He stared at her, saying nothing.

'I read your notes,' she said. 'I went into your office today when you were out. And I found them. Do you know what was the worst thing? It was the hope I felt when I found them — how, the whole way home with your notes hidden away beneath my clothes, I thought they were going to set me free. I thought that I would read the notes and finally all my terrible confusion would come to an end. But that's not what happened at all.'

She pulled the pages from her pocket and unfolded them. Her hands were shaking.

'You wrote that I was obsessed with the possibility of countertransference. What does that mean? That I was obsessed with whether you had feelings for me? How could you turn it on me that way? Of course I wanted to know what you thought of me. Isn't that perfectly normal, especially when you encouraged me the way you did, telling me that I shouldn't be ashamed of my feelings? You constantly led me back to how I felt about you, never letting me escape.'

'What would you like me to say to you, Evelyn?'

'I want you to say something, anything. I want you to acknowledge that these notes are a distortion of our relationship, leaving out everything about the role you played in getting me to this place. You need to take responsibility.'

'Why are you so afraid of letting yourself say how you really feel about me, Evelyn?'

'What do you mean? I have told you how I feel.' She snapped at him, her words taut with fury.

'No, I don't think you have.' He was so calm, letting her rave.

'What more am I supposed to say? How can I give you anymore of myself? It's frightening to think that ...' She stopped herself. She did not know if she could say the words.

He took a step towards her, his eyes penetrating. 'You were about to say something else. What is it frightening to think?'

Evelyn shook her head. 'I can't. I'm afraid of what will happen when you say nothing in return.'

'You can trust me, Evelyn. I'm not going to hurt you. Tell me what is on your mind.'

London seemed to slow down around her. Daylight had vanished, and Dr Daley was lit up by the lamp that hung above the porch. His hair shone, that strange mix of auburn black she could never quite describe. She took a deep breath and said the words that, once spoken, she could never take back.

'It's frightening because I've fallen in love with you.'

All she had left to give, there it was between them. It was up to him now: he had promised that he wasn't going to hurt her, not when he held her broken heart.

'How does it feel to tell me this?'

Evelyn stared at him, her eyes widening. 'No,' she said. 'Don't do that.'

'What is it that you think I'm doing?'

'You pushed me to say those words; you made me expose this most vulnerable part of myself. You told me that you weren't going to hurt me.'

'How am I hurting you?'

'You know how you're hurting me. Why don't you just tell me how you feel about me, whether it is love, or hate, or indifference, or something else. I need to know; I need to be able to love you or to move on from you. But you have trapped me here, imprisoned me in this turmoil of not knowing. How can I get over you if I think there is a possibility that you might love me? Or you can help me to understand that this isn't real, that, as Diana said to me, it's how psychoanalysis works, the delusion of transference. But you never do that. You've never helped me separate out reality from fantasy.'

His silence was more than she could bear. She took two steps backwards, onto the pavement. He did not move.

She kept walking, further back and back into the street. It seemed as though her body was detaching from her mind, the fabric of the houses vibrating strangely. Standing in the middle of the road, she struggled to understand the dimensions of the space around her. But her gaze never left him, searching for something in his face that would tell her what to do.

Quivering with anger, with desire, with a desperate sadness that she could not endure, she stopped, her legs too heavy to move another step. It was as though they were merging, bound by the thick coils of a snake.

She hated him and she loved him. She wanted to run to him, to take the knife from her pocket, to cut the pain out from her heart. Instead, she folded up the notes and returned them to inside her jacket, her eyes never leaving his.

The sound of traffic was growing from the east, but she could not turn away from Dr Daley. They stared at one another, a thread of energy growing between them. She hated that she was back in this place again, that she could have let this happen, this pathetic dependence, seeking love over and over again. It was an endless repetition: Mr Hardy, Dr Daley, even Henry, how he'd nearly succeeded in turning her own body against her with her unwanted pregnancy, the blood of her miscarriage. She loved these men and she let them destroy her.

The driver did not see her. Her clothes were too dark, her scarf hiding the blonde of her hair. She was standing in darkness and the taxi was moving too fast.

The Model Patient

Evelyn heard the taxi, though. She felt everything, the ground vibrating beneath her, the roar of the engine, the wheels grinding into the tarmac. And yet her legs could not move; she was frozen, trapped in Dr Daley's gaze.

The taxi was going to hit her. And Dr Daley knew it too.

He did not move.

Headlights illuminated the space around her. She closed her eyes.

An impact, hard and strange. Evelyn was falling.

The lights from the car vanished. Her body hit the road.

CHAPTER 32

The doctor closed the door, returned to his desk and pressed the record button on his Dictaphone.

'18 February 1963. E. Westbrook.'

A pause. The click of the record button once again. The Dictaphone returned to the desk, the bottom drawer sticking as the doctor pulled it open and closed.

Another pause, the sound of footsteps, the doctor checking the door. His chair scraping against the floor. A piece of paper ripped from a notebook, flattened against the desk, a pencil lifted from a pot.

An exhalation. A decision made.

Evelyn Westbrook, he wrote before scratching it out and starting again.

Evelyn Anderson.

I doubted myself for the first few weeks but there's no point denying it. I know who she is. While she is yet to mention my father, I know it's coming. I can picture that

The Model Patient

photograph on the living room wall at Winter Manor, the one I see whenever he finds time in his busy schedule to ask me to visit. It makes me so angry, how she came into our lives and took everything.

While I do know that I need to refer her to someone else, that treating her myself is fraught with complexities, I can't bring myself to do it. It's an opportunity, both for her and for me. Sometimes, when I look at her sitting there opposite me, I hate her. I can feel all that unresolved rage, everything I tried and failed to talk about in my own psychoanalysis when I was training. This, now, is my chance.

I can control my anger when I'm with her. It is important that she sees nothing of how I feel, that she never knows who I am. That is my way with every patient, of course, abstaining from showing anything of myself, letting them lead the way while I help them draw out and discuss the emotions their projections and transference evoke. I can tell how frustrating she finds my silences. I give her nothing of how I really feel, presenting myself as I have been taught: a blank slate on to which she transfers her desires and her fears.

And yet I can't help seeing her through the eyes of my parents. My father: how he desired her for himself. My mother: how conflicted she was, that terrible swing between hate and guilt. And to confuse it all, there is my countertransference, a force that tries to consume me every time she looks at me, mirroring how she feels. I can sense her response to me building with every appointment.

Before she came along, we were so happy. My parents,

me, my two sisters visiting at the weekends: all of us in that big house, Winter Manor, or back in our apartment in New York City. She seduced him, just as she tries to seduce me every time she walks into my clinic. She can't help herself.

For years I have been certain that she was the villain: it is easiest that way, shifting the blame away from my father. She made him fall in love with her, tore him away from us. We had no choice but to leave, returning to America with everyone thinking it was my mother's fault. I heard the rumours, how she had a lover back at home, a glamorous New York life, my poor father left behind. But that wasn't true. It was Evelyn's fault. She broke up our home. My sisters knew it too, how Mother wasn't to blame. But they didn't want anything to do with either of our parents after that, disappearing with their husbands and pretending we didn't exist. Evelyn tainted us all.

Now Mother is dead and Father didn't even come to the funeral. That was the first day I'd seen my sisters in years. They left the funeral quickly, before I had a chance to talk to them.

Sometimes when I listen to Evelyn, I can feel that version of the past slipping. It is tempting to see her as the victim when she is so tormented, all that anxiety and fear she brings to me. But changing the past is not what we are here to do. Instead, we need to understand it, even if it hurts.

Evelyn hopes that I will absolve her and help her to come to terms with the past and the present. And maybe I can, once she has accepted what she did. Maybe she'll frame it as

The Model Patient

an abusive relationship, my father taking advantage of her. Yes, she was young when it all began, but she let it continue even when she was old enough to walk away. If she had left him sooner, maybe my father would have found a way to return to us before it was too late.

I've seen the photographs, how beautiful and seductive, how knowing she looks, a dangerous young woman with the power to make a man destroy his life. And now I can feel what is going to happen: she is going to try to do the same to me. She is going to try to make me fall in love with her.

This time it will be her turn to feel as though the whole world is turning upside down. The signs are already there, how she is falling for me, her desperate need to know what I think of her. All I have to do is ask the right questions.

CHAPTER 33

Evelyn could not move. A weight was pressing down on top of her, the tarmac hard beneath her legs. She did not understand what was happening, what it was that held her immobile against the ground.

She opened her eyes, terrified of what she would see. But there was no car. The taxi had driven away. It had not even stopped.

He had changed his mind. He did not watch while a car's screeching tires mowed her down. He had not let her die. The weight on top of her, it was the man she loved, his arms flung beneath her head. At the last minute, he had run into the road, throwing her to the ground and out of the path of destruction.

But she had seen it. For a few moments, Dr Daley was going to let the car destroy her. He was going to watch, silent and still, while she fell.

'Are you okay?' he said, rolling off her. For the first time, he was shaken, a human revealed from beneath his performance of the powerful psychotherapist, always in control. His hands were bloodied, badly grazed from breaking her fall against the road, and one of his trouser legs was ripped at the knee.

Evelyn sat up slowly, her body gradually waking to the pain. Her back was aching, her tailbone throbbing, and her ankle was bleeding. One of her shoes lay in the middle of the road and her wrist was twisted awkwardly.

'I'm okay,' she replied. 'Nothing broken, I don't think. What about you?'

He was pulling himself to his feet, groaning as he straightened his knee. 'I'll survive. Cuts and bruises only.'

Reaching down to her, his hair fell forwards across his face. Evelyn looked up at him. She did not understand his expression: there was a new hardness emerging, erasing that brief moment of humanity. She did not think he had the power to hurt her any more than he had already, but that look – there was something hidden he was yet to reveal.

She shuddered as she placed her hand in his. He helped her up, catching her when she stumbled.

'You're in shock,' he said. 'And maybe concussed. Come inside and you can sit down.'

He led her across the road, unlocking the front door and guiding her up the stairs to a flat on the first floor. It was so different from the way he walked in front of her between the clinic waiting area and his consulting room, Evelyn following a few paces behind. This time, he held her.

'You sit there,' he said, gesturing to the sofa. 'I'll get some water and cloths to clean up these cuts. And a cup of tea? Or something stronger?'

'Definitely something stronger,' she replied, trying to smile. That coldness, a hard edge that terrified her: she needed to win him over.

He disappeared into the kitchen, and Evelyn took the opportunity to look around, absorbing everything. To be in this room was overwhelming. After months of knowing so little about him, just the few scraps that Diana revealed to her, this, now, was too much at once.

It wasn't a large flat, as far as she could see: one main room, a kitchen, bedroom and bathroom. She was intrigued by the way he had decorated the room. There were several lamps in red and burgundy shades, and a distressed wool rug covered much of the floorboards. Shelves lined one wall, packed with books but also a long row of records, and a collection of small sculptures that looked as though they came from the archaeological dig of some ancient temple. A circular wooden table next to the window was covered in books, a vase of dried and dusty flowers at the centre. In the corner, on top of a drinks trolley, was a record player and a radio. In the shelving beneath was a collection of glasses in different shapes and sizes, nestled around bottles of whisky, gin, brandy, some bitters. The room gave her the impression of someone who enjoyed curating their life, selecting art, objects, books, music. Perhaps it was essential for a psychotherapist, when he gave away nothing of himself to his patients, to have a home that defined him.

The Model Patient

This room was bursting with personality. Evelyn closed her eyes: it was too much to decipher. She could not sift through it quickly enough to work out who he was.

Dr Daley returned with a bowl of water and some towels. Although he had washed the blood from his hands, the grazes were red and angry. He'd changed out of his jacket and was wearing a black collarless shirt, his sleeves rolled up. Setting the bowl and towels down on the floor next to the sofa, he went to the drinks trolley.

'Whisky? Or I can mix you something.'

'A straight vermouth, if that's okay.'

'Of course.'

Evelyn leant down towards the water and towels. A pain shot through her neck and she groaned, righting herself and pressing her head back. The sofa was crowded with cushions, all in different shapes, colours, patterns. She picked up a green velvet one, decorated with golden pine cones, and held it tight in her arms. There was comfort, she found, in having something to hold.

He turned back to her, the sound of two glasses clinking against the bottle of Cinzano vermouth. Clearing some space on the wooden table by the window, he poured their drinks. When he handed the glass to her, he extracted the cushion from her grip, placing it on the far side of the sofa. Evelyn felt exposed, her body cold and shaking.

'Let me help you,' he said, wetting a towel in the bowl of water. He started with her ankle, wiping away the blood. Evelyn winced, the cloth too hard against her broken skin.

Moving up onto the sofa next to her, he took her wrist, cleaning the wound and washing blood off her hand and arm.

It was strange to be touched by him, after months of wondering how it would feel when he did. She looked at him, his head lowered to her wrist, the focus in his gaze as he cleaned her skin. As he touched her, it was as though a costume was falling off from him; he was becoming real, the mysticism stripped away, layer by layer. This room, every detail, every choice, his coat hanging over the back of a chair, the print of Jackson Pollock's 'The Mask' above the fireplace, the plant growing in a chipped terracotta pot by the window. Patrick Daley was emerging.

But then he looked up at her and smiled. It worried her, how impossible it was to understand the man beneath. Even as his costume vanished, Evelyn did not know if this version was real. One role had gone; but what was there in its place frightened her.

'Evelyn, can I see those notes?'

It took a moment for her to understand what he meant, but then she remembered. She was still wearing her suede jacket. Removing it and pulling it on to her knee, she was suddenly aware of the knife hidden inside. She was lucky, she realized, that it had not impaled one of them as they fell.

She found the notes, pulling them out and handing them to him. He took them, taking her jacket at the same time. Evelyn watched, terrified he would feel the knife, but he simply draped the jacket on the back of a sofa.

'You know these are not the only notes I make,' he said,

opening them out and flattening the pages. 'These are the official progress notes that I must keep for the clinic records. I write them with as much brevity as possible, to protect the confidentiality of what you tell me. But I do keep more thorough, personal notes where I record my thoughts and feelings after a session with you.'

'But the notebooks were empty. I looked inside every one and there was nothing.'

'The ones in my desk? I haven't used those yet. I keep my working notes here with me, at home. I record them on a Dictaphone immediately after the appointment and then write them up when I get home.'

Evelyn glanced to his bookshelves, an urgent desire to see where he kept these notes overwhelming her. Diana had failed to find them when she was searching. All she discovered was the photograph.

'Can I see?'

'You want to know what I write about you?'

'Yes, I want to know. These notes are so clinical and indifferent. You have removed yourself entirely. I want to see what you actually think about me.'

'I can't show you the notes, Evelyn. They are personal and they wouldn't make much sense. But I can tell you that they contain the truth of how I feel about you. I have not removed myself from them, not like these ones. On the contrary, I am entirely present.'

'How *do* you feel about me?' There it was again, the question that consumed her.

He took her hand again, turning it over and wiping the remaining blood from her palm. Then he let her go, picking up the cloth and the bowl of water and returning them to the kitchen.

Dr Daley was never going to tell her. She sighed, frustration making her tense painfully. Her body ached from the fall, and her neck was getting stiffer every moment. As she tried to roll her head, stretching out the tightening muscles along her shoulders, she caught sight of a photograph on the mantelpiece. It was a black and white photograph of a woman in her mid to late thirties, with thick and naturally curling hair that she had partially tied back. She was wearing a beautifully cut dress, large buttons down the front, tight at the waist and falling to below her knee. Judging from the style, this was taken just after the end of the war.

The photograph was too small to see properly from the sofa. It compelled her, and Evelyn knew she needed to look more closely. There was something about the woman, even from this distance away, that was familiar.

She got up as quietly as she could and walked to the mantelpiece. With that tightness growing in her chest, she tried to think. Evelyn knew she had seen this woman before, but her face was not falling into the correct recesses of her memory. It was like in those moments after waking from an elusive dream, how quickly the images faded from view.

Dr Daley was returning and there was no time to move

The Model Patient

back to the sofa. He found her standing next to the photograph, her hand resting on the mantelpiece.

'Is this your mother?' she tried. 'She's beautiful.' Evelyn reached up to touch the frame, her fingertips lightly brushing the edge of the glass.

'Don't touch her.'

Dr Daley was right behind her. His voice was angry and it shocked her to hear emotion in his words. Grabbing her wrist, he wrenched her around and into the middle of the room. She stumbled, her shoulder knocking into his.

'I'm sorry,' she replied, her wrist throbbing beneath his grip. She tried to pull away but he did not let go. Perhaps his mother was dead, she thought. It was the only way to explain his reaction.

'Why are you upset? I wasn't going to break anything.'

'Everything is already broken, Evelyn. My mother died last year and my father didn't even come to the funeral.'

'Oh, Patrick, that's so hard. I'm sorry.' He did not let go of her wrist, but rather seemed to grimace when she used his name, Patrick, for the first time.

She frowned, shaking her head as she tried to reason with him. 'But how could I have known that? I know nothing about you.'

His face had returned to that neutral calm. 'Come and sit down,' he said, gesturing to the sofa as he released the grip on her wrist.

She looked down at the piles of cushions, the two glasses of vermouth on a side table, balancing beneath a small burlap lamp. A dim golden glow was illuminating the alcohol. Evelyn tentatively lowered herself onto the sofa, groaning from the pain in her back.

Dr Daley sat next to her, his thigh touching hers.

'I'd prefer it if you called me Dr Daley. It's important that we don't let the boundaries slip.'

Evelyn tried to stifle her shock. How could he say that now? She was in his home. He'd thrown her out of the way of a moving car, just seconds after he was about to let it hit her. He'd cleaned blood from her wrists and ankle. His words, the way he demanded to keep the power for himself, it reminded her of Mr Hardy. He, too, had not liked it when she called him by his first name.

'Evelyn, I'm not being serious. Of course you can call me Patrick. It isn't a big deal.'

She looked up at him, uncertain. He was smiling. But she didn't like his smile, how patronizing it was, how pathetic it made her feel. She felt lost, as though her body could not find solid ground.

Reaching up to her, he pressed the back of his hand against her cheek. She sighed, rolling her head against his touch. This, she told herself as she felt a tremor of fear run through her, was what she had longed for, over and over again. Evelyn wanted to feel it all.

He kissed her, first her jaw and then her lips, and she could feel herself falling inside the sensation. Pulling her down beneath him, he kissed her harder, taking her hand and pressing it above her head into the cushions of the sofa.

'This is what you want,' he whispered to her, his voice at her neck. When he kissed her collarbone, his lips rising up her neck, she shuddered. This was what she wanted: she'd told him so many times.

And yet, now it was really happening, she was terrified. She did not know if this feeling was real, whether the terrible, desperate love she felt for him was a figment of her imagination, a fantasy just like the narratives she created in her mind. What was more frightening was that he knew this too. He knew it with much more clarity than she did: he understood the dynamics of erotic transference, this symptom of psychoanalysis. It was a fantastical creation within the analytic space, two people passing desires, fears, traumas of the past between one another, asking each other to hold those feelings in the strange world of therapy. This was the work they were supposed to do together – but not like this. He knew that. And yet here they were, trapped in each other's arms, the delicate space between them irrevocably broken.

As she continued to let him kiss her, his hand moving down to between her legs, she told herself that it was his responsibility to save them from this. She had relinquished all her power.

'How does it feel,' he said as he moved to unfasten her belt, 'to tell me you love me?'

'You know how it feels,' she gasped. She wanted him to touch her, for him to feel how her body responded to him. But there was another part of her that recoiled. Hidden deep inside was a young girl who screamed silently to be heard.

That scent again, rosemary, orange, honey, leather, cedar: it was more powerful than ever, Dr Daley's skin so close to hers. She could picture the bottle, English Leather, with its large wooden lid.

With a shock that jolted through her body, the memory sparked into life. There it was, the bottle of English Leather cologne positioned on a wooden dressing table in the bedroom of a man she longed to forget. It would elude her no longer.

Mr Hardy always wore the same cologne. She remembered now, the way Mr Hardy dabbed the liquid against his jaw as he was dismissing her. English Leather, a gift from his American friend in the advertising industry. After that first gift, he got it shipped over specially, never letting himself run out. There was something about the scent that he liked, the masculinity, the unashamed boldness, the privilege to fill a room: his signature smell. And now, Dr Daley was wearing the same cologne. Too many repetitions, the same relentless cycle once again. It had to stop.

'You have always wanted this,' he said, his mouth on the side of her neck. 'You want to be adored.'

'No.'

She tried to press him away, struggling up the sofa. The girl was emerging, her scream no longer silent. She was sixteen again and Mr Hardy was on top of her, whispering in her ear. You want to be adored, he said. You want to be loved.

'Get off me,' she cried. 'This isn't right. I don't want this.'

The Model Patient

'You do want this,' he said. 'Don't resist what you want. Don't punish yourself for your desires.'

'Not like this. Please. Don't do this.' He kissed her again and she felt her chest constricting, panic hitting her. She didn't understand what was happening, why he was refusing to listen to her. Did he think this was part of the treatment, some twisted way to help her learn about herself? It was enough. She had learnt enough.

Reaching behind her, she fumbled for her jacket. It was right there, the suede soft in her fingers. She needed to distract him. Wrapping her legs around his body, she drew him into her as she returned his kiss.

It was her only chance. She dug her hand into the material, desperately trying to find the opening to the pocket. And there it was, waiting for her. Closing her fingers around the knife, she pulled it out.

She stabbed him, slicing through the sleeve of his shirt and deep into his arm. He groaned, his body convulsing as he tried to get his arm away from her knife.

Using the distraction of his pain, she pushed him off and scrambled to her feet. The knife fell, the sound muffled by the rug, but there was no time to retrieve it.

She needed to get away before he tried to drag her back, either with his body or his words. For it was his words that made her most afraid. And it was herself, how easily he might persuade her back to loving him. She ran to the door and pulled it open.

Evelyn screamed. There was something, someone,

blocking her escape route. Stumbling, she stepped back into the room, away from the figure standing in the doorway. Evelyn felt a pressure against her lungs, a rage coming from in front and from behind her, an unyielding force that would drown her if she did not find a way to fight.

The figure in the doorway stepped forwards, her features sharpening like the final seconds of a developing photograph. Diana.

The two women stood on either side of the door. Diana reached out her hand. She was brightly lit, the hallway light shining around her. Evelyn was in the shadows, Dr Daley's apartment cast in a red and gloomy darkness behind.

'We have to go back in there,' Diana said, her grip on Evelyn's hand tightening. 'One more journey into the past and then I promise you will be free.'

CHAPTER 34

Patrick Daley was standing in the middle of the room, clutching his wounded arm. Blood stained his fingers.

'I know what you've been doing,' Diana said, and he looked up at her in surprise. The two women stood side by side, their hands touching. While they might look like sisters in their identical black trousers and sleeveless jumpers, everything else about them was in stark opposition. Evelyn's long blonde hair had fallen out of its ponytail and her eyes were dark with the unruly stains of her make-up; Diana was neat and precise, her perfect pixie haircut, subtle make-up, a tidy rim of black at the edge of her eyes. While Evelyn swayed with exhaustion, Diana was firm, her eyes fixed on Patrick.

'You've deceived us both, dragging us into your dangerous game. I will never forgive you for turning me against my best friend.'

'Diana, what are you talking about?' Patrick shook his head slowly, a look of pity on his face. Here were two deluded women: it was his role to save them from their hysteria. But it was a performance; Evelyn could see that now. Everything he did was a performance, a carefully planned act to make two women, his patient and his lover, doubt everything that they knew instinctively to be true.

'Tell me about this book?' Diana reached into her bag and pulled it out. A ragged-edged theatre ticket was sticking out from the front pages. It was an old and worn copy of a play, a red dustcover, theatre curtains opening onto the white space of the title: *A Streetcar Named Desire* by Tennessee Williams.

'What is this about, Diana? I lent that to you after suggesting it would be useful inspiration for your novel. Blanche DuBois seducing men in the Tarantula Arms.' He smiled at her, another attempt to assert his control, the calm doctor explaining reality to an irrational woman. 'I told you how I went to see the play when it first opened in London in 1949.'

'Yes, you went to see the play when you were seventeen years old and still living with both your parents at Winter Manor. But it wouldn't be long before all that ended and you and your mother returned to America.'

Evelyn froze. She did not understand what Diana had just said. Winter Manor was Mr Hardy's house. Why would Dr Daley be living there?

'There's no point denying it, Patrick,' Diana continued. 'Did you forget that you'd written your name and address on the inside of the book? Patrick Hardy, Winter Manor. Or did you give me that book deliberately, to make me doubt everything you'd ever said to me? You'd already driven Evelyn to the edge, and now I had to suffer too? It must have been a blow for you when you were forced to leave that big beautiful house. Did it hurt to realize that your father was not the man you thought he was?'

'I'm not Patrick Hardy.' He spat out the words, as though he was trying to repel some old and buried part of himself.

'Yes, you are,' Diana replied. 'You're Patrick Hardy and you're punishing the woman your father raped. Why are you doing that to her? Do you think she destroyed your parents' marriage? Did she end your childhood? How can you not understand that she was a child too?'

'I'm not Patrick Hardy,' he repeated. 'I'm Dr Daley.'

Diana laughed. 'Fine, you're Patrick Daley. Is that your mother's maiden name? Did you decide that you wanted to remove your father from your life, pretend he didn't exist? Well, isn't that ignoring the whole point of your psychoanalysis? To bring the hidden secrets of the past up to the surface?'

'This is crazy. What does it matter if he was my father? I haven't seen him in years and I no longer think of him as a parent. It has nothing to do with either of you.'

'Don't call me crazy, Patrick. It has everything to do with us. You took advantage of your power over Evelyn, of the transference she was experiencing. She fell in love with you, or some false version of you that emerged out of your dangerous methods, and you led her further and further down a path that was only going to end this way. Did it make you feel good to have a beautiful woman sitting in front of you, telling you her fantasies, with you as the central character?'

'It's a respected method of psychotherapy, Diana. I did no more than what hundreds of physicians are doing around the world.'

Evelyn took a step towards him, rage building inside her. All those times she had told him about Mr Hardy, what he did to her, how young she was back then, how vulnerable, terrified of all that she might lose. What had Dr Daley done but make her doubt herself, turning it around, reminding her again and again how she longed for love, how she was to blame, how it was her fault for being incapable of saying no?

'Is it still respected when you take advantage of my past to learn how to trap me?'

He shook his head, but it was different this time. His silence had changed, its power evaporating.

'Do you think I planned all this, Evelyn? How could I possibly have known you would end up in my clinic?'

'No, maybe you didn't plan this. Not at the beginning, anyway. But then when you worked out who I was, you knew this was your chance. Did you think you had the opportunity to punish me and you simply couldn't resist? You tried to make me feel that I was going insane.'

She was shaking, all those moments she had suffered as she sat opposite Dr Daley in his consulting room returning to her. He was a doctor, and she had let herself trust him. 'That painting you used in your dream images: did you find that in your father's house? I always suspected that I left it there, or that he took it out of my school satchel. Did you add it to your images to make me feel I was losing my sense of reality?'

'You were already punishing yourself, Evelyn. I did very little.'

'But you could have helped me, Patrick. You could have taught me that I didn't need the eyes of a man on me, a man with the power to make me feel whole and to destroy me. I relied on you. You drew me close, let me sense your attention, but you never quite let me know that you cared for me. Instead you made me doubt constantly. I worried that I was delusional.'

'You are delusional, Evelyn. You play the innocent victim so you don't have to take any responsibility for what you did.'

'What did I do, Patrick?'

'You seduced my father. Your actions forced my mother to leave him. You made my sisters want nothing to do with either of my parents. You destroyed my family. And then you stand there, next to the photograph of my mother, telling me that she is beautiful. I know she is beautiful. But somehow you made sure that your beauty eclipsed hers.'

'That wasn't my fault. How can you still think that after all that I've shared with you? I was fourteen when it all began.'

'But it didn't stop, did it? Even when you were old enough to make up your own mind, you kept coming back. Were you weak, or did you just love the attention he gave you?'

'Did you hate me every time I walked into your consulting room? Did you think I was trying to seduce you, like I seduced your father?'

'You were trying to seduce me.'

'Yes. Yes, I was. But I could have stopped, right at the beginning, if you had handled it differently. If you had only helped me to see that my love for you wasn't real, then maybe it wouldn't have been so painful. You should have put a stop to it. Instead, you encouraged me. And I thought that the way to make you like me was if I loved you. I gave you everything.'

Evelyn clenched her fists, anger throbbing through her.

'I said to myself over and over again: I love him and I hate him. Was it the same for you? Did you hate that you were falling in love with me? Did it feel as though you were betraying your beautiful dead mother?'

He stepped towards her. Evelyn and Patrick were inches apart and they felt the heat of each other's anger. Diana watched, her body poised and still.

'You know, Evelyn, you're right about one thing. I did want to make it hurt. I wanted you to be in so much pain that you begged me to love you. And then I wanted to kill you. I imagined it so many times, how I'd strip you naked, touch you exactly the way you wanted me to, and then I'd cut your throat.'

She threw herself at him. He fell backwards, his head hitting the coffee table. It stunned him and he was too slow to avoid her rage. Pulling him down onto the rug, she wrapped her legs either side of his waist. Her hands found his throat and she pressed down, too fast for him to react. She hated him and this time she was going to kill him. There would be no more repetitions of the past.

The Model Patient

He tried to lift his hands to her face, but she wrenched her neck away, pressing down harder, her knees trapping his legs, her fingers wrapped tight around his neck. Taking her shoulders in a furious grip, he shook her. She could feel the bruising deepen beneath his hands, but she did not let go.

Diana watched. She was, for an instant, hypnotized by her friend's rage. As Evelyn pressed harder around Patrick's neck, her legs weighing him to the ground, Diana began to move closer. To destroy this man would destroy Evelyn too.

Evelyn felt a force pulling her from behind. She tumbled, falling from the man she was trying to destroy, and into the arms of her best friend.

'That's enough,' Diana said, holding Evelyn tightly. 'He's not going to hurt you anymore.'

They looked at Patrick. His throat was bruised and he was struggling to catch his breath. Pulling himself up on to his knees, his gaze suddenly became still, fixed on a spot a few feet away.

A glint of metal. The knife was between them, caught in the lamp light. Evelyn saw it too, a sharp edge of silver, the small blade of the knife shining like the gleam of a pearl. It was hers, and she would not let him touch it.

They moved together. Evelyn was faster, drawing the knife into her fist and pointing the blade towards him. She was shaking, an exhaustion rising to the surface. Holding her arm steady took all the strength she had left. But Diana was right there with her. There was nothing he could do to hurt her now.

'I have imagined saying goodbye to you so many times,' Evelyn said, reaching for Diana's hand. 'In my mind, it was tragic. I couldn't stop crying, and you would tell me that it didn't need to be this way. We could, you'd say, continue working together. But I knew that the only way to escape from you was if I stopped loving you. And I was terrified that you'd never let me be free.'

She lowered the knife, and Dr Daley faltered, his legs buckling as his hand wrapped around the wound on his arm. Blood dripped on to the rug beneath him.

He was silent. There was power, Evelyn felt, in watching him try to find the words to make her stay. This time, nothing would keep her there.

The two women walked to the door, Dr Daley pressing his hand tighter over the blood. At the threshold, Diana turned to him.

'Try to paint us as crazy and hysterical women if you want. But I think you'll agree that the evidence is against you. It's not going to look good when your medical board realize you were treating the woman who was raped by your father. Or that you sought out her best friend, seduced her, proposed to her. How far were you going to go, Patrick? Would you really have married me to punish Evie? Or were you so in love with the power you held over us that you started to think you were invincible, a brilliant man who could save us or punish us, with no repercussions?'

He stepped backwards, lowering himself onto the sofa.

The Model Patient

Evelyn stared at him, remembering what he had said when he finally broke. He wanted to strip her naked and cut her throat. And she, too, had wanted to kill him: love and death in conflict. That was what they did, a doctor and a patient transferring the pain of the past between one another, trying to find redemption through love.

But it hadn't worked. Instead, they had come too close to destroying each other.

Diana and Evelyn did not go home, not immediately. They wanted to feel alive, the two of them together, everything unspoken between them finally exposed.

They walked for hours, their exhaustion slipping away as they paced the streets of the city. Evelyn and Diana linked arms, their steps synchronized as they walked down Oxford Street, through Covent Garden, to the water, along the Thames, up through Chelsea.

'I'm going to start a new novel,' Diana said as they walked along the King's Road. 'I couldn't work out how to end the last one. Nothing I tried was working. I found myself wanting the actress to kill all those men, but I also wanted her to heal. It was impossible to find a satisfying way to make it all come to an end.'

Evelyn nodded, but all she could think about was those pages falling onto the kitchen floor, her hands covered in blood.

'I'm sorry I destroyed your book. I was so angry. Every word felt like a betrayal.'

'She wasn't you, Evie. I know it might seem that way, but she wasn't. Maybe it was your experience with Roland Hardy that sparked the idea. But that was it. In many ways, I wish you had been able to kill the men who took advantage of you. Though you did come close tonight.'

'Yes.' Evelyn smiled. 'If you hadn't been there, then I might well have turned into your actress.'

Diana unlocked the door and they walked up the staircase they knew so well.

As they reached the landing, Evelyn faltered. A familiar anxiety hovered at her throat and for the briefest moment she felt that painful ache in her chest. Evelyn's heart was beating fast and her skin was hot, a flush of sweat beading beneath her jacket.

She stopped, and this time she let herself feel everything: the palm of her hand pressing into the banisters, the creaking wood beneath her feet, the cold air of the stairwell, the tension that collected at the base of her neck, the tightness of her jaw.

Resisting nothing, she experienced it all. When it began to move, there was no struggle. The strain swept down her neck, through her spine, along her limbs. It was her demon, and it was moving – a creeping fear that had lived inside her for so long set free.

It was time to let it go.

Closing her eyes, she could sense a new feeling gliding forwards. A settling, a sweep of energy absorbed back within her, calm and powerful.

The Model Patient

That serpent, the one that had terrified her, possessed her, then seduced her – once again it had changed.

Her monster. This time they held one another.

When Diana opened the door of Number Six, Evelyn felt a lightness dancing through her veins.

CHAPTER 35

It took Evelyn three more days before she decided it was time to face Henry. In those three days, Evelyn and Diana left Number Six only to eat, to walk through Hyde Park, to visit their favourite shops, trying on new clothes and drinking coffee in the King's Road cafés that played the newest music from their jukeboxes. Walking around the Serpentine, the softness of the breeze was healing, the brutal winter banished at last.

It was the Easter holidays and Diana did not have to work. She did, however, start planning her new novel. This time, she shared her ideas with Evelyn, the two of them throwing suggestions back and forth over their reclaimed tradition of wine, bread and cheese. Patrick Daley could not steal that from them, not anymore.

Evelyn decided to go on her own. Henry had called her the day before, asking when she was coming home. He needed to speak to her. There was something different in his voice, a vulnerability that she did not know existed beneath

The Model Patient

the regulated order of his life. Beyond the rote phrase of 'I love you', he had never been able to articulate the complexities of desire.

As Evelyn walked slowly through Chelsea, the Saturday morning shoppers moving at a fast pace around her, she was surprised to realize that she was not afraid. She knew that it was safe for her to see him. For the first time in her life, she had the strength to stay true to her choices.

Arriving at their house in Pimlico, she knocked before unlocking the door and letting herself in; it felt important to announce her arrival.

She found Henry upstairs in the bedroom. There was something about the messiness of the room that made her pause, her fingers pressed against the doorframe. His clothes were pushed into a pile on one of the chairs and the bedcovers were pulled untidily across the bed, so different from his usual packing away of each item of clothing into the correct compartments of the closet.

He was opening the curtains when she came in, and he turned, an anxious smile on his face.

That too frequent temptation rose within her, to smile, to forgive, to make him happy, to forget what he had done. But the feeling passed as soon as it arrived, and she steeled herself.

'Let's go downstairs,' she said. 'I'd prefer to talk in the kitchen. We can make some coffee.'

He followed her down the stairs. Neither of them spoke: there was too much to say to know how to begin. He filled the kettle, digging through the cupboards for some mugs.

Evelyn looked around her. There was no evidence at all that Henry had tried to cook while she was away. She did not dare open the refrigerator; if she saw evidence of her mother-in-law's Tupperware meals, she might find herself walking straight out the door.

They waited until the coffee was ready and they were sat together at the kitchen table. Henry spoke first, blurting out the words as though he could not contain them any longer.

'Evie, you need to know the truth. Your birth control pills for these three months were fake. They were dummy pills.'

Evelyn nodded. It hurt so much that he could have done this to her. But there was relief in knowing she hadn't been making this up. Her accusations were real.

'But I didn't swap them, Evie. It wasn't me. I know that's hard for you to believe, but it's true.'

'It was your parents then? The three of you together: it doesn't make it any better. It's worse, in fact, that you could let them do this to me.'

'Evelyn, I had no idea. I only found out what they did a few days ago. My mother finally gave in and admitted it.'

Despite all her suspicions, the fear that she couldn't shake ever since she found her mother-in-law in her bedroom all those months ago, Evelyn was stunned. To think that Ruth and Alec could do this, to plot against her, force her body to bend to their will: it sent a chill along her skin. She shuddered, remembering Alec standing at the end of the examination table, cleaning blood from between her legs. He did that to her, and then he drove her home.

The Model Patient

In the silence of the kitchen, she could feel her mind falling into a familiar pattern of blame and punishment. It was her fault, a repetition of the past, how she let others control her body, Mr Hardy all over again. But then she stopped, her thoughts catching themselves. This wasn't her fault. That terrible journey back to the past, Dr Daley's silences that tore her apart: he had taught her more than he knew.

She dug her hand into the edge of the kitchen table, her knuckles pale. Looking up, she saw Henry staring her. He was terrified, watching every emotion that crossed her face.

'I will never forgive them, Evie. They tried to make me see why they had done it, but everything they said made it worse. We don't need our life to be like theirs, I realize that now. I want us to create our own life, together.'

He leant forward across the table, his hand reaching for hers. 'I love you, Evie. And I'm sorry.'

For so long, Evelyn had waited for him to forge his own path, away from the control of his parents. In marrying her, a fashion model whose career was certain to horrify his mother, perhaps he had tried to break free back then. But he had slipped too quickly towards the comfort of what he knew.

Now she was afraid it was too late. She did not know how to go back to him.

'I can never forgive them either,' Evelyn said, shifting her hand away from Henry's. 'And I am not sure I can forgive you for letting them feel it was acceptable to do this to me.' She held up her hand, stopping him from interrupting her. 'I know that they did this without your knowledge. But don't you see that your inability to place any boundaries over their intrusion into our lives empowered them to overstep. And not just overstep, but violate my body.'

'Please, Evelyn. I will never see them again. I've told them not to try to contact us. They aren't welcome here.'

'What did your mother say to that? Do you really think it's realistic for you to never see her again?'

'I am going to try. At least let me try.'

'That's not going to be good enough, Henry. Every time I see them, the memory of what they did will come back to me. And you love your mother. It's not possible for you to simply walk away. I don't want you to give up your relationship with her if it means you'll resent me for ending that part of your life.'

One man had already punished her for the loss of his relationship with his father; she did not want it to happen again with Henry.

'It is possible, if it means I can be with you.'

Evelyn stood, taking her coffee mug to the sink. Part of her longed to go back to him. She had loved him. It was tragic to think of all they had lost, how their relationship had fallen apart as Evelyn struggled to cope with the changes to her life. If they were to recapture the warmth, the connection, the safety of their love from before they were married, Evelyn needed to rebuild herself. She could not go back to the same depressing existence, waiting at home for her husband, no career, no future, no outlet for her art, her creativity, her love. Despite all the pain, Dr Daley's therapy had helped her find a new path: she would not debase herself to bring happiness to a man.

'I can't, not yet. I'm going to live with Diana for a while. I am not saying this is for ever. But we need to find a way for this marriage to work for both of us. It won't happen overnight and I can't be with you while I work out what I want. You also need the space to learn whether you can love me as an equal. I want this to be a marriage of mutual love, no hierarchy, no inflicting punishments for failing to bend to each other's will. We need to learn to talk to each other.'

She walked to him and he rose to meet her. They embraced, Henry holding her tightly in his arms. She could hear his chest starting to heave, the sobs following fast. Evelyn thought her heart might break.

Gently, she pulled away from him.

'We'll meet soon.'

'How about we make a plan, Evie? Let's meet once a week, until you're ready for more. We can talk.'

'Yes, okay, I'd like that. Once a week. And we both need to agree if and when we start to increase the number of meetings; there must be no pressure.'

'No pressure. But, Evie, there will always be love. I am not going to stop loving you.'

She kissed him and then she left. Once a week. It was, she realized as she closed the door behind her, a repetition of sorts, replacing her psychotherapy sessions with Dr Daley. But everything else had changed. This, with Henry, was a search for a different sort of love, an equal love. Dr Daley had unravelled her, unpicking each thread that had kept her together, making her doubt herself, hate herself, again and again. It was up to her to form a new pattern, a fabric stitched afresh.

This time, she would hold on to herself and only from that place of self-love would she learn to love again.

CHAPTER 36

Eighteen months later

Evelyn waited for quiet to settle before she introduced Diana to the audience. It was a Friday night two weeks before Christmas, and memories of the brutal winter freeze more than eighteen months ago were fading. On this December night of 1964, the winter spirit was bold, young and determined: The Beatles were number one with 'I Feel Fine'; the cinemas were crammed for the premiere of Sean Connery in the latest Bond film; Harvey Nichols had a special Christmas shopping night; skirts with ever-rising hemlines could be seen in the windows of the most fashionable shops; and women were swapping their beige stockings for colourful woollen tights. But for this crowd of people who had packed themselves into a beautiful jewellery boutique on the King's Road, they were here for free drinks, endless conversation, and the celebration of a new novel: *Let Her Rave* by Diana Ashley.

Clinking the edge of her glass against Diana's, the party gradually hushed. There was little need to introduce her really, not when the room was filled with familiar faces: supporters, friends, family, lovers old and new, all of whom had congregated to celebrate the launch of Diana Ashley's debut novel. But Evelyn felt her heart swelling with pride as she lifted a copy of the novel into the air and the applause travelled like thunder through the room.

The two women stood next to a display of books, raised on a small platform at the back of the shop. Usually devoted to trying on the modern jewellery designs that Lionel stocked and celebrated, the platform gave them a good view of the room. A large mirror behind them illuminated the space, multiplying the pile of books, the audience, the jewellery displays positioned in glass cabinets and draped over mannequins. There was a Christmas tree in the corner, decorated with mock-ups of the shop's most popular jewellery. The branches were draped with long and large strings of faux gemstones; teardrop glass decorations hung like giant earrings and there were circular bands of gold bracelets, geometric silver triangles, ruby red flowers shining beneath an abundance of glitter. The window display, too, was dazzling. Colourful Christmas lights snaked through the space, along the floor and around a series of wooden stepladders that held piles of Diana's book, as well as long velvet mannequin arms that writhed, swan-like, from different levels of the ladders' steps.

Lionel Diallo had opened the shop six months earlier. He

described it as a salon for the intersection of art and fashion, inviting jewellery designers from around the world to exhibit and sell their pieces: wearable art, he called it, available to everyone. It was immensely popular, partly because of the accessible price range and also because walking into the boutique was like entering a fantasy land. He chose the music carefully, curating song lists that made one feel as though anything was possible. Between the glass cabinets and the velvet mannequins, the mirrors and the dressing tables, a person could make that ever-elusive quest to understand the beauty of their body, bringing their neck, throat, wrists alive with adornment. Lionel believed that jewellery did not have meaning without a body to give it completion: that was why he insisted on customers trying on the designs in front of a mirror. He asked every person who came into his store to think of each piece of jewellery as the start of a conversation with their body, their desires, their understanding of who they were and who they wanted to be.

Diana thanked Evelyn before opening the book at the first chapter. Evelyn had read this book many times already, but to hear it now spoken out loud by Diana was different: she fixed her eyes above the heads of the crowd and tried not to cry.

The title for *Let Her Rave* emerged out of a late night with Diana, the two of them trawling through the book to find a phrase that would stick. To let her rave: it sounded so familiar. It was Evelyn who remembered where she had first heard it: a line in a poem by John Keats, studied with Mr Martin when they were teenagers. There was something unsettling about the words, a man finding beauty in a woman's suffering. She'd read the lines out to Diana, and they knew it was perfect.

'If thy mistress some rich anger shows, imprison her soft hand, and let her rave and feed deep, deep upon her peerless eyes.' Evelyn used to love that poem; now she wasn't so sure.

Diana finished her reading and the energy in the room shifted once again. Glasses were refilled, the lights lowered, the music raised. Lionel was the perfect host, guiding lonely guests towards one another, and ushering those with deep pockets towards the books and jewellery available to purchase. Evelyn's and Diana's parents were here, and had finally left their place of safety in the corner. Diana's mother was determined to make an effort to talk to everyone as she handed round the home-baked Christmas biscuits and Evelyn's was showing off her daughter's jewellery collection. For there had been no doubt in Lionel's mind that he would choose Evelyn's jewellery to take centre stage.

Evelyn joined her parents, her father kissing the side of her head and her mother wrapping her arm around her waist.

'These are stunning, Evie,' her mother said, draping a serpentine gold necklace over her fingers. The pendant, held in the jaws of a golden snake, was a paisley teardrop crafted from metallic thread. This had become her signature over the past year, an integration of intertwined fabric in the shape of paisley tears, fastened to complex designs of gold creatures: she drew on her consortium of monsters, her snakes and spiders, the looping tails of mermaids, trees with tangled knots of branches. She experimented with colours, materials, shapes, sizes, but the paisley shape was always there, at times fabric, or often silver, copper or stainless steel. Her favourite design was a pair of paisley teardrops earrings. They had a silver spiderweb base, with black jade embedded into the casing and thread woven among the silverwork. Pride of place in the centre of each earring was a black pearl, a midnight lake under moonlight. Evelyn often used pearls in her designs. It was empowering, she found, to take the symbols of her past and make them her own. She had enrolled in a course on experimental jewellery design at the Hornsey College of Arts and Crafts, led by the designer Gerda Flöckinger. Combined with learning the technical skills of stone setting and engraving, Evelyn's designs had flourished.

It had not been easy, but Evelyn had finally told her parents about Mr Hardy. She'd taken the train home one day a few months after she'd ended her therapy with Dr Daley. They had listened to her and they had cried with her, and everything had changed. But Evelyn knew that wasn't enough. She'd written to every agency she'd ever worked with and set out her aims to protect young people from the men who were determined to abuse their power. She wanted to tell her story, in the hope it might help young women build the tools they needed to see the warning signs of abuse. It was dispiriting how little progress she had made, most of the agencies not even acknowledging her letter. But Evelyn refused to give up. This, along with her jewellery creations, was becoming her life's work. She was determined that change was possible.

There had already been so many setbacks, and it was easy to feel trapped inside a system that did not want to help women. When she put in her complaint about Dr Daley, she was warned it would not be straightforward. And that was true. Many times in the process of pursuing her complaint, she had been labelled as unstable, hysterical, a liar, a seductress. But she had not given up and she hoped that one day she would be believed.

Henry was over by the bar. Giving her parents a hug, she left them to continue boasting about her jewellery to anyone who would listen. Weaving through the party, she made her way to her husband. She smiled as she reached him. The man at his side was nodding enthusiastically, trying to keep up with Henry's chatter.

'My wife designed the front cover,' he was saying, holding a copy of the novel out in front of him. 'Look how the shape of the woman emerges from beneath?'

'It's mesmerizing,' the man replied. And he was right. Evelyn had painted the shadow of a naked woman, partially hiding her beneath thick strokes of red paint. It was abstract, but it was also absolutely clear. There were no riddles in this painting, no hiding beneath a veiled desire.

Evelyn kissed her husband, drawing her arms around him. It had taken a long time, but finally they were living together again. They had sold the house in Pimlico, returning the money gifted from Henry's parents. Now they were renting a flat in Wimbledon Village and were hoping to buy a place of their own soon. It had been a relief to give up that oversized home in Pimlico, the gleaming kitchen, the depressing dining room with all those long Sunday lunches. Now they spent Sunday mornings together in bed; they walked for hours through Wimbledon Common; and they talked. Evelyn told him everything: Mr Hardy, Dr Daley, the repetitions of her life finally releasing her. And he shared with Evelyn the truth of how he'd felt when he first met her, this hope that he could find a way to be more than the youngest son in a family of rules and expectations, his anger at himself when he failed to break free. They were discovering one another all over again.

'I'll find you again soon,' Evelyn said. 'I need to say hello to Diana's publisher.' Henry kissed her again and she turned back to the room. The heat and noise were building and it was getting harder to move through the crowd of people. Diana was perched on a stool near the raised platform as she signed copies of her book, surrounded by guests. There was an excited crowd of young women who looked as though they had only recently left school: ex-students of Diana's, delighted to be seeing their teacher in a different setting.

Evelyn walked towards the window display, a slow progress through the crush of the room. Diana's publisher and agent were close by, and she could hear them talking, but she decided to wait before she said hello. She wanted to pause, to take it all in, to let the images before her strengthen into the promise of solid, vivid memories.

The door opened and cool air rushed inside. Evelyn turned, instinctively stepping forward to greet the man who was walking into the shop. But then she stopped, her chest tightening, an old fear flooding through her. She watched as the man entered, her eyes narrowing in disbelief. To turn up now, after all that had happened: he had still not learnt to accept that his influence was over.

He was wearing a black jacket over a pink floral shirt and one of his trouser legs was tucked into the back of his boot. Patrick Daley had not changed, although his hair was even longer than before. Evelyn steeled herself. She had not expected him to dare turn up at Diana's book launch. She had not, in fact, expected to see him ever again.

In the instant before he saw her, she let the fear wash through her and away again, a receding tide of emotion. Evelyn did not need to be afraid, not anymore. A part of her was grateful to him: it was because of him that she had learnt to understand herself. Her whole life had been a battle of conflicting desires: the desire to be loved and the desire to be strong enough to love herself; the desire for men to want her and the desire to be free from their gaze. In a world dominated by men like Roland Hardy and his son, she had spent too long trying to make them love her, humiliating herself in the process. It was hard, she had realized over the past year, to free oneself from a dominant culture, even an oppressive one that tried its best to infantilize women. The mentality was ingrained so deeply. But she was not alone: Diana was with her every step of the way.

The Model Patient

Dr Daley, she had realized, liked her best when she was vulnerable, when she needed him, when she pleaded with him to help her. He had enjoyed playing the great saviour, the enigmatic man she craved to understand. Maybe he had thought that if she became addicted to him, then leaving would be impossible. It had taken the truth to break his spell.

She did not look away when he saw her. He was standing in the doorway and she was by the window, her face lit up by the Christmas lights. The conversation of Diana's publisher and agent drifted between them, filling the space like a strange, dream-like radio play. Patrick and Evelyn stared at one another as they listened to the two women speaking.

'So different from her first book idea, of course.'

'Did you ever read the full manuscript?'

'No. She changed her mind about the direction she wanted to take. It worked out well, obviously.'

'I will be interested in what readers think of the ending. I wanted her to kill him off. It would have been a more satisfying conclusion.'

'The doctor? I know, I felt the same.'

'I craved a good murder scene.'

A peal of laughter from across the room broke the spell, and the two voices lost their clarity. The conversation was absorbed into the noise of the party, and Patrick and Evelyn took a step towards each other.

'What are you doing here, Patrick? Are you going to read the book?' She could feel a smile forming at the edges of her lips, but it was not the smile that she used to offer him eighteen months ago. This was a smile for her alone, a smile that reminded her she would not let him make her feel small.

'Would you like me to read Diana's book?' he said. A flicker of annoyance passed through her, but then it was gone and she laughed.

'Don't try that on me now. Read it or don't read it, I don't care.'

'I didn't make you fall in love with me, Evelyn,' he said, taking another step towards her.

'Was I ever really in love with you? Maybe I thought that you wanted me to love you, and so I obeyed. You were only really interested when I was talking about you and my response to you. I should thank you, really. It was in liberating myself from you that I learnt who I could be.'

He was not listening to her, not really. Evelyn could see the signs, how his eyes flicked over her, how he was trying to find a way to reassert his power, claim his superior interpretation of her words. She tried again, and this time her words found their mark.

'I don't love you. And I don't hate you either. I used to think you were either a benevolent patriarch or a sadistic god. Now I see that you're simply a broken man. It wasn't my fault that your parents' marriage ended, but I know how much it hurt you.'

He shook his head, the smallest glimmer of pain travelling between his eyes. Evelyn took a step towards him. 'Patrick, you need to stop searching for satisfaction in the power you have over your patients.'

The Model Patient

There was another warm screech of laughter. Lionel had turned up the music again, rock-and-roll bouncing between the guests and the wine and the mirrors. A group of young women were dancing in the centre of the room, condensation dripping from the bottles of beer in their hands. As they drank and danced, the energy of their movements spread to those standing at the edges. Evelyn could sense a new pace building among the crowd, and from the corner of her vision she could see the slick shine of sweat, a fast beat marked out from the hips of the dancers. She wanted to join them.

'We need to stop now,' Evelyn said, impatient to end the conversation with Dr Daley. She walked to the door and opened it, the sounds of the King's Road traffic rolling beneath the music.

Patrick did not move. Evelyn understood the feeling, how hard it was to leave a room with all one's emotions unresolved. So many times she had walked out of his clinic, feeling as though her body and mind were falling apart. This time, it was his turn to leave.

Evelyn had thought about the moment of saying goodbye to him many times during those months of therapy. Never had she let herself imagine it this way.

Dr Patrick Daley walked past her and out onto the street.

'Taking away his pain is not your responsibility.' Diana was there beside her, watching as the door closed.

'I know.'

They stood together, side by side. The song changed. Evelyn and Diana stepped back into the crowd, took each other's hands, and started to dance.

Author's Note and Bibliography

The Model Patient is both a love letter to psychotherapy and a criticism of its fragile ethics. While the novel does interrogate concerns about the dangers of encouraging a transference-dominated relationship with a patient who, by the very nature of the treatment, is likely to become unhealthily reliant on the psychotherapist, *The Model Patient* should not be read as a criticism of the important and often life-changing work that people can do in therapy. Instead, it is an exploration of the problematic power dynamics that pave the way too easily for abuse.

In my research for this novel, I came across many fascinating theories and writings about psychoanalysis, mental health, changing access and attitudes to contraception in the 1950s and 1960s, relationships, love, patriarchal structures, feminism, dreams, advertising, fashion and art. My research was enhanced by taking a course on Freud's *The Ego and the Id* led by Dr Keith Barrett, visiting the Freud House Museum in Hampstead, exploring 1950s and 1960s fashion and jewellery in the Victoria and Albert Museum (London) and the Metropolitan Museum of Art (New York), reading the confessional poetry of Anne Sexton and Sylvia Plath, and experiencing over a year of psychodynamic therapy with a therapist who encouraged full and extensive analysis of transference as a therapeutic methodology.

Many books on psychology and psychotherapy are written by psychologists who place themselves at the centre of each case study, the heroes and saviours for their troubled patients. Reading so many of these books was unsettling, and I found myself craving an account of psychotherapy from the perspective of the patient. Very few of the case studies written from the perspective of the therapists showed, in my opinion, a real or meaningful attempt to understand the often bewildering and painful experience of being in psychodynamic therapy or psychoanalysis.

I am specifically focusing here on psychodynamic therapy and psychoanalysis, the therapies with their roots in Sigmund Freud's writings and theories, though they have, of course, taken new and interesting directions throughout the twentieth century. There are other types of therapy that are common today, for example cognitive behavioural therapy, acceptance and commitment therapy, parts work (internal family systems) that help people to understand and integrate the parts of themselves that are in conflict, and dialectical behavioural therapy. These modalities do not usually risk the re-traumatization that can come with therapies that encourage transference. There is, however, significant debate about

The Model Patient

the effectiveness of each type of therapy, and good therapists are able to acknowledge this uncertainty.

It wasn't until I was beginning to edit the first draft of this novel that I found the book *In Session* by Deborah A. Lott, a journalist who conducted extensive research and interviewing of women who were or had been in therapy. At last I had access to the patient's voice, beyond that of my own experience. Reading Lott's book was empowering and gave me the confidence to challenge many of the troubling power dynamics inherent in therapy, such as the unequal structure, the potential for gaslighting, and the way some psychoanalytically aligned therapists use the concept of transference as a catch-all to deny the patient agency in the therapeutic relationship, instead giving the therapist a convenient way to evade any responsibility for the dynamic between them.

The Hungarian psychologist Sándor Ferenczi critiques Freud when he suggests in his 1932 *Clinical Diary* that Freud's methods serve to help make an analyst's life more comfortable. He writes:

> the calm unemotional reserve; the unruffled assurance that one knew better, and the theories, the seeking and finding of the causes of failure in the patient instead of partly in ourselves, the dishonesty of reserving the technique for one's own person; the advice not to let the patients learn anything about the technique, and finally the pessimistic view, shared with only a trusted few, that

neurotics are a rabble, good only to support us financially and to allow us to learn from their cases: psychoanalysis may be worthless.

This interrogation of the role of the therapist interested me, and led me to examine the way two people, a doctor and a patient, might battle against their roles: the doctor determined to maintain control; the patient desperately trying to understand what is happening to them, but trapped in a bind where any attempt to challenge the therapist is turned back on them as being a symptom of their neuroses.

The Model Patient is written from the perspective of a patient who is troubled by the lack of informed consent in the methodology her therapist uses. While this book is fictional and the events go far beyond common unethical boundary violations, it does explore the complexities that a patient might face when having to decide whether to persevere with a therapist. The question that I kept returning to when writing this novel was this: how does the patient know if they're the problem, or whether it's their therapist? Or perhaps there is a third option, somewhere in the realm of the symbolic, within the safety of the clearly defined boundaries of therapy, only realized once the patient feels truly able to trust their therapist with all their feelings, vulnerabilities and fantasies.

Alongside the focus on psychotherapy, *The Model Patient* is set at a time of changing attitudes to contraception in the

The Model Patient

early 1960s. In December 1961, after much debate and uncertainty, the birth control pill, then called Conovid, became available for married women on the NHS. While the drug had already been on the market in the UK for three years previously, and had been available in the US since 1960, there was resistance from many influential voices. Enoch Powell, the Minister of Health, had to tread a careful line in making this medication available. There were concerns from some Conservative voters over the cost of the medication for taxpayers, as well as a fear that access to this pill was encouraging promiscuity. It wasn't until 1967 that its availability expanded to unmarried women also, and even before then, it was at a doctor's discretion whether they decided a married woman should be prescribed the birth control pill. While there were family planning clinics, for example those run by the Family Planning Association, they often held traditional values and did not provide contraception for unmarried women. There were, of course, other methods of contraception women could use, such as the diaphragm, but it was the arrival of the birth control pill that truly began to give women control over their own bodies. As this medicine gradually became more popular and more trusted, women started to find a new way to liberate themselves from traditional social pressures.

I hope the novel will transport readers back to this specific moment of time, 1963, a year when change was in the air. As Philip Larkin writes in his poem 'Annus Mirabilis',

Lucy Ashe

Sexual intercourse began
In nineteen sixty-three
(which was rather late for me) —
Between the end of the Chatterley ban
And the Beatles' first LP.

With the country emerging out of the 1950s, the austerity of war, the waning popularity of a Conservative government, but not yet embracing the youth culture and sexual revolution of the 'swinging sixties', this was a fascinating time of transition. And alongside all this budding change was the 'Big Freeze' of 1963, the coldest winter for over two-hundred years. The snow began on Boxing Day 1962, and it wasn't until March that the temperature rose above freezing. I highly recommend the book *The Beatles 1963 — A Year in the Life* by Dafydd Rees (published 2023) for any reader wishing to explore first-hand accounts of this bitter winter, while also learning more about the growing popularity of The Beatles during this formative year of their career.

It was also a time of change among artists and designers. For jewellery design in the 1950s and 1960s, there was an increased focus on jewellery as wearable art at accessible prices, with commonplace materials used such as copper, paper and textiles, rather than precious metals and jewels. A similar shift was happening in the fashion world. Mary Quant's boutique, Bazaar, opened on the King's Road in 1955, and on Carnaby Street the Glaswegian tailor, John Stephen, opened a number of male clothing stores in the early 1960s. The way

The Model Patient

young people were shopping was changing, and with more daring fashions and a faster production of clothes, the Mod culture was developing. As Mary Quant writes in her 1966 autobiography,

> It is the Mods . . . the direct opposite of the Rockers (who seem to be anti-everything) . . . who gave the dress trade the impetus to break through the fast-moving, breathtaking, up-rooting revolution in which we have played a part since the opening of Bazaar.

While Evelyn and Diana are very much a part of this culture, it is the modelling and advertising industry that dominates Evelyn's understanding of herself. Advertising was expanding alongside the growth of other industries, such as television and consumer goods, led by the success of advertising in the United States. Advertisements typically promoted a comfortable middle-class lifestyle, depicting women devoted to home life and motherhood. I was interested in how jarring this must have felt to Evelyn when the reality of her modelling experience was so different from the woman she presented herself as in front of the camera.

The Model Patient is also a novel about art and the power of creativity to help process and heal trauma. The 1950s and 1960s saw significant changes in the art world, led by movements such as Abstract Expressionism, op-art, and hard-edge and colour-field painting. I have included references to art that was meaningful for me while I was writing this novel, for example Bridget Riley's 'Movement in Squares' (1961), Helen Frankenthaler's 'Seven Types of Ambiguity' (1957), Arshile Gorky's 'One Year in the Milkweed' (1944) and Adolph Gottlieb's 'Blast, I' (1957). Jackson Pollock is a key influence for me, partly because of his interest in psychoanalysis and his own experience of analysis with a Jungian therapist. I was inspired by 'Greyed Rainbow' (1953) and his 'Summertime: 9A', a piece that was included in a UK exhibition of Pollock's work at Whitechapel Gallery in 1958.

In writing *The Model Patient,* I was drawn to artists who explore the unconscious impulses in the making of art, how hidden symbols and meanings might arise in both the act of creation and in the reception of art. And it was in my creation of this novel, the directions it led me and the characters that emerged, that I learnt how powerful and how frightening it is to let what has been hidden appear and unravel.

I have included a list of the texts that I found most inspirational when writing *The Model Patient,* for any reader wishing to explore these subjects further.

Marilia Aisenstein, translated by Andrew Weller, *Desire, Pain and Thought: Primal Masochism and Psychoanalytical Theory* (2023)
Martin Bladh, *The Rorschach Text* (2015)
Michaela Chamberlain, *Misogyny in Psychoanalysis* (2022)
Phyllis Chesler, *Women and Madness* (1972)

The Model Patient

Lucie Clayton, *The World of Modelling, and how to get the London model-girl look* (1968)
Sarah Clegg, *Women's Lore: 4000 Years of Sirens, Serpents and Succubi* (2023)
Melissa Dahl, *Cringeworthy* (2018)
Sándor Ferenczi, *The Clinical Diary of Sándor Ferenczi, 1932,* edited by Judith Dupont; translated by Michael Balint and Nicola Zarday Jackson (1988)
John Fletcher, *Seduction and the Vicissitudes of Translation: The work of Jean Laplanche* (2007)
Sigmund Freud, *The Ego and the Id* (1923), *Beyond the Pleasure Principle* (1920)
Lori Gottlieb, *Maybe You Should Talk to Someone* (2019)
Stephen Grosz, *The Examined Life* (2013)
Barbara Hess, *Abstract Expressionism* (2022)
Melanie Holcomb, *Jewelry: The Body Transformed*, The Metropolitan Museum of Art (2018)
bell hooks, *All About Love* (1999), *Communion: The Female Search for Love* (2002)
C. G. Jung, recorded and edited by Aniela Jaffé, translated by Richard and Clara Winston, *Memories, Dreams, Reflections* (1963)
Susanna Kaysen, *Girl, Interrupted* (1993)
John Kerr, *A Dangerous Method: The Story of Jung, Freud, and Sabina Spielrein* (1993)
Sara London, *The Performance Therapist and Authentic Therapeutic Identity: Coming into Being* (2023)

Lucy Ashe

Deborah A. Lott, *In Session: The Bond Between Women and Their Therapists* (1999)

Cherry Marshall, *The Cat-Walk* (1978)

Sylvia Plath, *The Bell Jar* (1963)

Mary Quant, *Quant by Quant: The autobiography of Mary Quant* (1966)

Alice Robb, *Why We Dream* (2018), *Don't Think, Dear* (2023)

Anne Sexton, *To Bedlam and Part Way Back* (1960)

Frank Tallis, *The Incurable Romantic* (2018)

Irvin Yalom, *Love's Executioner and Other Tales of Psychotherapy* (1989)

Acknowledgements

I wrote the first draft of *The Model Patient* in five feverish months. I could not relax until the story was complete, and my compulsion to write this novel was, at times, a joy, and at other times, a torment. The novel that you are reading today, however, took another eighteen months to finish editing, and I went back and forth on many drafts. I would like to thank Antony Topping, my agent, for his early guidance in helping my chaotic idea for a story find its shape. Thank you to my editors, Clare Hey in the UK, and Claire Wachtel in the US, for their expert suggestions. Thank you also to Jenny Parrott for her kind early support, particularly on the historical details. It really did take a village.

Thank you to the wonderful team at Simon and Schuster for their passion and enthusiasm. I will never forget our first meeting and all the brilliant ideas that everyone shared. I am very grateful to the team at Union Square & Co, and for the opportunity to work with Claire Wachtel for the third time. Thank you to Jennifer Weltz, my agent in the US, for all her support.

There are so many people who worked on the production, marketing and publicity in the UK and US. Thank you to Olivia Allen, Aneesha Angris, Gen Barratt, Jess Barratt, Moira Eagling, Diane João, Sabah Khan, Hayley McMullan, Juliana Nador, Alison Skrabek, and Patrick Sullivan.

I could not have written this book without the support of my husband, Erik. The book was inspired by my experience of psychodynamic therapy, and in writing *The Model Patient,* I was attempting to find a creative way to cope with the physical and mental effects of this therapy. Erik's unwavering love helped me to find the strength to challenge and change what was happening. Thank you also to those who were there for me during this time, for supporting me even when I could not explain why I was finding everything so hard, particularly Beth Armstrong, Natasha Bassett, Brittany Ashworth, Thomasin Bailey, Joanna Bratten, Nina Ellis, Bryerly Long, Amita Parikh, Nicole Nehrig, and Susie Wallat-Vago. Special thanks go to Alexa M.

As with my first two novels, I am immensely grateful to my parents, my sisters, Jo and Suzie, my brother-in-law, Ollie, and my husband, Erik, for reading early drafts and giving me the confidence I needed to continue developing the novel. I am very lucky to have family who are willing to read everything I write, often several times. The final edits were completed during the second and third trimester of my pregnancy, so I should also thank my baby girl for providing distractions in the form of kicks and tumble turns.

I would like to acknowledge the man whose psychotherapy

method started me on this journey. While writing this novel began as an attempt to impose some order and understanding over the confusion of our complicated relationship, my experience did gradually change, and I am grateful for all that I discovered along the way.